LOYAL TO A DEGREE

BY HORST CHRISTIAN

LOYAL TO A DEGREE

Growing Up Under The Third Reich: Book 2

BASED ON A TRUE STORY

Horst Christian

This book is a work of fiction based on a true story.

LOYAL TO A DEGREE

Copyright © 2013 Horst Christian

www.horstchristian.com

Second Printing 2019
First Printing 2013

ISBN-13: 978-1491068137
ISBN-10: 1491068132

For my wife, Jennifer.

ACKNOWLEGEMENTS

I would like to thank my friends, Greg and Jon, who egged me on to write this book. Without their prodding I would not have started.

Special thanks go to my editor Wanda Skinner, for correcting my second language, English, into a readable version. Her constant questions regarding particular subjects kept me in line to pay attention to what I was trying to convey. Thank you, Wanda, very much.

I found the writing of this book, with the assistance of Wanda, was pretty easy. But without the invaluable help from Christina Haas, owner of zenithbusinesssolutions.com, it would still be nothing more than a manuscript.

From formatting the book to designing my author's website, opening accounts and pages on Facebook, Twitter, and writer's forums, all the way to designing the cover art, creating a book trailer and finally creating my accounts at Amazon and actually publishing the book for me, without Chris I would still be stuck in the labyrinth of self-publishing. To top it off she answers my myriad questions on a daily and sometimes hourly basis. You are truly a beginning writer's best friend. You made it possible for me to concentrate on nothing else, but writing. Please accept my gratitude and my thanks, Chris; your guidance is priceless.

Last, but by no means least, I want to thank my wife, Jennifer, for doing all the physical work on our small ranch while allowing me to sit and write in an air-conditioned office. Thank you, Jenny.

PREFACE

Although this book is based on a true life story, the names of the
characters have been changed. However, the people the characters
are based on were real, the locations existed, the events actually took
place, and the story captures the factual experiences of a young boy
struggling to survive in the final days before the fall of Berlin during
World War II.

FOREWORD

During Hitler's reign in Germany, information did not flow as quickly or as freely as it does today. There was no Internet to check the facts and if there was, it would have been moderated completely by the Nazi government. Children growing up during that time knew only what they were told - by the government and by adults too frightened to contradict the government's propaganda. It was a time when neighbors could simply disappear in the night and it was a time of great uncertainty for the ordinary citizens of Germany.

In 1940, joining the Hitler Youth group became mandatory for young German boys. At the age of 10 they became members of Deutsches Jungvolk (German Young People) and at 14, they were members of Hitler Jugend (Hitler Youth). During that time, young boys were treated differently than they are today. By the time they were 14, they were considered to be "young adults" and as such, were expected to learn a trade and earn a living. And when it came to the war, they were fully expected to be soldiers.

There are many stories that have been written about World War II. Very few, however, have been written from the perspective of the young boys who were members of the Hitler Jugend (HJ) and served as ordinary foot soldiers. These boys knew only what they were told and they followed the orders they were given or suffered the consequences. Their stories are not about guts and glory but rather, about trying to survive during extraordinary times.

Loyal To A Degree is based on the true story of one young boy in particular and the events that took place in his life as a member of the HJ during the days leading up to the fall of Berlin. In the end, it all boils down to one very important decision - loyalty or survival.

ONE

Karl turned the radio off. He had just listened to the German special OKW report, which announced a breakthrough of Russian tanks at a German defense line 180 kilometers east of his camp.

This was the news Karl had anticipated and feared for the last seven days. He knew that he had to act fast if there was any chance left to bring the kids from the KLV camp back to Berlin. His camp was located in a 200-year-old cloister near Kosten in Poland. It had served for the past two years as an evacuation camp for children from Berlin.

The leader of the camp was Lieutenant Lothar Hardfeld, a former tank commander who had lost his right hand and the lower half of his right leg during an explosion of an ammunition depot. After his amputations and partial recovery in a field hospital, he was declared unfit to fight and had been ordered to oversee the "air attack evacuation" camp of school children from Berlin.

Since no teachers were available, he was also ordered to conduct some minimal teaching of the German language and also arithmetic. At 46 years of age he was the only adult in the camp of 122 boys, almost all of them under the age of 12 years.

Karl Veth, his assistant, was a brown haired blue eyed 14-year old. He was short for his age; only 5'3 and he weighed 124 pounds. Because of his physical build, he was trained as a sniper in the German HJ (Hitler Youth). He was in charge of food and personal hygiene.

Karl's best friend was another 14-year old HJ member named Peter Zahn.

Peter was in charge of physical education, which mostly consisted of long distance running and some ball games. However, after the only ball in the camp disappeared, it was only running; every day at least 2 kilometers, which was not much but still a good distance to run for the age group.

After Karl had turned off the radio he looked over to the other bunk bed and noticed that his friend was peacefully sleeping. "Peter," he whispered, and then louder, "Peter, wake up. The Russians broke the line and could be here within 24 hours."

As Peter looked up Karl added, "Run and wake Hardfeld, but don't wait for him to fire any questions at you because I have no further details. Just tell him that the Russians are coming and then ring the alarm for the camp. If he asks for me, just tell him that I am in the bathroom throwing up and that I will meet him at the front entrance."

While Peter fumbled around in the dark to find his uniform, Karl was already out the door and running towards the back of the hallway. The few candles on the walls of the cloister were the only illumination the camp had for the last few weeks, barely enough to keep you from banging into the moist cobblestone walls. But Karl could have found his way anyhow, even in total darkness, and as he approached the last door on the right he quickly entered and closed the door behind him. He did not like the room very much. It was very small, more like a closet and it was currently being used for storage of old broken down snow shovels.

It wasn't the shovels that gave him the creeps; it was more the many rats that scurried around and squeaked when disturbed.

It had been about six weeks back that Karl had found this room by accident when he was on night guard duty. He had followed a weird sound that seemed to emerge from the end of the hallway.

What he found was this closet. It covered an entrance to an underground passageway leading from the main living part of the cloister to the actual chapel. The sound came from people shuffling around and talking to each other.

He discovered Polish people; old people, mostly women and one old priest apparently trying to read mass or something.

Karl did not understand the Polish language, but he knew that this was strange because as far as he knew, the church section of the cloister had been sealed shut a few years ago. The Polish people who tended to the maintenance of the cloister had been forced to leave, and anyhow, church services at this place were not permitted.

As he tried to get a better look at the meeting he somehow locked eyes with the priest who proceeded to read from a book, but a slight movement of his hand told Karl that he had been detected and should stay at his place.

A few moments later the priest stopped reading and announced something that Karl did not understand, but all of the sudden the meeting broke up. There were actually only five women and one more old man besides the priest.

Karl counted them as they lined up behind a frayed but colorful curtain, apparently to enter another dark staircase leading down. The priest stayed behind and looked again in Karl's direction.

"Come on out, I see you and I think that I know you," he said in broken German, "I will not harm you, but I think that we need to talk."

Karl figured that he could easily overpower the frail looking priest and since he was detected already, he might as well find out what was going on here.

"What are you doing here and what do you want," he asked the priest.

The priest replied with a very thin smile forming on his lips, "This is my home and I am praying, and maybe we can help each other. Are you interested?"

"I don't need any help and I can have you arrested for conducting an unlawful meeting." Karl was weak in his response as he was unsure who would be doing the arresting.

"You are right. You don't need my help right now, but maybe soon. Sooner than you might think." The old clergy continued to smile, "Come, sit down over here and I will tell you what I have to offer and you just might wish to kungle."

Karl was stunned. First, that the old guy spoke a reasonable German, and second, that he used the word kungle, because kungle was not really a common word of the German language, but a recently developed slang word meaning the exchange of goods on the black market.

Let's see what the priest has to kungle, he thought to himself and came out from behind the trap door to sit down on a step stool beside the altar.

"What do you have that you think I might need," he asked locking eyes with the priest.

"For one thing," the old man answered, "I have civilian clothes for you and for your friend Peter. You will need them real soon. I might also have underground information you will certainly need to get back to Germany alive."

Karl thought quickly. This guy was right on both counts. Karl's only clothing was his uniform which identified him as a Jungschar leader and a sniper. Of course, he could get rid of all the insignia, but it was still a uniform, and if he ripped off the patches, it would show on the fabric. Also, getting back to Germany alive depended a lot on evading the Polish underground movement.

"You might be right, let's kungle. What do you want in exchange?"

"We need food and medical supplies. I know that you have access to them," the priest answered.

"You seem to know a lot about our present condition and about me. Maybe even too much, and yet I know nothing about you. I did not even know that you or your meetings here existed. And most of all, I don't know if I can trust you."

"You can't trust me, you know that, because you cannot trust anyone anymore, but we need each other and we need to establish what you call trust and what I call a common ground relationship. I show you my goodwill by offering you a pair of used but very well insulated winter shoes. With the shoes you are now wearing you will not get 10 kilometers from here, especially if it is snowing and it will, within a few weeks."

The old man had hit the nail right on the head. Karl had been worrying about his footwear for quite a while. It was badly in need of replacement and there was not even a remote possibility of getting a Bezugsschein, an entitlement form, but even those were by themselves useless.

The stores were empty of merchandise. The only way to obtain anything was by kungling, and shoes, getting them were nearly impossible, unless you knew of a family where someone had died and the family traded off the belongings.

"What do you want for the shoes," Karl asked.

"Soap," the priest answered.

"How do I know that the shoes will fit?"

"Try them on; they are right under the altar." The priest moved a curtain from behind the side altar and pointed to a pile of used but slightly clean looking clothes and a pair of heavy black leather boots.

Karl tried the boots on. They were maybe a size too large but this was perfectly fine with him as he was used to padding his shoes with old newspaper to make them fit. He smiled to himself. This turned out to be good because he had an idea of how to obtain soap from the camp without raising suspicion.

"I'll be back tomorrow," he said.

"I know you will," answered the priest.

"Be careful," Karl said, "You know too much."

"I know that we need each other. Let's try and build on that," the old man answered.

The next morning during the early drill which required that all the boys line up in rows of three and doing knee bends for 5 minutes and running in place for 10 minutes, Karl went through the personal belongings of his charges and collected all of the started soap bars he could find. He wound up with a bag of over 120 of partially used-up bars of soap of all sizes. He figured that it weight more than three pounds. Then he went to the camp supply room and took from the soap supply a fresh box and removed about 140 new bars and issued the new bars to the kids as they reentered the building.

"I had to confiscate all the old soap," he told camp commander Hardfeld, who stared at him in amazement as Karl handed him a new bar, "where is yours?"

Hardfeld went to his room and came back with 2 started bars.

"What's wrong with the soap we are using?"

"Beats me," Karl answered and mumbled under his breath something about a sabotage report from Berlin. Lieutenant Hardfeld just nodded, sabotage was on everyone's mind and coming from Berlin was frightening.

Actually, as of late, anything coming from Berlin or connected to Berlin was bad news. He just wished that the whole darn war would be over. He wanted to go home to Hannover and see if his family was still alive. Besides constant reports of bombing attacks by allied forces on Hannover, he had not heard a word from his family in weeks. It was starting to wear. Just as little as two months ago he was in weekly contact through the use of Feldpost, a term for military mail. But since then everything changed for the worse. Feldpost was not able to keep up with the constantly changing of positions and commands. He was more than discouraged; he knew he was a cripple for the rest of his life, however short that might be. The KLV camp meant nothing to him and he just wanted to see his family once more.

He nodded to Karl, "Yes, do what you can to keep us healthy and in compliance with Berlin's latest nonsense."

He knew that his last words were dangerous, because any criticism of Berlin in any form or way was strictly forbidden. He regretted his remark and was ready to back-paddle, but luckily Karl did not seem to notice. He was already on the way to the dump to get rid of a pair of dirty paper bags, or something.

Good thing that Karl and Peter are efficient, he thought to himself, I would not really know how to keep order in this place or keep the children occupied and healthy.

But, still he wondered about Karl and his connections to Berlin.

Lothar Hardfeld knew that Karl's connections must be powerful because every so often, Karl was ordered to Berlin for a one day meeting with HJ leaders and political officials. One of the latest achievements of Karl was a total and unexpected surprise for Hardfeld.

Karl was called to Berlin for a three-day stay and when he returned he did so on a motorcycle with a sidecar filled with cans of petrol.

"Where did you get this and what for," he had asked, and Karl had looked at him.

"This is for you," he said, "my orders are to get you and the boys back to Berlin in case the Russians break our lines by Warschau, and I am told that transportation at that time will be very limited, but I am supposed to act to the best of my ability in accordance with my orders. Do you like it?"

"What?" Lothar asked, "Your orders, which seem to override my authority, or the bike?"

"The bike of course, my older friend. You are unable to march for any distance and my orders are directly from the SS headquarters and in writing."

With this he started to hand Lothar two SS insignia envelopes, but before Karl let go of them, he kept one of the envelopes and put it back in the his pocket.

"I like the bike already," Hardfeld answered as he briefly glanced at the envelope, "but how did you get it? And where did you learn how to drive?"

"Wehrmacht and a crash course of the HJ," was the short answer.

"But where did you get it, and the petrol?"

Karl looked over the shoulder of Lothar and seemed to observe a bird in the distance. There was a moment of silence and then, "Don't ask."

"How are you supposed to bring the boys to Berlin if there is no transportation?"

Again, there was a moment of silence. Karl was by now concentrating hard on the bird. "My problem," he answered, "I will ask for your help when I need it." With this he turned away and pushed the motorcycle to an empty storage shed on the opposite side of the cloister.

It had been snowing for a while and the envelope in Lothar's hand was getting wet. It contained two sheets of paper informing him and ordering him that in the event of a breakthrough of Russian forces, the camp was to be evacuated to Berlin under the command of Karl Veth, Gefolgschaftsfuehrer, HJ. Furthermore, he was relieved of his command due to his physical inability to act in the face of the enemy.

The second sheet of paper was just an information sheet advising him that due to the need of keeping fighting troops and reserve units supplied with food and weapons, an evacuation of his camp by rails was highly unlikely.

It closed with the sentence, 'We wish you and Gefolgschaftsfuehrer Karl Veth all the best in your endeavor to bring the children home to their parents. Heil Hitler.'

It was signed Berlin School Evacuation Headquarters.

Dated February 6th 1945.

The Lieutenant could not help staring at the papers in his hand. All his efforts to be an example as an officer and all his sacrifices had been in vain.

He considered himself to be an officer of the Wehrmacht, and not subject to the command of the SS or the HJ. To be replaced by a 14-year-old kid in the uniform of the HJ was just too much for him to comprehend.

He considered for a moment to end it all, but the thought of his family and of the motorcycle in the shed made him hesitate just long enough to abandon his thought of taking his own life. There had to be a way out. How, he did not know, and neither did he know how to ride a motorcycle. Maybe the answer was with Karl. After all, if the SS and the HJ put him in command, then maybe the boy was also capable of getting him home. He took another pain killer pill and realized that he had only a few left.

TWO

When Karl was in Berlin, six weeks ago, he had thought of a possible way to get the children back to Berlin.

Actually it was not so much his plan, than a variation of a plan which was given to him in the first week of February during a meeting with a few of the remaining school officials in Berlin.

The instructions outlining the plan were titled "Extreme Evacuation Guidelines" and he had been told to "modify" as necessary. Karl had modified this plan immediately.

While still in Berlin, he went to the local HJ headquarters seeking additional authorization documents. Then he tried to find and see a certain SS commander who happened to be the father of one of the boys in his camp.

After about an hour of searching through the files of the school district, he found what he had looked for and decided to visit the local SS headquarters. The SS commander he wanted to see however was unavailable. So he left a note for SS Obersturmbannfuehrer von Glinski, informing him that his son Udo was one of his charges, but he could not assure the Obersturmbannfuehrer the safe return of his son in case of a Russian breakthrough. He ended the note, "I would appreciate any pertinent help." He signed the letter and hoped it would reach the SS commander.

Karl had also tried during this Berlin visit to find his own parents, which he had not seen since the previous May, but the apartment house where they had lived for the last 4 years was totally destroyed during an air attack in early January by allied forces. All that was left was rubble of broken cement pieces. On some of the larger pieces were scribbled messages from former tenants, in an effort to leave a message for relatives or friends who were seeking to find the whereabouts of survivors.

Karl found nothing, but he was not too worried. In one of the last letters from his mother, she had told him that she and his younger brother and sister were trying to leave Berlin and she had named an address of an uncle in Westphalia. Still, he was seeking to find a notice from his father who was drafted into the Volkssturm, but as much as he looked within the short time period he had available, he found nothing. No note, no address, and no indication from any neighbor he used to know.

He did find however, a larger piece of rubble with a list of people who did not survive the bombing of this house, and his family was not listed.

He considered this to be good news. Actually, much better than he had feared. He had scribbled with a sharp piece of broken metal on one of the cement pieces, his name and the current date. This way, he figured, if someone from his family was looking for him, they would know that on this date he was still alive.

Karl then hurried to meet the military transport column which took supplies to the fighting front in Poland and who was ordered to take him along as far as Kosten; about 10 kilometers from the children's camp. He was running late and he almost missed the convoy, which was just leaving as he turned the last corner leading to the supply depot.

While he was frantically waiving to the first drivers it was not until after the fourth truck had passed that he was able to jump on the running board of the fifth truck and show his credentials. The driver was an old gray haired reserve soldier, and he slowed down just enough for Karl to jump on the running board and climb into the back of the truck.

In a way he was lucky, because the first few trucks all had open truck beds while the one he was able to catch had a canvas top and seemed to carry medical supplies. It had started to snow and Karl crawled over boxes and crates to find some shelter from the cold wind which blew in from the rear through the holes in the canopy. He was exhausted and fell asleep as soon as he found a place protected from the howling wind. When he woke up it was almost daylight. The convoy had come to a halt and the drivers were busy clearing a massive and almost frozen snowdrift from an intersection.

Karl crawled to the loading gate at the rear of the truck and asked the next driver who walked by how much longer it would take to reach his drop off point by Kosten. The soldier just stared at Karl's HJ uniform and answered that he did not know the exact time frame, but it would take at least another hour. This was perfectly alright with Karl. He was afraid that the convoy had stopped for him to get off and that he might have to start his walk to the camp. He searched his pocket for some dried bread, which he had received from the school officials the previous day.

He did not really know how hungry he was until he started to chew on the bread. It was called Knaeckebrot and in a texture similar to rye crispy. Not bad tasting, but a bit salty. He ate every last crumb he had and then jumped out of the truck to help the drivers moving the snow away from the intersection to what appeared to be a major highway.

Thirty minutes later he was back in the truck.

After another hour and a half, he was awakened by his driver, who pointed out to him the general direction he had to walk to reach his camp.

The snowstorm was gone. However, the country road he was supposed to follow was buried under a foot of fresh snow. It made for some difficult walking, but after a little while the sun was penetrating the gray sky and the landscape turned from flat white to a sometimes blinding white with some glaring blue spots; it almost looked pretty.

It was the typical Polish flat plain with just enough of some straggly birch trees from time to time to mark the direction of the road. Karl was feeling great. The soldiers had given him some more Knaeckebrot, and a small can of margarine as well as a can of meat. He had also been given a field canteen of water, which he had not even started to open when he finally reached the camp.

During his walk he had tried to imagine what he needed to do if the Russians broke through the defense line in eastern Poland. He knew that the 'Evacuation Guidelines" given to him in Berlin were almost impossible to implement. He had been given some authorization documents which empowered him to stop any kind of empty vehicles, including military vehicles which he might encounter as he marched the children westward to Berlin. As a next step, he was supposed to hand the drivers of the vehicles the orders to take the children to safety.

Right on the outset, two things were almost impossible to achieve. For one thing, the children of the camp were all between the ages of 10 years and 12 years old, and marching in a snowstorm would be a suicide mission.

Besides that, what about the food and water?

The second part of stopping military vehicles might work, if there is an orderly retreat, and Karl was not too sure about that. Besides, he had not even seen any empty military vehicles. The few trucks he had seen moving westward were filled with wounded soldiers, and the ones moving eastward were filled with supplies and reserve troops.

His thoughts turned constantly back to his evolving friendship and arrangement with the Polish priest. He had started to like the old fellow and he had learned that his name was Stanislaus Dobrowski.

During the last week, Karl had kungled with him for additional used civilian clothing and now had pants and jackets for Peter and Hardfeld as well as for himself.

He had also asked Stanislaus if he could introduce him to some Polish guides. He needed some local knowledge to find a short cut through a birch forest to the railroad track, which connected Warsaw with Kottbus. This was two weeks ago, and in the meantime, he had supplied Stanislaus with some more canned food and some medical supplies.

His general idea was to obligate the priest to help him and the boys when the time came to evacuate the camp.

And the time was now.

The Russians had broken the German lines. There was not much the few retreating German tank and infantry units could do to stop the Russian onslaught towards Berlin.

Karl had entered the passageway to the chapel, and looked for his stash of clothes. He found everything just as he had left it and he kept on running towards the end of the underground passageway. He was trying to locate Stanislaus and hoped that the old fellow would really keep his word and help him. He did not need to worry. The priest had gotten the word of the massive German retreat through his resistance network before Karl had even heard it on the radio.

"Over here," he shouted at Karl, who just turned around the corner towards the altar.

Karl turned and was stunned for a moment. Next to Stanislaus were three young men, obviously Poles, maybe 17 or 18 years of age. At first he thought he was being ambushed and considered reaching for his service pistol, which he carried under his shirt. But then his worry turned into surprise because he saw several large baskets of apples standing between the three of them. Karl had not eaten an apple for over a year and he could not even remember when he saw

11

the last one.

"The Russians are coming," was all he was able to say as he still stared at the green and yellow apples.

"We know," answered Stanislaus, "but, according to our information, it is only a tank division. Their infantry is still standing down and will not move for a few hours."

"It does not matter, tanks or infantry," answered Karl, "the children have to leave immediately." At this time they all could hear the howling sound of the camp siren. Peter or Hardfeld must have triggered the alarm.

"Yes," said Stanislaus, "this is why you see my friends here. They will help you to get the boys to the railroad tracks. They will also help you to light a fire to stop the train." When he saw Karl's skeptical look, the priest continued, "You will need them."

"What for?" asked Karl, "You know yourself how difficult it will be to explain their presence to an SS patrol or commando. If they will be seen with the German children they will be shot regardless of what I say."

"I already thought of that." answered Stanislaus, "These fellows speak a good enough German to pass as Volksdeutsche."

Volksdeutsche was the term used for non-native Germans. They were actually Poles as far as their legal status was concerned, but they were of German ancestry.

Karl looked at the group in bewilderment. He could not believe what he was hearing.

"You cannot take the risk," he insisted, "you are lucky that you are alive as it is, and I don't understand what is in it for you?"

The priest answered by handing Karl an apple, "Don't worry, they have German papers, and if one of your little boys falls or passes out in the cold, you will be unable to carry him and you would have to leave him behind; so you will need these guys, and," he locked eyes with Karl, "don't ask me about my motivation again. It hurts."

Karl nodded, "I understand, sorry."

Karl turned towards the largest of the three, "What is your name?"

"I am Elu, this is my brother Lechek and we call the other guy Pilu. Here are my German papers." With this Elu handed Karl a German Volksdeutschen Ausweis, which was the identification card issued by the German civilian authorities.

"This one looks authentic to me." Karl said as he glanced at the seal and date of issue, "Let me see the other ones."

Lechek stepped forward and handed him two more ID's, which looked identical to the one which Elu had shown him.

"Well, let's hope you don't need them." Karl was satisfied with the quality of the Ausweise, he had seen worse. "What is with these apples?" he asked Stanislaus.

"They are for your children as a farewell present and as a thank you gift for helping us when we needed your support."

For a moment it looked to Karl as if the priest had some tears in his eyes.

But, time was pressing and he had more on his mind than to think about the sentimental attitude displayed by Stanislaus.

He turned to Elu, "Please place the baskets with the apples near the rear gate of the inner wall, and then watch for our group leaving in about an hour."

With that he turned to Stanislaus, "Watch out for yourself, you are facing a much worse enemy than we Germans ever were to you. If the Russians find out that you cooperated with us, you will be a dead man. Besides that, get rid of your clergy clothes. The first wave of fighting troops will be happy to have any excuse to shoot you."

The old priest all of the sudden did not seem so old anymore. He stood erect as he nodded to Karl. "I know that our days may be numbered, and even if the fighting troops spare us, the political commissioners might not."

"I wish you well," said Karl, "and thank you once more for all your help.

"I will not forget you old man, and I know that you are not a priest."

With that he turned around, waved once more to Stanislaus and disappeared into the passageway.

He heard Stanislaus asking a question but he could not afford to waste any more time to stop and answer. He had to get back to Hardfeld and inform him of his idea of stopping a train to get the boys back to Berlin.

As he returned to the main hallway, he almost ran in to his friend Peter.

"Where have you been? I think Hardfeld had a stroke or heart attack. He is lying on the floor in the kitchen." He grabbed Karl by the arm and pulled him across the assembly hall to the part of the cloister, which served as a kitchen.

Karl took a careful look at Hardfeld and decided that Hardfeld had neither experienced a heart attack nor a stroke. The skid marks on the floor indicated that he must have slipped on the greasy floor and then passed out. One of the two Polish women who served as a camp cook was kneeling by the Lieutenant and trying to push a towel under his head.

"Get me a pot of water!" Karl shouted at Peter. "No, cold water, quick!" he added as he saw Peter scanning the stove for a pot.

While Peter was searching for a suitable pot, Karl rose up and grabbed a bucket of water that stood next to the doorway. With one fast swoop, he threw the contents of the bucket over Hardfeld's head and shook him by the shoulders. "Wake up!" Karl shouted, "Wake up, wake up!"

As Hardfeld slowly opened his eyes, Peter approached from behind and dumped another load of cold water over the Lieutenant's head. It took another effort by Karl shouting questions at Hardfeld until the Lieutenant was able to answer.

"No, I don't think that I hit my head. I must have passed out from the pain when I fell on my amputated arm stump." Hardfeld sat up and noticed that he was sitting in a pool of dirty water. "Who did this to me?" Peter and Karl helped him up and pushed a wooden bench under his buckling knees. "And, what is going on?" Apparently he was clueless and pretty useless in the current situation.

"I'll bring you up to date in a moment," Karl answered, "but right now I have to know where you keep the Camp Evacuation Registration Box."

"In my office, should be on the top shelf, first box on the right."

"Good, and where is your pain medication?"

"Should be right here in my pocket." With this the Lieutenant reached into his pants pockets, apparently searching for his vial of pills.

"Run to the office and get the box with the registration forms." Karl shoved Peter in the direction of the door. He then turned to Hardfeld; "The Russians broke the defense line about 180 kilometer east from here. I will walk the boys through the woods to the railroad tracks and try to stop a train going west. I will then come back and get you out of here."

Hardfeld just stared at him in utter disbelief. "You cannot do that. It will be impossible to achieve. I have to command you to stay here with me!"

"You can command all you want, this is your privilege, but as you very well know, I don't have to obey. You can either try to walk with us, or you can stay here until I return. Your choice, Lieutenant!"

While Hardfeld pondered a reply, Karl went into the assembly hall where all the boys were seated at their designated dining tables. This is the easy part, Karl thought to himself. The camp had practiced for the last two weeks all kinds of emergency procedures, and this one here was indeed the easiest to implement and hopefully to execute.

As he entered the hall he overheard one of the boys whispering to his classmate, "This is no exercise tonight, Rudy, look at Karl, he is all serious. Not his regular manner and not a smile on his lips."

Karl turned to the boy, "You like to see me smile?" and then louder so that all the boys could hear him, "Listen up, this is not a drill, none of us will go back to bed, and all of us will be going home."

He had hoped for a happy response, but it was not as joyful as he had expected.

Most of the boys seemed happy over the news, but there were also boys crying in bewilderment, and more than a few were just staring at the floor. He knew right away what was wrong.

The mail had been slow over the last two weeks and some of the boys had not gotten a letter from home in over three weeks. These boys feared that they would not find their mothers alive. Some feared that their apartments had been 'bombed out' and in this case 'going home' was not possible. Where would they wind up, when there was not a 'home' to go to? Where would they go in Berlin when the little security of this camp and Hardfeld and Karl was no longer available?

Karl knew he had to inject some glimmer of hope otherwise some of the boys might just give up when they needed all their strength to endure the walk to the railroad.

"Listen up again!" he yelled through the tumult, "I know that some of you have been waiting from a letter from home, but there is really nothing to worry about. As you know, I was in Berlin just a few days ago and was told that the mail to the camps had been delayed in favor of the field post to our wounded soldiers.

I can also tell you that there was no major air attack on Charlottenburg during the last two weeks. Most of the air attacks had been targeted at Tempelhof and Neukoelln."

His words had the desired impact because the boys in his camp had all been from the school district of Charlottenburg and

Wilmersdorf.

"In one hour from now I will lead you through the woods to the railroad line to Berlin. Once we are there we will board a train and when we reach Berlin, we will proceed to the Fichte school in Wilmersdorf where you will be met by your relatives. Your relatives have been advised that you will be there within 48 hours."

Karl was lying to the best of his abilities. He knew that he could not provide any real answers, but he also knew that he had to keep the boys motivated enough to sustain the upcoming walk through the snow and the remainder of the night.

"Peter will call out your names and hand you your identification card. The card will be in an envelope attached to a string, which you will loop around your neck. All of you will stay in this hall. Eat as much as you wish in the meantime.

We will be on our way within 15 minutes."

As Peter proceeded to call out the names and hand out the ID envelopes, Karl noticed that someone was calling his name. The shouting came from the outside of the buildings, but there was no one supposed to be outside except for Elu, Lechek and Pilu, the three Polish guides he had met a while ago.

He looked at Hardfeld, who had followed him into the assembly hall.

"Did you hear that," he asked.

"Hear what," answered the Lieutenant, who could hardly keep himself upright.

A dreadful thought entered Karl's mind. Hardfeld is in worse shape than I thought, first a cripple and now also deaf.

"Jungscharfuehrer Karl Veth, is anybody in there?"

Karl heard it again and went outside into the cold wind and looked around.

The sky was clear and the moon was out and he could recognize a soldier at the gate to the camp's training ground.

"Coming!" he yelled on the top of his lungs and then he also saw what looked like a military truck outside the gate.

The gate was closed, but not locked. As he neared the gate, the soldier stopped shouting and waited for him to come closer. Karl looked over the soldier for a second and knew that he had an SS man in front of him. No rank insignia was visible, but Karl liked him instantly without knowing why.

Maybe because he saw two small military transport trucks lined up in front of the gate.

The SS man looked at Karl for a moment, "I need to speak with Karl Veth."

"That would be me," answered Karl.

"Cannot be," the SS soldier replied, "you are just a dumb kid from the camp."

Karl pointed to the insignia on his uniform and to the silver eagle on his cap.

"Believe it or not, I am Karl, and I am happy to see your trucks. I am authorized to command any empty military trucks to assist me in the evacuation of this camp. Here are my papers."

The soldier, who looked like he was about 50 years old, squinted first at the papers and then at Karl's insignia on the uniform and when he saw the silver eagle on the black winter cap of the Hitler Youth uniform, his mouth moved without saying a word.

He finally managed a few words, "My name is Brandt. I am coming here at the direct orders of SS Obersturmbannfuehrer von Glinski. I am supposed to bring his son Udo back to Berlin, and in doing so to render any assistance required by Jungscharfuehrer Karl Veth. I guess this is you, but I was under the impression that Veth was older then you are, and that Veth is trained as a sniper."

Karl just looked at Brandt and asked, "How many children are you able to transport in your trucks, and how much petrol do you have on board?"

Brandt still had trouble associating Karl Veth with the kid in front of him.

The uniform and the papers convinced him that Karl was the Hitler Youth he was looking for, and Obersturmbannfuehrer von Glinski had warned him not to underestimate Karl Veth in any way, but this boy looked so small and seemingly much too young to represent any authority at all.

"I can transport between 60 and 70 kids at the most and I have sufficient fuel to get back to Berlin," he answered to Karl's question.

"Sixty to 70 will not do; not even close Herr Brandt, but we will see. Come in and if you are hungry we have food to share. Please back up your trucks to the side entrance over there." Karl pointed to one of the several doors leading to inside the building and opened the gate.

THREE

Brandt went back to his truck and motioned to the driver of the second truck to follow him into the yard. As Brandt backed up his truck to the old wooden door of the cloister, he scanned the dark sky for clouds. There were none. The snowstorm had passed a few hours ago and he could see stars wherever he looked. He went over to his younger buddy in the other truck and told him about this Hitler Youth kid who was in charge of the boy's camp.

"You will not believe this fellow, Anton, but as you know, our orders are to assist him and to follow his instructions. But as of right now we are invited to go in and eat."

"How did he know that we are starving?" wondered Anton. "By the way, did you see the three fellows on the far side of the yard? It looked to me as if they were trying to hide from us and now I don't see them anymore."

"No," answered Brandt, "I was only looking at this kid in the uniform of an HJ leader. And I am still worried about our mission here.

"Sturmbannfuehrer von Glinski told us that we would find more boys here than we could accommodate. We might be triggering a panic when we leave some of them behind. I am glad that we are not in command or the decision maker."

He flicked his just started cigarette in a nearby snow bank. "Let's go in, and remind me to tell Karl about the three unknowns you saw."

Karl was standing in the hallway, next to Hardfeld and Peter.

"Everything changed," Karl announced, "we have a partial solution to our dilemma. The father of Udo von Glinski, the SS leader of our district in Berlin, must have gotten my message that I cannot vouch for the safe return of his son to Berlin. We have some trucks waiting to take more than half of the boys back to Berlin."

"Trucks," echoed Hardfeld "where? And Udo? I had no special

information about his parents, how did you know?" He really did not expect an answer to his question as Karl was always preoccupied and lately thinking ahead of him. But this time, to his surprise, Karl answered.

"When I received the order to bring the children back to Berlin, I reviewed the current school records to see if any of their parents had been killed during the air attacks and I came upon Udo von Glinski's father, listed as Sturmbannfuehrer of the 'Waffen SS'. I tried to find him and tried to call him to enlist his help in case we had to evacuate the camp. However, all I could do was to leave a message for him at the SS Headquarters."

Before Karl could finish his answer, Peter had sneaked a look outside the front door and then left for the assembly hall.

"Udo," he called, "Udo von Glinski, come to the front table." The boys in the hall repeated Peter's call until a blonde boy showed up at the front table. Peter knew him well. Udo was 11 years old and one of his best long distance runners and he also liked him because of his always-disciplined behavior.

"Udo," he asked him, "is your father an SS leader?"

"I am not supposed to talk about my parents." answered Udo, "Did something happened to my father?"

"No," Peter assured him, "Your father is all right. Now just get your belongings and bring your friends and sit down here at this table."

While Hardfeld limped through the outside door and looked at the two small trucks, Karl saw the two SS men who just came out of the kitchen, each with a dish full of steaming mashed potatoes and gravy.

"Sit down," he said, "how long will it take you to drive to Berlin?"

"Depending upon congestion around the towns, troop movements, delays and weather, we should make it within eight hours," answered Brandt.

"Do you have enough fuel to make a detour of less than two hours," asked Karl.

"Yes, we do." This was the first time that Anton answered. "But, I don't think that a detour is called for. We drove a pretty direct route to get here and I have been driving this route now several times, transporting wounded troops, and I know my way around the area."

"I am glad that you know your way," answered Karl. "The detour is not exactly a detour, but a side trip. We cannot fit all the boys in your trucks, and we cannot leave any behind. So I need you to drive some of them to the railroad line leading west, probably to Kottbus. You will then return to pick up the remaining group and take them to Berlin. I will be with you on the side trip, and then you will be on your own."

Brandt looked at Anton. "This sounds better than leaving screaming kids behind. Let's do this as fast as possible." He then turned to Karl, "You might not be as isolated as you think you are. Upon our arrival we saw three guys without uniforms, probably Polish resistance, trying to hide and stay out of view."

"Yes, they are, and they are also known to me. I will get them right now." Karl got up and left the surprised SS men to the remainder of their meal.

Peter, who had just approached the table, followed Karl. "You know Polish resistance members? I don't know any more if I really know you; I mean how can I trust you?"

Karl smiled at his friend. "Come along. I'll even give you an apple and introduce you."

Hardfeld, still standing at the door, overheard Peter's question and Karl's answer.

"Karl, I demand an honest answer to Peter's questions."

Karl stopped in his stride. "Yes, I understand that you are both confused, but we have not sufficient time for long explanations. So I'll make it short. By coincidence I met some Polish resistance members, solicited their help for the sake of the boys, traded some food to obtain some civilian clothes for you Hardfeld, and for you Peter, and if you don't trust me you might as well start walking to Berlin right now. You can also choose to help me to get the boys organized."

"Civilian clothes," mumbled Hardfeld, "Truck's, one miracle after another. What do you want me to do?"

"Yeah," Peter chimed in, "what do you need us to do?"

Karl looked at both of them. "Hardfeld, line up 40 boys and try to get them all inside of one truck. This will be a very close fit. See how many you can fit into one truck. Two or three might sit next to the driver. Once you know the number for both of the trucks select the youngest and weakest ones for the later ride to Berlin.

"Peter, select about 40 of the oldest and strongest boys and have them collect their bedding straw and blankets and pile them up at the exit where the trucks are standing. I'll be right back."

Karl broke into a short run towards the other side of the yard and Hardfeld and Peter returned to the main building. Elu came out of the bushes he was hiding in and intercepted Karl in his run.

"I see the trucks, is our plan dismissed?"

"No, but we don't have to walk, we will drive. Get your friends and bring the apples to the front door and prepare to leave with us."

Karl lifted one of the baskets on his shoulder and started his walk back to the trucks. Elu and his friends carried the rest of the baskets close behind him. As they approached the vehicles they were greeted by the first group of boys who climbed all over the first truck and over themselves. Hardfeld tried to get some resemblance of order into the bunch by shouting short and sharp orders. It seemed to work for a moment and then he had to repeat them again.

Karl set his basket down and called to the group. "Line up in a single line.

"One apple for each of you, come and get them while you can."

The boys were almost stunned as if they could not believe their ears and eyes. They did not remember that apples existed.

To the amazement of the Lieutenant, they lined up in a single file. Karl ordered the first boy at the bushel to stand by and give each of the other boys one apple. Not of their choice of course, just one unselected apple to each one of the group. Karl waved at Elu and Lechek and helped Pilu to bring their baskets into the hall.

It took only a few minutes and all of the apples disappeared from sight.

Every one of the boys had indeed received an apple of their own.

They stood around munching the juicy treat, and talking to each other, describing the taste of the yellow apple to the ones who had received a green apple and vice-versa.

Even Hardfeld had an apple and was debating with himself to ask Karl how he had managed this new miracle. But again, Karl was ahead of him.

"The apples are a present, I did nothing special. As a matter of fact, I am just as surprised as you are. Now tell me how many boys fit into one truck?"

"Forty-two," answered Hardfeld, "this includes two boys next to the driver. What's next?"

"Easy," said Karl, "just like I told you before. Line up eighty-four of the youngest or weakest boys and keep them busy carrying food from the kitchen to the door here. Also tell them to dress as warm as they can and no suitcases. Backpacks only, with a bare minimum of belongings.

"I will take the rest to the railroad and come back with the empty trucks."

"You mean to say that you will leave the boys alone at the railroad bed? What are they supposed to do? How will they survive," asked Hardfeld.

"You will see," answered Karl, "because you will be with me." He looked across the hall and went to see Peter.

"Hey, Peter, how are you coming along? Did you get all of the blankets?"

"Of course, no big thing, and I also figured the numbers between the railroad group and the truck group and I have the oldest boys standing by," answered Peter, "We are ready to roll at your word."

"Let's first get the canned food from the storage room to the trucks. Line up the boys and order fire brigade drill. Where are the drivers? They should help."

"Hmm," answered Peter, "I think Anton likes our kitchen helper, Regina. They made eyes at each other and disappeared a moment ago from the kitchen. Herr Brandt is outside by his truck."

Karl had absolutely no experience in handling a situation like Anton and Regina. He was old enough to shoot and to kill if necessary. He had been trained by extremely good teachers, but nobody had ever told him anything of sex or even a subject close to it.

However, he did know that the Russian soldiers mostly attacked when they were drunk and he had been told that when the fighting troops are drunk they would rape any women and girls they come across, even very young girls who are still children. But, this here had nothing to do with fighting troops or raping.

He went outside to see Brandt and told him about the disappearance of Anton and Regina. "I don't know how to handle this and we have to get on the way as soon as possible. Please help me," he asked of Brandt.

"I don't really know Anton that well," answered Brandt, "but this should not take me long. Get the boys on board and I'll take care of him."

Brandt went into the building and Karl signaled to Peter to bring his group of older boys to the trucks.

"All of you will listen to me and to me only," he addressed the boys.

"You will sit wherever you find a place to sit. Peter and I will throw all the blankets and bedding on top of you. Sit on it and cover yourself. The ride will be short, not longer than 30 minutes at the most.

You, Willy, will sit in the front, next to the driver of truck number two. Peter and Pilu will sit with the rest of you in the back of truck number two.

"Lechek and I will sit with the group in the back of truck number one. Elu will be in the front of truck number one, next to the driver. That's all, no questions. Load the canned food and then get on the trucks!"

Within twenty minutes the boys climbed on their assigned trucks. Peter and Karl proceeded to pile all of the blankets and bedding on top of them. As Peter lifted the last of the bedding into the truck, he looked to his friend and asked, "How come you decided to sit in the back with the boys, instead of in the front next to Brandt?"

Karl glanced at him, "Elu knows the nearest way to the railroad bed. I have never been there and could not be of any help to the driver, and I don't think that you have been there either. Besides, I want to talk to Lechek."

Peter nodded in agreement but then asked, "What gives with Lechek?"

"I don't really know for sure, but I think that Lechek is the younger brother or even the son of Wanda, our camp cook. And, I have the feeling that our Polish crew is just as much afraid of the Russians as we are."

Karl went back into the building to look for Brandt and get the civilian clothes for Hardfeld and Peter. He decided that he would leave his own jacket and pants in his room until he came back from the trip to the railroad.

The clothes for Peter looked like the right size, maybe a little too small for Peter's large frame, but they had to do. As he came out of his room he saw Wanda, the older of the Polish cooks come out of the kitchen.

"Hello Wanda, have you seen Regina?"

"Yes," answered Wanda, "she is outside talking to the SS driver. I think she is trying to hitch a ride away from here."

Karl did not care if Regina wanted to get away from the Russians, but he did care if this would mean that one of his boys had to surrender his seat on the truck. Still carrying the bundle of clothes for Peter and Hardfeld, he turned to the outside door but stopped when he saw Wanda's face. It was all red and tears were running down her cheeks.

"Karl," she said, "can you take us along? Please? You are our last hope. If the Russians find out, and they will, that we worked in this camp for the Germans, there will be no mercy for us."

"Even if we could take you along, where would you go to in Berlin?" Karl answered, as he hurried towards the door. "And what about Stanislaus? You told me that he is your father and that he is part of the Polish resistance. I am sure that he can find a way to hide you."

The disappointment on Wanda's face and her frightened eyes made him stop to reconsider. His thoughts raced through his mind. Just a week ago, everybody, he included, was afraid of the Polish underground spies. And now it looked like that they wanted to be friends with the Germans. He thought for a moment about Stanislaus, who had assigned three of his young members to guide him and his boys through the woods to the railroad tracks. That was just about an hour ago.

Things were changing fast, much too fast for him to comprehend. He needed to talk with adults who had experience. Hardfeld and Brandt were the only adults around him, and he was not too sure about Hardfeld's mental condition.

Karl thought about his father and wondered if he would have had an answer for him. The last time he had seen him was about one year ago; and right now he did not even know if his father was still alive.

Wanda was still looking at him. "Please," she whispered.

"I don't know myself what I am doing, Wanda. This situation is not in my hands and I am afraid of making any decision at all. But, let's talk with your father. Tell him I need to see him when I come back from the railroad."

Hardfeld had seen Wanda and Karl at the door and he had also seen the civilian clothes Karl had been carrying.

"Are they all yours?" he asked Karl.

"No, they are yours and Peter's. Hide yours in the sidecar of the motorbike. As soon as I am back we will get the boys on the road and you and I will take the motorbike and join up with our group at the railroad."

Karl handed a heavy insulated overcoat, a jacket, and a pair of trousers to Hardfeld. "Oh, I almost forgot, I also got you a packet of high potency pain killers. You will find them in the pocket of the jacket."

Hardfeld was speechless. He had always asked the military field doctor, who came by the camp every second week, for additional pain killers and was told every time that he could only get one pill for each day because they were in very short supply and needed for the field hospitals. And now he was holding in his hand a vial full of pills. There must be at least 60 tablets here, he thought.

He trembled as he put the vial in his pants pocket. He had no idea how Karl could get his hand on medication while he himself as an officer was unable to do so.

Karl handed the remainder of the clothing to Peter and turned to Brandt.

"Ready to drive? Let's go."

Elu took his seat next to Brandt and Karl climbed in the back. He found a place next to Lechek.

While the trucks moved out, Hardfeld turned to the remaining boys, "You will be going home within the next two hours. It will be cold on the trucks. See if you can get into your shoes with two pairs of socks on, and double up on your clothing as much as you can wear. Also, you cannot take any suitcases along, only backpacks.

"Go to the storage room and fill your back packs with canned food. If you don't have a can opener on your pocketknife, go into the kitchen and see if Wanda or Regina can find you one. Furthermore, go through all the rooms and bring all the pillows and blankets that the first group might have left behind. You don't have much time, so let's get going."

Hardfeld thought hard if he had forgotten anything, hoping that it would not be anything critical. He then looked at Udo who was still sitting on the front table. "Get two or three of your friends and help me to push the motorbike into the yard."

The lieutenant felt a little relieved that this camp assignment was almost over, but he was also deeply worried about the upcoming challenge at the railroad, and how, or even if, he would eventually get home himself. He went to his room and stuffed his backpack with some underwear and socks and then carried his last personal belongings and notes to the kitchen where he burned them in the wood stove.

Four

Elu knew the area and the shortcuts to the railroad as well as the back of his hand. He had hunted the woods with his father for rabbits and in the last 2 years during the German occupation, he had carried dozens if not hundreds of messages between the Polish underground and resistance members. With his German ID papers and his German language ability, he had traveled several times to Kottbus, and on one occasion, he even went on a German troop transport from Berlin to Warsaw.

But lately he was assigned to Stanislaus, and he had gathered with his friends, a bunch of wood and kindling and stacked it close to the railroad tracks with the intent to stop and raid German supply trains.

It was all planned by people he did not know other than by a few code names. He was pretty good at his assignments, but this latest one was different. He could not really understand why all of the sudden he was supposed to help the German kids to stop and board a train.

Stanislaus had told him yesterday that now was not the time to debate tactics and he trusted Stanislaus more than anyone else he knew. They had traveled for about 25 minutes at a much faster speed than he expected. The snow was only about 3 inches deep and on many spots the wind had cleared the road completely. He guided the small convoy through a few turn-offs and they were nearing his intended destination.

"Turn left at this tree. There is a turnoff to a small country road.

We need to follow this little road for only about 1 kilometer and then we come within 200 meters of the railroad tracks. I don't think that there will be room enough to turn around. Can you drive 1 kilometer in reverse?"

"Elu," answered Brandt, "you have no idea what I can do. Just tell me where to drive."

Within a few minutes Elu motioned to slow down and stop. While Brandt remained behind the wheel, Elu jumped out and knocked on the truck's paneling.

"Lechek, Karl, we cannot drive any further, but we are within a few minutes' walk to the tracks."

Karl jumped out and looked around. The terrain was almost too good to be true for what he had in mind. They were right next to a great bunch of bushes which would provide an excellent wind shelter if they needed one.

"Everyone out. Throw all the bedding and blankets over to the right side and then make a fire brigade and throw all the bedding and blankets into the center of the bushes."

A moment later Peter stood by his friend, "What's your plan? Any orders for me?"

"Yes, as soon as the trucks are empty I will be off to the camp. You will take all the boys to the center of the bushes and crush down the branches to make a small flat area. Throw all the bedding on the branches and try to build something of a windbreak in every direction. Stash all the canned food in one corner and heap all the blankets on top of the bedding.

"Then go with Elu to the tracks and have him show you how far you are from the wood pile he was talking about. If the pile is right next to the tracks leave it there. If not, make a fire brigade and transport as much of the wood as possible to the tracks. Don't forget the kindling. I'll be back with Hardfeld."

Peter just nodded to his smaller friend. He admired his fast decision-making and his sharp thinking. What Karl had missing in body strength he more than made up for with his mind.

"Don't worry, Karl, when you come back you will find everything in order.

You want me to leave Lechek and Pilu with the boys when I go with Elu to the tracks?"

"Your call. You will see as you proceed, but I will take Pilu with me to guide me back."

The unloading of the trucks took just a few minutes. Karl climbed in and sat next to Brandt.

"What was the deal with Anton and Regina," he asked as Brandt backed up the truck and tried to stay in the snowy grooves.

"Don't really know. Regina must have asked if Anton could take her along. That's all I go out of him."

Brandt would not say anymore and concentrated on his driving. After some sliding and slipping, they were back at the main road. The night had given way to the first daylight and it looked as if they had a nice and dry day ahead of them.

Karl wondered if the Russian foot soldiers had by now started to advance. He had been told that the Russian tanks initiated the first breakthrough by driving wedges into the defenders. He asked Brandt if he had any more information about this tactic and what he thought about their chances of bringing the children back to Berlin.

"When and how did you hear about the Russian advancement," Brandt was asking in return.

Karl was thinking for a moment, "It must have been about 1:30. I had been listening to the radio and woke up when the OKW blasted their team music which precedes their alarms."

"Then what, any phone calls from your headquarters, any other communication?"

"No, our phone lines must have been cut or destroyed by the storm yesterday evening. My standing orders are to evacuate the camp immediately upon any news pertaining to a breakthrough by the Russians. This is why I am asking you."

Brandt kept his eyes on the road as he answered. "Yes, I think that we will be able to bring the remainder of the children back to Berlin, and I know that we will not be able to do this trip twice in a row.

"I was actually on duty to drive ammunition trucks to the front when Anton reached me with the orders from SS Headquarters to assist you and to bring the son from the Sturmbannfuehrer to Berlin. So it stands to reason that Headquarters knew about the breakthrough before you heard it on the radio. I have to say that you have guts to try to stop a train to transport the boys westward. I mean, you know as well as I know that the railroad tracks back there do not directly connect to Berlin."

"I know, but I cannot think of anything else that might work. During my last meeting in Berlin I tried to reason with the school official in charge of the KLV program to bring the camp home. But I was told that there was no chance that the Russian troops would ever reach the German borders. Hitler was supposed to have Wonder Weapons ready to beat the Russian army back to Russia.

"I was told that the allied air attacks on Berlin were of a much greater danger to the boys than the camp in Poland. Therefore, it was decided to keep the camp where it was, but I was also promised that I would be relieved of my temporary authority as soon as some teachers or adults with experience became available."

"Let me tell you something, Karl, there are no teachers available. Hitler's orders are to draft any able adult into the Volksturm, and this includes you in the Hitler Youth."

Karl had the feeling that Brandt wanted to tell him more. But, he also knew how dangerous it was to even mention the possibility of defeat.

"What do you know about the Russian tank wedges," he asked again of Brandt.

"This is a relative new tactic and it works in several ways. Actually it is the Russian artillery, which is blasting for several hours at a specific spot in our defense line. When they are certain that there is no one left to defend, they roll in their tanks. These tanks are not allowed to shoot during the breakthrough, not even to defend themselves should they come under attack. Instead, they are ordered to move forward until they run out of fuel.

"However, once they run out of fuel, they will start shooting right and left into our side lines. This tactic is totally confusing for us because our fighting troops do not know exactly where the actual fighting front line is, or if it even exists anymore."

Karl pondered what he heard. "How much time do you think I might have with my group at the railroad?"

"Very, very little," answered Brandt. "You have to stop the first train which comes your way. There might not be a second one."

They passed a few abandoned farmhouses and the cloister showed up in the distance.

"Where are your parents?" continued Brandt.

"I don't know. I just hope they are alive."

Karl did not know what to add, but he found it somehow comforting that Brandt had asked about his parents. Nobody had asked him about them before. He wished that he could stay with Brandt for a while longer. They reached the gate to the yard and he saw Hardfeld standing next to the bike, topping off the tank from one of the fuel cans. He also noticed that Hardfeld had the fuel cans removed from inside the sidecar. He had them somehow attached and secured to the luggage carrier mounted on the back of the sidecar.

"Stay safe, I wish you well, and...thank you for helping," Karl reached over to Brandt and handed him an envelope, "Please forward this note to the Fichte school, the address is on the envelope."

Brandt looked in Karl's eyes and shook his hand. "Take good care of yourself, and if you know how to pray, do so and often."

Karl pulled his hand back. He had prayed for guidance just last night, but he was surprised to hear the advice. Maybe not all of the SS were the same.

"Thanks Herr Brandt, you do the same."

He turned abruptly around to avoid showing his moist eyes and walked toward Stanislaus, who he had spotted behind the tool shed.

"Stanislaus," he started, "Regina and Wanda are begging me and one of the drivers to take them to Berlin. I'd like to help them, but you know that this does not make any sense. Please talk them out of their idea."

Stanislaus shifted from one foot to another. "Karl, you have misunderstood. Yes, the girls are afraid that the Russians will rape them, but they don't want to ride all the way to Berlin. They just want to get to Luban, their home village, only about 65 kilometers from here." He took Karl by his arm and pulled him further around the shed.

"Look, we tied some baskets together. You can fasten them to the back of the trucks and load them up with some of the boys' backpacks. This should give you the room you need."

Karl considered for a moment the possibility of adding one more passenger to each truck. It should be doable as long as the original estimate of passengers was not too tight to begin with. Besides that, he really wanted to be of help to the Polish women. They were good cooks and he had enjoyed their food. It was not what he was used to from home, but it was good and tasty.

He also reminded himself that the girls had plenty of opportunity to steal supplies from his storage room, but he never found anything missing.

"Wanda told me that she was your daughter and that you are no priest, but a local organizer of the resistance. Why did you help me to obtain civilian clothing?"

"Karl, why don't you think before you ask stupid questions? It was you who thought that I was a priest; I never told you that. It was very simple reasoning for me to offer you clothing in return for needed medication and canned meat. I knew from Wanda about your ability to obtain food. Even medical supplies did not seem to be a problem for you. By the way, how did you get the medical supplies?"

"Now it is me who does not like stupid questions. I obtained for you what you wanted and you supplied me with what I needed. And we might not be done. I will take the girls to Luban, and you owe me one."

Stanislaus' face lit up like a Christmas tree. He had been worried that Karl might refuse. He was in no position to hide the women in this area, which soon would be a combat zone. However, his wife in Luban would know what to do.

He shook hands with Karl and watched him walk back to the trucks and to Hardfeld.

"We have two more passengers. The drivers will take the cooks to their village, which is on the road to Berlin. So for an hour or two the boys will have to squeeze even more than anticipated, but we will not leave the women behind."

The stern tone in his voice made it clear to Hardfeld that this was a decision and not up to discussion. The Lieutenant did not mind at all. He really liked Wanda, who very often brewed him extra strong tea and also helped him with his bandages. If he had not been married and committed to his wife, he might have tried to fool around with her. He was glad that he had not had to make the decision of what to do with the women. So, he just smiled at Karl and nodded in agreement.

The boys had loaded the trucks and jumped around to keep warm. They all were eager to get going and lined up to shake Karl's hand and then jumped over the tail gates to find a place to sit down between the back packs and themselves. Karl knew all of them by name and gave each one a few encouraging words and pats on the shoulder.

He then faced the drivers who were standing with the women. Regina had a small potato bag in her hand and Wanda carried something in a large bundled towel.

"Brandt, Anton, please take the women along to their home village. It is on your way to Berlin. No detour; just drop them off where they tell you. I wish you well. Travel safely and say Hello for me in Berlin."

Before he could turn away Regina threw her arms around Karl and kissed him on each cheek. She smiled through tears of joy and Wanda joined her to hug Karl, who all of the sudden did not know what to say or what to do.

Brandt smiled at him too and said, "Thank you Karl from all of us; we will never forget you."

Then, everything happened very quickly. The women climbed in the back of the trucks, the boys argued about where to sit, Brandt and Anton started their motors, and Hardfeld and Karl waived a last good bye as the trucks moved through the gates.

It was a sad moment for Karl who swallowed hard to keep his emotions under control. He really did not know in his young age about emotions and that he had any, but his whole body was shaking and he looked at Hardfeld for some support.

The Lieutenant tried to think of some comforting words, but all he could come up with was, "Keep your head up, and think of the Fuehrer who trusts your ability to remain stable under any condition. How else do you think you wound up with your authority and position?"

Karl did not blink and did not answer. He felt like running away, but there was nowhere to run. Not now, maybe later.

He asked Pilu, who was standing a few feet away, to help the Lieutenant to enter the sidecar of the motorbike, and then went to his room to retrieve his civilian clothing and his backpack.

The backpack was regular Hitler Youth issue and had a portion of a tarp over the top. The tarp was fabricated from a very stiff canvas-like fabric and cut into a triangular shape. Furthermore, it had short strings and buttonholes attached. It also featured a slot in the center that served as an opening to stick your head through. This way it served two functions; the first one being to serve as a rain cover. You placed the whole canvas over yourself, the narrow triangular portion went to the front, then you stuck your head through the slot and that was it. The wider rear part of the tarp protected your shoulders and your gear including your backpack.

The second purpose was that three tarps could be connected to each other and serve as a tent-like rain shelter for three people. In actuality, it was not very rain proof and when it got soaked, it was heavy to carry. But right now, it would come in handy to protect

Hardfeld in the sidecar from wind and snow.

Karl looked once more at the old stone walls and made his way to the outside. Hardfeld was sitting in the sidecar and Pilu stood next to the rear seat of the heavy KS 750 Zuendapp motorbike.

It was the heaviest motorbike in the Wehrmacht and advanced in its design. It featured a drive shaft and a locking differential connected to the side wheel. Karl's only driving experience was a short training course, which hardly covered anything more than starting, shifting and breaking. He knew nothing about motors and hoped for the best.

As he tried to recall his starting instructions he also glanced at the notes he made during the course. But, first he handed his canvas tarp to Hardfeld who stuck his head through the slit in the center and Pilu helped him to secure the loose ends to keep them from flapping in the wind.

Karl opened the fuel lock underneath the tank and then jumped up and down on the kick-starter. Nothing happened and he thought that he might not carry sufficient weight to turn the starter motor. So, he tried to jump harder on the starter, but no luck. Once more he studied his notes and found the answer.

He had forgotten to press down the key in the headlight. If it was not pressed down, the motor would not start. One more try on the kick-starter and now it turned over and the engine noise filled the air and made normal conversation almost impossible, but conversation was not on Karl's mind. He tried to get comfortable in the seat and pointed to Pilu and the backseat. Pilu jumped on and Karl found the first gear and drove slowly out of the gate.

Once on the road, he shifted up into the other gears and settled down to a cruising speed of a little above 45 kilometers per hour. Not much of a speed, but Karl was satisfied that he was moving at all.

The Lieutenant shifted his body in the seat of the sidecar to find some protection behind the partially broken windshield. He was in pain again. This time his arm and his leg were hurting and he blamed the sidecar for his discomfort. He was thankful for Karl's pain pills, but he suspected the whole trip would be nothing short of torture.

It was early afternoon and the sun had dried the wet spots from the ice on the road. From time to time Karl felt a push from Pilu on his back, who pointed him towards the turns they had to take to get back to the railroad. Just as Karl settled on a slightly faster cruising speed, he noticed a person ahead of him who was standing on the side of the road.

It turned out to be Lechek, who was instructed by Peter to watch out for the bike and to make sure that they would not miss the final turn-off. Karl breathed a sigh of relief as he saw the bushes and the make shift camp. He came to a stop and turned off the key, which he carefully put in his pocket.

As Pilu and Lechek helped Hardfeld out of his seat, Peter came up to Karl with a big grin on his face.

"Welcome back, Karl, you want some hot tea?" he asked his friend.

"Yes, do you have some sugar in it?" Karl asked in return. He liked everything sweet, especially the spicy herbal tea of which they had plenty.

"No, no sugar. We must have forgotten to take some along. You will have to learn to do without it." Peter's answer made Karl wonder if they had forgotten any real necessary essentials. But on the other hand, they could do without anything if they were able to stop a train. And then again, what if there were no more trains going west? He shuddered at his own thought.

"Did you find the wood? How far is it from here?" he asked Peter.

"Not far at all. It was real close and we just finished bringing it up all the way to the train bed. I think we have more than enough."

Karl wanted to ask something else, but decided against it. Instead, he told his friend, "Please find Elu and bring him along to meet with me and the Lieutenant for some planning."

It was getting late in the day. Some clouds had moved in and it started to get dark. In an hour it would be pitch black.

Karl was cold and thought about the heavy overcoat from Stanislaus, and then he looked at the boys who were all bundled up and figured that he had to set an example for the kids. However, this did not make him feel any warmer, so he did some jumping jacks and went to see Hardfeld.

The Lieutenant was leaning against the motorcycle in his full uniform. He was not ready to change into civilian clothing. If he were to get caught by SS patrols he had to be in uniform, but if the Russians were to overrun him, he was better off without the officer's uniform. On the other hand, he wanted to be in uniform when they stopped the train. He had also decided to ask Karl why they could not simply join the kids on the train, if there was one, and leave the motorcycle behind.

Karl started the meeting by asking Elu if he had any information gathered during the past week about the timing of trains to the west. Elu answered that there were very few trains using this line and the westward trains were down to one or maybe two trains per night. Almost always, transport trains of wounded soldiers.

"What time," asked Karl.

"After midnight," answered Elu. "We think that they load the wounded on board after dark sets in."

"Are these high-speed trains," asked the Lieutenant.

"I don't know what high-speed trains are. To me they are all pretty fast."

Peter had nothing to say at the moment. He also wanted to ask Karl when they were alone, why he wanted to drive with Hardfeld on the bike to Berlin instead of boarding the train with him. It seemed that Karl anticipated the question, because he started to explain that he had no set plan in mind.

"We need to play this by ear. First of all, we need to get some rest until about 11:00 PM. At that time we will move all the wood on top of the tracks and wait for the train. If the train runs through the fire, we are back to square one. If the train stops, Peter and I will board the locomotive and the boys will immediately start to climb on the train.

"Hardfeld, you will stay out of sight at that time because I want to tell the locomotive driver that these are all German children abandoned by the KLV leaders. I intend to tell them that the boys are hungry and cold and apply to their mercy. If this works, I will tell them that we also found a wounded officer wandering aimlessly around who needs medical attention and care. If this works too, we are all on board and Elu can drive the motorbike back to Stanislaus."

"I will stick close to the Lieutenant and if we make it to Cottbus or any other station close to Berlin, I will disappear with him. You, Peter, will stay with the boys. If you don't make Berlin, try to get in touch with Udo's father. The SS might be able to assist the boys to get to safety. Here is the number from the SS Headquarters."

He reached in his upper pocket and handed Peter a yellow piece of paper.

"There are a few more numbers, which should help you. Some of them are from the German Red Cross and some of them are from the Catholic Caritas group. These organizations were supposed to help us, where are they now?"

To Karl's surprise, Elu spoke up, "Your plan should work. I can assure that the train will stop, leave it to me."

Karl turned to face Elu, "How?" he asked.

"We will set a few small fires alongside the tracks in front of the big fire. They will confuse the locomotive driver. His headlights are going to be unable to penetrate behind the big fire because it will blind him. He has no choice but to stop. But you have to be very fast to get the boys on the train."

Karl thought for a moment, and then stood up.

"I think if there is a train at all, it will come within an hour. Because of the Russian advance, there will be a fast effort to bring the wounded to safety. Elu, start lighting the small fires you suggested, right now. Have Lechek and Pilu listening for any noise on the rails.

"Peter, start the big fire too, but just start it. Don't burn the whole thing down, watch it carefully."

Peter took off and the Lieutenant understood immediately what needed to be done and limped over to the boys to get them ready to move to the tracks. Karl joined him and addressed the group.

"You will lie down next to the track. Take your blankets along to cover yourself. As soon as the train stops, you will need to board it. Don't wait for any orders. You will have to help each other. If you want to get home, you need to get on the train. I know that you can do that."

He looked around and noticed a small glimmer in the distance. This must be the first small fire he thought. The Lieutenant was searching through the small pile of canned food and supplies and grabbed a can with his left hand and threw it in the sidecar which was parked a few feet away. Karl walked over to him, "Remember Lieutenant, stay out of sight. Whoever is on the train must be convinced that he has only abandoned children on his hand. Be close by and ready to move."

Hardfeld did not reply. He was willing to follow Karl's orders, which he considered in his own mind as mere suggestions. He had adopted this mindset since this helped him to accept Karl's authority.

Peter helped the boys to drag their backpacks and blankets and even some bedding to the shallow trench next to the tracks. He was glad that there had been no new snow and that the trench was almost dry. He dragged some of the straw-filled bedding to the deeper parts of the trench and some of the boys followed his example. If they had to sleep or just lay down for a while, the bedding would serve as a barrier from the moisture of the ground.

Karl had decided to talk once more individually to each of the boys.

He wanted to give them some personal words of hope and assurance that very soon they would be home and with their families. He also reminded them to stay on the school grounds in Berlin in case their parents or relatives were not there when the boys arrived.

The boys liked Karl because he always helped when they needed something and they listened to every word he told them. They felt like they had a big brother explaining to them the world of the adults. Except, Karl could not explain to them why there were bombs and burning buildings and dying people all around their hometown. He did not know, nor could he imagine that there even was a reason for this chaos. But, he understood that the boys were afraid of what might be waiting for them once they reached their hometown.

He understood, because he was afraid himself.

Five

The boys settled down and Karl and Peter replaced Lechek and Pilu on their listening posts. The rails were ice cold and Peter placed the side flaps of his uniform cap between his ears and the rail. He was worried that his ear might freeze to the rail if he fell asleep while listening.

Karl lifted his ear off the rail from time to time and shifted his position every few minutes to avoid falling asleep. He thought about his father who was somewhere on the eastern front serving as an infantry soldier, probably just as cold and worried about Karl as Karl was worried about him. Elu showed up next to Karl.

"How are you doing?" he asked.

"If it wasn't so cold, I would write myself some notes," answered Karl, "because if I survive the war, I will write a book about this madness."

When Elu did not answer, he added, "You will be in it too, Elu, I will write about how you helped us."

"What would you write about tonight?" asked Elu.

"How cold and quiet it is. The remainder I don't know yet, the night is not over," he added.

An hour later, Lechek and Pilu showed up again to take over listening for some noises or rumbling on the rail. Karl went to find the Lieutenant in the darkness when Pilu's voice stopped him cold.

"Train is coming, I hear it," and right afterwards he heard Elu and Lechek running towards the glimmering side fires, stoking them to full flames.

Peter was already by the big fire and threw dry pine tree branches on the top, causing the whole pile of wood to almost explode. The flames must have been over 15 feet high and in the flickering light, the boys huddled next to each other, touching each other with their outstretched arms, just as the lieutenant had told them to do.

Their line along the railroad bed was about fifty feet long with Karl and Peter standing closest to the fire. They all could hear the train approaching.

As it neared the first small fires, they could hear some brakes screaming.

It seemed that the whole night went from dead quiet to shouting and screaming steel on steel within less than a minute.

As the locomotive slowed down, Karl could see that it was a rather small engine, not the big 03 he had seen in the Berlin railroad station. He could not see the full length of the train because he concentrated on jumping on the running board of the engine as soon as it stopped. He could hear Elu, who shouted over the noise that it was a short freight train. This meant no passenger cars with small doors, but wide freight doors in the box-like short wagons. He did not know if this was good or bad, but he knew that he had to cross the tracks because Peter was on his side and he wanted them to board the locomotive from both sides.

The engine stopped the train within maybe 5 feet of the main fire, which by now was a tower of flames. Karl jumped so fast into the cab that he almost overran the machinist. He was an older soldier maybe in his early sixties. He was in infantry uniform without any rank. His gray hair and face were dirty and sweaty.

Karl had at first decided to use a heavy-handed approach, maybe pulling his gun and forcing the machinist away from the controls. But after seeing the old man and his fearful eyes in front of him, he decided in a split second to try a helpless plea.

"Please take us along. We are about forty boys from a KLV camp. Our teachers and leaders abandoned us when they heard that the defense line by Warsaw was broken."

As soon as the words had left Karl's mouth, he realized that this was the wrong approach. He had made a mistake. The fearful eyes of the infantryman turned into a very angry expression.

The old guy screamed at Karl's face, "You damned kids! Do you realize what you have done? You stopped a transport of deadly wounded soldiers and officers. Because of this delay they might die. Get off my locomotive before I knock you off!"

He had stopped the train because he had thought that the Polish resistance had sabotaged the rails. When Karl and Peter had jumped in his locomotive he had thought that he would die, but once he realized that he had kids in front of him his initial fear turned into rage.

Before Karl could answer, Peter moved in front of him and kicked the old man with all his might into the groin.

"Shut up. You will take us along, like it or not."

It was clear that Peter was just as agitated as the old soldier who now sat on the floor covering his groin with both hands. He rocked back and forth and then it looked like he was about to pass out.

"Hands up, both of you," the commanding voice came from the tender behind them.

As Karl and Peter raised their hands they saw a corporal with a handgun pointing at them. Neither of them had thought about the possibility of a fireman or second soldier in the tender.

The Corporal, who was about 30 years of age, looked at both of them, and when he could not detect a weapon, he lowered his gun. He was large and strong enough to handle both of them in case they tried something. He also noticed the rank insignia on Karl's HJ uniform.

"Your leaders left you behind? How many of you and how old," his voice was now almost concerned.

Karl had hope again, "We are forty boys. My friend and I are 14 years old; all the rest are twelve years old or younger," he answered the corporal and added, "Please, take us along, we are freezing."

"You boys have guts, I give you that."

The Corporal's answer was encouraging to Karl, but the next few words from him were even more electrifying, "The only room we have is in the second freight car. You might have to stand all the way through the trip, or lay on top of each other. The doors are unlocked. You have five minutes and not a second longer to jump in."

Karl was off and running before the Corporal moved his hand as if to wipe him off the locomotive. Peter wanted to follow him, but the Corporal blocked his way. He looked at the old soldier, who was still groaning and whimpering, and then at Peter.

"You should have not kicked him in the balls, kid, at least not that hard. I would stay out of his sight forever, if I were you. Beat it."

He bent down to help his machinist get up and then jumped down from the engine to look and check if he could just drive the train through the fire. Peter set off running behind Karl who was already helping and pushing the boys into the freight car.

It was Elu who had called the boys to the unlocked doors on the second car after he had tried the first car only to find that they were locked. As Peter was running to the huddle of boys, Karl motioned him to climb on board to help from the top. There was a bottleneck because some of the boys were still crawling on all fours when they reached the floor of the wagon. Elu and Karl were busy lifting the next one up and pushed them right on top of each other. Peter saw immediately what was needed and pulled on arms and legs as hard and fast as he could. There was not much of a protest from the boys as they were being now pulled from the top and pushed from the back. The ones who were already in the car tried to help too, but Peter shouted at them to get away and to the rear of the car.

Just as the last of the boys got through the door, the train started to move.

Karl shouted a last "Thank you!" to Elu and jumped on a portion of a running board on the slowly accelerating train.

He glanced back once more to make sure that no one was left behind when he remembered the Lieutenant. Hardfeld had tried to limp to the train when the last boys boarded it, but at the same time the train began to move and Hardfeld's limp was too slow. His leg prosthesis limited his forward movements to a slow pace. There was no way that he could make the now faster moving train. He was in severe agony as he stopped his effort and gave up.

Karl's mind raced. He could not leave the Lieutenant behind and he had to jump off the train right now if he did not want to get seriously hurt.

"Peter!" he yelled, "Take good care of the boys!" He jumped just as the freight car passed the last flickering pieces of wood.

Before he hit the ground, he protected his head with his hands and rolled sideways as he was trained to do. The motorcycle driving course from the HJ had also covered crash positions in case he rolled the cycle. Luckily there were no rocks were he had landed, just hard dirt with a few semi-frozen grass bushels.

Karl had to sit down once more before he could get up. The impact with the ground had shaken him up. He looked around to get his orientation back. The train had left a fiery trail and was moving out of sight. He could make out the figure of Hardfeld who was supported by Elu or Lechek, and they were limping in his direction.

Karl tried to guess what time it might be and hoped that he had still the majority of the night ahead of him. He slowly walked over to Hardfeld who had stopped again. It was Lechek who supported the lieutenant and who now looked at Karl with a little admiration showing in his eyes.

"I think you are crazy to jump from the train among the flames, but boy, I am happy to see that you are back to take care of the Lieutenant. I don't know what we would have done with him."

Hardfeld said nothing. He was in severe pain and it showed in his face.

"Help me to place him in the sidecar," said Karl "I think that the boys left most of their food behind. Share it among you, or take it back to Stanislaus. I hope there is some other stuff you might be able to use. We don't need any of it."

Karl missed his backpack, which he had tossed into the freight car while he helped the boys. When they had waited for the train he had his warm civilian topcoat secured to the pack and now it was gone too. Karl fished around in his pockets and found the key for the Zuendapp.

"Lean on me and let's go," he encouraged Hardfeld, who now tried to walk on his own.

As they approached the motorbike they noticed that the turning radius of the heavy bike with the sidecar was too large to turn it around on the narrow field way. Elu was trying to push it back and forth by himself without much success, but now it was not much of a problem. Karl and Elu pushed the bike and Lechek pulled and pushed on the handlebars and with a few back and forth movements, the bike was pointing in the right direction.

Elu wanted to place some canned food into the sidecar, but Karl stopped him, "We will find some troops and something to eat within the next day. You keep it Elu, you will need it."

"Where is Pilu," Lechek asked. Nobody had seen his friend since Karl had jumped off the train.

Elu looked worried, "Pilu!" he shouted in the direction of the train tracks, "Where are you? Are you all right?"

Before the others could join in they heard Pilu answering, "I am coming!" and he came carrying Karl's backpack with the heavy overcoat still attached.

"I saw that something was thrown from the train. I could not see what it was and it took me a while to find it." He was grinning from ear to ear as he handed Karl his pack.

"I guess I will never find out who acted this fast," said Karl as he took the backpack from the young man. He opened a side pocket of the pack and removed a pack of cigarettes and handed them to Pilu. "Thank you, please take them, they will come in handy when you need something to trade for food."

Karl did not think it was possible, but Pilu grinned now even more. He admired the cigarette pack from all sides and tried to fit them into his shirt pocket.

"Thank you, thank you, Karl, I will not smoke them. I will just keep them."

Hardfeld had watched the exchange in amazement. He did not smoke, he never had, but he knew that cigarettes were almost impossible to obtain.

However, he was not too surprised. Nothing that Karl had or did surprised him anymore. He was getting used to it. But, he had not expected that Karl would jump off the moving train to help him to reach safety. He was still too much in shock to talk to Karl about it or to thank him for it.

He fumbled in his pockets to find his pain pills, and when he thought that nobody was looking, he swallowed two of them. This was the first time he had taken two at once, but he had taken none since they had left the camp. He wanted to save them. They gave him some comfort, and even some pain relief. He had saved a few, just to have a small reserve, but right now he felt again like passing out. He hoped that he could talk Karl into taking him to a field hospital instead of delivering him to Berlin.

Any doubt about Karl's ability to drive them safely to Berlin was a thing of the past. By now he knew that the Jungscharfuehrer, in spite of his young age, was extremely capable and he would trust him with his life. He limped to the bike where Elu was waiting to help him into the seat but first, he sat on the back of the sidecar and remove the prosthesis from his leg. Something had come loose as he tried to make the train and now he was bleeding. He had some sterile bandages in his pocket, which he applied before he was sliding into his seat.

In the meantime, Lechek was busy giving Karl directions to the nearest major highway leading west. Karl was not sure if he wanted to risk using a major highway as it was possibly congested with troop movements and supply caravans. On top of that, he was concerned about being stopped by the military police because he did not have the correct papers for the Zuendapp. All that he had was some temporary certification from the HJ that entitled him to drive the bike and he had the orders from the HJ and the Berlin school district of Wilmersdorf to bring the Lieutenant from the camp back to Berlin.

His major concern was the fact that the bike was registered to the Wehrmacht, (the German army) and if the military police stopped him and needed a bike for themselves, they could just order him to surrender the bike. On the other hand, if he decided to avoid the major routes and make a detour to Kottbus, it could also prove to be a mistake because who was to tell if there was less military police by Kottbus than in Posen, or Frankfurt; on the Oder River.

He listened to Lechek's instructions and made himself some notes and then had the idea to ask the Lieutenant for any advice he might wish to offer. Hardfeld was surprised but glad that Karl had asked for his input.

"Look, Karl, I think that you can talk us out of any situation, but as long as you ask me, I would favor taking the route to Kottbus. I was in their field hospital some months ago. You can just drop me off and continue on your way to Berlin without me. If we get stopped between here and the hospital you can tell them that I am a medical emergency and I will play my part and whine and groan and show them my amputations without the leg prosthesis."

Karl remembered his orders to evacuate the camp and then to bring the Lieutenant back to Berlin, but delivering Hardfeld to a hospital was a viable option. Nobody in Berlin would ever know if this really was a medical emergency or not.

Then he had another idea. He looked at Hardfeld and asked, "What do you really want, Kottbus and a hospital, or the nearest field hospital?"

"At this point, I would really like to see a doctor as soon as possible. Look I am bleeding all over from my leg and I could not strap the prosthesis back on if I tried."

"So Posen it is. We are less than two hours away from it."

Karl started the heavy bike and looked to the three men who had become his friends during the last few hours.

"I doubt if we will ever see each other again. Thanks for your help and take good care of yourselves. Please give my regards to

Stanislaus." One last wave and he drove back to the road. The night was still pitch black and he was out of sight within a flash.

Six

When Karl entered the main road, it started to snow and he had to slow way down to see where he was going. It seemed to him that the wheel of the sidecar had a mind of its own, but then he told himself that this was probably normal on the slippery road.

After about 90 kilometers, the motor started to stutter and then it died all together. He had run out of gas and Karl fumbled in the morning dawn to open the connection to the reserve portion of the tank. After he started it up again, he wondered if he had missed a turnoff in the dark and decided to stop and wait for daylight. As the snow continued to fall, he was glad that there was no wind. Just heavy snow flakes piling up on him and on the Lieutenant, who was again under the cover of the canvas. This time, Hardfeld had his head underneath the tarp.

Karl thought that it might be fairly warm under the canvas and the snow and he envied the obvious comfort of the Lieutenant. He slowly climbed off the bike and walked around it to keep himself warm. As he looked around to see if he could spot a tree or bush for some protection, he noticed that he might be able to find some shelter underneath the bike.

Better than nothing, he thought to himself as he crawled and pushed himself underneath the steel bottom of the sidecar. As soon as his face was out of the falling snow, he realized how tired he was and he fell asleep within minutes.

When he woke up it was daylight and it had stopped snowing. At first he just wanted to turn over and sleep some more, but then he noticed that his pants were wet, but only on one side. He pushed himself backward and after his head had cleared the bottom of the sidecar, he stood up and examined his uniform. It was not as bad as he had feared. The moisture from his wet pants had saturated his shorts and part of his shirt. It could have been worse considering that he had been sleeping on a layer of snow.

As he looked around he saw that the snowfall from last night did not amount to more than maybe 3 inches, and he noticed what looked like some tire tracks across the street. Some kind of a vehicle must have passed as he was asleep. Maybe this was a good thing, because he knew that it must have been a military vehicle; there were no civilian cars anymore any place in Poland and the tracks might lead him to the next larger town.

But first he had to look after Hardfeld. The snow on top of the canvas covering the sidecar looked undisturbed and he wiped it off and opened the slit in the tarp to see if the Lieutenant was still asleep. Hardfeld was groaning as he tried to adjust his eyes to the bright sunlight. His face looked flushed and when Karl placed his hand on the forehead of the Lieutenant, it was obvious that he was fighting a fever.

Karl hoped that the fever was just the beginning of a head cold and was not related to the Lieutenant's injuries. Hardfeld was groping around under the canvas as he tried to lift himself up and straighten out in the seat.

"Karl," he asked, "do you think that we could find a hospital today?" His voice was strained but not hoarse, which made Karl think that the Lieutenant was not getting a cold. It must be something of a wound fever, he reasoned to himself.

"Yes, of course," he answered, "we should find one within a couple of hours of driving. I saw you yesterday throwing a few cans of food under your seat. Maybe we can eat some of it now. I am hungry besides having a wet behind." He tried to cheer Hardfeld up and it worked.

The Lieutenant painfully smiled, "I thought you would be potty trained." He shifted around in his seat and produced a can of liverwurst from below the tarp. "This should be enough to last us for a while. Do you have a can opener handy?"

"I have something here which will serve just as well," answered Karl as he handed his HJ knife to Hardfeld. "But I don't think that we have anything to drink." He rummaged through the saddlebags hanging from the rear seat of the bike. "No, I did not think so. Let's eat and then get going. What time is it anyway?" Karl did not own a watch. Very few boys of his age owned a watch. None of his friends ever owned one. He had hoped to get a wristwatch from his parents for Christmas, but Christmas had come and gone and he had to stay with the boys in the camp. He had not made it home to see his parents.

"It is 10:35," answered the lieutenant as he handed to Karl a big portion of the canned liverwurst on a few pieces of Knaeckebrot.

While Karl was eating he walked over to the tire tracks to see if he could determine in which direction they went. Judging by the splashes of frozen dirt next to the sides of the tracks he determined that the vehicle must have been moving in the same direction he wanted to go. He finished his last piece of bread and filled up the tank from one of the two remaining fuel containers.

Hardfeld had lifted himself out of the seat and examined his leg. The bandages had stopped his bleeding; however, he was reluctant to remove them out of the fear that doing so might reintroduce the bleeding. He rearranged the blankets in his seat and slipped down again and found a more comfortable position.

Karl checked the tire tracks one more time and was just about to start up the bike when he saw a vehicle coming his way. He got off the seat again and walked to the middle of the road to flag the vehicle down and ask for directions to the next field hospital. It turned out to be a Kubelwagen, an all terrain vehicle developed by Ferdinand Porsche and built by Volkswagen. It had a light machine gun mounted on the hood and was driven by what appeared to be two infantry men who stopped immediately and got out to inspect the Zuendapp with its passengers.

Hardfeld cringed when he recognized that the soldiers were actually SS men. As an officer of the Wehrmacht, he had no use for the gung-ho and overbearing demeanor of the SS. When the first of the SS men, a Rottenfuhrer, realized that the officer in the sidecar was a Lieutenant with the insignia of a tank commander, he stopped for a moment and then decided to salute. Hardfeld observed that the salute was more than sloppy and waved back with his right hand prosthesis in a likewise manner.

Karl stepped forward and informed the SS men that he was from the KLV camp by Kosten and asked how to get to the next field hospital. The Rottenfuhrer, one of the lowest ranks in the SS, looked at the insignias of the HJ uniform worn by Karl and at his silver eagle at the cap. His name was Konrad and he was in his early twenties, tall and lanky and polite in his answer.

"You should have taken a left turn about one kilometer behind you. If you continue to drive in your present direction, you will wind up in a restricted area. You will have to turn around anyhow so you might as well do it now."

The second SS man was a Sturmman, which was not a rank, just a designation for a private. He looked at the Zuendapp and the Lieutenant and then addressed Konrad; "We could take them along to the entry of our area. We could sign in and out and lead the Lieutenant and the Gefolgschaftsfuehrer to the hospital. We need medical supplies anyhow, and this might give us an excuse to get them now while they still might be available."

Karl was a bit uncomfortable with the idea, but Hardfeld blinked at him to be quiet. Konrad seemed to like the suggestion of getting medical supplies and he nodded his agreement. "Please follow us. We need you there to establish the urgency, otherwise we are unable to come back and guide you."

Before Karl could voice his opinion about this arrangement, Hardfeld spoke up, "Let's do that right now. I need to see a medic as soon as possible. We appreciate any help you can give us. Just drive slowly because this Zuendapp is slipping all over the place."

Karl looked at Hardfeld in surprise. After all, it was him who was doing the driving and not the Lieutenant. He did not remember much slipping last night and now it was daytime and he could not see any ice on the road if there was any at all. But then he figured to keep his mouth shut. There must be a reason that the Lieutenant wanted to take the detour to the restricted area. He wondered what kind of a restricted area it was anyway. He had never heard of one this side of Posen.

The two SS soldier turned their Kubelwagen around and started to drive back in their old tracks. Karl started up to follow and then asked Hardfeld, "Why did you agree and why are we driving slowly and most of all, where are we going?"

"You did not notice the small inscription on their sleeves?" Hardfeld asked Karl in return.

"No, I was watching you and the eyes of the Sturmman. He seemed to like this bike and I don't trust him, in spite of his friendliness." Karl's answer was clipped and his voice was serious.

49

"I wanted you to drive slowly, so that we could talk. These are not ordinary SS men. They are prison guards, and the restricted area is a prison camp for political prisoners and homosexuals. It is not on any map, but I heard about it. The SS troops guarding these camps are known for their sadistic tendencies and they have practically unlimited powers, especially in the face of the Russian advance. If our request for assistance to find a field hospital gives them an excuse for a side trip, so be it. Better to have them on our side than to worry if they are plotting to get the Zuendapp from us."

Hardfeld's face was sweaty again, and his speech was slow and halting. Karl hoped that the prison camp was not too far. His wet pants and underwear started to get ice cold and extremely uncomfortable.

Within a few minutes he was passing several warning signs advising him to turn around and that he was about to enter a restricted and guarded zone. The first and actually only thing he saw was a long row of double barbed wire and a large guardhouse. Then came about 150 feet of open land and another, this time triple row, of barbed wire with another gate and guard shed. There were at least five large shepherd dogs running back and forth on the open stretch between the wire barriers.

The Kubelwagen stopped at the first guardhouse and Karl came to a halt about ten feet behind it. Karl watched as Konrad walked into the building and shortly thereafter, three SS men came out and helped Karl to turn the heavy bike around. At first they wanted the Lieutenant to get out of the sidecar, but when they saw the bloody bandages around his leg stump they just started to push the bike with Karl and asked him if he had any cigarettes to spare. When Karl told them that he did not smoke, but that he had a package of pipe tobacco, they were happy to accept his treasure. The oldest of them was about 30 years old and told Karl that he was from Dresden and that his 8 year old son was also in a KLV camp someplace on the Baltic sea. He gave Karl an empty envelope with four different addresses on the front of it.

"My name is Berchthold. My address is on the back of the envelope. When you get to the HJ headquarters in Berlin, please see if there is a central information system in place to reunite the KLV children with their parents or their relatives. I would really appreciate if you could feed these addresses into their system."

Karl placed the envelope in his side pocket and promised to see what he could do. They started to talk about the role of the HJ in regard to the KLV camps, and Karl's position and authority impressed the SS Sturmman.

"I can only wish that my son has someone like you looking after him." He shook Karl's hand, saluted the Lieutenant and the three soldiers went back to the building. Shortly thereafter, Konrad appeared again. He stepped into the Kubelwagen and as he backed up and turned the vehicle around, Karl could see that there were now three SS men altogether in the car. They moved past the Zuendapp and motioned Karl to follow.

It was now early afternoon. The sun was still out and the weather was dry.

Karl signaled the Kubelwagen to go faster and pretty soon they passed their rest stop from last night. Konrad had told them that it would take them about one hour to reach the next little town where there was a field hospital with limited facilities. But none of the field hospitals featured any extensive follow-up medical treatment. Karl hoped that they could and would care for the Lieutenant. Once they were at the hospital and the responsibility for the Lieutenant was lifted off of his shoulders, he would gladly surrender the Zuendapp to anyone who desired it. A short time thereafter the village showed up.

The field hospital was located in a small factory building and Karl noticed that there was a side spur of railroad tracks leading up to an entrance with some kind of makeshift sliding doors, which were open. Male and female orderlies carried wounded soldiers on stretchers toward two freight railroad cars. The front entrance of the factory was on the opposite side of the rail tracks and the Kubelwagen parked right next to it. Konrad got out and went through a side door into the building, but first he waved to Karl to drive further down to what seemed to be some kind of a loading dock.

The whole area was a congestion of arriving and leaving vehicles. Most of them were light infantry support trucks, similar to Konrad's Kubelwagen.

Karl pulled up as far as he could and parked sideways by the dock where he was immediately greeted by two orderlies who grabbed the Lieutenant by the shoulders and arms and lifted him out of the sidecar. Hardfeld tried to stand upright on his left leg, but the long time period of his immobility took its toll and he was unable to support himself. He just simply slid down to the ground and the two orderlies reached for a stretcher to carry the Lieutenant away. They had completely ignored Karl who was obviously just a driver and capable of taking care of himself. This was fine with Karl who was happily surprised to see the speed and efficiency of the facility.

He removed the key from the Zuendapp and was about to trail behind the Lieutenant when he was pulled roughly back by his shoulders. A big, red-faced sergeant was yelling at him to move the damned bike or he would roll the sorry thing into a pile of garbage. Karl mumbled something about big people having small brains, but luckily for him, he kept his voice too low to be understood. The sergeant took it as an apology and pulled his vehicle right into the free slot after Karl continued down the factory driveway to find a parking space. There was actually plenty of space to park, because all the arriving vehicles took off after unloading. Everybody was in a hurry to keep on moving.

As Karl walked back to the factory, he noticed that most of the arriving wounded were very young infantrymen. He did not see a single soldier older than maybe 20 years old. He did not know what to make of it, but he thought that it was odd. The inside of the building was a massive open space, divided into rows of operating tables and rows of straw mattresses. Right in the front was something like a waiting area for the wounded. Several female nurses tended to the individuals and sorted out the most serious and immediate surgical candidates.

Karl had never seen the inside of any hospital, let alone a military field hospital, and he was shocked at all the blood on the coats of the orderlies.

Actually there was a lot more blood on the floor in the entrance area than in the operating area. This was probably due to the leaking bandages of the arriving wounded. As he went further into the hall he found the smell almost overpowering his will to find Hardfeld. There was moaning and groaning everywhere he looked and went. In spite of his shock, he was impressed by the apparent underlying order in all the tumult. Whoever was in charge knew what he was doing and did it well.

Alongside the back of the rear wall was again a separate row of mattresses. There were also some benches and even some chairs that were occupied by freshly bandaged and partially sedated soldiers. Karl noticed that there was no apparent separation between ordinary privates and officers. He was still winding his way around the benches trying to find Hardfeld when he heard someone calling his name. It was a female nurse who had called to him. She was standing at the sliding doors leading to the railroad cars. In front of her was a small folding table covered with sheets of paper, which turned out to be destination passes and transfers. Next to her stood a tall military policeman who inspected and stamped the transfers before they were pinned to the uniforms of the wounded leaving the hospital. She looked in Karl's direction and pointed at him and then to the MP.

Hardfeld must have given her my description, thought Karl, as he made his way between the waiting soldiers. The MP took a look at Karl in his HJ uniform and shook his head when he recognized the sniper insignia.

"Well, you made it; we thought that you left already. You must be Karl Veth, Lieutenant's Hardfeld driver."

"Yes, how is the Lieutenant and where do I find him?" replied Karl as he looked around the exit, hoping to see Hardfeld.

"I think that your lieutenant is alright. According to my notes he will be transferred out of here, probably with the train sitting outside. You are supposed to wait for him. Don't wander off or disappear, he wants to talk to you."

Karl looked around to find a place to sit, but there was none. "I'll be right back," he told the MP, "need to change my underwear."

His pants had somewhat dried, but he still felt uncomfortable and he could not stop thinking about the set of warm woolen underwear in his backpack.

He went out of the building, found his way back to the Zuendapp and was relieved when he saw that his backpack was still attached to the rear seat.

Unfortunately, the reserve canisters of gasoline had disappeared. He cursed himself for not stashing them into the sidecar. Without gas, the bike was useless but maybe he could still trade it for something. He was sure that he would be able to think of something.

When he got back to the MP, he saw to his astonishment a very young major standing next to the folding table. It was not so much the appearance of the officer, but the medal around his neck. It was the Ritterkreuz with swords. One of the highest medals ever bestowed upon a German warrior.

Karl had never met a recipient of a Ritterkreuz before and snapped a sharp salute at the officer. The major returned the salute and locked eyes with Karl. Karl did not know what to think; he knew these eyes and then again he did not remember how he could have known them. The Major's eyes were gray, strong and unblinking, but not cold or unfriendly. Karl had the strangest feeling that he knew the Major, but he knew that he had never met any officer beyond the grade of a first Lieutenant and for sure he had never met anyone with that many medals of courage and achievement.

"There he is," announced the MP to the Major, "this is Gefolgschaftsfuehrer Karl Veth, the driver of Lieutenant Hardfeld."

The major took his eyes off Karl and started to ask the MP where he could find Hardfeld when the Lieutenant appeared. Hardfeld stretched his right arm out in an attempt to salute but the major waved him off.

"No need to do that, Lieutenant." He spoke in the dialect of a native Berliner. "I understand that you were in command of the KLV camp by Kosten. Where are the children now?"

Hardfeld told him briefly about the events of the last two days and praised Karl's performance and abilities. The Major listened to the Lieutenant and asked about some details in regard to the prison. All the Lieutenant was able to tell him was that he thought that it was a facility for political prisoners and homosexuals. He also told the Major that they actually did not see any prisoners at the entrance to what seemed to him a severely guarded compound. "We were not allowed into the facility," he told the Major.

The Major turned to address Karl, "When you are done with getting the Lieutenant on the train, come and see me. Sergeant Werner, the MP here, will know where to find me. I need to talk with you." He then asked Werner if he had seen the SS men who had guided Karl to the field hospital.

"No," answered the Sergeant, "but if they were obtaining medications, they are required to sign out with me. They must still be within the facility."

Hardfeld motioned to Karl to follow him outside and started to walk towards the train. He seemed to be in a much better shape than just a short while ago. His prosthesis was strapped to his leg again and he limped pretty fast along.

"Karl," he started, "I have a transfer to Hannover, my home town. The transfer allows me to use this train until Kottbus. All we are waiting for is the locomotive, which is supposed to bring additional freight cars. I want to thank you for everything you have done for me. I will recommend you for recognition, and I hope that you find your parents. Most of all, take good care of yourself. You are a credit to the Hitler Youth and our Fuehrer would be proud of you."

"Thank you," answered Karl, "I will take your advice and will look for my parents, but first I have to present myself to the school administration and our KLV headquarters in Wilmersdorf. If I am still alive after the war, I will also try to look you up in Hannover. Do you have any messages I need to relay in Berlin?"

"No," answered the Lieutenant, "just an order for you. Stay alive!"

Karl shook Hardfeld's left hand and then stretched his right arm to salute the Lieutenant, "Heil Hitler," but the Lieutenant just waved him on and limped slowly towards the freight cars. It was getting dark again and the few shaded lights hardly illuminated the immediate area around the train. The Lieutenant disappeared into the darkness.

Seven

Karl had changed his underwear and was now feeling warm and comfortable. The Major still wanted to talk to him later on in the evening.

In the meantime, he had ordered Karl to help the orderlies with the stretchers to bring the wounded to the train, which had been supplemented by three additional cars and a small steam engine. When the locomotive was ready to roll, Karl went along the cars to catch one more glimpse of his Lieutenant, but it was too dark in the boxcars to make out anything at all. Most of the freight cars had been improvised with wood frames and mattresses to allow two and three tiers of wounded soldiers on top of each other. Again, there was no separation of officers from the common foot soldier. Each freight car had a box of medical supplies at the sliding doors and was accompanied by one or two orderlies.

As the train started to move, Karl waived a last good bye to no one in particular and went back into the building to find the Major. The MP directed him to a table along one of the side walls and encouraged Karl to help himself to some stew. The stew was mostly potatoes and vegetables, no meat, but it was nevertheless, tasty and hot. Karl ate until he thought that he might burst if he had one more spoonful. There was also some coffee ersatz in a gray colored tin can. Whatever the ersatz consisted of, it was lukewarm and smelled like molasses. Karl passed on that and had some cold water instead. In accordance with his instructions from the MP, he went out of the main hall to find the side building, which must have been the office building for the factory.

The small entrance led to a short hallway with several doors leading into individual offices. Karl entered, as directed, the first office on the right and looked around the small room. It had no resemblance of an office. It looked like a makeshift bedroom for three people; a couple of mattresses on the floor with a chair next to them and a wall cabinet in one corner. There were a few pieces of clothing on the mattresses and Karl assumed that this was a sleeping room for the orderlies and sat down on one of the chairs. He was dead tired. It had been a long day and the hot meal almost immediately induced the desire to sleep. He wished that he could stay in this room until the next morning. He did not mind if he had to sleep on the bare floor. It was warmer in this room than in his old bedroom at the camp. There could be no harm in lying down on the floor and resting his head on the side of a mattress. Might as well get some sleep while he could. The worst that could happen was that he had to get up again. He stretched out and fell asleep as soon as his head touched the mattress. The next thing he knew was that the Major stood in front of him. He did not know if he had slept at all, but he was kind of refreshed and scrambled to his feet to salute the Major.

"Stop that, Karl," said the young officer, "Do you know who I am?"

Karl squinted at him very carefully. The eyes on the Major looked a bit familiar, but the face did not trigger any memory and for the first time he noticed a big red scar, which started over the Major's right ear and extended all the way to below the chin. This was not a scar from a bullet. It must have been something like a knife or a bayonet. Probably inflicted in hand-to-hand combat. Karl's respect for the Major increased. This was a real war hero in front of him and he could not think of a reason why this officer was interested in him.

"No," Karl shook his head, "Herr Major, I don't know who you are. I don't even know your name."

"My name is Siegfried Zahn, and I am the older brother of your friend Peter Zahn." The Major smiled at Karl who all of the sudden knew why the eyes of the officer looked so familiar. It was like he looked at his friend Peter who just had aged by ten years.

"This is just in regard to my name and not the real reason I wanted to talk with you. But first, do you think that Peter is alright?" the Major asked.

"Peter was alright when he boarded the train with the boys. The train was destined to Kottbus. They should be there by now. How and if your brother and the boys found further transportation to Berlin I do not know." Karl tried to answer as precise as possible. He was still impressed that his friend had a brother who was a Ritterkreuz recipient. Peter had told him about his brother, but only that he was an officer someplace on the eastern front, and that he hoped that his brother was still alive. The last time he had heard anything about him was a long time ago. He had told Karl that he thought that his brother had been in many combat situations and one time he had thought that he even heard his brother's name in an official report from the OKW, the military headquarters, but he could have been mistaken. In any event, Karl knew that Peter wanted to prove himself worthy of his older brother; he wanted to be a true Hitler Youth.

The Major hesitated for a long time before he decided to continue. "Karl, I have been in difficult situations, but this is hard for me to explain. Anyway, I will try.

"I received the Ritterkreuz just two weeks ago and was granted a special four-day leave to see my parents in Berlin. I only found my mother, who told me that my father had been arrested one day before my arrival. There were no formal charges. The SS showed up in the middle of the night, arrested my father, and told my mother that her husband was now a political prisoner. That's all she knew. This was four days ago. I tried in the meantime to find out what I could, but when I asked the Berlin SS Headquarters about my father, I was told to accept that my father was a political enemy of the Third Reich. I was not to ask questions and to continue my duty to our Fuehrer and to the Fatherland." The Major stopped for a moment before he continued.

"I know that my father is not a traitor; he is not smart enough for that. Matter of fact, I know that his only fault is a very loose mouth and that he is too stupid to keep it shut. But I also know that political prisoners do not live long enough to tell a tale. They will be executed, or if they are lucky, they will be ordered to serve in the front line to prove that they love the Fuehrer. Either way, they are as good as dead."

Karl was shocked to hear that the father of his friend was a political enemy and that he has been arrested. He was also shocked to hear that even a Major of the Wehrmacht, with one of the highest medals for bravery, was unable to obtain information about his father's arrest by the SS. He knew that the SS and the Wehrmacht were at odds, but he did not realize the extent of it.

Major Siegfried Zahn left no doubt about it as he continued, "Karl, there is absolutely nothing that I can do; except that I heard about the prison camp you almost visited. I know that the political prisoners in this camp are destined to serve in the next front line to stop the Russian tanks, which of course, they are unable to do. But they will serve as cannon fodder so that the enemy is hopefully out of ammunition when they meet our real fighting line." Siegfried stopped again, not sure how to continue.

Karl ventured a guess, "You want me to find out if your father is in the camp?"

"I don't think that you are able to obtain any names or information about the prisoners. You have to remember that the SS is not your friend," answered the Major, "but I wonder if there is a way for you to find out when they are breaking their camp or when they intend to move the inmates to the front line."

The Major thought some more before he continued, "Because, if I would know the approximate date, I could volunteer for front line leadership duty. I did this twice before. It would fit right in with my regular behavior. This might or might not give me a slim chance to see my father once more. But honestly, I don't even know what to think or do. I was always ready to give my life for the Fuehrer, but now, it does not make any sense. Nothing makes sense anymore."

The Major sat down on a chair and loosened his uniform buttons. He looked tired, almost defeated. The last words of the Major echoed in Karl's mind; nothing makes sense anymore.

Karl, who never had a problem balancing his loyalty to Adolf Hitler and his sense of duty and honor, was beginning to understand the gravity of the Major's words. He was to him a real hero, but right now he looked utterly confused and helpless.

"Herr Major, I think that there is a way for me to find out what you need to know." Karl had at this moment no real idea on how to do that, but he felt that he had to offer some hope.

"Karl, why don't you get some sleep? I don't think that I want to involve you. I just needed to talk. You can sleep on that mattress there. I will see you tomorrow morning."

Karl wanted to salute again, but Siegfried just shook his head and said, "Good Night Karl," and walked out. Karl tried to sort out his thoughts, but his need to sleep was stronger. He fell into a dreamless sleep within a few minutes.

The next morning was cool, but clear and sunny. When Karl woke up, he found the hospital in a frantic haste to serve the still arriving wounded and at the same time, it was beginning to evacuate. During the night another locomotive had brought five boxcars, which were already partially loaded. The MP who was at his usual place told Karl to grab something to eat and then to wait for the Major who was busy on the telephone. The only food available consisted of the usual dried Knaeckebrot, canned margarine and some kind of diluted fruit marmalade.

While the Major was still talking on the phone, Karl went to check up on his Zuendapp. It started right up but then stopped immediately. Karl suspected that his tank had been siphoned and a look into his tank proved him right.

Nothing he could have done to prevent that from happening. He figured that maybe he could have slept in the sidecar, but as tired as he was, he would not have noticed the thieves.

When he returned to the main hall he found the Major waiting for him. "Any thoughts about our conversation last night," he asked Karl.

"No, but here is what I could do," answered Karl, "I could drive back to the prison and ask for the SS guard Berchthold who gave me the addresses for his son. I might be able to explain to him that I need to know his whereabouts during the next week to relay any possible messages to him. He seemed like a very concerned family man. If I can gain his trust he might even tell me what we really want to know." Karl became excited at his idea as he continued, "I could take the motorbike, if you could get me some fuel, and I could be back within three to four hours."

Siegfried Zahn considered the possible consequences of Karl's plan. The more he thought about it the more he liked the proposal. It was simple and without any serious implications. The fact that Karl needed fuel was not a problem. The major had arrived at the hospital with a small staff car driven by his personal driver. And as far as he knew, they had several cans of spare fuel.

"Come on," he said to Karl, "we'll gas you up to get you on your way."

"Will you still be here when I return or how will I find you?" asked Karl, who was happy that the Major approved of his idea.

"I don't have to be back before tomorrow morning. I will wait for you right here. In the meantime, I will help the hospital staff with their transition."

The staff car was parked behind the factory, and as Karl and the Major approached, the Major's driver snapped to attention. He was a young looking sergeant, maybe 20 years old, or thereabout. The major asked him to carry a can of fuel over to the motorcycle. Within a few minutes, Karl was ready to leave.

As he started the bike he asked the Major, "What time is it now?"

The Major looked at him in surprise, "Where is your watch?"

"I never owned one," replied Karl.

The Major turned to his driver and asked him if he could produce a watch out of nowhere within the next fifteen minutes. The sergeant contemplated the question for a moment and then answered, "Not much of a chance unless we have something to trade."

"Will fifty grams of cigarette tobacco do it?" asked Karl, "I have an unopened package of a navy ration," he continued.

"Willy, take the tobacco and don't come back without a decent watch. You have about twelve minutes left."

The Major turned his attention from his driver back to Karl, "You have any more tobacco or other surprises?"

"Hmm, yes, I think that I have one or two more tobacco packages. I wanted to use them for emergency trades in Berlin," answered Karl, "But, if you need them, they are yours."

The Major seemed at first unwilling to accept, but then he thought better of it. "I don't smoke, but if you would give me a package, I will distribute the tobacco to the most severely wounded. It will do them a world of good."

Without a further word, Karl handed the Major a blue and white embossed package of finely cut cigarette tobacco. He closed his backpack and was just about to place it in the sidecar when he took it out again. He rummaged around in it and found two large, heavy bars of antiseptic soap, which he offered to the Major. "You asked me what else I had. I am sure that you will put them to good use."

The Major accepted the soap bars with gratitude and was just about to remark that he had not seen this brand and quality of soap when Willy came running up to them.

"Sorry that it took so long, but I have here a good working Anker Pocket Watch, and it cost me only half of the tobacco." He handed the watch and the remaining tobacco to the Major who gave him back the tobacco and passed the watch on to Karl. The watch was dirty, silvery looking, with a white dial. It showed 10:30 and as Karl thanked Willy and the Major, he wondered to himself how long the Major had slept. He started the bike, placed the watch in his front breast pocket and took off in the direction he had came from the day before. The weather was almost perfect and he hoped to make good time.

As he shifted up the gears, he thought about his new possession and remembered that he had forgotten to salute the Major when he left.

Too late now, he thought, and then contemplated how he could approach the SS Sturmman Berchthold to obtain the information he needed. Within an hour, he noticed the first warning signs that he was traveling close to a restricted area. He recognized the last turn he had to make and right afterwards, the warning signs came up again. This time however, they were not simple warning signs as before, but stern warnings advising him to turn around. He knew that this was the short and final stretch of the road to the prison camp.

As the guardhouse came into view, he slowed down and continued the last few hundred feet in second gear. He stopped next to the gate and was immediately greeted by two large German shepherds who seemed to observe every one of his moves. It was kind of eerie because they did not bark. So far, none of the guards had noticed him, but he saw on the other side of the gate several SS men next to a convoy of six trucks.

In order to get their attention, he yelled as loud as he could. "Heil Hitler!" As he expected, they turned in his direction and one of them even answered with a likewise outstretched arm. Karl figured he might as well get right to the point of his visit.

"I am Gefolgschaftsfuehrer Karl Veth and I am looking for Sturmman Berchthold."

Two of the guards opened the gate and stepped in front of Karl. They studied his uniform and his motorcycle, and then assumed a threatening stance.

"We do not know of a Sturmman Berchthold. If you would not be a member of the HJ and a kid on top of it, we would have to arrest you because you are trespassing on a restricted area. Now let's see your ID."

Karl was not the least bit intimidated. He had encountered enough bullies before and knew their behavior. He knew that they could not help themselves; certain people just had to yell and shout. He suspected that it had something to do with their training, or it was just simply in their blood.

Karl handed them his papers with confidence and said, "If Sturmman Berchthold is not here anymore, then I need to see Rottenfuhrer Konrad."

The first guard looked up at Karl and studied his face, comparing it to the picture attached to Karl's ID. "Do you carry a weapon?" he asked.

"No, no weapon," answered Karl.

"Wait here by your motorcycle. We will see if Rottenfuhrer Konrad is available."

He went to the guardhouse and the second SS guard stayed with Karl. As they waited for Konrad to show up, another column of trucks approached the gate from the outside. Karl counted five vehicles; all of them empty except for the drivers. After they had passed the gate, they lined up next to the first group of trucks. Karl observed that all of the drivers were SS men. None of them had to show any ID when they passed the gate, and judging by the lively conversations between the new arrivals and the other waiting drivers and guards, it looked very much that they knew each other.

The SS guard who had remained with Karl pointed to the second gate inside the compound where the shape of the Kubelwagen showed up. "Rottenfuhrer Konrad is coming. He must know you to show up this fast."

As the Kubelwagen came to a stop inside the last gate, the familiar shape of Konrad jumped from the passenger seat and came towards Karl and the guard. Both of them saluted the Rottenfuhrer who dismissed the guard and asked Karl about Lieutenant Hardfeld and why he had came back to see him.

"The Lieutenant is in good shape and on a Lazarett train. I did not come to see you, Rottenfuhrer Konrad. I came to see Sturmman Berchthold, who was on guard duty when I was here before. When I asked to see him, a few minutes ago, the guards said that they did not know of a Sturmman Berchthold. So, I asked for you because the guards ordered me to turn around and leave."

"Why do you want to see Berchthold?" asked Konrad.

"Sturmman Berchthold asked me to take these addresses to my school headquarters in Berlin and to enter them in an information center for the purpose of giving his son contact information." Karl reached into his pocket and gave the envelope from Berchthold to Konrad and hoped that this would establish sufficient credibility for his return to the facility. Konrad studied the addresses on the envelope and handed it back to Karl.

"So, that still leaves the question why you came back to see him?" Konrad asked in a friendly tone, his official manner gave way to a relaxed conversation.

"I was able to phone the KLV headquarter in Berlin and they told me that Berchthold's son's KLV camp has been evacuated from the Baltic Sea to Stettin. I am ordered to travel to Stettin to assist in the further evacuation of the camp," Karl lied without hesitation. He thought back to what the Major had said last night, nothing makes sense anymore. He figured that Konrad had more important things to do than to check up on his story. Konrad had no reason to doubt Karl, who had proven to his satisfaction that he was a true HJ leader.

"I thought that if I could see Sturmman Berchthold once more before I leave for Stettin, I might bring his son a handwritten note from his father," Karl continued.

"That is very kind of you and I am sure that Sturmman Berchthold would have loved to write a short encouraging letter to his son. But he is not here anymore. We are leaving this camp tonight and he was one of the first to get ordered out. Sorry that you made this trip for nothing." Konrad admired Karl for being so concerned about his charges in the KLV group.

Karl was unsure how to proceed. His first mission was accomplished. He knew that the camp would be dissolved and that the prisoners would be transported in the waiting trucks. He decided to play dumb and confused.

He reached in his pocket where he had placed the envelope from Berchthold and took it out again. He also took out a bunch of other papers, which he laid out on the canvas of the sidecar. He looked at Konrad as if pleading for help.

"Could you spare some water or coffee? Please, I have to get some order in this stuff and I would like to sit down for a moment. I am sure that you know that the hospital is also evacuating, and I don't know if I will get a chance to rest before I make Frankfurt."

Konrad took pity on the young boy who was obliviously trying to live up to some demanding obligations. "Sure, Karl, you can sit down with me in the guardhouse. We have some coffee, good coffee, not ersatz. Would you also like something to eat?"

This question reminded Karl how hungry he was. "Yes, please," he answered.

Konrad took some of Karl's papers and guided him through the gate into the building. The room Karl entered was empty of guards. There were some folding chairs and tables, and a great steaming coffee pot. On one of the tables was a field telephone with a hand crank, otherwise, the tables were empty. The Rottenfuhrer laid Karl's papers down and grabbed an empty mug. He pointed to the chairs, "Take a seat, relax, bring order to your papers and I will get you some soup, if we have any left. Otherwise, I will get you some bread."

"Thank you very much," said Karl, who still debated with himself how he could find out about a prisoner named Zahn. He smiled thankfully at Konrad who filled the coffee mug for him and then went to the door to tell his driver to bring something to eat for Karl. "If possible find some hot soup," he added.

While Konrad stayed at the door and observed the guards and drivers, Karl's eyes scrutinized the walls, which were covered with sheets of paper. He almost cried out in astonishment when he realized what he saw. There where sheets of papers listing names of barracks, complete with names of inmates, and right next to them he saw lists of truck numbers.

He also noticed that some of the names had been crossed out or marked. Karl could hardly believe his luck but before he could study the names, one of the guards passed by Konrad and entered the room. He took a look at the wall and compared the lists to a notebook in his hand. Karl took his eyes of the wall and concentrated on his own paper work. And then it hit him. The last name of his friend was Zahn. It started with the last letter in the alphabet. He did not need to search all the lists on the wall. All he had to do was to find the last list.

As soon as the guard left, he studied the wall again and saw right away what he was looking for; Erwin Zahn, Barracks Seven, Truck Seven. He had it right in front of him in black and white, however, he did not know if Peter's father's first name was Erwin. But this did not matter at the moment. Konrad received from his driver a small terrine of hot soup and some bread. He placed it in front of Karl and asked him to eat up fast because he could not leave him alone in the room, and he had to attend to the guards. Karl did not need much encouragement. He was hungry anyway, so to eat real fast was not a problem and he had the information he was seeking. He could hardly believe his luck.

"Thank you Rottenfuhrer Konrad. I appreciate the food and the rest. I wish you well on your trip west."

"I wish we would be going west. No Karl, we are going east, somebody has to face the enemy. It is up to us, the SS, to do the fighting. You are lucky that you are so young. You might just be lucky enough to survive, but in any event, I wish you well. Now, get out of here."

Rottenfuhrer Konrad went back with Karl to the bike. A last salute and Karl hit the road faster than he ever drove before. Before he had started the bike, Karl had glanced at his watch. It showed two o'clock. He should be back at the hospital shortly after three o'clock.

Eight

It was exactly half past three when Karl parked next to the Major's staff car. The trip back was without incident except that the warm soup and coffee had caused Karl to stop more than once. When he entered the main building he saw Willy, who was carrying bags of medical equipment to the train.

Karl looked around to ask somebody where he would find the Major, but there was no one left in the main building. There was no orderly or nurse in sight. They all seemed to be at or on the train. Even the Sergeant was not at his usual position on the sliding doors. The hall was empty and deserted, except for boxes of equipment. The doctors had already started an emergency treatment facility in one of the freight cars. All in all it looked to Karl that he had just made it in time before the Hospital shut down completely.

Karl decided to check the train when he heard footsteps behind him. It was the Major who was eager to see him, and his face was one big question mark.

"How did you do, Karl?"

"If your father's first name is Erwin, then he is leaving the camp tonight in a truck, numbered seven. I counted a total of eleven trucks, but I did not see if the trucks displayed any numbers," Karl's answer was direct to the point, like always.

The Major stared at Karl. "How did you obtain this information? Did you see my father?"

"No, I did not see any inmates at all. As to the information, I just got lucky."

"There must have been more to it than just luck," insisted the Major.

"No, just dumb luck, Herr Major. But, I think that they will be leaving before tonight. Rottenfuhrer Konrad was in a great hurry to get me out of there."

The Major considered what he had heard and went to the office building to make a phone call to his division headquarters. He had to be back by tomorrow morning at the latest and he needed to find out if he had any options to choose a specific frontline command. Karl wanted to get on the road towards Berlin, but he doubted that he could obtain the necessary fuel.

Right now he had hardly enough left to reach Posen. And from there, it was still around 300 kilometers to Berlin, maybe more. He had to figure on detours and destroyed highways. Of course he could just leave the Zuendapp here, but then he would have to try to hitch a ride with this train to Frankfurt.

The more he thought about it, the more he liked the idea of a comfortable train ride instead of driving the unruly bike. Once on a train he could unwind and maybe even sleep. He started to relax and went back to the bike to collect the last few items from the saddlebags. There was not much left and it all fit into his backpack. When he returned to the hall, he found a doctor waiting for him.

"You are Karl Veth," the doctor asked in an assuming tone in his voice. He was gray-haired and looked overworked and tired. There was a uniform under the somewhat soiled and bloody coat, which might have been white at one time. It did not show any rank, just his name, Dr. Felder.

"Yes I am," answered Karl, "Do you need any help with a wounded?"

"No," replied the doctor, "but I might need transportation later on and I heard that you are driving a Zuendapp with a sidecar. I wanted to ask you if you could possibly take me along to Berlin?"

There goes my sleep again, thought Karl, but he assured the doctor that he would be honored to drive him. However, he added that he was short on fuel and he was hoping to hitch a ride with the train. While Karl still talked with Dr. Felder he saw Willy again, who was gesturing towards the side door, which lead to the office building. Apparently he was to hurry up and see the Major. He told Dr. Felder that he had to see Major Zahn once more and promised to be right back.

"If you don't find me here, when you come back, I might be at the train. Be sure to look for me. I will try to find us some food for our trip. The kitchen shut down already, but I think that I saw some cans of liverwurst in one of the supply bags on the counter. I hope that they are still there."

He went in the direction of the kitchen and Karl could hear him asking for supplies and blankets. In the meantime, Major Zahn left the office building and was on his way to his staff car. It was the first time that he was wearing his heavy lined leather officer coat, which indicated to Karl that he was also ready to leave the hospital. He waved at Karl to follow him to his car.

"I have to get back to the division and I wanted to thank you once more for your excellent service." he spoke slowly as if he had a problem talking. He handed Karl a brown envelope and continued, "I wrote a recommendation for you. Please give this envelope to your commanding officer. I wish that I was able to do more for you, and I will, if I am given a chance. If you see Peter, please tell him that I am proud of him and that I hope to see him again. Stay away from the SS. Remember, they are not your friends."

Karl wanted to salute but instead he received a warm handshake.

"Keep your salute for the wounded on the train and at home. They deserve it more than I do. Try to stay alive." His eyes were hard as he looked at Karl, but they also seemed to be moist.

Willy reached them and started the car. As they drove out of sight, Karl wondered how many more times he had to say until we see each other again, without much hope to see it come true. He turned back to the building to see if there was any possibility of obtaining fuel. When he reached the sliding doors to the railroad track, he almost ran into the MP who was carrying two canisters of fuel.

"There you are," he said to Karl, "Dr. Felder asked me to find some fuel for your bike. I searched the supply shed of our motor pool, but all the fuel reserves are gone, however, I found these two cans. They were hidden under a workbench. Somebody must have stashed them away and forgot about them. Anyway, they are yours now." He handed one of the canisters to Karl and then fell in step with him to help him carry the gas to the bike. Karl was sure that he had now sufficient fuel to get close to Berlin.

After he topped off his tank, he fastened the canisters on top of the sidecar. Then he told the Sergeant to hop on for the short ride back to the main entrance of the old factory. Dr. Felder was waiting for them. His white coat was gone and his insignia on the long and heavy infantry coat showed Karl that his new passenger was a Captain. "Thanks for finding us the fuel," he said to the MP. "The train will leave any minute. Better hurry up."

Willy did not even bother with a salute. He ran towards the sliding doors, grabbed his backpack, which he had left there before and boarded the train.

Captain Felder asked Karl how he wanted to secure his meager luggage on the bike. It consisted of a medium-sized valise and a small bag of food.

"This depends where you like to sit Captain. If you sit behind me, we can just throw it in the side car, otherwise, we will have to tie the valise on top of the back seat and you can stow the small bag below your legs."

As the captain considered his options, Karl looked longingly towards the train and dared to ask a question, "Excuse me, Captain, but, why do we bother with the bike? It looks like we are in for a new snow storm and we are driving into the night. This will slow us down. It might even force us to stop completely."

It was obvious that Dr. Felder was not used to answering questions from subordinates. He was also surprised that someone would question him at all. After all, he was a respected surgeon and an officer, and for a moment it looked like he wanted to pull rank. He glared at Karl but then seemed to change his mind. He looked up at the blackening sky and over to the steaming locomotive and hesitated before he answered.

"Karl, I have orders to get to Berlin the fastest way possible. This train provides much better transportation, I'll give you that, but it only goes to Frankfurt, and it might be delayed. Troop transport and supply trains have first priority." He checked his wristwatch and continued, "If we can make it to the Posen field hospital before the snow starts, we can rest for a few hours and then continue in the morning and be in Berlin by late afternoon."

Karl did not know what to answer, so he just said, "Thank you, Captain." He was happy at the prospect of spending the night in Posen. He should be able to make it within two hours and if he could use the main road, it should be even faster. Dr. Felder was done fastening his valise to the rear seat and stepped into the sidecar. Karl checked once more that the gas cans were secured, turned the key, and jumped with all his weight of barely 120 pounds on the kick-starter. The Zuendapp responded immediately and within a few minutes they were on the main road. However, they were constantly ordered by MP's to pull over and stop at the side of the road in order to let conveys of troops pass. The troops were driving to the east while the Captain and Karl were westbound.

While they were stopped again and standing on a cross road for longer than 20 minutes, the Captain fished out a flashlight and studied the map again. He pointed to a mark on the map and showed it to Karl. "If we turn here to the northeast, we should be able to miss all that traffic and then we should be able to turn west again. It might cost us twenty minutes at the most."

Karl welcomed the suggestion to keep on moving, but he thought that it might not hurt to ask the MP on the crossing how much longer he had to wait.

"You could still be standing here tomorrow morning, if you are lucky. These are all combat ready troops and the first ones might engage the Russian tanks at any given time. In this case you are in a combat zone. If I were you, I would have taken the crossroad a long time ago."

The MP's answer helped Karl with his decision and as he repeated the advice to the Captain, he turned the bike away from the main road. The road he was following now was a neglected Polish secondary road and according to the captain, they were driving east by northeast. Not the ideal direction, not at all. Karl did not have any driving skill to speak of and the little experience he had was barely sufficient to keep the bike in the center of the unpaved road. Luckily for them, the anticipated snowstorm did not materialize. Maybe it was too cold for snow. In any event, the road was frozen solid and started to get very slippery.

Karl had again the sensation that the side wheel wanted to pass in front of the bike, and he spent most of his energy pushing and pulling on the handlebars to maintain a straight, forward direction. After driving for about a half hour, the road finally turned towards the northwest and a deserted farmhouse showed up beyond a curve. Maybe it was the driveway to the farm that distracted Karl's attention, or it was a frozen rut. Karl did not know how it happened, but the bike slid off the road. The sidecar was a few centimeters in the air and the side wheel was without traction. He found himself in a ditch, and the front wheel was stuck in an almost impossible steep angle.

The Captain said something that sounded like "Shit, shit, shit" to Karl, but he could have been mistaken. He pushed on the handlebars to free himself and as he got off the bike, the Captain climbed out of the sidecar.

"Are you hurt?" he asked Karl and as Karl shook his head, he added, "I don't think that we broke anything on the bike. Fortunately, you were not driving too fast."

Karl did not know if this was a complement or a criticism, but he did not really care. He had to get the bike back on the road. As they tried to move the bike, they both realized that the Zuendapp was far too heavy to be pushed out of the trench. They had to either dig the front wheel free or bring some traction under the side wheel. Either way, they had no tools to dig or to move dirt. The motor was still running and Karl shut it off. It seemed as if the silence and the darkness of the night made him feel cooler than he really was.

"Maybe there is a shovel at the farmhouse," speculated the Captain and Karl set off towards a broken down shed, which was close to the driveway. A few minutes later he was back with a spade. "How lucky can we get?" he asked the Captain, who took the spade from Karl and started to loosen the frozen ground around the front wheel. He worked fast without looking up and a short while later he stopped to remove his long coat. Karl took over and shoveled the dirt away from the front and threw it under the side wheel. He was not sure if this would help to get traction, but they had to get it out of the way anyhow, so why not try?

He was about to take a breather when the Captain signaled him to stop. He looked up to the Dr. who motioned him to be silent and then he heard it too. It was the unmistakable sound of a chained vehicle. It was a deep growling of a motor, together with the rattling and clanking of chains.

"Great," he said, "we are almost done and now we get the help we need to pull us out." He looked back down the road trying to penetrate the darkness, except now he thought that the sound came from the front and to the right. He was just about to ask the Captain for the flashlight to signal to the approaching vehicle when he felt the hand of the Dr. shaking his arm. But it was not so much his arm that was shaking as the Dr. himself.

"This is not a chained vehicle, Karl. I know this cracking sound of the motor. This is a T34, a Russian tank."

Karl's first instinct was to fall flat on the ground, but the arm from the Captain was not shaking anymore and was holding him up. "Don't even move," said the Captain. He had to almost shout because the sound of the approaching tank was getting very loud and it came almost directly from the front. "If they have night vision glasses they might have seen us already. However, if it is the spear head of a tank column, they will not shoot unless they happen to run out of fuel right in front of us."

Now it was Karl's turn to shake and he did so unable to control himself.

"Steady," said the Captain, as he laid his left arm around Karl's shoulder and then they both saw the terrible form of a T34 materializing out of the darkness. They were not in the direct path of the beast. If it continued in the direction it was moving, it would pass them within maybe ten meters. The frozen ground seemed to shake and if the tank driver adjusted the direction by a degree, it would roll right over them. To Karl's amazement, he could now make out the shape of the tank commander standing in the turret. He was holding binoculars at his eyes and he was looking right at them. Karl's mind all of the sudden adjusted to the terrible reality. But his thoughts were not racing each other anymore as they did just a split second before. His mind became crystal clear. There was no doubt he could be dead in a second or two. He wanted to close his eyes, but they would not obey him. His body was literally petrified. It was to him as if he could see himself, unable to move, but full of hope to survive the next few seconds, because that was all it would take for the tank to pass.

And then he saw out of the corner of his eye the most incredible thing.

Captain Felder was straightening out his posture and lifted his hand to the brim of his officer's cap and threw a salute in the direction of the tank. Karl's mind snapped back to the reality on hand and his only thought was, this asshole will get us both killed. But, to his astonishment, he saw that the tank commander returned the salute before he disappeared into the darkness. The sound diminished and there were no other tanks within hearing distance.

They had just witnessed the daring strategy of the Russian spearhead tank offensive. These guys would really drive through the German lines without shooting, but cause havoc of confusion.

Karl was still speechless when Dr. Felder shook his hand and said, "You are a brave boy, Karl, and I am glad to have you as my driver." He pulled back his hand and reached again for the spade. "Let's see how fast we can get out of here." Their effort paid off faster than Karl had feared.

As soon as the front wheel pointed forward, he started the engine and the rear wheel of the Zuendapp gained traction. The captain crawled on the sidecar and his weight added to bring the side wheel down. Karl kept the bike in the ditch until he found a relatively flat spot to get back on the road.

He stopped for a moment to give the Captain a chance to assume his seat and then he shifted up through the gears to get away from the place he was sure he would remember for the rest of his life. He would also remember that he had learned to pray. He just did not know exactly when that was, before the tank had passed, or afterwards.

They reached Posen within two hours and asked their way to the field hospital. Dr. Felder's credentials helped them to obtain a room to sleep and for the third time this week Karl was asleep as soon as he pulled his blanket up to his chin. The Captain decided to file an official report of their encounter with the Russian tank before he went to sleep, but he was almost ridiculed out of the MP's office. They told him that he probably experienced extreme fatigue and as a physician, he should know better. However, one of the officers believed him and forwarded his report to the next command center.

The next morning came faster than Karl's sleep ended...

He was awakened by Dr. Felder at about 7:00 AM and was told to get dressed as fast as he could possibly manage. No time to wash up or eat.

"Come on, come on," urged the Captain, "We are lucky. I obtained for us two passes on a special express train to Berlin. We will be driven to the railroad station by a staff car but if you are unable to speed it up, I will have to leave you here."

That was all Karl needed to hear. He almost jumped into his uniform, took his backpack from the chair and ran behind the captain who stormed out of the door. It was almost daylight and he could see his motorcycle, which he had parked the night before alongside the wall by the entrance. There was a soldier standing next to it and as Karl ran by him he threw the soldier the key to the Zuendapp and said, "It's yours now." The surprised soldier caught the key and turned to see who had hollered at him, but all he could see were an officer and an HJ boy jumping in a staff car, which took off immediately.

Dr. Felder looked at Karl, "Good thinking."

"What?" Karl managed to say.

"Throwing the key of the Zuendapp away. Now we have to make the train."

The railroad station was heavily damaged and some of the tracks were out of commission. The driver of the staff car guided them to track 1A, where a train consisting of five 2nd class passenger cars and one first-class passenger car was waiting for its 03 express locomotive. Several MP's were guarding access to the train and the Captain had to present his travel passes twice. The passes entitled him and Karl to a 2nd class compartment all the way to Berlin. There was only one scheduled stop in Frankfurt.

As they settled in their upholstered seats, Karl started to make himself comfortable by placing an extra blanket behind his back. He felt as if a weight had been lifted off of his shoulders and he watched the Captain opening a can of corned beef.

"Breakfast," he announced to Karl, who forgot for the moment that he was still tired. They shared the can of meat together with some fresh bread the Captain had secured in the hospital. Dr. Felder turned to Karl and said, "You know that the MP's at the hospital did not believe our encounter with the Russian Tank?"

Karl looked at the doctor and replied, "I don't blame them. Looking back, I cannot believe it either, but I will never forget it."

Captain Felder locked eyes with Karl and took out of his pocket a large notebook. "I will write a short report of our encounter and also a separate recommendation for you. You deserve it."

Oh no, thought Karl, not another one. They will only get me into trouble.

Nine

The express train was fast when it moved, but most of the time it was sidetracked and delayed and had to wait for passing transport trains. It was almost dark when they finally entered the city. In Berlin itself, it stopped over and over again. Many of the regular tracks were demolished and out of order and they finally arrived at the Zoologischen Garten, or Zoo Bahnhof, as the Berliners referred to it. Karl shook, for the last time, Dr. Felder's hand and got out to use the subway to bring him near the HJ headquarters. The rest of the way he would have to walk.

The Captain changed to a subway train to Friedrichstrasse where he had to report for hospital duty. He had exchanged addresses with Karl, who told him that his civilian address was useless because the apartment house in which his parents had lived was totally bombed out. But he gave him the KLV school address and the HJ headquarters address. Dr. Felder gave him in return a civilian address in Essen an der Ruhr and he invited Karl to look him up after the war.

"In the meantime, try to stay in touch if you can and if you need medical help in Berlin, do not hesitate to call on me. The personnel office in the Zoo bunkers medical facility should always know where I am located."

"I will do that," Karl assured the doctor.

Instead of saluting, they waved at each other as they parted. It was evening and for the first time Karl was not tired. He had slept soundly on the train all the way from Posen to Berlin. His orders for

Berlin instructed him to report to the KLV headquarters at the Hohenzollern Damm and also to report to the HJ Dienststelle in Halensee. Since it was already evening, he figured that the school headquarters was probably closed and decided to try the HJ Dienststelle first.

He arrived there at 9:00 PM and found it closed until the next morning.

Looking around the entrance for a bulletin board, he found a name on a piece of paper tagged on the door. The name Franz Wiese Scharfuehrer did not ring a bell, but the address next to the name was close enough to give it a try. He had no place to go, very little money, and he needed a place to spend the night. His other option was to go to one of the public air raid shelters, which were never closed. Air raid or not, they provided warmth, shelter and sometimes even food on a twenty-four hour basis for the bombed out population. The streets and individual houses were dark due to the blackout regulations and while he knew the area by heart, he had a hard time deciphering any house numbers.

Before he reached the address, multiple air raid sirens interrupted his walk.

The regular procedure was to seek immediate shelter. All the houses had signs painted on the walls with directions to the nearest basement. Karl knew from experience why it was important to get off the street as fast as possible. Soon it would rain shrapnel from anti-aircraft shells. Many of his former schoolmates had been severely injured by the hot and sometimes very heavy steel fragments. He turned towards the nearest apartment house and stood for a moment under the covered entrance area to find his way to the basement.

It was not a moment too soon. The anti-aircraft batteries opened up in the attempt to create an aerial fire wall and huge beams of searchlights crossed the heavy clouded sky. Two women came running down the main staircase. One of them held a small child close to her and the other was carrying a suitcase and blankets. They went right past him through the hallway to the cellar entrance. Karl was slow to follow them because he feared the apartment house cellars almost more than the bombs and the iron rain of the flak. While he still hesitated, many more women and even some men came rushing down the staircase. Most of the men were very old and slow but all of them were carrying some kind of luggage and some of them were chasing children in front of them.

Karl had good reasons to be afraid of the cellars. Most, if not all of the apartment houses in Berlin, were connected with public gas lines. If a gas line busted from the pressure of a collapsing building, the gas crept through the basements and cellars of the apartment houses and poisoned the unlucky refugees who were not fast enough to get back out into the open air. When Karl was still attending school in Berlin during the beginning of 1944, he attended a funeral service every week for his classmates or their parents who had not survived the previous week. Many of the casualties were not due to falling buildings or by being trapped in fire, but by the deadly consequences of seeking shelter in cellars polluted by escaping gases. The casualties often included children and old people who were simply trampled to death at the exits.

When Karl started school in 1936 at the Goethe school, his class consisted of 64 boys. There were no girls in his school. All of the teachers were men. By 1940, many of the school buildings in Berlin served as army barracks, police stations and later on, as emergency hospitals. This meant that certain schools were combined to serve boys and girls in the same classroom. Karl's classroom in 1941 numbered 122 pupils, girls and boys together and due to the fact that most of the able male teachers had been drafted, to the horror of the boys, they had for the first time female teachers.

The introduction of female teachers to 11 and 12 year old boys who were only used to male teachers and male authority figures was, for most of the boys very difficult. With the possible exception of their mothers, there had never been a female authority figure in their lives. It was not that the boys resented the female teachers; it was simply that they did not believe that a female could teach.

During the beginning of 1942, most of the schools in Berlin had to double up again and introduced the 10-hour school system. This meant that Karl's class of 122 pupils started at 7:30 AM and lasted until 1:00 PM. It was only interrupted each hour with a five-minute break. The next class of about 120 students started at 1:10 PM and lasted until 6:10 PM, again, only interrupted by five-minute breaks each hour. To make it equal, the morning and afternoon school sessions were alternated every week. One week Karl's class started at 7:30 AM and the next week it started at 1:10 PM. This would have been all right but by 1943, it was constantly interrupted by air attacks.

During the day time air attacks, the school children were ordered into the basements of the schools and most of the time the lights went out due to hits to the power transmission lines.

They learned the multiplication tables and spelling of words in the darkness of cellars and they learned it by endless repetition. While the bombs were falling and the buildings shook, the children were huddled together in fear and repeated over and over again:

7 times 17 equals 119

8 times 17 equals 136

9 times 17 equals 153

And they learned how to spell in the very same way.

These conditions led to the mandatory evacuation of the school children from Berlin and other targeted cities to less populated areas, which were not subjected to the constant bombardments. This was known as the KLV system (Kinderlandverschickung). The KLV system tried to designate one adult teacher to about 120 children. If the children were under 12 years of age, the adult was assisted with 13 and 14 year old boys to maintain order and sanitary conditions. Karl was one of those 14 year olds. Entrusted with the safe evacuation of his KLV camp in Poland due to Russian advances, he was now back in Berlin but without his charges. He knew that he had done his best. He had recommendation letters to prove it.

Right now he would rather take his chances in the hallway of the apartment building than in the cellar. There was one more reason why Karl hated the school cellars. Some clueless school official had decided to use the time spent in the basement to have the teeth of the children examined, and if necessary, treated by the school dentist. This was all right as long as there was electricity but when the electricity went out, it was almost sadistic. The student sat on a regular chair and the dentist sat in front of him. Next to them was a contraption like an old-fashioned spinning wheel and while the dentist was paddling with his feet to operate the wheel and the gears, he was also drilling the tooth of the student.

No Novocain or pain medication. Just two or three children restraining the helpless student patient in his chair, another student shining a flashlight in the patient's mouth and the dentist paddling and drilling while all the while the bombings were shaking the building above them. Hitler had it all summed up in only two words: "Total War"

Indeed.

And now, as Karl had to decide between seeking shelter in a

basement or taking his chances in the entrance hallway of the building, he leaned against the wall of the hallway and then slid down to sit. He thought back to what he could have done different in evacuating the camp, but nothing constructive came to his mind. He tried to concentrate his thoughts to the next important phase. He had to find his family. The best place to start would be to visit once more the ruins of the apartment building they had lived in. Maybe his mother had come back and left him a note. Maybe his KLV headquarters had some updated personal information for him. And, where might his father be?

He thought of looking up SS Sturmbannfuehrer von Glinski to inquire about the well being of his son, Udo, and also to ask him for help. How should he go about finding his father?

His thoughts were interrupted by an air raid fire marshal who came running through the entrance shouting for attention. He informed the few people who came out of the cellar that a housing block in a nearby street was burning down due to a carpet-bombing. The fire threatened to spread in their direction. Karl asked for the street name that was ablaze. The marshal ignored him and stormed out of the building to alert the next one down the line. Karl got up and followed him out to the street.

The fire was almost blinding and he wondered if a fire of this size could ever be fought in a productive way. There was a large group of fire engines and military fire fighting vehicles standing between him and the blaze. Hopefully they would contain the fire and keep it from spreading. It was over two blocks away and the heavy clouds above seemed to open up, promising a massive rainfall.

When he went back into the building the air raid sirens announced the end of the attack and shortly afterwards it started to rain. Karl looked at his watch. It was a quarter past one in the morning and due to the stormy weather, he hoped that this would be the last air raid of the night. He knew that if he went outside he would be drafted to fight the fire and he was in no mood to do this tonight. Not unless he was forced to do it.

He directed his attention to the main staircase and noticed for the first time that it was heavily carpeted. He was in the lobby of one of the elite apartment houses on the Kurfuersten Damm. He turned towards the cellar entrance to see if any more people were coming up. Nobody came. They must have all gone back into their apartments. Karl decided to walk up to the second floor or higher to be out of the cold draft from the entrance and to sleep on the soft padded carpet. He climbed the stairs, found a warm corner, placed his backpack under his head and went to sleep.

When he opened his eyes it was past 7:30 AM and an older infantry soldier kicked at his backpack to wake him up.

"Got surprised by the rain and the air attack last night?" He asked. "Want something to eat? Come on, I live upstairs," he continued before Karl had an answer for him. Breakfast sounded too good to be true, so his was an easy decision.

Karl got up and introduced himself and apologized for sleeping on the stairs.

"Don't worry about sleeping here. My name is Walther," said the soldier by way of introduction. They went up to the fifth floor where Walther opened a door to a nicely furnished apartment.

"I lived here with my brother until last year, and then we both got drafted to the infantry. I have not seen him since. This is the first time that I am back for a short leave, but I know that he was here not too long ago. He left me a message on my night stand," Walther said as he opened a breadbox and placed a jar of jelly on the table. He fixed two cups of coffee ersatz and invited Karl to sit down.

"Tell me about yourself, I can see that you are a trained sniper. Be careful that the Russians don't make you out in combat. They have the nasty habit of tickling snipers with a flame thrower."

Karl answered that yes, he was trained as a sniper, but he could not imagine killing anyone. Maybe just wounding them to make them unable to fight. "Maybe a shot in the shoulder or a hand, but not much more."

"Hmm," answered Walther, "Don't make that decision now. When you are face to face and it is either you or them, you will know what to do. Why did you sleep on the staircase?"

Karl decided to give him a short version of the last week and finished by saying that he will need to see the HJ leader in charge to get new orders.

Walther shook his head and suggested that Karl should first go back to see if he could find a note from his mother.

"Once you report back for duty they might send you anywhere. You might not get another chance for a while. Go back and search while you can."

He went to a hall closet and came back with a dark blue woolen sweater.

"Here, wear this under your uniform. It is too small for me and it will keep you warm."

Karl thanked him and folded the sweater in a small bundle and placed it in his backpack. "Thanks for the breakfast. I will follow your advice and look for messages first before I report to the HJ," said Karl as he prepared to leave. Walther opened the door for him and wished him luck. Karl did not hear any noise until he was down to the third floor. Then he heard the thump of the closing door above him.

Nice fellow this Walther, he thought as he went out to the street. He was not used to being invited by strangers. But then, he was not used to sleeping on staircases either. The rain was gone but there were still dark clouds above him as he made his way to the nearest subway station. The street was wet and at times he had to walk around puddles filled with ashes. There was debris everywhere he looked and the nearer he got to the fire from last night, the harder it became for him to breathe.

What was most appalling to him was the gut-wrenching smell coming from the burned-out buildings, which were still smoldering. It was not the first time that he smelled the terrible stench of burnt flesh, but this time it seemed to be all around him. He changed his mind about using the subway. His former home was only two stops away and he decided to walk a detour in order to get some cleaner air.

When he arrived at the ruins of the building that served as his former home, he had no problem finding the site where he left his name a few weeks ago. Quite a few names and addresses had been added to the major pieces of rubble. Some of the older messages were harder to read than the newer ones.

Karl decided to start searching next to his name and then almost cried in relief when he saw a circle around his name and an arrow pointing to a recently scratched message.

It read: 'Uncle Herrmann', followed by his mother's name. Karl sat down on the sidewalk and then got up again to read the message again and again. He was so happy that he actually started to cry. Now, all of the sudden, everything seemed bright and light. He felt that he was not alone anymore and jumped up to get to the nearest post office to mail a post card to the address he had copied in the back of his service book. He found the post office had also been bombed out and there was a sign with a new postal address. It was not far away from the old one. He obtained a pre-stamped card from a one-armed soldier behind the counter and asked how long it would take for the card to reach Westphalia.

"I wish I could answer that," replied the soldier, "but I guess it should get there in about a week."

Karl thanked him and left the temporary post office, which looked like it could collapse any time. He also silently thanked Walther for his advice. He felt refreshed, strong and ready to tackle whatever waited for him. Since he was now only about six blocks away from his KLV school headquarters, and it was still early in the day, he decided to walk there first. He had to walk a detour around a street that was blocked off due to the danger from partially collapsed buildings and when he arrived at his destination, it was still before noon.

The first thing he saw when he entered the KLV office were some children's coats. Then he heard his name, "Karl, Karl, come over here." He differentiated several voices and moments later he was surrounded by four of his former camp children. They must have seen him entering the building. He was just about as happy to see them as they were to see him. They were members of the group who left the camp with the trucks provided by SS Sturmbannfuehrer von Glinski. He remembered their names and was just about to ask them about their return trip when another door opened and an older woman entered. Women teachers always seemed old to Karl, but this one must have been in her late fifties. He had never seen her before but she walked right up to him and said in a warm voice, "So, you are Karl Veth, the HJ boy the children bragged about. I am Frau Becker." She shook Karl's hand and then told the boys to quiet down.

"I am to report about our camp's evacuation, but I see that this has been done already," said Karl as he pointed in the direction of the boys.

"No, not really," said Frau Becker, "We only know about the children who came with the SS trucks. Where are the other ones?"

"They should be here too," answered Karl, and he proceeded to tell Frau Becker about the freight train destined for Kottbus with Peter Zahn in charge of the older group. Frau Becker had question after question, made some notes, and finally asked him about a copy of his HJ report.

"I came here first," answered Karl, "I will go to the HJ after I leave from here. I will bring you a copy afterwards."

Frau Becker told him that it would not be necessary because she would type a report for the KLV files based upon what he had told her already.

"Now, what I would like to know," asked Karl, "is what are these four boys doing here? I thought that school had been discontinued. Why aren't they with their parents or relatives?" He looked first at Frau Becker and then at the boys. When Frau Becker hesitated with her answer, he asked the boys directly, "What are you doing here? Why aren't you home?" He started to worry when one of them answered that they were waiting for their parents to pick them up.

He looked at Frau Becker again who finally answered. "We notified the parents that the camp was being evacuated and that they should check with us daily. The trucks with boys arrived here two days ago and all of the boys have been picked up by either the parents or their relatives, except for these four."

Frau Becker answered Karl's questioning look with a stern look of her own.

"We will provide food, care and shelter until they are picked up," she added as Karl was still looking at her.

"Boys," he called over to the children, "please go into the next room; I need to be alone with Frau Becker."

As the boys left the room he turned again to Frau Becker and asked, "How did you notify the parents? Do you know if they are still alive?"

"Now, now," answered Frau Becker, "no reason to jump to conclusions. We notified the parents as instructed in our KLV files. You have seen that most of them have been picked up and these four will get picked up too."

"And what happens when nobody picks them up? What do your files say about that?" He was getting warm under his collar because he could clearly see that Frau Becker resented his questions and his tone of voice.

"Karl, you have to understand that we are understaffed. We cannot go from house to house and look for, or for that matter through, collapsed buildings to find parents or relatives of each boy who comes back from the camps."

Karl tried to control his emotions. "I'll tell you, Frau Becker, what I do understand. You or whoever is in charge of the KLV system is greatly incompetent. You put cripples like Lieutenant Hardfeld and boys like me in charge of hundreds of children to get them out of your hair. And when we return them, you don't do a damned thing to actually go out and find out if the parents or relatives are still alive. And now I also understand another thing. Unless I or one of our HJ boys goes out and does the job for you, it will not be done." Karl got up, went to the room the boys were in and told them that he would be back tomorrow. When he started to leave Frau Becker stopped him.

"Karl, you don't know what this means, but Herr Hitler declared 'Total War'. Personally, I do not know what Total War means, but if we don't go by rules and by the book, we cannot function. When you come back tomorrow and the boys are still here, I will go with you to the addresses of the boys, I promise."

She looked at Karl with tears in her eyes, and he almost regretted what he said before, but he knew that he was right. He also knew that this situation had nothing to do with being right. It had everything to do with what she had said, 'Total War'.

"I'll be back tonight," he said, "I need to eat and a place to sleep."

Frau Becker nodded in agreement as he left.

Ten

An hour later Karl reported to the HJ Dienststelle. He was happy that his friend, Harold Kellner, was the Gefolgschaftsfuehrer in charge. Harold was the same age as Karl. In contrast to him, he was taller, dark haired and about 30 pounds heavier. They had been close-knit friends for about three years. It was Harold who supplied Karl with all the goodies like painkillers and tobacco and cigarettes. He was also the guy who had helped Karl to "find" the Zuendapp motorcycle. Harold's ability in "finding" things for Karl was not so much due to some hidden talent, but more the fact that Harold's father was a leading civil servant and in charge of supply and food warehouses in Berlin. The common bond between Harold and Karl was that both of them were "subway rats".

They were so named because they were part of the Berliner children who liked to play in the subway tunnels. While the other children played with balls, they jumped on subway cars and traveled the dark tunnels of the subway system. Not so much that they liked to play in the dark and damp tunnels, but more to be able to move quickly all over the city. It was a dangerous game because of the hot (electrified) 3rd rail, and entering the tunnels was strictly forbidden by the subway authorities. This only added to the challenge. Karl had started to play in the subway system when he was about eleven years old and probably knew it just as well as the engineers who designed it, or drove the trains. He knew every station within the numbered system. He knew how the hot rails were covered and where they ran and connected.

He knew every airshaft, which allowed him to enter and exit the system without going through the train stations. He knew the control and substations and the tool and maintenance sheds. He even knew about the sewage tunnels, which at times ran parallel but a bit deeper than the subway rails. Harold was not as savvy as Karl in regard to the electrical system, but he also had an extensive knowledge of subway connections. Karl was happy to see him on duty. He walked up to the desk, clicked his heels, stretched out his right arm, his fingertips extended as required, raised and level at the exact height of his eyes.

"Heil Hitler!" he shouted, and a startled Harold jumped up and returned his salute.

" Mensch, you must be nuts to scare me like that," he said to Karl. They shook hands and Harold handed Karl a partially preprinted sheet of paper, which Karl was required to fill out. Karl started to write immediately and was done within 15 minutes.

He looked up to Harold and told him of his visit to the KLV headquarters.

"Harold, can you get me eight HJ boys tomorrow morning to meet me at the school to start searching for the boys' parents?"

"We might not get eight, but I will see what I can do for you. Why don't you ask Sturmbannfuehrer von Glinski for help? He called here several times and wanted to talk with you. You are supposed to call him when you check in." He handed Karl the phone and a note with a phone number on it.

Karl dialed and his call was answered on the second ring. He identified himself to the switchboard operator who recognized his name and asked him for his phone number. Karl told him that he would be at this number only for a very short time and hung up.

The phone rang almost immediately. Harold answered: "HJ Dienstelle Halensee."

"Obergefolgsschaftfuehrer Veth, please."

Harold handed the phone to Karl and whispered, "Obergefolgsschaftfuehrer?" Karl answered the phone.

"Karl Veth, here."

The voice rang strong and clear, "Congratulations on your promotion to Obergefolgsschaftfuehrer. This is von Glinski. I want to thank you for the note you left me two weeks ago, and for taking such good care of my son. Your official promotion will reach your Stamm Headquarters tomorrow. I would like to invite you to come and visit with me, but I am awfully busy. However, if I can do anything for you, don't hesitate to call me. Don't forget this number, understood?"

"Thank you, Sturmbannfuehrer," answered Karl, "I do need some help, if you don't mind. I need three or four of your SS men to help me find the parents of four boys from my camp. They are without hope at the Brandenburgerstrasse KLV School. I need them for five hours at the most."

Sturmbannfuehrer von Glinski listened to Karl's request. "You will have four of my men tomorrow morning at 8:00 AM at the KLV Headquarters, he said. "Will there be anything else, Obergefolgsschaftfuehrer?"

"No, Sturmbannfuehrer von Glinski. I thank you in the name of my boys and also for my promotion." Karl's voice sounded almost cheerful. Von Glinski ended the call and Karl handed the receiver back to Harold. Harold beamed at him.

"Mensch, Karl a promotion to Obergefolgsschaftfuehrer, directly from the SS Defense commander of Berlin-Wilmersdorf. Tell me how you earned it and about the camp and the evacuation." Harold was happy for Karl and as he listened to him they were interrupted by another air raid attack. The sirens wailed up and down in their intensity. Karl started to get up but was waved by Harold to sit down again.

"Nothing to worry about, Karl," he said, "This is the regular nuisance attack. They come every day at about the same time, hardly any heavy bombs. I think that these are Russian planes, but I am not sure."

The heavy 8.8mm flak opened up. It started with the deep boom and ended shortly afterwards with the high and sharp, almost eardrum piercing crackle, when the shells exploded. Karl moved his chair under the somewhat protection of the nearest doorframe, but Harold kept sitting on his desk and encouraged Karl to continue his story. A little later the sirens started in again. This time it was a steady high tone, the all-clear signal. Harold got up and told Karl that he would send him some HJ members tomorrow morning to the KLV office.

"Come back tomorrow afternoon to get your new ID. If you cannot make it tomorrow then come back the next day. I should have your new orders by that time."

Karl walked back to the KLV office. This time he walked a slightly larger circle detour to see if there was any additional and new damage to his familiar neighborhood. The last few times he was in Berlin, he did not have the time for it. He was shocked at the additional damage. There was simply no building without deep scars from the constant bombings. Most of them were permanently evacuated and many of them were reduced to hills of rubble.

He arrived at the KLV office in time to see Frau Becker before she left for the night. She had a room with a folding bed ready for him. His room was in one of the abandoned classrooms and located right next to the temporary bedroom of the four boys. She had also a soup prepared, ready to be heated up.

Karl asked Frau Becker what time she would be back in the morning. She told him that some lightly wounded and recovering soldiers would take over for her in a little while. They would be sleeping in a room down the hallway from him and help him with the boys in case of an air attack which would certainly happen. The soldiers and the boys actually preferred to spend the whole night in the air raid shelter, which was equipped with a few folding cots and a restroom. This way they did not have to get up in the middle of the night.

Karl thought that he would be better off sleeping in the classroom, but did not mention this to Frau Becker. Instead he asked her again what time she would be back in the morning. He added that he would have some SS men and a few HJ boys helping him to find the whereabouts of the parents or relatives of the four boys.

"It would be nice if you could lend me the KLV files pertaining to the information roster of the parents. This way I can plan tonight and not waste any time tomorrow morning when my helpers show up,"

Frau Becker told him that she would be back before 8:00 AM and agreed to get him the files right then. A few minutes later Karl had the rosters he needed. Karl thanked her and wished her a good night. After she left, he went to visit with the boys.

They were already waiting for him and wanted to hear about Peter and their older friends they had left behind. Karl told them how Peter and his group took a train to Kottbus and should be on their way to Berlin. He did not tell them about his own trip back to Berlin other than that he had the luck to hitch a ride.

"Where is Lieutenant Hardfeld?" one of them wanted to know.

"I delivered the Lieutenant to a field hospital before I hitched a ride," Karl told him. The boys did not really want any details. They were happy to hear that everyone was safe and on the way home.

Karl asked them when the last time was that they had received any mail from home. The answers varied, but Karl summarized that it was fairly recent. The wounded soldiers showed up and Karl introduced himself and at the same time excused himself. The soldiers believed him when he said that he was tired. They were nice guys with the oldest maybe 30 years old and they went with the boys to the basement to set up their beds for the night.

Karl studied the home addresses of the kids. All of the addresses were supplemented with secondary information about relatives and even friends.

He laid out a plan of forming four individual groups, each one targeting the primary address for each boy. He also copied for each of the groups, all of the remaining information. Before he went to sleep he wrote another postcard to his mother. He planned to send about five cards, each one a day apart, and hoped that one of them would reach her.

The folding bed turned out to be more comfortable than he thought. He fell asleep only to be awakened a few hours later by another air attack. This one lasted longer than the one he remembered from the previous night. The target however, was way on the north side of the city. Again, he did not seek the basement shelter, but he did get up and dressed. He wanted to be ready for any emergency. It even crossed his mind to sleep during the day and to volunteer with a HJ fire commando for night duty. He would talk to Harold about it, but in any event, he would have to wait for his new orders. About two hours after the all-clear signal, the night was interrupted again by another alarm. He reasoned that he could get more rest during the day.

Tomorrow night I will not get undressed, he thought.

At 8:00 o clock in the morning, he was surrounded by four SS men who arrived in a Kubelwagen, five HJ members and Frau Becker. He had washed up in the bathroom on the end of the hallway and asked Frau Becker if she wanted to stay with the boys or if he had to designate an HJ member to stay behind. She told him that she had taken his speech of incompetence personal, but that she understood his frustration and she had arranged with the soldiers from the night watch that two of them would stay with the boys and also watch the phone in her office. She was determined to go with him.

"Good," said Karl, "let's go."

"Not without eating something first," replied Frau Becker, "it is barely daylight. We will have a few minutes time for a cup of coffee and a jelly sandwich."

Karl agreed and told the group that whatever the results, he wanted everyone back at 11:30 AM to discuss their progress. He designated to each SS man one of his HJ members and gave the driver of the car the furthest destination. The fifth HJ member would go with him and Frau Becker. His intention was to double-up with one group and then split when they had multiple leads or perhaps messages to follow.

"In the event that an address is bombed out, be sure to leave a message with the boy's name, address of school and date. Don't forget the date," Karl repeated more than once.

One of the SS men spoke up, "I know this address at the Guentzelstrasse. I assisted a bomb removal squad, maybe three weeks ago. The bomb was in the middle of the street. The building itself was blasted off the foundation by an air mine. However, all of the residents who took cover in the air raid shelter survived. We should find plenty of messages on the rubble."

Karl did not know if this was good news or bad news. He wished the SS man good luck in finding a helpful message and gave the signal to get going.

The weather had cleared up, but the temperature was still near freezing. Karl's group hit their address within minutes. The apartment building was part of a housing block, which was still standing. The particular building itself had been evacuated. It seemed to have burned in several places, mostly in the upper floors. There were several signs warning visitors to stay out of the building because of the unstable walls. There were scratched messages all over the place and Karl's group split up to search through the messages.

Frau Becker was the first one to find a contact address, apparently left by the boy's mother.

"What is the date of the message," asked Karl.

"No date," answered Frau Becker, who was copying the contact address.

"How far from here?"

"Half an hour maybe. We need to use the subway," Frau Becker looked up and continued, "At this point we have no way of knowing if the contact address still exists. What do you suggest, Karl?"

"You found the address, you should go. Take one of the boys

along in case you have to split up again. See you, at 11:30. Good luck."

"Wait," interrupted the SS man, "if you want me to go I can get a car within 20 minutes."

"Great, take Frau Becker along, please. The boys and I will search here some more before we join one of the other groups."

Karl waved to the two boys to follow him towards the courtyard to search along a small wall, which was full of scratched messages. They did not find what they were looking for, but it seemed to Karl that most of the tenants must have survived the attack. At least they did not find a single note indicating otherwise. After a while they decided to join the nearest group.

When they arrived, they were pleasantly surprised to see a fairly intact housing block. The designated search team was on the street, ready to split up and notify the mother, who was drafted a week ago on a work order to work for the BVG, the Berliner traffic company in charge of the busses, streetcars and subways. Everyone was eager to continue his or her search and ready to proceed towards the next destination.

Karl decided to send the SS Sturmman to the employer. "Pull rank when you get there. Tell them you have direct orders to escort the woman to her son. Go."

The Sturmman smiled and said it would be his pleasure to act heavy-handed and went on his way. Karl looked at his watch. It was 10:00 AM and he decided to send the remainder of his teams to the other addresses. He wanted to get back to the school.

He planned to use the phone together with the authority of the KLV Headquarters to call someone in Kottbus to find out what had happened to his friend Peter and his charges. He did not know who to call, but he figured he could start with the local HJ headquarter in Kottbus. He was sure that Peter would have left a message for him. He also wanted to call Harold and ask him if he had heard from Peter, and if his new orders had arrived.

He knew that many, if not most of the phone transmission lines, were damaged. The use of any workable phone was practically limited to emergency calls, but he figured that his purpose of finding missing KLV children justified an emergency. He also reasoned that if he did not attempt to find Peter and his group today, he would be questioned later on by some school official about his lack of effort.

When he reached the school, he was greeted with happy faces.

Everyone was excited because one of the teams had located the aunt of one of the boys who was now sitting next to her nephew, prepared to take him along. They were waiting for Frau Becker to execute the paperwork releasing the boy into the custody of his aunt. Karl asked the aunt to join him in the office and asked point blank about the whereabouts of the parents. The aunt replied that the father of the boy was serving on the western front and she had no contact with him. The mother had been injured in an air attack and was in a local hospital. Karl made out a simple report in duplicate, signed it as the HJ leader in charge of the evacuation of the KLV camp, and asked for the aunt's counter signature.

"You are now in charge of your nephew, and free to take him to his mother." Karl shook the aunt's hand and went to say goodbye to the little 10-year old boy. His name was Dieter and he formally shook hands with Karl.

"Goodbye Karl. When you go on another trip to a KLV camp, please do not forget me. I want to go with you." Dieter was absolutely serious and Karl had the impression that the little boy regarded the past six months in the camp, and the trip home, as a great adventure.

Eleven

The phone lines within Berlin were working. Karl reached Harold, who told him that he had not heard from Peter, but that he could send three more HJ members in the afternoon to help him with the search parties for the unclaimed children. Karl accepted. He needed all the help he could get. He had tried to reach Kottbus, but the line was out of order. He also tried to call Stettin to forward the addresses from Sturmman Berchthold, but that line was also dead. He considered his next move when all kinds of shouting and banging on the door interrupted his thinking.

The door opened and he recognized a woman teacher from two years earlier. There was also another woman trying to enter, who he did not know. The first one looked at him but apparently did not remember him. He was just one of a class from 120 children and now he was in uniform.

"Where is Frau Becker, who are you and what are you doing in her office?" she demanded of Karl.

He remembered her high-pitched voice and her name, and greeted her politely, "Heil Hitler, Frau Heinrich. My name is Karl Veth and I am one of your former students. Frau Becker will be back at 11:30. I am in charge of the remaining boys from KLV Camp Kosten."

Frau Heinrich stared at him in the same way he remembered from years ago.

"What boys," she asked in her loud and demanding voice, "and what are you doing in Frau Becker's office?"

"I am trying to use the phone," answered Karl in an even voice, "but you can have it, it's useless."

He ignored her and left the office. As he entered the hallway, he saw a bunch of school children, maybe thirty or forty boys and girls, all about 10 or 11 years of age entering the Aula, the main hall of the school. Apparently another evacuated camp had reached Berlin and was gathering at the school to meet their parents. These must be the charges of Frau Heinrich, he speculated. He turned around and asked the other woman who was following him, "Where are these children from?"

"Albeck," she answered.

Karl remembered the little village of Albeck. He had been there about a year ago. It was seaside resort located on the island of Usedom in the Baltic Sea in front of Stettin.

"Are you a teacher too?"

"Yes, my name is Frauelein Wegberg. I am the camp leader from Haus Seeblick in Albeck."

"Were there any KLV camps from Dresden in Albeck?"

"There were KLV camps from all over the country on Usedom and also on the island of Wollin, but I don't know about a camp from Dresden."

Karl told her about Sturmman Berchthold's request. He asked Frauelein Wegberg if she knew about any kind of a central office for the KLV camps.

"There must be a place where the names of the parents and relatives can be matched against the evacuation records of the KLV camps."

None that she knew of, she answered, but she agreed that if there were none, it would be time to start one. She suggested that Frau Becker might be able to help.

"Frau Becker already has some unclaimed children on her hands," said Karl, "and as far as I can see, the whole KLV information system has to be brought up to date. Nobody knows where anybody is. And, we are talking about scared and helpless children." He saw one of his search teams entering the schoolyard and went out to meet them.

His hopes for his boys swelled when the team reported that they found the relatives for the third boy. By noon, he knew that two of his boys would be taken care of by some relatives. This included the relatives Frau Becker had located. One of the boys had already been dismissed into the custody of the boy's aunt. However, the search results for the relatives of the fourth boy were absolutely negative. The building where his parents had lived was burned out and no messages in regard to his name were found. Karl thought that it was kind of strange that his team members could not locate a note in regard to the fatalities. Most of the totally destroyed buildings he had seen did have such a 'list of casualties'.

"Did you leave a dated message of your own," he asked the SS men who were ready to leave.

"We left messages in several different places around the immediate area," they assured him.

Karl thanked them individually. He was grateful for their help and told them so. In the meantime, the three additional HJ members Harold sent reported to him. Karl considered at first to send them back to Harold's office, but then decided differently. He brought them up to speed on the first team's results and then told them to canvass the remainder of the housing block next to the burnt out building.

"Knock on doors," he told them, "identify yourselves as acting on behalf of the KLV district. Ask for help. Leave your name, your HJ Dienststelle address, and the school's address. Search as if you are searching for your own parents. However, if you are interrupted by an air raid, discontinue and seek shelter."

As the three were preparing to leave, he walked them out and added, "Stop your effort at 4:00 PM, this gives you time to report back to me. Don't bother to report back to Gefolgschaftsfuehrer Harold. I will take care of that."

The HJ members from his morning team left with the SS men and Karl started to look for Frau Becker. He found her busy cooking pots of soup in a makeshift kitchen. It was again a converted classroom. There were no kitchens in this school. He asked her if he could help.

"Yes," said Frau Becker, "tell them to come and eat; Frau Heinrich and Frauelein Wegberg, too. You will find them in the basement."

Karl took off for the basement and found the two women setting up additional folding beds. All the personal luggage of the children was distributed next to the beds and nametags on the beds. The boys were separated from the girls by a privacy curtain. There must have been a heating system in the basement because it was warm and really comfortable.

Maybe I should move down here too, thought Karl. Something to consider if it gets real cold some night.

He asked the women to come up to eat. When they were all together in the Aula, he brought up again the need for a central name or register system. The women agreed that this would help and speed up the relocation of the arriving children. However, Frau Becker pointed out that they already had the data for all of the KLV children on file.

"This is not the issue on hand," insisted Karl, "yes, you have the data, but it is not up to date. Every night that we have an air attack and casualties, the data shifts. I will get you help from the HJ. They can do the legwork for you. You told me yesterday that you are understaffed, so let me help you."

The women agreed that any kind of help would be more than welcome. Even Frau Heinrich had a smile for him. Karl got up from the table and went to find Herbert, the last boy of his group. He found him in the middle of the other boys who listened to him as he apparently related stories from his camp in Poland.

"There is my big friend," he said to the boys around him when he saw Karl approaching.

"Great," said Karl in return, "and here is my younger friend. How are you doing Herbert? Did you have enough to eat? There is more in the kitchen. Help yourself, just like in camp," he added.

Herbert pointed at Karl and smiled proudly at the group around him. "See what I told you? He is taking care of me."

"You better believe it, my friend," said Karl, "see you later."

He made his way back to the teachers and was about to ask if he could use the phone once more, when he saw his three HJ members entering the Aula.

One of them approached him. He had a serious expression on his face and told Karl that in the hallway of the next building to the house in question, they found a list of the casualties, and Herbert's mother was among them. He had copied the whole list and handed it to Karl. This was really getting to Karl, who had hoped to get some better news. He thanked his team and dismissed them.

Frau Becker, who had observed the short meeting, came to ask him about the news.

"Not good," answered Karl "what do we do now? How long can you take care of Herbert? And if you wind up with more homeless children, how can you handle this?"

Frau Becker answered that the German Red Cross and a Catholic Church group would support them.

"Hmm, yes, that might work, but before we ask them for help let me call Sturmbannfuehrer von Glinski. I think his son Udo and Herbert were friends in Kosten. Maybe the Sturmbannfuehrer is willing to take Herbert in for a while until we find some other relatives."

Frau Becker was quiet. She had just realized what might happen in the coming weeks. She refused to think that the war could be lost and that the Russians might conquer Berlin, but if that should happen, what would become of the children? She could not think of an answer. Karl used her phone and got connected to the Sturmbannfuehrer.

Von Glinski listened quietly, and when Karl mentioned that Udo and Herbert might have been friends in Kosten, he told Karl that he would discuss this matter with his wife.

"If my wife agrees, we will take care of Herbert as long as he needs us," he assured Karl, who felt a bit better when he ended the phone call. Just to be sure, Karl decided to ask Herbert if he was a friend of Udo's.

"Oh, yes, Udo and I cheated together on tests," he confided in Karl.

"Let's hope that Frau von Glinski is as charitable as her husband," said Frau Becker when Karl told her about his phone conservation with the Sturmbannfuehrer. Karl remembered that he was supposed to check back with Harold. He had seen enough of the destroyed section of his hometown and decided to take the subway.

When he arrived at the office he was greeted by a group of friends who had heard about his promotion and who wanted to know how it was possible to earn two advancements within one year. To top it off, he was also surprised to find a winter uniform waiting for him. It was a used uniform, but this one here was heavier and warmer than his present one. It was made of heavy wool and there was even a new shoulder belt, and his new arm patch. Usually you had to buy the uniform of the HJ yourself, but first you had to obtain a buying permit, which in itself was difficult to obtain due to the shortage of any kind of clothes. Secondly, even if you obtained a coupon, you were unable to use it because the stores were all empty of goods.

Harold told Karl that the uniform was delivered to the office by a civilian older guy, who did not identify himself. The shoulder belt and the new arm patch were a gift from the HJ headquarters. There was a note attached to the package, which only read 'Thank You'. No signature or address.

Karl could really use the uniform. The one he had, he wore daily. It was over one year old, and he had not found a chance to wash it during the last few weeks. He wondered who could have sent him this nice present, but stopped guessing when the sirens warned of another air attack. Frau Becker had told him that since January they had more than two and mostly three, or even four air attacks during any 24-hour period. Karl went into the bathroom and changed his uniform. The new one was a bit too big, but he could offset the effect with the sweater from Walther. His shoes were still the same he had kungled from Stanislaus a few weeks ago. They were sturdy and waterproof and with the help of inlaid newspapers, they were warm and fit him well. He took the old uniform and threw it in the garbage can.

Instead of new orders, he received from Harold a choice of assignments.

He could either travel by train to Stettin and assist the KLV camps with their evacuations, or he could assist locally with the training of the old men in the recently formed Volkssturm. He asked Harold what he thought of it and Harold suggested that he should stay in Berlin and train the Volkssturm.

"You know how to shoot and could make a difference as a coach," he said, "besides, this is your hometown. You have friends here and you were gone long enough." The telephone rang. It was Sturmbannfuehrer von Glinski for Karl.

"Thank you for the nice uniform, Sturmbannfuehrer," said Karl.

"What uniform?" came the voice through the phone.

"The one which was delivered to me this afternoon," answered Karl.

"I know nothing about that. I just wanted you to know that I will send a car to the school to pick up Herbert. My wife and I have decided to take him in. You are welcome to visit him anytime. My driver will leave our address at the school. Take good care of yourself." Before Karl could answer, there was a click and the line was dead. The booming voice of the Sturmbannfuehrer was loud enough to be overheard by Harold.

"Be careful Karl," he warned his friend, "sometimes it's dangerous to have powerful friends. If they find it convenient for their purpose they will use you."

"I know," answered Karl, "but I had to help Herbert. He was the only one left from my first camp group. He is unable to go home because his home is gone and we don't know of any relatives or loved ones. Now he can be with a friend." He looked at Harold "I have been warned of the SS before, but in this case, you would have done the same."

"I guess so," answered Harold.

Twelve

Karl had decided to take his friend's advice and stay in Berlin and was now in the third week of training the Volkssturm. He was in charge of a group of 65 to 70 year-old men. His specific training course covered the extinguishing of cylinder phosphor bombs and the use of hand grenades in hand-to-hand combat. The extinguishing of the cylinder bombs was easy to teach.

The bombs featured a heavy six-cornered steel tops attached to a longer, but like-sized six-cornered cylinder. The heavy end of the bomb penetrated the roof of the building and the ceilings and floors of the upper floors. When it came to a stop, it was most often lying on its side and ignited the contents of the cylinder, which sprayed phosphor flares from all six sides of the canister high into the air and in the surrounding area. The extinguishing technique consisted of holding a paper bag filled with sand right over the top of the most upward shooting flare. The flare would burn through the paper bag and the sand would fall down and over the cylinder causing the fire to suffocate from the lack of air.

It was an easy technique to teach because the procedure was always the same; you had to approach the burning cylinder from the front or the rear; never from the side. When you approached it from the front or the rear, you could hold the paper bag right over the bomb, even without gloves and without getting burned by the spouting flares. If, however, you approached the bombs from the side, you would get hit by the flares, which contained phosphor. The phosphor would stick to your clothing and skin and burn you badly.

Very badly.

Karl taught the method outside in the middle of a neighborhood park.

He used real bombs collected by the HJ and which, for one reason or another, had failed to ignite. Besides the members of the Volksturm, he was always surrounded by a mass of civilians; mostly women, invalids and some children. He never suffered a burn, and neither did anyone he trained.

The method in itself worked great, but the trick was to find the bomb right after it came to rest and before it ignited the whole apartment. Anti air raid measures dictated that each apartment had to place in front of their door, one bucket filled with water and two paper bags filled with sand. This assured that there was always some sand nearby. When the siren sounded, the tenants had to seek shelter in the basement but leave their apartment doors unlocked.

This allowed the fire marshals, and in this case, the Volkssturm, to enter the apartment if they suspected it was penetrated by the phosphor bombs. It was not so much a guessing game, because the planes threw out the bombs in sheets of hundreds at a time. If you saw one igniting on the street, it was a sure bet that the surrounding buildings had been hit too. In this case the fire marshals and members of the HJ, and now also the Volkssturm, raced up the stairs of the building to the top floor, searched the apartments for igniting or already burning bombs and proceeded with the extinguishing technique.

Some of the old men in the Volkssturm, who could not climb the stairs fast enough, were required to take up observation stations under the temporary shelter of door frames the very moment the air raid alarm sounded.

This observation duty caused many casualties. Many times the observers were directly killed by the incoming bombs, and many of them suffered terrible burns. Nevertheless, they had to be trained and Karl was good at it, but he also understood the limits of the capabilities of his charges. When he saw a trembling old man shaking in front of a burning bomb and unable to proceed, or even to move, he wrote out a relief document certifying that the holder was relieved from the fire extinguishing detail. Karl's signature was known throughout his district of Berlin-W15, and he was proud that his certification was never questioned.

During this time, he earned the trust and respect of the men he trained. As the Russians troops advanced towards Berlin, the training became more combat-oriented. Karl's job was to instruct the members of the Volkssturm in the proper use of the carabiner, the German infantry rifle. Karl himself was an excellent shot. He had been trained by sniper experts and he found it difficult to impart his expertise to old men who had a hard time holding a heavy rifle steady enough to fire at all, let alone hitting a target. The only exceptions were some of the WW1 veterans, but there were not too many of them around. Karl was convinced that this training of old men to fire a gun was not productive.

If they ever stood eye to eye with the Mongols from the Russian infantry forces, they would be killed before they could find the trigger. He voiced his concern more than once to the local commanders of the Volkssturm until some of the officers thought that he might be right and replaced the shooting instructions with hand grenade instructions. Karl was ordered to conduct the training in the Grunewald district, and on the first day, he lost one of his men.

They had started right after daybreak with simple throwing exercises. The defense headquarters had supplied them with several boxes of live and innate Model 24 Stick hand grenades and two boxes of model 24 smoke grenades. They were accompanied by a combat-experienced sergeant because Karl himself had no training with hand grenades. The sergeant explained the differences of the old model 24, which was still in use, to the newer model 43, which was not as heavy. The model 24 dated back to WW1. He pointed out that the smoke grenades had a slightly grooved handle.

There were some little techniques to improve the throwing distance and within a few hours they averaged between 25 and 35 yards. The afternoon instructions proved to be more difficult. While the platoon was busy learning to throw a grenade from a kneeling and prone position, the sergeant showed Karl advanced uses of the stick grenades. Karl paid undivided attention to the instructions because he was to teach this the next day to his platoon.

The first instruction was how to make a "geballte ladung". This was done by removing the throwing handle from six of the grenades and tying the grenade heads with wire around a seventh stick grenade. The geballte ladung was very effectively used to stop and destroy vehicles. The next instruction consisted of attaching a fragmentation sleeve over the top body of the grenade. This was very easily done and due to its nasty effects, almost doubled the devastation radius.

The third exercise was a bit different and the platoon went to a different area of the exercise field, which simulated a combat zone. It was complete with dug out holes and winding trenches. The sergeant took his time to point out two different advantages of the stick grenade vs. the egg shaped grenade. The first advantage was obvious; a stick grenade was unable to roll back to the thrower. This would not matter too much in street-to-street fighting, however, in hilly terrain, it was a definite advantage. The second advantage pertained more to the older model 24. Both of the models functioned on the same principle. Both required that you had to unscrew the cap on the bottom of the handle, which caused a porcelain ball to fall out. The ball was attached to a fuse-like cord/ratchet, which ignited the grenade. Karl and his platoon learned that there was a five second delay from the time they unscrewed the cap until the grenade exploded. As they started to train with live grenades, they would unscrew the cap and count 21, 22, 23, and throw the grenade. Counting for three seconds made it unlikely that in actual combat the grenade was thrown back at them. The sergeant proceeded to instruct Karl and his men how to set up a booby trap.

The model 24 allowed that you could unscrew the cap without igniting the grenade. You just had to hold it straight so that the ball would not fall out of the handle. He showed Karl how to string a wire across trenches and carefully hang up a live model 24. If someone would trip the wire, the grenade would fall and explode. The sergeant set up several variations of the booby trap and demonstrated how they would be triggered.

As they were still training, the air raid sirens sounded the afternoon alert and Karl ordered his men to get out of the trenches and to double-time to a nearby shelter. In the ensuing confusion, the men urged each other to hurry up and one of the members of the platoon ran through the trenches instead of getting out. He tripped over the wires of the booby traps. He must have thought that all of the live grenades had been detonated. In any event, while he took his time to get up, a grenade exploded right next to him and shredded him to pieces.

Fortunately, the explosion was triggered in a short section of the combat ditch and none of the other members of the platoon were injured. While most of the men continued to seek shelter, Karl, the sergeant, and some of the platoon members stayed behind and collected the grisly remains. When Karl reported later on in the afternoon to the Volkssturm base commander in Wilmersdorf, he found a very understanding infantry captain. He tried to console Karl and assured him that his record would remain unblemished. Karl replied that he was not concerned about his record, blemishes or not. He told the captain that he was under the command of the HJ and his assignment to the Volkssturm was a temporary one and that he would ask for reassignment.

The captain listened to him and said, "Karl, you don't want a reassignment, you have been very good at what you were doing. Take a day or two of rest and then check back with me. I will contact the next of kin of the soldier and arrange for a speedy burial of the remains."

"Captain, I am unsure of what you are able to bury. I think that most of this soldier is buried already out at the training grounds."

With this, Karl left the command center and went to see Frau Becker at the school. He had made good on his promise to help her. He had three HJ members stationed at the school to assist her with the identification and notification process. During his time with the Volkssturm, he had slept at their center in the Brandenburg Strasse. Now he wanted to see if she needed any additional help. He also wanted to sleep in the school again, if he could.

When he got to the school it was late and Frau Becker left for the day. He found the classroom, which served a few weeks ago as his bedroom, occupied. All of the classrooms seemed to be filled with refugees. Karl knew that there had been wave after wave of refugees from East Prussia, Pommern, and Poland. He also knew that the Berlin defense headquarters had issued an order to the effect that none of the refugees were allowed to stay within the city limits in excess of 48 hours. They were supposed to keep on walking towards the west and away from the Eastern Front.

Karl was wondering how this order was or could be enforced. There were thousands of refugees and more were coming every day. Who was there to control them? He walked through the school to see if he could find some KLV children. He found over one hundred of them in the Aula, which had been converted into a kind of dormitory. He also found that two more classrooms had been turned into temporary kitchens. There were some pots with potato soup on the burners and a note next to them, suggesting to help yourself. He took this as a personal invitation to eat and helped himself accordingly.

It was a rather watery soup without any meat and not too many potatoes in it, but nevertheless, it was tasty enough that it warranted a second helping.

Going back to the Aula, he found a place to sleep on one of the benches. It was 10:00 PM and he hoped to get some rest before the nightly air raids started. Tomorrow he would see Harold at the HJ center in Halensee.

During his stint with the Volkssturm he did not have an opportunity to see his friend. He also lacked information about the current situation of Berlin.

He had only heard rumors that the Russian troops had bypassed Berlin in an effort to surround it. Most of the rumors came from the refugees who supported them with horror stories about atrocities committed by the fighting Russian forces. However, the radio of the German High Command still proclaimed that victory was absolute. Supposedly Hitler had "wonder weapons" in reserve, ready to be employed when enough Russian and Allied troops where deep within Germany and therefore unable to retreat. Karl had asked the Volkssturm captain about these 'wonder weapons' and inquired as to why so many had to die before Hitler would avenge their sacrifices. The captain had answered with one word, "Horseshit, but you did not hear this from me." Then he added, "What I meant to say was, I only know what horse manure smells like. I know nothing about tactics of warfare."

He was obviously scared that his remark could be reported. But, Karl dismissed the captain's answer. It did not tell him anything. He thought about the father of his friend Peter Zahn, and his loose mouth. He had no desire to report or repeat anything to anyone. He only wished to know how and when this drama was supposed to end.

Thirteen

Karl dreamed about hand grenades and mutilated bodies but still managed to sleep right through the air raid. When he got up in the morning he decided to wait for Frau Becker before seeing his friend in Halensee. By the time Frau Becker arrived, it was already 9:00 AM and Karl was anxious to get moving.

He was, however, happy to have waited because Frau Becker gave him the good news that many of the children from the other camps had been reunited with their relatives. The not so good news was that she was still taking care of over 150 children who stayed at the school and that over nine hundred children were missing and this, just in the school district of W-15.

Missing meant that there was no information about their whereabouts since the evacuations orders had been given. The camps from East Prussia were totally unaccounted for. Karl asked Frau Becker if she needed additional help from the HJ to cope with all the refugees using the school.

"Food" was the short answer. "We are running low on any kind of food. Our allocated rations are not even enough for the remaining children. In order to feed the refugees, we had used up our reserves."

"What about the emergency food storage facility in the Brandenburger Strasse?"

"Where? I never heard of any food in the Brandenburger Strasse. Can you find out for me?" Frau Becker's voice had changed from desperation to hope.

"If you don't know about the storage facility, I hope that I am not mistaken," answered Karl, "but I will let you know either way."

When he arrived in Halensee he heard from Harold that last night's air raid had been a minor one with a minimum of reported damage. "Things are looking up, Karl. Our boys can relax for a day. They have been constantly called upon to assist the air raid marshals to find survivors. How are things with you?"

"Harold, I need your help. I need a transfer to a different assignment," answered Karl, "here is what happened." He finished his report of the training fatality by saying, "I don't think that I am personally responsible for the loss of the soldier, but I still feel guilty. This should have never happened during a training exercise. With all your information and requests, there must be a more suitable task for me."

"I don't have to search very far to find you a different assignment. Matter of fact, I received this morning a request from the SS in charge of the BVG for a subway rat. I would have called you back from the Volkssturm anyway. We might even have to team up for this job. I will fill you in on the details as soon as you read this letter." Harold opened a drawer on his desk and handed Karl a gray envelope.

"It came yesterday. I sent it out to you last night by messenger, but you were not at your base. I had instructed him to bring it back if he could not find you."

The letter was dirty and it had been opened. It was impossible to determine the date it was posted. Karl instantly recognized his mother's handwriting.

It was a short letter, but contained all the good news Karl had hoped for. His mother, brother and sister were on a small farm close to Detmold. They had not experienced another air raid since they left Berlin. It was written before his mother had received any of his postcards. It contained a short remark that his father might be serving in Berlin, but no indication of the name of his unit. The letter closed with his mother writing that she missed him and loved him very much and hoped to see him and Dad again and if possible, soon.

As short as the letter was, Karl still read it over and over again. He was interrupted by Harold, "I can tell by your face that it must be good news. I am happy for you. Now, settle down and listen to this." He waved a piece of paper towards Karl, who had gotten up from his seat and was pacing the room. His face was red and he was too excited to sit still, but he followed his friend's request and stopped in front of the desk. His hands were still busy sticking the letter in his pocket and pulling it out again. Harold observed for a moment his friend's agitated behavior and then decided to proceed.

"Listen up, Karl, this is important. They need someone with intimate knowledge of the subway system to guide various units through the tunnels in case of enemy penetrations. That's the basic requirement. You and I can do that. No question. However, what worries me is that the SS will be calling the shots. They are competing for the command of the defense of the inner city, including the entire subway system.

"The civilian authority of the subway system, the BVG, is apparently out of knowledgeable technical personnel. The SS will use us any way they can. This might get very messy for us."

"What do you mean by messy?"

"Dangerous, you idiot. Should the Russians enter the city, we will see hand-to-hand combat. Depending upon the various front line locations, the SS might want to use the U-Bahn tunnels to lead our troops behind the Russian lines. In this case we will be used as guides. Just picture this; you will be in a tunnel with the Russians in front of you and the SS behind you."

Karl interrupted again, "This is crazy. To lead, or guide like you said, a company or two behind the fighting lines will not help. If the Russians enter Berlin, we are done. No street-to-street fighting will turn this thing around. No matter how often we, or the SS, are using the tunnels. At best, it will be a temporary fix. At worst, it will only cost additional lives. Maybe even yours and mine. Hitler better get his wonder weapon going before it is too late."

Harold stared at Karl in total disbelief. "How can you talk like that? Have all the good spirits left your mind? You know better than that Karl, talk like that can get you shot."

"Come on Harold, don't tell me that thoughts like that have not crossed your mind," Karl was not about to stop.

"Right, Karl, they have. But, I am not stupid enough to open my mouth and talk about it. What is the matter with you? The loss of your Volkssturm man must have scrambled your mind."

"Maybe so, maybe I have to take a day off, as the captain suggested. You are right, I should know better, however..." Karl was unsure if he should finish his sentence, but then he continued, "Horseshit."

"What?"

"Horseshit." repeated Karl "This was the answer from the Volkssturm captain when I asked about the timing of the wonder weapon."

"Now I know that you are deranged. You questioned your captain about Hitler's defense strategy?" Harold had an honest expression of worried disbelief on his face as he studied his friend. "On second thought, it must be mental fatigue. I never heard you talk like that. Pull yourself together. We will go to my home later on and you will enjoy a home cooked meal. You can sleep on the couch in our living room. And tomorrow you will be yourself again."

"Thank you, Harold, I'll be happy to go home with you," Karl was pulling his letter out of his pocket again to read it one more time, but then he decided to stop reading and asked Harold if he had any other information about the possible new assignment.

"I am glad that you asked," answered Harold, "after your verbal garbage, I was not sure that you were interested."

"Of course I am interested. Besides, I will always do what I am ordered to do, even if it makes no sense to me. What you said about the Ruskies in front of us and the SS behind us does not worry me at all. After all, we know our way around down there and also how to get out of the way. Between the two of us, we could disappear any time we feel like it." Karl pulled the chair away from the desk and sat down. "By the way, you mentioned that we might be able to share in this task...how so?"

"I don't know, not exactly, but I think if the Russians are invading Berlin, all hell will break loose and we will have no choice in our assignments at all. We will just be ordered to fight wherever we are. In this case it would be nice to have a place to hide after all.

"On one hand it would be nice to survive. On the other hand survival might not be worth it. But if there are any wonder weapons, and if they are employed in the last minute, we could wait them out. To have an ongoing SS assignment to guide troops around the U-Bahn system might be the best we can hope for. It surely beats house-to-house combat." Harold looked out of the window and stopped talking. It was now Karl's turn to digest his friend's comments.

"Are you saying that you are planning to hide in the tunnels until the war is over?"

"No, that is not what I am saying, not at all. I do think however, that as long as we have a choice, we should choose wisely. Don't you think so?"

"I agree that when it comes down to hand-to-hand combat, we will have a better chance to survive in the tunnels than on the streets." Karl's answer came slow and deliberate. He was thinking of a particular ventilation shaft. It was a little wider on the top than the regular ones. He knew it well; it was close to the Uhlandstrasse subway station. Not far from their present location. He made a mental note to visit it as soon as possible.

"We might need some canned goods, just in case. That reminds me, do you think that there is a way to get some of the food reserve from the Brandenburger Strasse depot, to Frau Becker? She used up her rations for the children by feeding refugees in her facility. Are there any applications to submit? Or, do you have any suggestions?"

"Yes, on the canned goods, just in case" Harold parroted Karl. "Maybe, on the food reserve for Frau Becker. Here is a requisition form. Have Frau Becker fill it out, stamp it with the KLV rubber stamp and sign it. Have her double the amount she needs." He looked at Karl. "We try the legal way first. If the request will be cut in half, it will be still sufficient for her needs. Go, no better yet run, and get her signature now, while you still have the time. I'll expect you back before 3 PM. This way we can still submit it today."

Karl took the form, in triplicate, and went to the door. He stood there for a second and then asked Harold, "Submit? Harold, tell me, why do you send me out? Do you really ever submit anything?"

"No, but I need to cover my ass. You dummkopf. Go!"

Karl did not run, but hurried anyway to reach Frau Becker. She was happy to fill out the requisition form and Karl told her to apply for enough food to last her until she would receive her next monthly allowance. She used her school stamp twice on each sheet, once on the top of the form and once more over her signature, on the bottom. Karl was always amazed to see the official stamping of forms. It seemed to him that any kind of an official in Berlin, in any kind of capacity, had at least one important looking rubber stamp and loved to use it. He had seen that Harold, in the HJ Dienstelle, had at least five stamps neatly arranged on a miniature carousel devise.

Maybe, I should get a rubber stamp too, he thought, and was amused by his idea. It must be good for something.

On the way back to Halensee, he remembered to inspect the airshaft by the Uhlandstrasse U-Bahn station. He knew that the actual entrance to the Uhlandstrasse station was on the

Kurfuerstendamm, but the ventilation shaft was in the courtyard of a stately apartment complex in the Uhlandstrasse.

When he arrived he saw that the luxurious housing unit was partially destroyed and closed to the former residents. He had some difficulty finding the former courtyard because it was filled with large chunks of broken cement walls and rubble from the collapsed portions of buildings. It must have been brought in from the streets by bulldozers. Karl had lined himself up with some of the still standing walls and found the approximate location of the airshaft. He was happy to see that it was buried under some of the smaller pieces of rubble.

As he tried to move some of the pieces, he thought that it might be a better idea to leave everything the way it was until he could come back with Harold and move the debris around to suit their purpose. With any luck this could become a perfect hiding place.

He left the courtyard thinking that the next step would be to enter the subway tunnel from the main entrance and walk to the airshaft and inspect it for any possible damage. But first he wanted to tell Harold about it and go home with him to eat dinner with the Kellner family. Harold hardly ever talked about his parents, but Karl knew that Herr Kellner was exempt from military duty and that he held a major position in the food reserve and distribution organization. It would be interesting to talk with him. Besides, the dinner might be much better than what Frau Becker was able to serve.

Karl looked forward to the evening and walked a step faster to be in Harold's office before 3 PM. It had been cloudy all day, not too cold, and now it started to drizzle. Typical winter weather for Berlin. Karl hoped that the Kellner residence would be heated.

When he rounded the corner towards the HJ headquarters, he saw one of the ever-present gray Kubelwagens parked in front. At first he feared that the Volkssturm had sent for him but when he saw that the driver was wearing a navy uniform, he relaxed but wondered why the navy would pay the HJ a visit. Harold was already waiting for him.

"Menschendkinder, you took your sweet time, didn't you?" Harold was in his cheerful mood again. Karl looked around for a navy messenger or officer.

"There is a navy staff car waiting in front of the door. Who is our visitor?"

"No staff car. No visitor," said Harold.

"Then I must be seeing things. What kind of a car is it and for whom is the driver waiting?"

"The driver is corporal Kost. He is on special assignment and waiting for you." Harold reached behind the desk and came up with a handful of official looking documents. "Here are your immediate orders. Corporal Kost will drive with you to the storage facility in the Brandenburger Strasse. This first paper will give you access to the facility and authority to go anyplace within it. You will proceed to the Navy section and get 2,000 pounds of pipe tobacco. Corporal Kost has the necessary authorization papers. You will then ask for the civilian section and get the food for Frau Becker. Let me see what she asked for."

Karl gave him the forms and saw to his bewilderment that Harold did not even read them. He just stamped them with a big round stamp that read 'APPROVED'. He used a red ink pad. It looked impressive. The imprint of the stamp left a line open for a counter signature and another line for the date. Harold grabbed another stamp, set the date for the current date and applied it in the designated space, this time he used a blue inkpad. He then signed the paper as required on the bottom. On the counter signature line he signed again, this time using his left hand.

When he saw Karl's questioning face, he shrugged his shoulders, "Nobody will question you, trust me, but you need to hurry again. Corporal Kost would have left already if he would know the way to the Brandenburger Strasse. I told him he needed to wait for you to guide him to the correct facility. Take him around some detours to make it look difficult. I also asked him to bring you and the food to the KLV Headquarters." He motioned Karl out of the door, and shoved him towards the car. "Wipe your stupid expression off your face. Look and act as if you are in command." He pushed a pack of cigarettes in Karl's pocket. "Give this to Corporal Kost if he hesitates to take you to the school. If not, then don't. I'll be waiting for you."

Karl wanted to close the car door and was stopped once more by Harold, who gave him another piece of double stamped paper. "Here, I almost forgot. This will get you a carton of Fliegerschokolade. I don't know in what section it is. You will have to ask for it. This is for us, by the way. Don't leave it with Frau Becker."

Karl told Corporal Kost to turn the car around and take the first right turn.

He followed Harold's advice and went in a zigzag circle around the Pruessenpark before entering the Brandenburger Strasse. The supply depot was in an annex of a former high school. Harold was right that they encountered no difficulty entering through a large cobblestone paved gateway. The supply manager was a silver haired man on crutches. He glanced at the authorization papers, stamped them again and wrote the time of day on it. Apparently the date and the time of entry and exit were important enough to be verified and recorded.

The requisition forms were sufficient to get a storage worker to fetch for them the tobacco for the navy and the food for the school. However, the request and authorization for the Fliegerschokolade was another matter. The civilian official seemed to find no record of this item in his inventory.

He gave Karl a helpless soldier shrug with his shoulders and gestured towards his extensive file cabinets. "We don't carry Fliegerschokolade. See for yourself."

Karl remembered that Harold had told him to act as if he was in command.

"Look here mein Herr, I don't have the time to search your inventory sheets. So I ask you nicely, but only once, to find the box of schokolade. If you don't find it in the next three minutes, I will call a Gefolgschaft of HJ or the SS to help you search. My papers state that you have over 20 boxes. I only want one, but I want it now." Karl had no idea if there were 20 boxes or none. He just did not like the behavior of the civil servant.

The navy corporal was about to leave the building when he heard Karl's angry voice. "Trouble?" he asked.

"No, I don't think so," answered Karl, "Our friend here is just about to get the last item." Karl's suspicion was right. The bare mentioning that he would call the SS to search the depot was sufficient to spark the memory of the supply manager.

"Now, that you mention 20 boxes, I think I saw a pallet of unmarked packages. It might be what we are looking for. Wait just a moment." He left the front office and entered an adjoining room. Karl could hear him giving some orders to another clerk. When he came back he carried a brown cardboard box in his hand and a wide grin on his face.

"Sorry, Obergefolgsschaftfuehrer, my mistake. We are overworked and understaffed. This box is part of the pallet I mentioned to you. They were among a few items that came in recently. We simply had not had the time to add them to our inventory." His eyes were darting back and forth between Karl and Corporal Kost, trying to seek understanding for his demanding job.

"Please sign here for this carton, and if there is nothing else you need, I will clock you out and you are good to go."

Karl knew that he could use this incident to wrangle maybe a tin of lard or margarine from the manager, but he did not have the heart to do it. "Thank you mein Herr, we appreciate your assistance. Heil Hitler." Karl and Cost snapped their salute and left the building.

"This box of must weigh about 10 pounds," said the Corporal as he started the car. "How can you miss 20 of them?"

"I guess when you are an overworked civil employee, things happen that way," answered Karl.

The KLV headquarters was only a few blocks away. The Corporal pulled up at a side entrance and helped Karl to unload and carry the food through the hallway to the nearest empty classroom. He wondered aloud if the canned liverwurst tasted anything like the fresh wurst from pre war times.

"Try it yourself," said Karl and handed him a can. "I wish I could give you more. These supplies will feed homeless school children otherwise, I would kungle you for some of your tobacco."

It looked as if the Corporal wanted to hand the can back to Karl, but then thought better of it and the can disappeared underneath his big uniform coat.

"You need a ride back to your office?"

"No, you better leave the city while you are still able to make it through the lines. Turn left on the next corner, drive four blocks straight and then turn left again. Keep on going straight and you will see signs guiding you out of the inner city. I wish you well. Heil Hitler." The big Navy Corporal returned the salute. He looked happy and as he accelerated to the corner, he waved back once more.

While they were unloading they had been watched by some of the KLV children and Karl called out to one of them to get Frau Becker. When Frau Becker arrived, she started to count the supplies. She saw at once that the food in front of her exceeded her requisition.

"How," she began, "how did you do that, Karl? So fast, and so much more than I expected. I have not seen tins of meat for at least 3 months."

"I always get credit I don't deserve." Like always, Karl was not at all at ease when people remarked about his apparent magic. A few months ago, Harold had told him that he had various channels to get him nearly anything he needed. Subject to one condition, "Never, tell anyone about me. Never. Take all the credit you can handle, but leave me out of it." He knew that he could trust Karl, and Karl trusted him. They did not even shake hands on it. This was an arrangement in which Karl's word was as good as gold, and Harold did not even exist.

Karl handed Frau Becker the revised form and told her that he got lucky to get immediate approval. "I think they like kids in uniform. Or, maybe I look very helpless and needy."

"You might look helpless," she agreed, "but you are sure an asset to have around. By the way, I still have not heard a word from the children who took the train to Kottbus. Some of the parents and relatives are asking daily. Is there any way you could make contact to the Kottbus HJ headquarters?"

"Yes, I have asked them to check with all the hospitals and also field hospitals in the area. They promised to notify me as soon as there was anything to report. I also instructed them to check with the local schools and I was told that the KLV Dienststelle in Kottbus was not operational. No explanation given. However, I know that my friend, Peter, will find a way to make contact with us . . . if he is still alive." Karl was slow with his answer. He had heard that the Polish underground had sabotaged the rail lines leading in and out of Kottbus and he feared the worse for his friend and the boys. "I will check back with you tomorrow."

The slight rain had turned the ashes and the debris on the streets into a dirty mushy substance, which clogged the drain gates to the sewer lines. The water had started to back up almost to the height of the sidewalk. Karl had greased his shoes with motor oil to make them waterproof, but that was a few weeks ago. By the time he reached Halensee, his newspaper linings were soaked and had dissolved.

Harold was happy to see the Fliegerschokolade. He locked the box in his desk and went to the door. "Any difficulties?"

"Not really," answered Karl, "but I had to threaten them with a search team before they decided to find this carton. They told me first that there was no Fliegerschokolade in their inventory."

"Yeah, that's about right," grinned Harold, "There was none as far as I knew. This stuff is hard to come by, unless you are part of the Luftwaffe. But I figured as long as you were there, we might as well ask for it. You did good." He slapped a surprised Karl on the shoulder and locked the office.

"Time to go home and eat."

Fourteen

Harold's parents lived in an apartment house in the Paulsborner Strasse. Because of the ongoing rain, the boys decided to walk part of the way through the connected air raid shelters. This was actually forbidden. Most of the apartment house cellars had long been linked to each other to allow the people trapped under their own collapsed building to escape.

In a way it was a good system and saved many lives. On the other hand, it invited looters to use the passageways and to disappear in the maze. For this reason, there was constantly a civilian patrol or HJ patrol on duty. Harold had used the passageways very often; sometimes during air raids and sometimes during bad weather. He knew all the short cuts and crossings to make the way home in record time.

The Kellner family lived on the second floor of a 4-story apartment house and occupied a 5-room apartment, including the kitchen. It was divided into a living room, dining room, kitchen and two bedrooms. Like all the high-priced apartments in this area, it also featured a bathroom with a bathtub. Harold was the only child and he was proud of his own bedroom. Karl had met Harold's mother before. She was pleased that her son was a friend of a well-known KLV leader and greeted him with a spoon in her hand.

"Welcome, Karl. We are happy to see you back in Berlin. Dinner is almost ready."

"Thank you," Karl managed to say before Harold dragged his friend to the bathroom where they washed up. There was no hot water, but there was a bar of soap and a few towels. "Harold, you don't know how lucky you are to enjoy a functioning apartment." Karl was washing his face two times to make absolutely sure that he was clean. He looked around to find a comb.

"Can you help me out?" he asked his friend.

Reaching up to a glass shelf, Harold handed Karl a new comb, still wrapped in gray and white striped paper, "Here, keep it. I don't think that you ever owned one."

"No, I never thought that I needed one. I've always kept my hair short; not longer than a pocket match. Regulation length, but thank you." Karl was still examining his face in the mirror and rubbed his forehead. He noticed a few scratches, which he did not know he had.

"Come on," urged Harold, "you don't get any cleaner if you wash yourself for a third time. Your face is just a bit scarred up. You will get used to it."

The dining room table was large enough to serve six people and was covered with a checkered white-on-white tablecloth. Ferdinand Kellner, a gray-haired man in his early forties, entered the dining room after the boys were seated. He had a pleasant voice and a strong handshake when he greeted Karl.

"So, I finally meet the friend of my son. He always talks about you. 'Karl said this, and Karl did that', but when I asked him, he knows nothing about your parents. I understand that your father is presently serving with the artillery. What does he do in civilian life?" Ferdinand's eyes were meeting Karl's when he asked his questions.

"He is an electrical engineer. He worked for AEG before he was drafted. I do not know where he is now." Karl helped himself to potatoes and canned beans. Frau Kellner had handed each of them a plate with some kind of meat on it. He did not care about the meat. As long as he had potatoes and any kind of gravy, he was happy. His favorite meal was potato soup with frankfurters. He knew that other people favored all kinds of meats and vegetables and he had always wondered why.

"I really miss my father. He would always answer my questions and always gave me great advice. During the last few weeks, I've gone through all kind of circumstances and I even met some officers. Now I have more questions than ever before, and he is not here." Karl looked up to Harold's father who had stopped eating.

Ferdinand thought for a moment and then offered, "I realize that you went through a tough experience with the KLV. This would have triggered many questions, which would have been difficult to answer, even for your father. But, I'll be happy to listen to you." Ferdinand got up from the table and opened the door to the living room. "Let's sit in here." He pointed to the couch and seated himself in an armchair. "Shoot," he invited Karl to speak, "I'll answer the best I can."

"I will not ask about the war," began Karl, "even if you explain all about it, I doubt that I would understand the answers. What I would like to know is more about the present circumstances. I am drafted to teach old men how to defend themselves and how to kill. I am 14 years old, and I was in charge of 120 boys below the age of 12, and had no adult to guide me. We are told every day by the OKW that we have wonder weapons standing by and that, in the end, we will win the war. We get bombed every night and have no air defenses left. The Russians have nearly completed their ring around Berlin and we might be in house to house combat within a week or two. If you would be my father, Herr Kellner, I would ask you, is everything lost already? And should I try to reach my mother? Since you are not my father, I am afraid to ask this question of you, Herr Kellner, but you are the father of my best friend, and I need to trust someone."

Ferdinand appeared uneasy. "There is no short and easy answer, however I will try." He looked over to his son, "You might as well take note too, of what I say."

"When we grow up, we develop a set of values. We develop these values based upon what we learned from our elders and from our own experiences. As we grow older, our values become our most prized possessions. Therefore, your values Karl, resulted from your experiences and include besides your love for your parents, your oath to the Fuehrer, and also how much you value your own life."

He paused and leaned closer to the boys, "Here is my short answer. It is certain that we will see hand-to-hand combat in Berlin. We will fight for every street and for our lives. Should you decide to abandon your oath and your duty and seek to protect your own life, your decision will have nothing to do with the war, or for that matter, with your age Karl, but it will have everything to do with how much you value your values. Both of you, regardless of how long you might live, will always adjust and readjust your values. This is part of growing up and maturing, but the eternal answer to every decision in your life is always determined by how much you value your values. It is that simple."

Karl was stunned. He had not expected to hear from Herr Kellner a firm answer to the possibility of hand-to-hand combat in the streets of Berlin. He had hoped to get a positive answer in regard to Hitler's wonder weapon. He loved his Fuehrer and he wanted to believe in a final victory. The short speech from Herr Kellner had not contained a single word of reassurance, far from it.

"Thank you very much, Herr Kellner," said Karl, "You don't know how much I appreciate your answers."

Ferdinand got up and asked his wife, "Can you make up a bed on the couch for Karl?"

"It will only take me a minute," answered Frau Kellner.

Karl was happy to accept. He had hoped to stay with the Kellner family for the night. The bed on the couch was soft and warm and just what he needed.

He thought about Herr Kellner's answers and tried to think if he had any values he was prepared to fight for, or at least defend. The sleep came faster than the answers he was seeking.

The usual night air raid started late and lasted a lot longer than usual. There was a rumor that the Russian planes had started the bombing raid and that the British planes had been reinforced by Canadian planes. Ferdinand Kellner was also the fire marshal of the apartment house, and he asked the boys to accompany him in his rounds during the raid. They checked first the water transmission lines for the building and then shut them off. It was a precaution in case a water line got hit or damaged. They did the same to the gas line. Next, they went to the top floor of the four-story building and checked that members of the Volksturm were at their assigned posts. They also checked that none of the tenants had elected to stay in their apartments. Ferdinand was so concerned about this that he had posted a list on the cellar entrance and every tenant had to sign in and out.

Karl marveled at the difference between Ferdinand and Harold. While the father was an example of correctness, Harold seemed to do everything on a whim. Ferdinand seemed to have a plan and method, and even notes for everything. No wonder, Karl thought, that Ferdinand Kellner was in a leading position in the civilian government. He did not really know what this position was and if Harold's father was a member of the Nazi party. Members of the Nazi party wore buttons on their lapels. He had not noticed one on Ferdinand's suit last night. Maybe the button was on his winter topcoat. He never wanted to ask Harold about this. He liked their friendship just the way it was. Besides, he could care less. Most of the teachers he knew were members of the party and otherwise he did not know many adults.

After the air raid, they went once more up to Harold's apartment. Frau Kellner fixed a cup of coffee ersatz and some jelly bread. Karl asked Harold when he would prepare the transfer papers to the special subway unit of the SS. When Ferdinand heard about this unit and Karl's possible position as a guide, he made a doubtful face. "This might be just another one of these suicidal last-effort commandos. However, it might give you an option between combat in the streets or possible refuge in the tunnels. Not a bad idea to freshen up on your local knowledge, Karl."

"I think that I understand what you are trying to say, Herr Kellner. Thanks for the hint." He shook hands with him and thanked him and Harold's mother for the dinner.

"We hope to see you again, soon," she said when the boys left for the Dienststelle.

The steady rain from the previous night had given way to a light on-again and off-again drizzle. The boys stayed in the middle of the streets. This made for faster walking than skirting the hills of debris, which lined the sidewalks. There was not much traffic.

Most of the bombing damage from last night's air raid had been in the eastern part of the city, and the few available fire trucks and emergency vehicles had been dispatched to the area of Wedding. Harold wanted to phone the liaison officer, Lieutenant Ebert, at the command center at the Tiergarten Flak Tower. He needed to know the exact reporting location for Karl, but when they got to the office, they found out that the phone lines were out of order again.

He took his seat behind the desk and pulled out first the request and then the transfer forms. He filled in all the details regarding Karl's familiarity with the subway system. He also attached a list of assignments completed by Karl. "Here is what I think we should do," he told Karl, "you will leave right now and report to Lieutenant Ebert at the Zoo bunker. I will send Dietrich, you remember him, one of our older HJ members, as your replacement to your former Captain at the Volkssturm. He will inform the Captain of your transfer to the SS." He was interrupted by the ringing of the phone. "Great, it's working again, don't leave yet, I have something else for you."

He answered the phone and listened. "Jawohl, I understand.

Please tell the Captain that an HJ member with the name of Dietrich will be reporting to him by noon. Heil Hitler." He ended the call. "That was easy. You are off the hook. They were just asking if you are available or if they could get a suitable replacement for you." He searched through the paper files in his wall cabinet and handed Karl an envelope. "I made some notes you might find helpful. These are updates of the subway system, including damage reports of the last six months. Read them when you are alone and surprise everyone with your up to date knowledge."

Karl took his papers and left before Dietrich reported for duty. He decided to take the subway to the Zoo bunker and to stop for a moment at the Uhland Strasse U-Bahn stations. He had not had the time to do an inspection of his airshaft. He would do this later or the next day. All he wanted to see was if the other nearby ventilation shafts were undamaged. He wanted to be sure that he had different access points to his intended hideout.

When he got off of the train, he had to work his way towards the end of the platform. He knew the station pretty well. When the Station Master was going back into his cubicle, Karl stepped down the few stone steps leading into the tunnel. The steps and the walkway were installed for the maintenance workers.

He remembered where he could cross the tracks without any danger of the electrified third rail, and found within minutes the first ventilation shaft.

Karl climbed up the small iron ladder and checked the locking mechanism of the air gate. The gate needed cleaning. It was covered with cement dust and ashes, allowing only a limited amount of air to pass through. The gate was secured with a padlock, which seemed undamaged. Hanging on the top rung of the ladder was a crowbar. Karl was about to use it to remove the lock when he noticed that it was unlocked. He removed it and put it in his pocket. He then removed the four bolts securing the ladder to the top of the shaft assembly. This allowed him to move the ladder around from the bottom. The removed lock now granted him access to the passageway from the outside. It also enabled him to scurry out of the tunnel should the need arise.

He was satisfied with his little handy work and went down to the bottom of the shaft to wait for the next train to pass. The trains were running about seven minutes apart, and he could hear the roar in the tunnel before he felt the air pressure wave. In spite of the partially blocked air vent, it seemed normal.

This could only mean that most of the other airshafts were in working order.

All together it had cost him a little over half an hour, and once he was back at the platform, he took the next train to the Zoo.

Fifteen

When Karl entered the 6-story bunker, he had to show his transfer orders to the Flak officer on duty. He was told that Lieutenant Ebert's office was on the fifth floor. There were two elevators in the structure, but they were mostly used to transport the 128mm Flak ammunition to the rooftop. Karl used the nearest staircase and passed the restricted area of the second floor, which was guarded with a special unit of the SS. He knew from Harold that it served to house and protect the inventory of several art galleries, coin collections and various art treasures from museums.

As he passed the third floor, he saw signs to nursing staff and operating rooms. When he arrived at the fifth floor, a member of the HJ, who was officially assigned to the Flak division, greeted him. He directed Karl to a door at the center of the long hallway. Lieutenant Ebert occupied a small office without windows. In one corner were some filing cabinets and a desk with two chairs. On the other side of the office was a field bed with several blankets on top. Karl could see no evidence that he was five stories up.

Lieutenant Ebert served officially in the First Flak Division, which operated the anti-aircraft guns on the rooftops of the high-rise bunkers. Most of the requests for HJ members came from him. In addition to his regular duties, he also served as a conduit between the HJ Flak detail and the SS Sonder Commandos.

"So, you are the special subway rat." Ebert took the transfer documents from Karl without answering his salute. "You will need to go to the Friedrichshain bunker to see Untersturmfuehrer Bernd to obtain your specific assignment. He is hoping to get more than just one rat. Do you have any friends who know the U-Bahn as well as you?"

"Yes, there is Gefolgschaftsfuehrer Harold Kellner. He is currently in charge of the HJ Dienststelle Halensee. I think that he knows the subway system as well as I do."

"Hmm, yes, I know Harold; he is our main contact in the HJ. Don't tell Untersturmfuehrer Bernd about him, at least not yet. Try to think of someone else." Lieutenant Ebert was a young officer with an easy-going manner. He took his time reading Karl's qualifications. "Do you understand your transfer," he asked.

"No, not really," answered Karl.

"Officially, Harold transferred you from Halensee to us, the First Flak Division. However, we have the request from the SS for someone of your knowledge. Therefore, you are now on a temporary assignment to the Waffen SS. If and when Untersturmfuehrer Bernd does not need you anymore, you will have to report back to us here in the Zoo bunker. In the meantime, I will give you a pass for unrestricted travel within Berlin."

Karl pocketed the pass, saluted, and walked down to the third floor. He hoped to obtain some kind of a medical kit to stash away at the hideout in the Uhlandstrasse ventilation shaft. As he tried to enter the restricted area an HJ guard stopped him.

"Who do you need to see?"

"Nobody in particular, but I am trying to locate Captain Dr. Felder. I understand that there is a personnel office on this floor." He showed the guard his new pass and was directed to a small office-like cubicle. He was surprised that his pass allowed him access to the confinements of the hospital floor, and marveled at the very efficient ventilation system. The air in the bunker smelled fresh and clean.

The HJ member in the cramped office informed him that Dr. Felder was expected to start his turn at the Zoo bunker within a few days and that he was currently stationed in Wilmersdorf in the Gertrauden Krankenhaus.

Karl asked the clerk if he could get some bandages and sterile solutions to take to the Dienststelle in Halensee. "We also need some ointment or salve to treat minor burn wounds," he added.

The clerk offered to get him an operation pack, called number one, which contained bandages and some basic sterile instruments. For the other requirements, he was unable to help and suggested to

Karl to come back when Dr. Felder would be on duty.

Karl had to sign a receipt for the number one pack, which was wrapped in yellow waterproof paper and had the number 1 stenciled on each side. This was better than he had imagined. He walked down to the ground floor and out of the confinements of the Zoo bunker and took the next subway train to Friedrichshain.

The Friedrichshain bunker was built like the Zoo bunker. He had been told that the walls were solid concrete. Over three meters wide on average and on the ground floor even five meters. The public entrance of the bunker was congested with civilians, mostly women with small children and little backpacks and small suitcases. It took Karl several minutes until he cleared the crowd. He noticed a wide exit ramp with two elevators nearby, which transported ammunition to the Flak located on the rooftop. Further into the bunker were two staircases leading upward which were also cramped with sleeping civilians. However, a little way down the main passageway, he found a directory attached to the wall. Apparently the office he was seeking was located on the second floor.

Karl observed that while the offices of the Flak commandos in the zoo bunker had no special guards, the offices of the SS leaders had security patrols in their hallways. Untersturmfuehrer Bernd occupied a similar office like Lieutenant Ebert. After Karl passed the inspection by the guard, he was allowed to enter. This was the first time he was face to face alone with an SS officer and he was eager to keep this meeting as short as possible. He could not help remembering the warning from Major Zahn, 'Stay away from the SS. They are not your friend'.

"What kind of a weapon are you carrying?" asked the Untersturmfuehrer after he had studied Karl's file.

"None," was Karl's short answer.

"It says here that you are an excellent marksman and trained as a sniper."

Bernd took of his reading glasses and motioned Karl to sit opposite from his desk.

"Correct. That was my training." Karl kept to his game plan.

"It says furthermore that you know the subway system. You want to be just as short as in your previous answers, or do you care to elaborate?"

Karl shifted in his seat and looked the Untersturmfuehrer in his eyes. "I am trained to answer my superiors directly to the point. Yes,

I am familiar with the subway system. I know the stations and crossings of the U-Bahn and the S-Bahn. I also know individual shortcuts within the inner city." Karl stopped. He hoped that his answer would suffice.

"You did not mention access shafts, ventilation shafts, emergency exits, bulkhead control chambers and third rail avoidance." The Untersturmfuehrer's voice was smooth and even encouraging. "Are you familiar with them as well?"

"Yes, I am. Somewhat."

"What do you mean by somewhat?"

"I know about everything you asked, except the bulkhead control chambers. I mean, I know pretty much where they are, but I am not familiar with their operation."

"Good enough. You don't need to know about the bulkheads and their operation, other than where they are located. For the next week I want you to reacquaint yourself with the system. I want you specifically to become an expert on every emergency entrance and exit as well as the nearness or possible access to sewer and water lines. For this I will get you copies of plans from the engineering staff of the BVG. All the rest you should be able to figure out by yourself. You will report to me every morning before 8:00 AM. You are dismissed. Heil Hitler."

Karl snapped his salute and departed. The meeting went far better than he had expected. He had feared to be permanently assigned to a special SS unit. Instead, he had been told to work on his own. This could only mean that the SS needed him only to serve them as a guide.

A look at his watch told him that he had time enough to catch Harold in his office. He took the subway back to the Uhland Strasse Station and walked the rest of the way. Harold was about to leave for the day when Karl arrived.

He liked the medical pack and then asked Karl, "How did it go? Is there a chance that we might be working together?"

"If you want to give up your position here at the office, I can arrange to have you join me. You were right on your guess that they want us on stand-by until the Russians invade the city. I am sure that they want us to guide SS and demolition units underground to strategic locations, or behind the fighting lines. In the meantime, this will give us a chance to place some emergency rations and maybe some civilian clothes in a subway airshaft close to the Uhland Strasse station. You want to see it?"

"Yes, how much room will we have?"

"Hardly any, you will have to see it for yourself."

"Lead on," said Harold, and he grabbed a dynamo flashlight and the box with the Fliegerschokolade, "Let's take this along. I have been told that we can survive on this alone for about a week. We have to find room to keep it safe."

It was already dark when they arrived at the courtyard and Karl moved quickly between the mounds of rubble to the covered entrance of the shaft.

"What do you think," he asked Harold, after he moved the last piece of concrete aside.

"The location is just what we need," answered Harold, "the buildings around us are pretty much leveled. There is nothing left standing that could fall on top of us. We will need to arrange the rubble in a way to cover us and still afford us with a wide field of vision. Let's go through the subway entrance and see what it looks like on the bottom. We should leave our packages right here." Harold placed his carton of chocolate next to Karl's medical package close to the vent grate and covered them with debris.

They went back to the station and had no difficulty finding their way back in the tunnel. Karl was the first one up in the shaft and used the crowbar to break the padlock on the grate. He used his friend's flashlight to see how much room they had in the opening.

"Harold, come up, there is some unattached cable in a side space. We can drop it down and stash our goodies right up here."

Within minutes, they decided to make this their hideout if they needed one.

Karl dropped the cable to the bottom and found that the exposed space was large enough to accommodate two people. There was also something like a toolbox in the clearance. He decided to leave it in its place and reached outside for their packages, which they had left behind.

"Water," he said to his friend, "we will need a few containers with clean water."

"There is running water in the station," answered Harold, "we can always get some if we need to."

"Not good enough," argued Karl, "the water might get shut off, blown up or whatever. Plus, we might not be able to go through the tunnels. We could find ourselves completely on our own. We should have at least a week of rations including sufficient water."

As they went back to the station, they had to pick their way through the mob of civilians who used the subway platforms nightly as a bomb shelter. Most of the children huddled under blankets, and the adults slouched under several sheets of clothing on the tiled floor. Many had cardboard signs with their names either next to them or on top of them. Most of them sat on suitcases and boxes. These were the people who were bombed out of their homes. The few belongings around them were all they had left.

Once in awhile someone would get up and walk a few steps down into the tunnel to relieve themselves. Harold estimated that there were more than 800 people in the Uhland Strasse station, however this figure would certainly increase as the night went on and the air raids began.

When they got back to the street level, Karl asked Harold once more if he wanted to give up the present assignment as Dienststellenleiter and join him in his subway detail.

"I guess that I should wait at least another day. I need the time to place some provisions in our hide out," answered Harold.

Sixteen

Karl decided to spend the night in the KLV Headquarters. The evening was cold and when he looked at the sky, he could not see a single cloud. Perfect flying weather for the Russians, he thought, and feared another massive air raid. The clear weather always induced the Russians to fly several missions without any intervals, and the air raids could easily last all through the night.

When he arrived at the place where just two days ago he had slept, he found the old school building gone. Instead of the massive gray building, there was nothing but a wide field of utter devastation. The whole housing block where the school complex was located was almost totally destroyed. It must have been hit last night by at least one, if not several air mines. Karl was stunned by the extensive damage. He could not even find the former entrance. Instead of an indication of the main building, there was only a massive pile of concrete slabs, bricks and still steaming rubble. Where was everybody? Where was anything?

As he climbed through the ruins to find the entrance to the former air raid shelter, which was located under the rear building, he was stopped by a patrol of air raid marshals. "Halt, stand right where you are. Hands over your head." The voice sounded old, but strong enough to make him freeze on the spot. He knew that the marshals were authorized to shoot looters on sight and feared that he might be accused of plundering. The commander of the patrol had a small flashlight, which he directed at Karl's face. While Karl was momentarily blinded he relaxed as soon as he heard his name.

"Oh, it's you, Karl. I was afraid that we had to arrest some HJ punk. You can take your hands down."

Karl had started to shake beyond control. The shock of seeing the familiar building destroyed, the absence of life, the frightening command, the fear of being mistaken for a looter, together with the cold of the night took its toll. He wanted to turn around to see who was recognizing him, but was unable to do so. He had to sit down to get a grip on himself. He felt that someone was sitting down next to him and grabbing his shoulders.

"Take it easy, Karl. We think that most of the children were in the shelter when it happened, and we got them out alive. There is nothing you are able to do right now. Let me help you get up and I will walk you out of here."

Karl looked up and recognized the face. It belonged to Herr Stein, one of the oldest Volkssturm members he had trained to extinguish the phosphor bombs. "Tell me," he said to Herr Stein, "did you see Frau Becker today? Is she alright?"

"Frau Becker was here all day. She was the only one who knew all the children by name and sight. We worked with her to find a shelter for the survivors. Some of the wounded children were taken to the extension of the Gertrauden Hospital."

Karl tried to get up and was glad that Herr Stein was there to help him. "I am on duty all night," he told Karl, "but if you like, you can sleep in my apartment tonight. I live only a few minutes from here."

Karl decided against it. "Thanks a lot, Herr Stein, but I think that I will sleep in the Friedrichshain bunker tonight. I have to report there anyhow in the morning. If you need to reach me, you can contact SS Untersturmfuehrer Bernd. His office is in the bunker." Karl wanted to get away from this place.

He thought that he might walk to the next subway station and take a train to Friedrichshain. The walk would give him some solitude to straighten out his thoughts. He felt very dizzy, almost disoriented. It seemed to him that his mind was somehow scrambled. Matter of fact, he was unable to hold any thought for any length of time.

He tried to think of his parents, the KLV camp in Poland, his friend Peter, but was interrupted by mental images of SS uniforms, burning buildings, and disappearing faces of people. This is no good and of no use, he said to himself. Just walk, put one foot in front of the other one and concentrate on reaching the nearest subway station. By the time you reach the shelter you will feel better.

This line of thought helped him to reach the subway. When he boarded the train, he heard the whining air raid signal. It was certainly a late warning because almost immediately after the sirens stopped, the heavy flak started to fill the sky with ear shattering explosions. The train stopped at the Zoo station and while some of the passengers elected to stay in the station below ground, others stormed the exit in the direction of the bunker shelter. Karl hurried along with the group towards the high-rise bunker. His mental fog lifted as he started to run.

The entrance to the shelter was as congested as always at the onset of an air attack. It took Karl over ten minutes to get through the heavy doors. Once he was inside, he could not stop to look around. The throng of people pushed him towards the staircases. It seemed that he had to make up his mind to either go up or down. He would have preferred to go downside to the lower level. People around him told him that it was warmer and that he might even find a place to sit on a bench. As he moved toward the staircase, he noticed two HJ Streifendienst members who were in charge of maintaining order. They directed some of the women with the smallest children to the steps leading to the lower level. The staircase to the upper stories was already filled up with women and older children, who tried to sit on the steps. Karl managed to move over to the HJ detail, which was something like an HJ unit equivalent to military police. He saluted and showing his ID, he asked if he could go downstairs.

"This is signed by Lieutenant Ebert. You must have some special qualifications to carry a pass like this." The Gefolgschaftsfuehrer on duty mustered Karl intently and then added, "You could try to go downstairs, but it is already filled to capacity. With this pass you may also proceed all the way to the fifth floor. However, if you want to sleep, you might find a place on the staircase between the fourth and fifth floor. If you need to find a toilet, you may use the ones on the hospital floor."

Karl thanked him and carefully made his way upward. He could not find an empty place to sit or lay down until he passed the third floor. The hard concrete floor was not an ideal place to sleep, but Karl did not care. Any small place to stretch out was fine with him. He used his backpack to elevate his head from the floor and covered himself with the heavy jacket from Stanislaus. He was rudely awakened by an SS officer who kicked the backpack with his boots. "Get up and help the women with the children. The attack is over."

Karl got up, dusted off his uniform and stuffed the jacket back in the rucksack. On his way down, he passed a young woman who carried a little baby. In her other hand she was carrying a small suitcase. In front of her was a little girl, maybe 3 years old, who was holding on to the suitcase.

"Here, let me help you," said Karl, "I can either carry your suitcase or your little girl; your choice."

The mother looked at him and handed him the suitcase. "Thank you, you are very kind. There is nothing of value in the case," she added, "just some clothing and a bit of food."

Karl was surprised by her remark. It would have never entered his mind to use the congestion in the bunker to disappear with her belongings. But later on he heard that it happened all the time. Even some young women who offered to assist the helpless mothers made off with their belongings. Right now, he was still sleepy and just hoped to get back in the bunker after he escorted the threesome to wherever they were headed.

"Where are we going," he asked, "I mean once we are out of the shelter."

"We are not going outside. I hope to find a bunk bed on the sub-level. It is only 2:00 AM and there might be another raid before the night is over. Besides, we never leave the bunker before 8:00 AM."

This sounded like a good idea to Karl. He also liked the thought of finding a bunk bed for himself. On the way back down, Karl listened to the young mother who explained to him that there were three different kinds of 'bunker occupants', as she put it. First there were of all the bombed out, the homeless, who used the shelter on a 24-hour basis until they found some relative or friend they could stay with. Then there were the people from the immediate neighborhood, like herself, who used the bunker every night. They preferred the high-rise bunker because it offered better protection, especially from the air mines that caused the buildings to collapse, often blocking the basements exits. The third group consisted of people who were in the vicinity of the bunker when the sirens sounded and needed to seek immediate protection. These were the people who were leaving the bunker right now to resume their way to their original destination.

The sub level was also thinning out and Karl found by sheer luck, a place with a bunk bed for the woman and her children. There was however, no bunk bed for him. He remembered that he had never fully investigated the extensive ground level. He had nothing to lose by searching. His efforts were interrupted by another air raid alarm. It was just as he had anticipated; the Russians were flying back-to-back missions.

He made his way to a different staircase and found a place on a step just before the first turn around. By now he knew just how to position himself on the stairs for maximum comfort. He rested his upper body against the wall, stretched one leg out on the step he was sitting on, and tucked the other leg for leverage on the step below. Not exactly ideal, but he could rest this way for a while.

He woke up when the all-clear signal reverberated through the hallways. His watch showed that it was a quarter past 6:00 AM. As he entered the main hallway, he had no problem making his way almost to the front of the throng. For an undisclosed reason, the doors were still closed. The minutes ticked by and he stood patiently waiting to get out on the sidewalk and get some fresh air. In spite of the usually efficient air purification system in the bunker, the air in the hallway became harder and harder to breath. Karl could not tell whether this was because of all the people piling up around him, or for some other reason.

There were rumors flying around that the ventilation system had failed, and that they would suffocate if the doors did not open. Karl tried to make his way backward, but this was simply not possible. The people behind him were like a solid wall. To top it off they were increasingly pressing harder and harder towards the exit. The seemingly limited air supply caused him to think of all possible scenarios.

For one thing, it was clear to him that the moment the doors opened he could be swept off his feet. Since he was short anyhow, he also feared that he might fall and be trampled upon by the masses rushing to the door. He had heard that this had happened many times. It had happened to bigger and stronger men than he was. Right now, he was pressed with his face against the chest of a large man. He looked up and saw him smiling down to him. It looked like the man was in a blue navy uniform, or, it was a black panzer grenadier uniform. It was hard to tell in the limited light. In any event, the owner of the uniform also had trouble breathing, but his smile encouraged Karl.

"You might want to stand on your Rucksack. Then you are not so much squeezed in your face. But, then again, you will lose the pack when we start running for the doors."

Karl considered the advice for a moment. His backpack was almost empty.

Only his warm jacket, a change of underwear and some canned liverwurst and Knaeckebrot. He thought that Harold could replace the clothing. Better to get some breathing room than to have his face squeezed to the point of being unable to breathe.

He looked up again, and this time he focused beyond the head of the soldier. There were many thick pipes running along the ceiling. It was some type of steel tubing, maybe 10 to 20 cm thick. Ventilation or water or steam pipes, he could not discern what they were. However, if he would be able to reach them, he might be able to wrap his shoulder belt around them and support himself.

Would they hold his weight? They might. He knew that he only weighed a little over 120 pounds.

While he considered his options, he received another push from behind and someone was pressing down on his backpack. The crowd was now yelling in chorus. They demanded that the SS guard detail on the exit open the doors. It felt like a wave moving from the rear towards the doors, and Karl was momentarily lifted off his feet. He moved his shoulders out of the loops from the Rucksack, but due to the pressure from the people, it still stayed right up on his back.

"Help me up," he yelled at the soldier, who looked at him dumbfounded.

Karl could not lift his arms and tried to communicate with his eyes. Somehow he connected his intent and he felt a strong hand grabbing his belt and lifting him up. At the same time, the people behind him and beside him pressed in the empty space under his body, and within a second, he was laying flat on the heads and shoulders of the crowd around him. Now there were many hands on his body. Some were trying to push him away and some were trying to pull him down. To Karl's surprise, he was eye to eye with the soldier. He was wearing the uniform of a navy officer.

"Up," Karl shouted, "lift me up so I can reach the pipes." Then he almost passed out because someone had punched him in his kidney.

Seventeen

It was not a fist that had hit him. It was an action of someone who had understood his plea and tried to help him by pressing his head upward against Karl's body. Unfortunately, he was pressing against Karl's kidney.

"Up, where, how?" The sailor shouted in his ear.

"If you help me to kneel on your shoulders, I might be able to reach the pipes and pull myself up!" Karl answered at the top of his lungs to make himself understood. The crowd was starting to panic and the noise was deafening. Karl knew he had only a few seconds to get up to the pipes because more and more hands were pushing and pulling him down. He pulled his legs close to his chest and with a quick turn, his knees rested on the shoulders of the navy officer. The strong hands of the officer pushed up Karl's chest, enabling him to stretch for the different sized steel tubes.

Karl was truly in luck. He could see now that the pipes were not directly attached to the ceiling. They were suspended every few meters by metal straps. This provided some room between the ceiling and the top of the tubes. Room enough for him to lie on the top of them. He reached across the first one and stretched for the nearest metal hanger. At the same time, he felt the hands of the sailor on his feet providing the needed leverage. When he managed to get one of his legs over the first two pipes, he knew that he was succeeding.

The mob below yelled at him, but he did not know why. Besides, he couldn't tell the difference if they were cheering for him or cursing him. His eyes searched for the face of the officer who had helped him and saw that he was winking at him. So far, so good, thought Karl, and he removed his shoulder belt from his waist belt. He then pulled himself under the V-hanger and secured the shoulder belt around the stringer then reattached it to his waist.

The shoulder belt was about two centimeters wide, made of leather and standard HJ issue. It would hold him securely above the tubes. Karl relaxed for a moment and started again to breathe regularly. He was happy that the pipes felt neither cold nor hot to the touch. They were too thick to be conduits for electrical or phone cables. Probably part of the ventilation or water system he thought.

He craned his neck to look at the SS detail guarding the exit doors. They did not look like regular troopers. They were more likely officers. He could not make out their rank, but he could see the metal shield dangling from their neck in front of their chest. This meant that they were presently in the service of the SS police. It was the kind of shield which was also worn by the HJ Streifendienst.

One of the officers held the receiver of a wall phone pressed against his ear.

He waved his head back and forth and stomped his feet. Clearly he was arguing with whoever was on the other side of the line. Karl saw him placing the receiver back in the cradle and reaching for another phone. This must have been the public address system because Karl could immediately hear a crackling and screeching coming from the loud speakers, which were placed in intervals along the upper part of the walls.

"Stand back, we will open the doors. Proceed in an orderly slow fashion. Once you reach the doors, you will need to form a double line. No running or pushing."

Karl could hardly understand the words over the roar of the crowd. They had only heard the first words that the doors will be opened when the crowd started again to shout and to push. Karl could not comprehend why they were not more patient. After all, you could not push through concrete or steel. He assumed that the panic was due to the rumors of the broken ventilation system.

As the steel doors slowly opened, he saw the throng of the people moving forward. It looked to him that the horde of people was running over three of the SS guards. He looked down to see if he could make out the head of the helpful navy officer, but it was impossible to identify anybody. It was like a human wave without a single body.

All of the sudden he could hear pistol shots from the exit. He could not see who was shooting or why, but now he could hear unhuman-like cries coming from the exit. He could not understand the cries and neither could anyone else. He could however, see that the people in the front wanted to stop.

Everyone in the front of the mob wanted to come back into the bunker. It was a terrible scene. Unlike anything he had ever witnessed before. There was a herd of people below him who shoved, without mercy, the people in front of them out of the doors. The rabid firing of handguns at the exit increased and the screaming became more unreal and louder. And then he smelled it, the unmistakable horrible stench of burning human flesh.

The tar and asphalt on the street in front of the bunker was melting and burning. And so were the people being pushed into it. Karl could not see it, but he surely smelled it. There was no mistake; the Russians must have laid a carpet of incendiary bombs right in front of the bunker. He knew a bit about high temperatures from his training with the phosphor bombs. This here was a lot hotter. Asphalt melted and burned at about 480 degrees Celsius (900 Fahrenheit). Roads paved with tar melted at a lower temperature.

The reason he thought that the streets were burning was the sudden draft of air rushing though the hallway and out of the bunker. The flames needed oxygen, and the fresh air from the bunker filled the need. The doors had to be closed immediately or they would suffocate. He could feel the pipes vibrating. Whoever was in charge of the ventilation system must have had good training and thrown a switch to affect maximum air intake. Karl wanted to close his eyes, but his survival instincts kicked in and he forced himself to watch out for any immediate danger to himself. His position above the pipes allowed him to observe the chaos below him. The panic of the crowd before the doors opened was nothing compared to what was happening now.

The pungent stink of burning flesh crept through the bunker and the mob storming the exit started to reverse itself. People climbed and hustled over each other in every conceivable form. He saw children disappear below adults, old people being knocked to the floor and trampled upon, and above all, the deafening noise of people screaming in panic. He was scared to death that he might fall into this mess of hysteria and at the same time he was thankful for being relatively safe. At least for the time being.

The public announcement system was working, but it was not loud enough to be understood by anyone. If anything, it added to the confusion. Karl could see that the doors started to move again and to close. He could not see how. He did not know if they were hand-operated or pushed or pulled shut. But he could feel that the blast of air rushing towards the exit subsided and finally stopped.

The wave of people who first stormed the exit and then flooded back, stopped too. Only the terrible cries from the trampled, wounded and burned that needed help kept on and on. There was no one rendering any help to anyone. Everyone was for himself. It seemed to be an eternity until Karl noticed that the crowd was thinning out. There were now less people below him. People who could walk moved to the rear of the bunker. He could see SS men and HJ Flak details moving through the people lying on the floor. They must have come from the upper floors, possibly from the hospital, because some of them had a Red Cross sleeve on their arms. He wanted to help where he could.

Carefully he disengaged himself from the shoulder belt and jumped down. At the same time he hit the floor, he crouched down and crawled to the next body. It was an old man who lay motionless on his side. Karl was glad that the man was still breathing and he tried to lift him up. When this did not work, he pulled the man out of the center of the hallway. He moved him to the wall where he found some rags, which he used to elevate the man's head. His eyes opened up and he caught a thankful glance. Karl thought that the old fellow would be all right, and got up.

In the meantime, more and more HJ Flak details moved among the bodies on the floor and sorted out the most severely injured, which they carried away on stretchers. Karl assumed that they were moving them up to the hospital floor. He kept on working his way to the exit in the hope that he might find the navy officer among the wounded. However, he could not find anyone in a sailor's uniform. He feared that the mob might have pushed him out of the doors into the burning inferno. He tried to think when he saw him last, but there were so many horrible impressions in his mind that he felt that he was better off to concentrate on the task on hand.

As he reached the exit area, he was overwhelmed when he saw the horrible burn injuries of the people lying on the floor and by the unbelievable smell coming from the burned flesh. He leaned against the wall and tried desperately to keep his stomach under control, but to no avail. His vomit was bitter and the heaving of his stomach did not stop, even when there was nothing left to bring up. He felt that he would faint at any moment, but the pain of his convulsions kept him from it. It was a vicious cycle and Karl tried his best to stay in control of his body and of his mind.

Eventually he succeeded by saying to himself, you are safe, and your reactions are normal. Breathe deep or at least in an orderly fashion. Stand upright, walk up to the hospital. He did not really know why he wanted to reach the hospital, because he also remembered that he had to report for duty at the Friedrichshain bunker. In any event, he wanted to get away from the main floor and he climbed the stairs until he reached the fifth floor. He found the office of Lieutenant Ebert without any effort.

There was a note on the door stating that the Lieutenant was on emergency duty on the third floor. Karl went down again and entered the third floor.

This time there was no guard on duty. Instead he saw a hand written cardboard directory leaning on the wall. Lieutenant Ebert was not listed, but he saw Dr. Felder's name. 'Section B' it said behind the name. Karl had not realized how big the floor was, and it took him some time to find section B.

The moment he entered, he was stopped by an orderly, "You stink like shit, and you puked all over yourself. What do you want?"

Karl showed his pass and asked for Dr. Felder. "Do you need medical attention," was the next question.

Karl answered that he needed to locate Lieutenant Ebert, who was supposed to be on this floor. He also told the orderly that he knew Dr. Felder on a personal level.

"Wait here," said the orderly and disappeared. Karl looked down at his uniform and saw that he was indeed a sorry sight. But so was everybody else, he told himself. He started to wipe himself off when he was addressed by Lieutenant Ebert.

"Our favorite rat. Now you even look your part. Just like a sewer rat. How come you are here and not in Friedrichshain?"

Karl told him that his trip to Friedrichshain was interrupted late last evening by the air raid. "Understood," said the young lieutenant, "I will have someone call Friedrichshain to explain your absence. In the meantime, we need you here." Lieutenant Ebert looked at Karl's soiled uniform and added, "Clean yourself up; second door on the right. Then report back to me." He left Karl and disappeared behind a door on the left.

The clean-up room turned out to be a simple toilet with a washbasin. There was some disinfecting liquid, but not much else to clean his uniform. He did the best he could and went back out to report to the Lieutenant Ebert, who liked what he saw.

"Better, not much, but better." He handed Karl a clean white jacket, which was too large for his size, and a Red Cross sleeve. "Stay on my side. Do as I tell you and we will get along just fine."

Karl wanted to ask how long this work detail would last when the Lieutenant added, "Nobody will be able to leave this bunker for at least another day. The streets are burning and there is chaos all around us. Some animals escaped the zoo, but they are probably dead by now. Let's get to work."

Ebert's tone of voice did not invite any questions and Karl knew when to shut up. He learned more about first aid during the next six hours than he ever cared to know. He also saw his sailor again.

Eighteen

Karl followed Lieutenant Ebert who went to the staircase, which was crowded with people trying to reach the hospital floor. Ebert decided to convert the small entrance area into a makeshift screening room. The burn victims were directed to the A section, where they received immediate attention from trained medical personnel. Karl's job was restricted to cleaning minor wounds and to assist an orderly with rendering first aid.

After several hours, the stream of help-seekers declined and Karl was ordered by the Lieutenant to take a break. This was his first opportunity to continue his search for the sailor. As he went down the staircase and approached the ground floor, he finally saw the blue uniform he was looking for. The navy officer was sitting on the second step from the bottom. His face was a bloody mess and he was moaning and crouched over in agony. Apparently he was suffering from some internal injuries.

Karl stopped two HJ members who passed with an empty stretcher and asked them to help him to bring the officer to the third floor. Internal injuries were treated in the B section, and there was a long line of people waiting to be seen by a doctor. Karl went directly to the operating room and approached the HJ guard on duty.

"I need to see Dr. Felder. My patient is a navy officer and he is dying from internal injuries." Karl did not know if his patient was dying or if he even needed emergency care. All he knew was that this sailor had saved his life.

That was reason enough for him to invent something to get to

Dr. Felder. "Tell Dr. Felder that my name is Karl Veth," he added when he saw that the guard was not moving.

"You will have to wait until the doctor is done with the current surgery. I am not permitted to interrupt." The guard motioned Karl to place the stretcher next to the door.

Karl started to clean up the officer's face when he realized that he might get faster attention if he left the face as it was. Rank had its privileges, but blood added urgency. It was a short wait and Karl was rushed into the operating room together with his patient and two others who had been waiting their turn. Dr. Felder was dressed in a white coat, which was almost clean except for large bloody spots around his sleeves. He was one of three physicians in the room and did not recognize Karl right away. But then his face broke into a smile and he greeted Karl with a concerned look.

"Karl, so good to see you, how are you? Are you hurt?"

"No, but I have a navy officer here who needs your help. I cannot tell what his injuries are, but I am afraid that he is bleeding internally."

Dr. Felder gave Karl a slight tap on the arm, "Don't worry, we will take care of him. Check back with me later."

Karl looked at his watch, 40 minutes had passed since he had started his break and he went to the third floor to report back to Lieutenant Ebert. There were no more injured people coming up the stairs. The entrance area to the hospital looked normal again and Lieutenant Ebert had returned to his office. Karl went up and knocked on the door. Ebert asked him where he had been and Karl told him about the navy officer and Dr. Felder.

After the Lieutenant listened to him, he told Karl that he was supposed to report to Untersturmfuehrer Bernd's bunker as fast as possible. He wrote out a direct order, which he handed to Karl. "Be happy that I give this to you. It will allow you to proceed immediately to the Friedrichshain Bunker. Without this order, you might be detained to clean dead bodies off the street. Not a pleasant detail, I assure you."

Karl turned to leave the office when he was stopped by the Lieutenant. "You still have time. The doors will not open for a few more hours. You should get some rest until you see the Untersturmfuehrer. Use the cot by the door and help yourself to the blankets. Try to sleep. You will need it. Untersturmfuehrer Bernd can't wait to send you into the subway tunnels."

Karl thanked the Lieutenant and stretched out on the bunk bed. He was asleep before he pulled up the blankets. It only seemed like minutes to him, but a few hours had passed when he became aware that someone was standing next to him.

"Here is a clean uniform for you. You have to get out of the one you are wearing. Take this key for the shower room at the end of the hall. You have about ten minutes until the bunker doors open. Make the most of it."

Lieutenant Ebert shook Karl's bed. In one hand he was holding a clean HJ uniform and in the other a key. Karl stretched, took the uniform from the lieutenant, thanked him, and got out of the office. Ten minutes was not much time. He did the best he could and even managed to cut off the insignias from his old uniform. He did not have a sewing kit to attach them to his new uniform, so he just put them in his pocket.

When the front doors opened, he was one of the first to leave the bunker. It was late afternoon and he was not sure if he had lost one day or two. However, the terrible stench was still in the air and almost made him vomit again. He gagged when he saw all the dead bodies in front of the entrance. He could not believe that human bodies could shrink so much. Wherever he looked, he saw corpses the size of children stuck in the tar and asphalt of the street. SS commandos stopped the men coming out of the bunker and ordered them to carry the corpses to some trucks, which were parked a few streets away.

Karl was thankful for Lieutenant Ebert's orders, which exempted him from any clean-up detail and allowed him to make his way to the U-Bahn station. After all the happenings during the last 36 hours, he was surprised that the trains were running. Not exactly on time, but nevertheless they were running, and within a relatively short time he was at the Friedrichshain Bunker.

SS guards stopped him again until he was allowed to get up to the second floor. Untersturmfuehrer Bernd was in his office when Karl arrived.

"Welcome. You are two days late. From now on you will sleep here in this bunker until I tell you otherwise. What does it look like around the Zoo Bunker? No, better not tell me. I heard enough and I don't think that I have the stomach for details."

The SS officer offered Karl some bread and jelly and a canteen with hot coffee. "Here are the plans from the BVG engineering department. They will help you to refresh your memory. I also want you to learn about the distances and breakthroughs to the sewer and canalization systems. Study the plans as well as the notes indicating the location of expansion tunnels and bulkheads you might not know about. I really wish that I had an experienced subway engineer at my disposal, but almost all of them have been drafted into the corps of engineers and God only knows where they are."

The senior SS officer reached in the drawer of his desk and handed Karl an unusual looking instrument. It was recently machined and consisted of a three-cornered piece of steel pipe with three cross handles. The cross handles by themselves were also short stems of steel pipe with different indentations.

"Here, take this along. This is not an original, but a combination key. I have been told that it will open any door, tool chamber, and bulkhead you might encounter. Try it out. I need to know if it works. If it does, I will have some more made for us. That is all for now. You can eat in our officer's mess, which is located on the end of this floor. Next to it you will find a room with some bunk beds. You can sleep on any one of them, but I advise you to not leave anything on or below them. And I mean anything; you will never find it again. You will report to me every morning at 7:00 AM to bring me up to date on your progress. If you think that you saw or heard something I might need to know about, you can reach me here any time before 9:00 PM. Any questions?"

"Yes, how do I get access to the sleeping quarters and to the officer's mess? There are SS guards all over the place, and I have a hard enough time just to reach your office."

Untersturmfuehrer Bernd thought for a moment and then produced an SS identification card. He wrote something on it, dated it and signed it. "Here, this will give you more access than you need. Don't misuse it."

Karl took the card without looking at it and placed it in his shirt pocket. "Thank you, Untersturmfuehrer, Heil Hitler." Karl clicked his heels together, turned and left the office.

It was now after 6:00 PM and Karl wanted to see Harold at the Dienststelle in Halensee. When he arrived, he found it closed. There was no note or advice for him on the bulletin board. He had a decision to make. He could try to reach Harold at his home or check out the hideout near the Uhlandstrasse. He was sure that Harold had used the past day to gather some supplies. He decided on visiting the hideout and when he entered the subway station, he saw Harold coming out of the tunnel. Harold was fuming, "You could have called my office! I feared the worst!"

Karl brought him quickly up to date and asked if there was any news about survivors from the old school and the KLV headquarters.

"We were asked to send some guys over for a search and rescue detail. As far as I know, there are still about ten or twelve children missing and one teacher. But the search will continue tomorrow morning. There is hope to find some survivors in a storage cellar which is still under tons of debris." Harold sniffed on Karl's uniform. "I thought it was the uniform, but it smells clean. I hate to ask you, what is this awful stink you seem to be extruding?"

"Burned flesh," answered Karl, "not much I can do about it. The fresh uniform does not seem to cut it. I could use some new or clean underwear. You are not the first to sniff me like a puppy. I think that I also offended the nose of my commanding officer, because I received this uniform from him. I still need to attach my insignias. Now, before you continue to criticize me, how are you coming with supplies for our place?"

"We have food and water for maybe two weeks," answered Harold, "I would like to stay in my office until the Russians enter the city. I think that I can do us more good by keeping my position here than going with you, at least at this time. Oh, I almost forgot to tell you about Hitler's birthday."

"What about it? I know that it is on the 20th of this month."

"Everybody knows that, but what you don't know is that I have been selected with twenty or so other HJ and Jungvolk members to be in a birthday delegation to the Reichskanzlei. I think that we will receive a medal or something, directly from the Fuehrer."

"A medal? From the Fuehrer himself? Will he shake your hand? What did you do? Is there something you are not telling me about?" Karl could hardly believe what he was hearing. He had seen the Fuehrer many times up close when he was with the HJ on parade and barricade duty. Sometimes the Fuehrer would shake hands with the boys who formed a living barrier, six rows deep, to keep the jubilant crowd at a safe distance. Karl, because of his small size, always served in the front row, but he was never able to lock eyes with the Fuehrer.

Harold could hear the excitement in Karl's voice and was happy that his friend showed so much enthusiasm. "I did nothing special,

Karl, but I think that my father's position had something to do with it."

"Could be, Harold, could be, but I still think that you are holding out on me." Karl could feel no envy. He suspected that his friend had somehow deserved this honor. "Since you mentioned your father, I would like to talk with him again if he has the time and you are able to arrange it."

"Sure thing," answered Harold, "you want to come home with me right now?"

"No, I better get back to Friedrichshain before another air raid starts. Untersturmfuehrer Bernd expects me to be in his office in the morning." Karl shook Harold's hand and boarded a train to the Zoo station where he changed trains to Friedrichshain. As soon as he arrived in the bunker, he made his way to the SS officer's mess where he was served some hot soup and dark rye bread. No butter or jelly, but the bread was fresh and Karl was hungry enough not to care that is was dry. He had been pretty hungry most of the last few days and was glad that he was allowed to eat with the SS officers.

As he was dunking the last of the bread in his soup, he took a look at the SS I.D. card, which he had needed to show to a few guards before he was allowed to enter the second floor and the mess room. It was a white card with the black SS insignia in the center. It showed his name and HJ rank. Under the HJ rank was a remark: "Special aide to Untersturmfuehrer Bernd. Unlimited access to the second floor."

Together with his other passes, he now had high-quality credentials and started to feel good about it. He got up to enter the sleeping quarters when he was approached by the SS guard who had him checked when he entered the bunker. The Rottenfuhrer, who was at least 1.8 meters tall (5 ft 9 in) and about 30 years old, smiled down at him and handed him a paper package with his name on it.

"For you, my friend. This is from Untersturmfuehrer Bernd, with the suggestion that you use it at your earliest convenience."

Karl opened it and found a double issue of new underwear. "If you had been where I was last night...you would need this too," he told the guard who smirked when he saw what was in the package.

"Hey, I didn't say anything, my friend. I am only the delivery guy. Besides, I am glad that I am not in your shoes."

Karl thought for a moment that this was a strange remark. Maybe the Rottenfuhrer knew more about his upcoming assignments than he did himself, but he did not put much value on it. If the Rottenfuhrer did not like to be in the shoes of the HJ...so be it.

"Thanks," he said, "My name is Karl, and I am not sure if I am your friend."

"Take it easy," answered the guard. "My name is Fritz Weinert and Untersturmfuehrer Bernd told me that you had a bad experience last night, and that you are on a special assignment for him. You are also entitled to extra food. When you leave in the morning, check with me at the exit. I am on duty at 7:30 AM."

"Thanks, Herr Weinert. I did not mean anything, it is just...I am new around here."

"Yes, I know. I would be skittish too if I were your size and surrounded by giants. Get a bunk next door, don't worry, and get some sleep; tomorrow is another day." Fritz Weinert waved a friendly good night and disappeared down the hall.

Damn, thought Karl, I should have kept my mouth shut. They really treat me decent and even supply me with clothing. But there was always the warning from Major Zahn in the back of his mind to stay away from the SS, and now he slept in their officer's quarters. He decided again to say very little and to stay as low as possible.

The night went fast. If there was an air raid he did not hear it. He woke up refreshed, showered and put on his fresh underwear. It was a bit too large, but it was new and did not smell. Breakfast was coffee and jelly on dark rye bread. He reported to Bernd at exactly 7:00 AM. The officer motioned him to sit down and went to a stack of messages and notes. When he got to his phone messages he looked up at Karl

"Do you know a submarine commander Korvettenkapitan Siegler?"

"No, Untersturmfuehrer." Karl did not know anyone who served in the submarine fleet.

"I guess you do, anyhow. I have here a note from a Dr. Felder, which says that by your correct diagnosis and determined action in the Zoo Bunker, you saved the life of the highly decorated Submarine Commander Siegler."

Karl sat in stunned silence. His sailor, who had saved him from being trampled to death by the mob in the bunker, turned out to be a submarine commander.

"I am unable to diagnose anyone. I saw that the navy officer needed help and I knew Dr. Felder. That's all I did." Karl was happy about saving the sailor's life, but he was unwilling to accept any special credit for it. "And, I told you about it yesterday," he added.

"Yes, I remember that you told me about helping some wounded in the hospital. But you never told me about a submarine commander and about your correct diagnosis. Now it seems that you are a hero, and they want you back in the hospital."

Karl knew that he was not a hero and most of all, he knew that he was not cut out for hospital work. "Untersturmfuehrer Bernd, I did not diagnose the sailor. I only told Dr. Felder that I was afraid that the navy officer was bleeding internally. I don't want to be transferred to the hospital. I know nothing about injuries. But I do know the subway system better than anyone around here. I want to serve where I can truly contribute to the final victory."

The SS officer did not know what to think about Karl's answer, but he did know that he wanted Karl on his team. "Don't worry Karl, you will stay with me. If you are truly a life saver, even only by accident, then I need you more than the hospital staff."

He turned away from the desk and went to a subway system chart, which was taped to the wall. "Now pay attention to what I tell you. I will answer this call from Dr. Felder and tell him that you will see him this afternoon, but no transfer. You will start today with learning about the bulkheads. Then, I want you to record exactly how long it takes you to move from here to the first bulkhead close to the river."

"I want you to remember every emergency exit, every ventilation shaft and tool shed in between. Begin here," Ebert pointed to a spot on the chart, "at the Friedrichstrasse subway station, and proceed towards the Spree River and the nearest canalization. Don't forget to try the key I gave you. We need functioning keys and I depend on you. You can stop work by the early afternoon in order to visit Dr. Felder and your submarine commander in the hospital."

He turned away from the wall and faced Karl again. "One more thing, you need a good flashlight. Your little dynamo light will not allow you to set it down." He handed Karl a bulky battery operated contraption. It was more of a durable work light than a flashlight. It was also too heavy and too large to be carried in a pocket.

"And don't be too modest. If Dr. Felder calls you a hero, or recommends you for promotion; accept it."

Nineteen

Karl left the high-rise bunker and enjoyed for a few minutes the early sunshine. In spite of the smoke rising from some burning buildings and the distant rumble of artillery, he perceived that there was a hint of spring in the air. After he crossed the street he entered the U-Bahn station. The lower platform was again densely occupied by sleeping civilians who were still resting from the air attacks of last night. As he waited for the next train, he noticed that there was fresh propaganda leaflets pasted on the walls. They did not say anything new, just the old slogans in different colors: The end victory is near. The wonder weapons will destroy our enemies.

Karl was reading this with some contempt. If Hitler really had any wonder weapons at all, why did he not employ them? Up until yesterday he was a loyal patriot and willing to give his life to the cause of the Fatherland and for the Fuehrer, but now his confidence was deeply shaken. He did not know if it was the mob in the bunker who had trampled over the weak and the children, or if the shrunken corpses in the melting asphalt affected his thinking and reasoning, but his experiences and the promises on the leaflets simply did not add up. The more he thought about it, the more he wished that he could talk to his father about it, but he did not know where his father was and this thought alone added to his mental distress.

First things first he told himself, and one thing at a time. No use thinking about something you cannot do anything about; at least not at the present time. Right now you have to do what you are ordered to do...let's see if the keys from the Untersturmfuehrer opened anything. The subway tool sheds and bulkheads close to the Spree River had always intrigued him. They would be his first targets.

The train to the Friedrichstrasse Station was late. Usually the trains operated in 5 to 12 minute intervals. Today, however, they were more like 15 minutes apart. Friedrichstrasse Station was even more crowded with civilians than the Friedrichshain Station. It must have had something to do with the fact that the bunker across from the Friedrichshain Station served as an air raid shelter as well as temporary housing for the bombed out families.

Before Karl entered the westbound tunnel he checked the time. It was 8:15 AM, and he started a time-line in his notebook. The tunnel in the vicinity of the platform smelled of urine and feces. He walked fast to leave this area behind him and he reached the first pen in a matter of a few minutes. The door was made of metal and large enough to accommodate two people walking next to each other. It was secured with a large padlock. Karl used one of the smaller pipe keys and the lock opened on his first try.

The space behind the door was mostly empty. The right wall had built-in shelves, which were crammed with large and small boxes filled with hand tools of all kinds. On the opposite wall was a rack with tar torches, shovels, picks and empty buckets. The room was dry and dusty. Karl stepped it off and recorded the measurement. It was almost 3 meters wide and 8 meters long. The air smelled a bit stale, but not too much. The floor was plain dirt and there were footprints all over the place. A sure indication that this shed was in constant use.

Karl found a light switch, which operated a single light bulb. Then he selected a small file from one of the toolboxes and marked his key with a single notch. Instead of placing the file back in the box, he slipped it in his pocket. He checked once more for anything unusual in the room and when he saw nothing of interest, he added maintenance room to his notations, turned off the light, stepped out of the room and closed the door. The padlock snapped shut and Karl continued his way along the rails.

Before he reached his next destination, he heard a train coming from behind.

The reflexes from his childhood kicked in and he laid down flat away from the rails. He could have remained standing, as the tunnel in this section was wide enough to allow a person to walk or stand along the wall. Furthermore, he was now authorized to be in the tunnel, but habits are habits and they had served him well in the past.

After he got up and going again, he passed a few ventilation shafts and all except one could be used as an emergency exit. The padlocks securing the grates on the top were all the same as the one on the tool shed, and he opened all of them without any difficulty. The one ventilation shaft without an apparent exit puzzled him and he wondered if it was a ventilation shaft at all. He made a note in his book as to the distance from the other shafts and added a double question mark. He would come back to re-examine the two-foot wide and upward-leading opening. But right now, he wanted to inspect a particular door because it was on the updated system map, which Harold had handed him a few days ago, but it was not on the original BVG map he had received from Officer Bernd.

It was either an oversight by the engineering department from the BVG, or it was something that was newly created. According to Harold's map, it was not really a door. While the symbol on the map referred to it as a door, it also had a waving line below it and a circle above it. Karl could not see a likewise note or symbol on either map, and this was the real reason that he wanted to inspect it. Besides, it should be pretty close to his present location. The way he figured it, the door should be within the next 150 feet or so.

He counted the steps as he continued to walk. When he reached the approximate area, he doubled his attention but he could not find any indication of a door. He decided to walk another 100 feet and then to double back. He made a small mark with his file on the wall where he turned around and walked all the way back to the last ventilation shaft. Nothing. Maybe the BVG map was correct and there was no door. He studied both maps again and wondered if he missed something. Not on the map, because they corresponded pretty close to each other and he was sure of his present location.

Another train approached and this time he just pressed himself against the tunnel wall. He knew that the average speed of the train was only about 30 kmph, but the shock wave in front of the train always took his breath away and gave him the impression that the trains traveled at a much higher speed.

There was also the difference between top speed and average speed. The further apart the stations, the higher the speed and in some cases, in the center between stations, the speed could approach 70 kmph. The train passed and Karl let the beam of his work light play over the upper section of the wall.

He remembered that before he had only directed the light at the lower two feet of the wall, assuming that a door would have to open at floor level. He turned around again to check this portion of the tunnel for the third time, but this time he made sure to look at the total height of the wall. And there it was, right at about 150 feet from the last airshaft he saw a square indentation in the wall. It was maybe 3 feet above the ground and 3 feet across. The indentation was old, like the rest of the wall. But in the center, there was a round steel bulkhead and it looked like a fairly recent addition. The bulkhead featured two large hinges on the left-hand side and could only be opened by lifting a lever on the right side. The lever was solid steel and secured with two different locks.

Karl tried all his keys and was only able to open the upper lock. The lower lock was a combination lock and he had no idea what the combination might be. He made another note in his book and this time he added a question mark with the word "combination" behind it. He also added the word "content" with another question mark behind it. So far, the amount of questions in the book almost outnumbered his answers.

He speculated as to the purpose of this partition. There had to be a good reason to secure it with two different locks. He pounded first with his fist against the steel and then with the handle of his file, and the reflected sound told him that there was empty space behind the bulkhead. Since the door symbol was not on the BVG map, he decided that he would not tell the Untersturmfuehrer about his find until he learned the purpose of it. He would also confer with Harold about it. After all, the map with the symbol came from Harold and maybe he had an idea as how to obtain the combination.

He continued his survey for the next few hours. There were no other surprises or mysteries and he followed the tunnel all the way under the Spree River to the Oranienburger Tor station. By the time he left the tunnel, it was 3:00 PM and his notebook featured pages of detailed notes. Karl had found that his pipe keys could open all of the doors and locks.

He took the next train to the Zoo Bunker and noticed that the streets in front of the bunker had been somewhat cleaned or washed down. Only the terrible smell was still in the air. Or, it was in his imagination. He was not sure about it. Once inside the bunker, he took the stairs up to the hospital floor. Dr. Felder was busy like always, but Karl was able to see him anyway.

When Karl entered Dr. Felder's office, he was not sure if he should greet the doctor with 'Heil Hitler'. He knew that it was the required greeting, but every time he had shouted 'Heil Hitler' at the doctor, his mandatory greeting had been ignored or was waved down.

"Karl, my boy, we have been waiting for you. Untersturmfuehrer Bernd had called and told me that that you would be here before evening." Dr. Felder smiled and shook Karl's hand. "The Korvettenkapitan wants to see you and talk with you before we dismiss him."

"How is he doing?"

"He lost some blood, but he will be alright and we will release him the day after tomorrow. He was extremely lucky that you found him and brought his condition to my attention. Internal injuries like this very often get missed in the rush to attend to the obvious." Dr. Felder rubbed his eyes and pulled up a chair before he continued, "Karl, we would like to detain you here for hospital duty, but Untersturmfuehrer Bernd told me that he has first dibs on you and big plans for your future. He said that a transfer is out of the question and he was very firm about it. Frankly, that really worries me. We know each other now for a while, and know that we can trust each other," he paused and looked Karl straight in the eyes, "Karl we will be in street to street and house to house combat within a few days, two weeks at the most, and after that there will be no future for you in the SS. The Russians will execute them or condemn them to a lifetime of hard labor to Siberia. Whatever is being offered by the SS commander, please, be very careful what you accept and leave yourself a way out, if possible."

Karl understood completely. Not only what Dr. Felder told him, but also what he did not tell him. "Thank you, Doctor. When the time comes, I will remember what you told me." Karl understood that if by some miracle he lived through the combat action in the coming days, he would have a better chance of surrender in the hospital with a medical team than with an SS commando in the subway system. But the decision had already been made, so there was not much use thinking about it. And, if he was honest with himself, in a weird way he even enjoyed the idea of pitting his subway system knowledge against the Russian combat troops. There was no doubt in his mind as to his abilities. He just wished that there was a chance of a final victory. But his gut told him differently. He knew that the days of the third Reich were numbered.

Dr. Felder got up from his chair, "Let's see if the Korvettenkapitan is awake." Karl followed the doctor out the door and was surprised that they went up to the fourth floor. "These are rooms reserved for our most valuable patients," explained Dr. Felder as he opened a door, "here is our submarine commander. This room was recently occupied by Colonel Hans Ulrich Rudel, the highest decorated officer of the German Luftwaffe; our most famous patient. They amputated his left leg below the knee. This was two months ago. Now he is flying again."

Karl had heard that Colonel Rudel had been shot down over Germany, but he did not know about the amputation in the bunker hospital. Karl entered the room and looked around. It was a rather small room without windows, like all the others he had seen in the bunker, except that it was painted stark white and smelled of disinfectants. Korvettenkapitan Siegler opened his eyes when he heard the voice of Dr. Felder. He strained to sit up and succeeded on his second try. Karl went to his bedside to help him, but Dr. Felder held him back.

"Hello Kommander, your young friend came by to see how you are. So sit up straight to show him that you are alright." Dr. Felder's voice was cheerful. "How do you feel," he asked the submarine commander.

"I feel great, when can I get out of here?"

"Eat, sleep, eat, sleep and again eat and sleep for the next days and we will let you go in two days." Dr. Felder turned to Karl, "Keep your visit short. Not more than five minutes, and see me once more before you leave the bunker." He turned and left the room.

"I just came by to thank you for lifting me up to the pipes and thereby saving my life," began Karl.

Commander Siegler smiled and stretched out his hand towards Karl, "Well, it seems then that we are even. Dr. Felder told me that I owe my life to your quick and accurate diagnosis."

Karl winced when he answered, "I can't take credit for any diagnosis. I only saw that you needed help and I knew that Dr. Felder would take good care of you. Besides, I could not have helped you if you hadn't helped me first." Karl wanted to steer the conversation away from the sentimental topic. "I never met a submarine commander before. Are you on furlough in Berlin?"

"I returned two days ago from a 28-day mission and was on my way to report to the SS High Command when the air raid trapped me in the bunker," Answered Kommander Siegler. "I need to get out of Berlin again. I have a crew waiting for my return," he continued, "Any reports about the Russian effort to cut off the city?" The Kommander's voice was strong and clear. There was no indication of any impairment.

"Nothing definite. Mostly rumors, but judging by the increased shelling from the Russian artillery, we know that that they are closing in on us."

Karl's answer was tentative because he really had no idea how far the Russian artillery could shoot. But he did know that the outlying areas of Berlin were still in German hands. "Is there anything that I could do for you?" he asked of the Korvettenkapitan.

"No, not really, except asking your doctor friend if there is any way that I could leave the hospital earlier than two days from now."

"I'll be happy to ask him," Karl answered, "but I think that I better leave now so you can get some of the ordered sleep." Karl got up from the chair and shook the officer's hand, "Thanks again, Kommander, and all the best to you."

"Halt, for a moment, Karl, I want to give you something. If we survive and win the war, I might ask you for it back. In the meantime, don't mention it to anyone and keep it secure." The U-Boat Kommander leaned over towards his uniform jacket, which was hanging on a hook next to the bed. He took a small, brown narrow carton from the inside jacket pocket and handed it to Karl. It was about the size of a cigarette pack. "This is for you and for you only. It might save your life. You will find instructions inside the box."

Karl did not know what to say and stammered only a "Thank you". "Take good care Karl, I am glad that we met," said Kommander Siegler with his great smile, "You got me in here, now please get me out again."

Karl returned the smile "Will do, Herr Korvettenkapitan." He turned to leave but had a second thought. "Would it save you time if I could get an officer from the high command to debrief you here?"

"Of course it would, but I doubt that you can find a high ranking SS officer with that kind of authority," answered the U-Boat captain.

"We shall see about that," mumbled Karl to himself, and left the room.

Twenty

Karl went back to the office of Dr. Felder and told him about Kommander Siegler's request. "He is recovering rather rapidly and we might be able to let him go by tomorrow, but he needs sleep and rest." was Dr. Felder's answer, "But to get SS officers with sufficient authority to come and debrief him here in the hospital is highly unlikely."

"Do you know, by any chance, about the Korvettenkapitan's last assignment?" asked Karl.

"No, we looked at his papers and found nothing but sealed envelopes marked confidential. His destination was the high command of the SS," answered the doctor.

Karl's face lit up like a beacon. "If you could let me use your phone, I might be able to call someone I know."

Dr. Felder was wondering who Karl might call, and allowed him access to his phone. The next thing he heard, to his astonishment, was Karl's determined request.

"Yes, I understand that the defense Kommander is not accepting any calls but if you value your soft position as a phone operator, you better tell Obersturmbannfuehrer von Glinski that my name is Karl Veth and that I need to talk to him personally, and now." Less than a minute later Karl continued his dialog, "Heil Hitler, Obersturmbannfuehrer von Glinski. I am calling from the hospital in the Zoo Bunker on behalf of Korvettenkapitan Siegler, who needs to be debriefed by your officers. He is injured and unable to travel to your office and he needs to get out of Berlin by tomorrow." Karl listened to the voice on the other end of the phone. "Yes, the name is Korvettenkapitan Siegler, U-Boat commander. No, I know nothing about his past or future assignments." Karl listened again. "You're welcome Obersturmbannfuehrer, Heil Hitler. Yes, I understand, goodbye to you, too."

Karl gave the phone back to Dr. Felder, who stared at him with a curious expression on his face. "You say 'goodbye to you, too' to the defense commander of Wilmersdorf?"

Karl had the most innocent twinkle in his eye, "Hmm, yes, I know him. He is the father of one of my former charges and I met him a while ago. And, yes, he will be here within an hour to debrief the U-Boat Kommander himself."

Dr. Felder said something of running an orderly hospital and wounded officers who needed to recover without visits from the SS, but Karl was not paying any attention.

"I have to get back to Untersturmfuehrer Bernd. Thank you, Dr. Felder, for your offer to work for you, and thank you for your advice. I will try my best." Karl did not define what he meant by "trying his best" and Dr. Felder did not ask.

As Karl left the Zoo Bunker, he fingered in his pocket the small carton from Kommander Siegler and wondered what it might be. He transferred it from his pants pocket to the outside pocket of his uniform jacket and by the time he entered the train to Friedrichshain, he forgot about it. The Friedrichshain Bunker was swarming with civilian refugees from the outlying areas from Berlin and was nearly filled to capacity. Untersturmfuehrer Bernd was not in his office, but there was a message board next to the door with a note for Karl, which instructed him to come back at 8:00 PM.

Karl looked at his watch. He had a little over an hour to kill and decided to go to the officer's mess to find something to eat.

The mess was nearly empty and the fare of the day was pea soup with gray rye bread on the side. While he was eating, he wrote a description of the places he had visited in the tunnel. He also added particulars regarding the keys he had used and the walking time between the different ventilation systems, airshafts and tool sheds. Next he made a short list of things to do during the next few days. Depending upon the possibility of new instructions from officer Bernd, he wanted to see Frau Becker and Harold to ask him about the combination lock. He also wanted to find out if there were any messages about Peter and the missing train with the children.

Before the hour ended, he saw Officer Bernd entering the mess room. He looked around and when he saw Karl, he took a seat next to him. "I hoped to find you here. This will save us some time. Tell me about your day."

Karl gave the officer a detailed verbal account of his tunnel inspection but did not mention his encounter with the bulkhead and the combination lock. He closed his report by giving the Untersturmfuehrer the notes he had just prepared. They were in excess of two pages and Karl hoped that they were sufficiently detailed.

Officer Bernd listened to Karl and seemed to be especially happy about the notations and markings on the keys. "Well done, Karl, better than I expected. Now let me give you the complete scope of your assignment."

Karl took out his notebook and was ready to write. "No, put that away, you don't need notes, Karl. You only need to understand the purpose of your assignment." The Untersturmfuehrer moved Karl's empty soup dish to the side and unfolded a map of Berlin. "When the Russian troops enter the city, we will need to move special assault units behind their lines. Therefore, we need to know which of the various subway exits are operational. Some of them might be buried under collapsed buildings. In order to infiltrate the enemy behind their fighting lines, we also need to know exactly where we would surface. I need to know if an airshaft or exit leads to a courtyard, a side street, or wherever they break the surface."

Karl interrupted the officer, "I know where most of them end, however, whether or not they are operational to accommodate a group of troops will change from day to day. Whatever I know today might be totally useless tomorrow."

The officer pushed the map closer to Karl and pointed with a pencil to the location of the Friedrichshain bunker. "Don't underestimate yourself. I agree that it will be impossible to keep up to date, but we have to prepare as well as we can. Right now, and for the next week, I want you to survey as far away as the Samariter Strasse station."

The officer started his pencil mark at a subway station on the other side of the Spree River and proceeded to draw a line around the inner city. "To make it short, your real assignment is to keep current within this circle and to inform me of any pertinent changes." He looked into Karl's eyes as if to make sure that Karl understood. "I requested from your headquarters more HJ members to assist you. So far we are out of luck. Almost all of the available HJ units have been assigned to the Vistula army group, and their Kommander General Heinrici is not cooperating to share any of them with us or any other SS unit. Most of the local HJ units are already assigned to the flak towers and the remaining ones are being trained to use the Panzerfaust in combat against the Russian T34 tanks. In my opinion, these are suicide commandos."

Untersturmfuehrer Bernd made a movement across his own throat and Karl was tempted for a moment to tell the SS officer what he thought of the subway infiltration assignments, but then he thought better of it and kept his mouth shut. He only nodded his head as if in agreement and made himself a mental note to ask Harold about the Panzerfaust training. He was also wondering how much longer it would take for Harold to join him. He felt that he had to say something to officer Bernd.

"Tomorrow evening, I will contact my friend Harold Kellner, and ask him to join me in my assignment. He knows the subway system as well as I do and since he is a Dienststellenleiter for the HJ, he might not be subject to the Wehrmacht."

Untersturmfuchrer Bernd liked what he heard, "I would be very happy to have him on our team."

Hmm, thought Karl, so now we are a team, what's next? Hopefully not an official induction into the SS.

Untersturmfuehrer Bernd got up, folded the map, and handed it to Karl. "I forgot to ask. Did you meet with Dr. Felder and the submarine Kommander; what was his name?"

"Korvettenkapitan Siegler," answered Karl, "we talked only for a few minutes. The Kommander seems to be all right. But he needed sleep and rest," he added.

"Did he tell you about his past or future assignment?"

"No, he did not mention it to me." Karl did not volunteer to tell the officer that he had arranged for a debriefing by Obersturmbannfuehrer von Glinski.

"Did he tell you his first name? The name Siegler sounds familiar; however I am not able to connect him to the submarine units." The Untersturmfuehrer seemed to search his memory, and Karl was unable to help him. "Hey, now I know where I heard this name. It is SS Sturmbannfuehrer Joachim Ziegler, the commander of the XI SS Panzer Grenadier Division, presently located close to the

Tempelhof Airport. No wonder I could not place him in the Navy. It is just a likewise sounding name." Bernd seemed satisfied that his memory was serving him well and Karl was glad that the questioning was over. They left the officer's mess together.

They could hear again the heavy flak on top of the tower opening up. It was the allied forces evening air attack, except it lasted several hours longer than normally.

Karl did not sleep very well, and he was also hungry. He thought that he should have helped himself to a second bowl of pea soup. The next morning started with another air attack. This time it consisted of nothing but Russian planes dumping their bombs as soon as the flak opened up to engage them. It was a massive assault on the government district, and Karl was glad that his assignment kept him underground.

He climbed every shaft he encountered and unlocked all the ventilation grates and exit doors. Some of the exits were indeed covered under a load of wreckage and most of the debris was too heavy to move from below. He made himself notes of only the operational exits. At noon, he stopped his work at the Warschauer Station and took a train back to the Zoo Bunker, then changed to a streetcar to the Fehrbelliner Platz. The air raid, which had stopped at about 10:00 AM, left several apartment houses along the Brandenburgische Strasse burning.

Karl passed civilian firefighters, mostly women and HJ units, who were battling the flames as he made his way to the bombed-out building of the former KLV headquarters. He was searching for a message or a note indicating that Frau Becker was alive. What he found instead was a message printed in chalk on a piece of wall in the courtyard.

It was short and simply said, "For information regarding KLV contact HJ headquarters Halensee"

This was Harold's office, which Karl wanted to visit anyhow. Karl figured that he had the time to go there right away. When he got close to the headquarters, he could see that the door to Harold's office was locked and the entrance area in front of the office was crowded with a group of shouting and crying women.

There must have been at least 20 of them and when he tried to enter the office, he was stopped and besieged with questions. He made an effort to answer individually, but then realized that he really had no answers. The women were evidently either the mothers or at least the relatives of missing children. The women asked questions ranging from abandoned KLV camps he had never heard of obtaining information in regard to survivors of the collapsed KLV headquarters building.

Karl could see that this was not an angry mob demanding information, but a group of helpless women hoping to hear something positive about their loved ones. He knew that it was nearly impossible to obtain any true answers to their questions, but on the other hand, he felt that he should try to at least instill some order to deal with their situation. He told the group to give him a few minutes to talk to the Dienstellenleiter to try to ascertain what kind of information was presently available.

Harold answered his friend's request to open the door. His face was ashen and his expression almost lifeless. "These bastards from the civilian school authorities, they left messages all over the Wilmersdorf and Charlottenburg district that my office has information regarding missing children, but they gave me no information whatsoever. They just closed up and disappeared, but not before they shifted their problems to me."

"Well," said Karl, "then we need to handle this by ourselves. Hopefully without causing any more fright or pain. Let's start right now to make a list and take from the women all their information as well as their specific questions." He did not wait for an answer from Harold. He opened the door for the waiting women and ushered them into the small meeting room next to Harold's office.

He told them that the Dienststellenleiter had no pertinent information at the present time, but that he realized their questions needed to be answered. He added, "We have a challenge on our hands. Give me a bit of time to decide upon a viable method." Harold interrupted Karl by asking how this information taking would help anyone.

"You will see. If the school authorities decided to simply close up and shift their burden to us, then we can do the very same. Is it alright that the women use your meeting room?"

"Yes,' answered Harold, "as far as I am concerned they can have the whole darn office. I am about to abandon it. Believe me, I am about to do it. There is no order anymore, not even in the high command of Artur Axmann. They are asking me for HJ units which I don't have.

"Yesterday, I had to assign every available HJ member to

establish a bridgehead by Pichelsdorf. As of this morning, they are asking for reserve units to defend some outlying units of Brigadefuehrer Krukenberg. Every day I am getting different orders, which are always in contradiction to the previous ones. Nobody knows anymore where anybody is, or who is in charge of what. And now look at the mess they dumped on me." He looked helplessly from Karl to the worried women. "Do whatever you can to get me out of here and preferably transferred to your assignment. I would rather be with you and the SS in a subway tunnel than face another day in here."

Karl was alarmed by his friend's tone of voice and his response. He had never seen him defeated or in despair, and he had always admired his resourcefulness. The Harold he knew had been transformed into a stranger.

"What happened," he asked, "you changed, and I don't believe that this is due to conflicting orders."

"I lost contact with my parents last evening. A direct hit by an air mine leveled the apartment house. Now it's just a huge mountain of rubble. There seemed to be no survivors. No place to go home to."

Harold's answer devastated Karl. It was clear that Harold needed his support and for a moment, he felt as if the walls were closing in on him. He needed some time to think, but he knew that even with time, nothing would be the same again. Karl went to his friend and placed his hands upon Harold's shoulder.

"I am closing this office right now and I am taking full responsibility for this action. You will come with me and we will make it together. I will talk to the women and then we leave. Give me your keys."

He went into the meeting room and addressed the women again, "I was just informed that the school authorities of Wilmersdorf and Charlottenburg closed their offices. So, it is up to you to find a solution. I suggest that some of you volunteer to use this office to collect, establish and maintain a database. Frau Becker from the Hohenzollern District had started one, which included the KLV camps in Poland and the Stettin area. I don't know how complete it was, but it might help you. I will give you her last known address. I will also give you written authorization to use this office, and as of right now, you need to decide if you wish to proceed with my suggestions."

Karl placed the keys on the table and wrote a short

authorization, which he dated and signed with Karl Veth, Oberscharfuehrer.

The women listened to him and decided right then and there to take matters in their own hands. As Karl left the meeting room, they asked for his present address. He took another piece of paper and printed 'Zoo Flak Tower, Lieutenant Ebert's Office'.

On purpose, he did not write Flak Tower Friedrichshain. He did not want to make it too easy for the HJ to find him. Actually, he did not worry about any possible fallout from his decision to close the Dienststelle. After all, Harold had just told him that nobody knew anymore who was in charge. If anyone should come looking for him, they had better hurry to catch up with him. He knew that SS Untersturmfuchrer Bernd would back up his actions. And, if he didn't, so be it.

The war would be over in another few weeks and he was determined to survive, whatever it might take. He grabbed Harold by the arm and dragged him through the door leading to the outside. He had the feeling that his friend was either fainting or falling into some kind of deep depression.

Harold had not said another word since Karl took over, and now his feet were somehow moving automatically. His eyes were almost closed and he constantly mumbled to himself. Not a good sign, thought Karl. I liked it better when he was cursing the KLV authorities and the Axmann administration.

He started to ask questions to get his friend out of his trance and when this did not work, he told Harold bits and pieces about his assignment. He was almost to the point of stopping and finding some cold water to throw over his friend's head when he sensed that Harold tried to respond to his last question.

"Ask me again," said Harold, "what combination lock are you referring to?"

"The double lock on the raised bulkhead near the Friedrichshain Station. One of them is a combination lock and we need to know the combination. Do you have any ideas?" Karl was relieved to see that his friend was searching for an answer.

"1944," said Harold.

Karl thought that Harold was referring to last year. "No," he said, "we are in 1945 now, why are you talking about 1944? That was four months ago."

Harold focused his eyes on Karl. "Hey, Dummy, don't blame me when you are slow on the uptake. I am not talking about a year. You asked me about a combination and it is 1944."

It sounded like Harold was snapping out of it and Karl was thankful that his efforts worked. He continued to ask questions, but avoided the subject of last night's air attack. By the time they reached the Friedrichshain Bunker, they started to make provisional plans for the next day, which included a visit to their hideaway in the Uhlandstrasse.

Twenty One

It was late in the evening when Untersturmfuehrer Bernd listened to Karl's report and welcomed Harold to the team. Karl had left out the part of Harold losing his parents. In the month of April, civilian casualties in Berlin were a common and daily occurrence and Karl was determined to keep Harold's mind busy and away from the tragedy. Unless Harold brought it up he would not mention it.

"Do you want to work together or separate," asked the Untersturmfuehrer.

"As far as the present assignment goes, it would assure better and faster results if we could work together," answered Karl, "Once you order us to guide your commandos, we will split up of course," he added.

"Done," said Officer Bernd. He wrote out another ID card for Harold and then turned again to Karl. "Please tell me in more detail why you decided to close the HJ office in Halensee."

"Simple decision," answered Karl, "you told me that you needed another subway rat and the office was no longer functional. Of course, I would appreciate if you could give me a written request for a subway rat."

"Done," answered the Untersturmfuehrer for the second time, "I had previously submitted numerous requests to Lieutenant Ebert, so we have a backup established. But, I will write you another one with yesterday's date on it. And, if necessary, I will also back up your action of closing the office. You did the right thing. Don't worry. Get yourself something to eat and find a bunk bed to sleep. I expect another report by tomorrow evening."

The next two days went fast as Karl established a working routine with Harold. Once they arrived at an exit or ventilation shaft, they took turns climbing up, unlocking the gate or grate and looking around where they were. The one boy on top of the shaft would shout to the one on the bottom what he saw; 'Side street, courtyard, or exit buried, unable to open'. The one on the bottom of the shaft would write down the location and results of the investigation. They would also add a note if the buildings around the exits were standing, or to what extent they were damaged.

Since they worked with the map from the BVG, they even found two exits that they did not know existed. But all in all, it was fast and accurate work.

In the evening, they handed their notes to officer Bernd, who kept the original and made a copy for each of them. When their survey approached the Uhlandstrasse Station and their 'hide a way', they entered in their notes 'Buried under rubble, unable to open'. Their actual visit to their hideout however, confirmed that their supplies were still there and undisturbed.

On the third day, they decided to take some time out to explore the bulkhead with the combination lock. The bulkhead was close to the Friedrichstrasse location and Karl found it right away. Harold had told him that he had obtained the secondary map of the subway system from the archives of the engineers who had mapped the Spree River and the Landwehrkanal. He thought that the bulkhead was an access to the city sewage system. Karl was not so sure. "Why would the U-Bahn transportation system want a direct access to the sewage system? There must be plenty of primary access points for the purpose of observation and repairs." He kept on speculating.

"Maybe they wanted a convenient or secondary access in case of failures. Or maybe they wanted originally just to verify and confirm the distance between the sewage system and the subway tunnel and then just closed it off." Harold guessed.

"How did you know that the combination is 1944," Karl asked his friend.

"The engineer who gave me the map told me that any combination lock on this map could be opened that way. Who knows? Maybe he lied to me."

"Here goes nothing," said Karl when he tried the lock. But the lock did not open.

"Try again," said Harold.

"What is there to try again," wanted Karl to know, "It does not open."

"Let me try it."

Karl stepped to the side. He had been standing on his toes because the lock was pretty high above his head. Harold was taller than Karl and he did not even have to stretch to reach the lock. "One, nine, four, four," he recited and as he turned the dial, the lock opened. Harold removed it and Karl wanted to see it to determine why it had not opened when he tried it.

"Don't look for excuses. You are unable to count to four," informed Harold.

"Anything is possible," answered Karl,"but I still want to see it."

"Later," said Harold, and put the lock in his pocket. He then turned to face Karl. "Do you really want to open the bulkhead? What if we open it and drown in shit?"

"Bang on the steel and listen. When I tried it before, it was a hollow sound. There was no indication of any liquid behind it," said Karl as he stepped backward.

"You must be nuts if you really think that I would open this thing," answered Harold as he pounded his fists against the bulkhead. While the sound was kind of hollow, there was no way to know for sure what was behind the bulkhead unless they opened it. "Why do we need to know what is behind this thing?" demanded Harold.

"Don't you want to know?"

"No, I am perfectly content by being ignorant. Man, Karl, we are talking of potentially massive stinky soup. Let's keep this darn bulkhead unlocked, but closed. We don't need to tell anyone about it." Pleaded Harold.

"Step back," said Karl, "or better yet, run to the next exit. I have to know and I will open it."

As Harold made some room, he saw that Karl was unable to lift the heavy lever by himself. Karl tried and pushed as hard as he could, but it did not move until Harold stepped up and helped him. There was no pressure of any kind against the backside of the bulkhead and Karl opened it all the way. The opening was about waist high, and Harold pointed their work light into the darkness. The light illuminated a wide channel of liquid, which lapped about 3 feet below the opening. The smell of raw sewage confirmed Harold's first guess.

This was indeed an access to the city sewage system.

"I hope you are satisfied," said Harold, "Let's close it and get away from the stink. I did not sign up to breathe manure."

"Manure is cow shit. This here is human excrement," Karl corrected, "and no, I am not satisfied. I want to know how deep this channel is and if it could be used as an emergency exit."

"Are you insane? You want to go in and walk around in this pudding?"

"No, of course not. Please go back to the maintenance shed and get me a long pipe or pole. I think that I saw something close to the entrance. In the meantime, I will use the work light to ascertain if I can see anything else."

Harold took off. He was relieved to get away from the horrible smell, which seemed to get stronger the longer they stood in front of the canal. Karl directed the light around the opening and saw that there were three steel bars imbedded on the outside wall above the bulkhead. He also detected another steel bar attached to the inside wall of the sewage tunnel. This bar was also above the opening. He speculated on the purpose and thought that it might serve as a handrail for the maintenance workers to lift themselves in and out of the bulkhead. This meant the channel could not be very deep. Unless of course, there was something of a boat attached to the inside.

Karl directed the light again against the sides of the canal. There was no boat, just a gently heaving of sewage. Karl observed that the sewage canal did not run directly side by side with the subway tunnel. The main channel was about 5 meters away and appeared to have a calm current. Because the work light was not strong enough, Karl could not see or estimate how wide it was. The small channel, which connected to the bulkhead, was maybe 3 meters wide.

Harold showed up again and the pole he carried was at least 3 meters long.

Just about perfect. Before Karl could proceed to measure the depth of the channel, his friend handed him an old pair of leather gloves.

"Here, I found these on the bottom shelf of the shed."

"Thanks. You just saved your shirt." Harold stared at him. "What? I would have needed something to dry my hands on."

He stuck the pole in the channel but he could not reach the bottom. However, the pole was at an angle and Karl pushed the pole all the way through the opening and lifted it straight up, then proceeded again to measure the depth on the inside wall. It appeared that there was a very small ledge, maybe 10 centimeters wide, about 2 meters below the bulkhead. But then it dropped off and Karl was unable to reach the bottom.

"This will definitely not serve as an emergency exit. Unless you want to swim in it."

"No, thank you, just the same," said Harold.

Karl pulled the pole out of the opening and laid it on the side. "Should we lock it again?"

"What for? Let's forget about it and find your other shaft, the one without an exit," Harold answered, and reached in his pocket and threw the combination lock far into the sewage channel.

"I wanted to see why I could not open the lock," protested Karl.

"I was afraid of that," muttered Harold, "if it is that important to you, go ahead and dive after it."

Karl closed the bulkhead and placed the regular padlock back in place, but did not lock it. While they had been working on the bulkhead, several trains had passed by and they were thankful that the tunnel was wide enough to allow them to keep standing. However, every time a train had passed, it also sucked a wave of the sewage air into the tunnel. They were glad to leave this evil smelling place.

The shaft without an exit remained a puzzle. They banged at the walls to find a weak spot or a hollow sound and only the ceiling, about 4 meters above the ground, appeared to sound differently than the walls. Karl decided to inform the Untersturmfuehrer of the mystery shaft, but not of the sewage connection. He was afraid that officer Bernd might want a further investigation. He reasoned that since it was not indicated on the map from the BVG, it did not exist.

When Karl and Harold reported at their usual time to officer Bernd, they found him to be disturbed and agitated. He was walking in circles in front of his desk, which was cluttered with papers and messages. He kept his eyes on the phone as if he was waiting for some bad news. Harold placed their notes on the desk and headed back to the door. Karl broke the silence and asked if he needed to come back later in the evening. Untersturmfuehrer Bernd was about to waive him out of his office when he changed his mind and motioned to the boys to stay with him.

Harold leaned against the door and Karl was about to sit on a cardboard box when the SS officer addressed him. "Did you see

Korvettenkapitan Siegler after your initial visit?"

"No, I did not even go back to the Zoo Bunker," was Karl's answer.

"Well, I don't know if I should tell you this, but apparently some high ranking officers of the SS have disappeared. The rumor is that Kapitain Siegler was visited in the hospital by the SS defense Commander of the Wilmersdorf district, Sturmbannfuehrer von Glinski. That was the last time that the Kapitain was seen." The officer wanted to say more but was interrupted by the ringing of the phone. He jumped to pick it up.

After several times of shouting "Jawohl, I understand" into the receiver, he shook his head in disbelief and then said once more, "Jawohl, Heil Hitler," and hung up. He looked at Karl and Harold, "Come back in twenty minutes. In the meantime, don't talk to anyone about what you just heard. Out, out," Officer Bernd waived frantically at the door.

"I wonder what that is all about," asked Harold as the boys entered the mess room.

"It sure was disjointed," agreed Karl, "let's wait until we hear more before we start speculating."

The short conversation with Officer Bernd had triggered his memory about the small package he had received from Kapitain Siegler. He had forgotten about it until now and he did not know if he should mention it to the Untersturmfuehrer. There had been no witnesses in the hospital room and he did not know what the little box contained. He decided not to talk about it. Not even to Harold.

Twenty minutes later, they stood again before Officer Bernd's desk. The Untersturmfuehrer was now more composed. Karl also noticed that the desk was orderly and clean again, all the papers were gone.

"First things first," began the SS officer, "Officially, the battle for Berlin has begun. The Russian troops are only one or two days away to complete the circle around Berlin. The missing SS officers have been accounted for. They were ordered by the high command of the SS to evacuate by submarine, commanded by Korvettenkapitan Siegler, for Argentina. This was done with the consent of General Hans Krebs, Commander of the Wehrmacht in Berlin, who also authorized the evacuation of some leading scientists who were working on Hitler's final weapon. This leaves us to think that Hitler's wonder weapons are not operational. We don't even know if they exist. Presently, there is not a joint defense plan for the city. Not by the Wehrmacht or by the SS, and it is not entirely clear who is or will be in command."

"The SS is forming 'flying court marshals', which are authorized to shoot any retreating troops, regardless if they are members of the Wehrmacht or of the SS. Tomorrow is the Fuehrer's birthday and I expect that he will personally take over the command of the city. Because some of the brass was evacuated, I have been promoted to Sturmbannfuehrer and presently I am in charge of all the remaining SS demolition teams. But because I am not willing to destroy bridges or blow up food or water supplies, I expect that this will change within a few days. I promise you that you will stay under my command wherever I go. I will not have you reassigned to the suicidal HJ Panzerfaust commandos."

The newly appointed Sturmbannfuehrer paused from his long speech. He looked first at Harold and then at Karl. "I have another piece of bad news," he continued, "As of this afternoon, we lost the last stronghold outside the city. We lost a major battle at Seelow Heights. There are no more armored divisions between us and the Belo Russian forces. We have a little hope that Hasso von Manteuffel's tank division will render us some relief. I know Hasso personally and he is about the best Division Commander there is, but I fear that our fate is sealed. I expect that we will be in house to house combat within the next few days. Get a day of rest and then get ready for action. Any questions?"

"No," answered Karl, "but you can count on us and congratulations on your promotion." Both of the boys saluted the officer and were glad to be excused.

"Man, what a mess," said Harold when they reached their sleeping quarters. "He made it pretty clear to us. He expects to be relieved of his command and we should disappear and take care of ourselves as soon as it happens. What do you think?"

Karl shrugged his shoulders. "I think that there will be more confusion, just like in the HJ leadership, but I don't think that he will be relieved. If there is no orderly defense plan in place, who would displace him? In any event, I believe that he will go out of his way to protect us and we should stick with him as long as possible," answered Karl.

"What do you make of the remark by the Sturmfuehrer about the flying court marshals?

"I don't think that this was a remark," answered Karl, "I think that he was only bringing us up to date. It will be easy for us to stay off the streets and I doubt that these commandos will be in the subway. Tell me about the Panzerfaust Kommandos. I know nothing about it."

"You don't know what a Panzerfaust is?" asked Harold.

"Sure I do. The Panzerfaust is a self-propelled anti tank weapon. Supposedly it is pretty accurate up to about 150 meters and is able to penetrate 20 centimeters of hardened steel. What I don't know is what the Sturmfuehrer referred to as the suicidal HJ Panzerfaust Kommandos." Karl looked questioningly at Harold.

"The so-called suicide Kommandos are mostly HJ members who are supposed to get as close to the T34 tanks as possible and place a direct shot to blow up the tank," answered Harold.

"Why are the Kommandos mostly made up by HJ members?"

"For one thing, the Panzerfaust has no recoil. It is fired from the crotch of your arm. You don't have to be a good shot, you just have to get close enough to the tank, aim and pull a lever. The weapon does not even have a trigger. And finally, it is a known fact that the members of the HJ are more fanatical and therefore will try to get nearer to the intended target. They hardly ever miss. On the other hand, their casualty rates are extremely high."

Karl had feared that Harold would tell him something like that. He changed the subject. "Will you still go to the Reichs Chancellery tomorrow to see the Fuehrer? I mean, now that your office is closed you might want to skip on that birthday invitation."

"Yes, I will go," answered Harold, "I want to see the Fuehrer. I might also hear something of benefit for us. Besides, I doubt that anyone has noticed that my office is closed."

"Alright," said Karl, "I will tell the Sturmfuehrer tomorrow morning where you are going and unless there are new orders for me, I will check up on the women's progress. It could be that they heard from Peter or from Kottbus."

Karl was hungry again. They had not eaten during the day, simply because they had nothing to eat and the watery soup in the evening was not nutritious enough to alleviate the hunger pang. He thought of Fritz Weinert, the SS Rottenfuhrer who had told him at the beginning of this assignment that he was to supply him with extra rations. He had not seen him since then because he had always left the bunker before Weinert started his duty in the morning. Karl resolved that he would see him tomorrow.

Twenty Two

The next day started with a heavy barrage by the Russian artillery. The outskirts of Berlin took a constant beating. It seemed to Karl that the Russians wanted to celebrate Adolf Hitler's birthday in their own way. He had reported to the Sturmbannfuehrer as usual at 7:00 in the morning. He told him about Harold's invitation to see the Fuehrer and that Harold intended to attend. He also told officer Bernd that he wanted to visit the women in the former HJ Dienststelle to ask about their possible success in finding their children.

Sturmbannfuehrer Bernd was impressed about Harold's invitation to congratulate the Fuehrer. "How did Harold deserve this honor?" He wanted to know.

"He did not tell me," answered Karl, "Maybe he will tell us when he returns."

"I don't think that you are able to render any help to the women in Halensee, but if you feel that you need to know about their effort, go ahead. But be back within three hours. I might need you here." Officer Bernd motioned Karl out of the office without returning Karl's salute.

It made Karl wonder. It seemed that all the required salutes went by the wayside lately. They were either sloppily returned or not at all. Karl went to find Rottenfuhrer Fritz Weinert to ask about the special food rations he was promised. He found Fritz in the mess room and came right to the point. "Heil Hitler, Rottenfuhrer. Harold and I are hungry during the day. Can you help us?"

"Yeah, Heil to you too, Karl. Keep it up and snappy and you might get another promotion before this charade is over. I can maybe get you some canned meat, as this is all we have at this time. We are running low and as a matter of fact, we are down on our food because our storage facilities have been ordered to be destroyed." He looked at Karl as if he was expecting another question. When Karl did not say anything he added, "The storage depot was ordered to be destroyed by the SS command. We don't want the food to fall into the hands of the advancing Russian troops."

"Why," asked Karl, "Why don't you open the storage facility to our hungry civilian population? And what do you mean by 'ordered to be destroyed'? Is the building still intact? And if it is still standing, is it really empty?"

Fritz did not answer. Karl could see that he did not like the questions. "I don't know about that. I only know what I have been told. Why don't you see for yourself? I cannot leave here, but I can give you the location."

Slowly it became clear to Karl what was going on. There were apparently some orders in place to destroy storage facilities, to prevent them of falling into enemy hands. But it was not entirely clear if the orders had been carried out. In the meantime, it seemed that certain SS troops would have liked to get their hands on the supplies. Karl knew that if you had food and cigarettes, you could kungle for anything. Jewelry and gold coins were high on the list, at least for the SS. For the civilians it was more the need for warm clothing. While the conversation started to make sense to Karl, he still could not make out what the Rottenfuhrer expected from him. After all, it was not him, but Fritz who had started the subject. He figured he might as well ask direct questions.

"Why me, where do I go, and what do you want?" he asked point blank.

"You have access through the subway tunnels. Where? Fehrbelliner Platz, specifically, the Arbeitsfront building. Cigarettes or tobacco," answered Fritz without hesitation.

"It might take me until late this afternoon. Where will I find you?" Karl was not sure if he wanted to get involved with Fritz and his SS friends, but he wanted to see and know about the possibilities.

"When you return I will find you," was Fritz's short answer.

Karl left the bunker with a small can of Teewurst, similar to liverwurst, in his pocket. It was better than nothing. When he reached the former Dienststelle, he was surprised and glad to see Frau Becker again. She was surrounded by three other women and each of them was busy comparing notes with lists of names. Frau Becker greeted him like a lost son and introduced him to her co-workers. One of them, a Frau Griese, shook Karl's hand over and over again.

"I cannot thank you enough for bringing my son back from Poland." Karl tried to remember the name Griese, but he could not connect him to any particular boy. "It was the SS trucks with the driver Herr Brandt in charge. He is the one who brought your son back, Frau Griese. I just told the boys to climb in and to hold on, that's all."

Frau Griese shook her head, "That is not what my son told me. He said that he was selected by your Lieutenant Hardfeld to a different group, which was to board a train. But in the last moment you intervened and ordered him to join the group with the trucks. If he would have been with the train group, he would be still missing."

"Oh, now I know who you are talking about. You must be the mother of Dettlef. Yes, I felt sorry for him. How is his knee?" Karl remembered the little boy who had told him at the time that due to a knee injury he had a problem keeping up with the other boys. Karl had told him to mingle quietly with the second truck group and left him behind when the first group took off for the railroad tracks. "I am glad that he made it," Karl added.

Frau Griese beamed at Karl. "You remember Dettlef. He will be so pleased to hear that you asked about his injury. You are his hero, you know? He wants to be an HJ leader just like you."

Karl shook his head, "Tell him there are better role models and that I wish him well". He turned to Frau Becker, "How are you coming along?"

"Fine, Karl. Every day we are able to reunite some children with their families. But there are also many children without much hope."

"How many? And where are they now," asked Karl.

"I don't know. In our district alone there must be over 800, which are abandoned, and every day we seem to have more. We asked every family we reunited to take along one or two more children as temporary guests. It works fairly well because the families are so glad to see their loved ones again that they don't mind helping out."

"That is a great idea," said Karl, "anything I can do to help?"

"Yes, there is Karl. I hate to ask you again, but we are out of food. Until yesterday, we received some help from the churches in the neighborhoods, but this morning they told us that their supplies are exhausted."

Karl thought for a moment about the Fehrbelliner Platz Depot, which Fritz had mentioned, but without knowing anything about it he could not offer any help. Then he had an idea. "Do you know if the depot in the Brandenburgerstrasse is still intact?"

"I think it is," answered Frau Becker, "but as school officials, we have no access to it. As far as I know it is a final reserve depot."

Karl told Frau Becker to make out a list of her food requirements and have it ready for him when he returned. As she got busy writing, he looked over to Harold's desk and for the little carousel of rubber stamps, but they were gone. "Where are the stamps from this desk," he asked Frau Becker and pointed to the old desk.

"Oh, do you want them? They are in a box in the other room. I will go and get them for you." Frau Becker disappeared for a moment and came back with a box full of seals, rubber stamps and inkpads, and handed them to Karl.

"I cannot promise you anything, except that I will try," said Karl and helped himself to the sheets of requisition forms, which were still on the shelf behind Harold's desk. "Did anyone from the HJ headquarters show up," he asked Frau Becker.

"Yes, but when I told them that this office was closed and when I showed them your authorization to the use of this office, they had no further questions and left. You must have some weight."

"No," laughed Karl, "it is not me, but the way I stamped the authorization. It is incredible how much weight a little seal in the right place and an unreadable signature carries."

Frau Becker stepped back from the desk with a deep frown on her face. She just realized how often she had been impressed by a piece of paper from the school authorities when it was stamped and signed, and how little she cared about a communication without a seal. Of course, she had been in charge of the KLV headquarters' rubber stamps. But they had been lost when the school building collapsed and she had never missed them or thought anything of it. I must be truly brainwashed, she thought. But then she caught on fast. "Let me have one or two of the stamps," she said to Karl.

"Of course," answered Karl, "but Harold has first choice. I will bring you back the remainders." He smiled at her and pressed her hand, "Take good care, I will try to be back as soon as possible."

He had to be back at the bunker to see the Sturmbannfuehrer as ordered and hurried accordingly. Actually, it was one of Karl's characteristics to always be on time. His HJ training had been very strict and he had been taught that 7:45 meant 7:45. It did not mean 7:40 or 7:50. To be five minutes late meant that he had no respect for other people's time. To be five minutes early was also not being on time. Because of his training, he had developed the habit of doing everything as fast as possible. In a certain way, he admired the people who acted slowly because it seemed like they did everything very deliberately. On the other hand, he thought that moving slow or walking slow was just a form of laziness. In any event, he would rather run than walk and he was back in the Friedrichshain Bunker before his three-hour allocation was up.

Sturmbannfuehrer Bernd was just addressing a group of junior SS officers when Karl arrived. After showing his ID to the double guards at the door to the conference room, he was allowed to join the meeting. Officer Bernd announced that as of this morning, there was a new directive from the Fuehrer himself to dissolve all the SS and armed forces headquarters in Berlin. They were supposed to be relocated near Premnitz to the west of Berlin. Dr. Joseph Goebbels, the former minister of Propaganda, now had a new title; he was now to be addressed as Reich Minister. He was also to dissolve his office in the Zoo Bunker and to relocate to the Fuehrer's bunker located under the Reichs Chancellery.

Karl noticed that the Sturmbannfuehrer was furious. Hitler had announced that an artillery General by the name of HelmuthWeidling was now in charge of the defense of Berlin. Officer Bernd was convinced that the individual officers under Weidling's command had hardly any combat experience. He told his assembled officer corps that they should only follow orders issued by SS Brigadefuehrer Wilhelm Mohnke, who was in command of the inner city.

Karl was stunned by what he heard. He actually liked General Weidling. He had met him once at an HJ rally in Stettin. He seemed to him everything a General should be. Weidling was, in his opinion, in stark contrast to SS Brigadefuehrer Mohnke, who was one of the most feared SS Officers in Berlin. Karl knew that there was no love lost between the Wehrmacht and the SS. Officer Bernd's comments confirmed his fear that there was greater rivalry to come. He was about to quietly leave the meeting when Sturmbannfuehrer Bernd saw him and asked Karl to join him in front of the group.

"This is Karl Veth, Obergefolgsschaftfuehrer in the HJ, and my personal aide in the defense planning of the U-Bahn system. I expect each one of you to extend to him courtesy. The day might come when you will need his knowledge."

Karl felt uncomfortable in front of the officers, but none of them paid him any special attention. He asked the Sturmbannfuehrer to be excused. "I'll be back before evening," he promised and went to find Fritz.

He found him at his usual post near the bunker entrance. However, Fritz was not alone. The guard detail at the entrance tunnel had been beefed up during the last hour. There were now three SS privates with Fritz, as Rottenfuhrer in command. Karl figured that this might not be the right time to talk to him and ignored him as he passed the guards. The Russian artillery had not stopped since morning, but so far the sound had not increased. They were still shelling the outer suburbs. Nevertheless, it was disturbing that there was no let up in the intensity. Karl wondered how much longer it would be until the shells would hit the inner city.

When he used the U-Bahn to get to the Fehrbelliner Platz, he was surprised to see several subway wagons being converted into an emergency hospital. They were presently parked along a third track near the Gleisdreieck Station and he remembered that this track was normally used for maintenance purposes. He left the train and identified himself to the stationmaster on duty. "Will this be the only subway hospital train, or are there other ones planned," he asked the white haired WWI veteran.

"I only know about this one for certain," answered the station master, "but there are supposed to be several more."

Karl feared the looming consequences. If there were really several hospital trains to be parked in the tunnels, he had to know exactly where they would be. "Will this train stay here at your station, or do you expect that it will be moved?"

"No idea. It would depend upon too many factors." The old man studied Karl for a moment. "Don't I know you?"

"Might be. I've been around," answered Karl, and turned away to avoid any further questions.

He boarded the next train to Fehrbelliner Platz and located the food depot. It was guarded by soldiers of the Wehrmacht and was a beehive of activity. Karl could see military trucks coming and leaving and even some trucks with the Red Cross painted on top. As far as Karl could determine, it was a fully functioning supply facility. He crossed the Hohenzollerndam and went to the entrance of the depot where he addressed the guard on duty.

"Heil Hitler. I am representing 150 hungry children from the Goethe school. What do we need to do to obtain some food?"

The soldier returned his salute in a far more orderly fashion than any of the SS officers ever did. "You have to acquire exact authorization from the district commander and then I can let you pass. But even then don't expect to obtain any food. This depot is only for the military."

"Are you saying that there is food available, but none for hungry children?"

The soldier shrugged his shoulders and did not answer. Karl saluted again and went back to the U-Bahn Station. He would have to talk to Harold about this depot and Frau Becker's needs. Harold was the expert and Karl smiled in his anticipation of Harold's action.

On the other hand, he did not think too much about the comments from Fritz. This changed, however, as soon as he entered the Friedrichshain Bunker. Fritz was waiting for him by the staircase and approached Karl with a single question, actually with two questions, "Is the depot still standing? Is it accessible from the subway tunnel?"

"Yes, it is operating just fine," answered Karl, "but there is no subway tunnel underneath. The depot stands on one side of the plaza and the subway runs on the opposite side of the Hohenzollerndam." He added, "Why don't you obtain authorization from our bunker commander and just drive up and get what you need?"

Fritz was not happy with the answer. "We are talking about a Wehrmacht depot and they are not cooperating with us, the SS."

"I am starting to understand this, but our bunker commander is a Wehrmacht officer, so what is the problem?"

"The problem is that we are practically out of food, that's what the problem is." Fritz was agitated.

Karl nodded his head, "Yes, I know that the Fuehrer himself had said, 'Hungry people are angry people'."

Fritz was now really upset. "He said that when we attacked Poland, you idiot!"

Karl knew that Fritz was just trying to use him. "Easy now, I am hungry too, but I remember that you did not ask for food. You wanted cigarettes or tobacco. I might be able to get some for you if you can get me some food to take to the KLV children."

"Are you saying that you want to kungle? We don't do that here." Fritz was righteous in his answer.

"I understand," said Karl, "and yes, that is exactly what I am saying. These children don't smoke, they cannot help themselves to food, and they are hungry." Karl started to climb the stairs but turned to face Fritz once more. "Let me know when you are ready. Your call."

Karl entered Sturmbannfuehrer's Bernd office and waited for the officer to hang up the phone. "We have three separate Russian armies attacking us and they are about to close the circle around Berlin," announced the Sturmbannfuehrer. "Hitler's directive is now officially code named 'Clausewitz'.

Karl raised his hand to interrupt the officer, "How can this be? We have a division named Clausewitz, fighting close to our HJ division Scharnhorst somewhere by Stettin."

"I agree it is confusing. Maybe the general staff is running out of names. No, that's not what it is," he corrected himself, "Karl, it does not matter what they call it, but you can relax now about your action of closing the Dienstelle in Halensee. You were just a few days ahead of time." Sturmbannfuehrer Bernd looked at the few notes Karl had prepared in the subway on his way back to the bunker. "What is this note about a Red Cross subway hospital train?"

Karl reported to him what he had seen and also mentioned the conversation with the stationmaster. "If we guide SS units through the tunnels and the Russians are using the same tactic, we could easily wind up with hospital trains in the cross fire." Karl was voicing his concerns. "Another thing that is bothering me..." he started to say when officer Bernd interrupted him, "I will send details of SS men to every subway station to report back as to the location of possible hospital trains." He looked up, "What is bothering you?"

"Two things," said Karl, "you had Harold and me inspecting and identifying the location of all the bulkheads between the U-Bahn and the Landwehrkanal. This makes me think that there is some plan to blow up the connections and flood the subway system. If I am correct, we will flood the hospital trains too. Secondly, and again, if I am correct, and given the water level of the Kanal and the Spree River, the water will only rise to maybe two meters and then start to recede. This would mean that we could potentially drown our own troops and shelter-seeking civilians before it would settle at a level of less than one meter. Also, the resulting low water level would not stop any advancing Russian troops. At best, it could only delay them." Karl stopped. He wanted to say more, but remembered in time his decision to say as little as possible. As it was, he might already have said too much.

Officer Bernd was very stern and serious when he asked Karl, "Why do you think that there is a plan in place to flood the system?"

"Why did we identify and mark the nearest bulkheads to the Kanal?" asked Karl in return.

"I could tell you that it is none of your business. But since it is bothering you, I decide to answer. Our objective is to use any means possible to inject special teams behind enemy lines. The subway system lends itself perfectly for this purpose. We might also want to use the Landwehrkanal and the Spree River for the same purpose." Sturmbannfuehrer Bernd was obviously not happy about the concerns raised by Karl. He was not aware that there was a plan to flood the subway, but he had to agree that Karl's fears were justified. "Is this all, or is there anything else bothering you?" He asked in a more friendly tone of voice.

"No, Herr Sturmbannfuehrer," answered Karl, "except, that because of our daily work schedule, Harold and I are down to one meal a day, which we receive in the evening. Are we really out of food reserves in this bunker?" He wanted to add or does it get converted to the black market, but he thought better of it. He feared that he might strain his relationship with the SS officer to a point of no return. There was nothing to be gained by it. He knew from his visit to the Fehrbelliner Platz that there was still food in depots, but he was also hungry and wanted the officer to know about it.

"One meal a day," echoed Officer Bernd. "Don't you receive breakfast?"

"Yes, sorry, I forgot. We receive two slices of rye bread, kunsthonig, and a cup of coffee." Kunsthonig (a mixture imitating honey) was the only sweet concoction Karl could not stand. Otherwise he liked everything sweet, but this stuff dried out the very moment he spread it on a slice of bread. It resembled somewhat the taste of honey, but not much.

"Hmm, I agree that this is barely enough. However, it is better than nothing. I will see what I can do for you." Sturmbannfuehrer

Bernd picked up the phone and indicated to Karl that he could leave.

Twenty Three

Karl went to the sleeping quarters and found Harold waiting for him. "How was your birthday party with the Fuehrer?"

"Disappointing. He told me that I was nothing," he added when he saw Karl's questioning expression.

"The Fuehrer really talked to you? And he told you what?" Karl was not sure that he had heard correctly.

"Yes and no, he did not tell me individually that I am nothing," answered Harold, "We had to line up in the courtyard and stand at attention in front of him. Then he shouted at us 'YOU are nothing, your Country is everything!' then he shook our hands and told each of us how proud he was of us."

"Let me see if I have this straight," said Karl, "the Fuehrer told you that you are nothing, and then he shook your hand to tell you that he was proud of you?"

"That's it, you got it."

"No, I don't think so. This is absurd. Why don't you tell me about the whole day?"

"Not much to tell, there is nothing more," said Harold, "well yes there is. There were newspaper reporters and cameramen from the propaganda staff who took pictures of us. At the end of the assembly, the Fuehrer asked us if we wanted to go home or to the front to fight the Russians. We all shouted that we would go to the front. Then we were invited to a meal in the Chancellery, but I did not feel like it. I showed them my SS ID and was excused to leave. Oh, I almost forgot, I received a medal, the iron cross, 1st class. Here take a look at it."

With this he handed Karl his medal.

"Congratulations," said Karl and studied it for a moment. He had always admired the soldiers who received medals for bravery, and now his friend had earned one and he was happy for him. He did not know of any special bravery performed by Harold and he speculated that this medal might have been awarded for leadership or management or something like it. However, he still had difficulty understanding what Harold had told him.

"You are nothing, the Fuehrer is proud of you, and you got a medal. What a birthday party and I thought that I missed something." Karl summed it up.

"Do you believe what he told you?" he asked Harold.

"What?"

"I mean, we are always told to believe in Hitler and what he says is supposed to be the ultimate truth. So, I am asking you, do you believe that you are nothing?"

"Karl, leave me alone, I am disappointed enough as it is without you taking things out of context. I love the Fuehrer, you know that, but you are right. Now I am not so sure anymore of the Fuehrer's doctrine regarding unquestionable loyalty."

"Interesting," said Karl, "I think that we are on the same page."

Harold readjusted his bedding on the cot for the third time.

"You want to sleep?"

"No, I don't think I can. I am still thinking of all the military and party leaders who were assembled at the ceremony. Artur Axmann, our Reichsjugendfuehrer, was actually the one who pinned the medal on me. I think that the Fuehrer was too weak or something. I think that he had some problems with his left arm. I also saw Dr. Joseph Goebbels. He was there with his wife and two of his children. We were introduced to them as role models."

"Hmm," mused Karl, "one moment you are nothing and the next moment you are a role model."

"Karl, give it up, will you?" pleaded Harold.

"Yes, of course, but please understand that I am also disappointed. I was hoping to hear something inspirational. The Russian artillery has not paused since this morning and we could really use some encouragement." Karl changed the subject, "Let me ask you something different. If you had still the requisition forms and the seals from your office, would you still be able to obtain some food for the KLV children?"

"If the Brandenburger Strasse facility is still operating, we could most certainly try. As far as any of the other food depots, well I doubt it," answered Harold. "But how do we get our hands on the papers and seals? I don't have the keys anymore and by now I am sure that the office has been ransacked."

"Not really ransacked," replied Karl, "but I took your requisition forms and your seals and rubber stamps. Frau Becker told me that she is out of food and I thought that you might be able to arrange something."

"As I said, we could try, but we would need a vehicle and a driver because I doubt that we could pull it off for a third time. Somebody will figure out what we are doing. Let me see what you have."

Karl proudly showed him the forms and the seals. "I even got your inkpads," he informed Harold.

"Good thinking, this will help us a lot." Harold looked over the assortment and was satisfied with what he saw. "We should not try to hide this stuff here in the bunker. Maybe we could make a trip to our place in the Uhlandstrasse. It would be safer there than any place else."

Karl agreed with his friend's suggestion. He had wanted to go there anyhow, to add some blankets and first aid kits to their stash. Then he remembered that Frau Becker's requisition papers and her school stamps had been buried when the school collapsed, and he asked Harold if he could write authorizations without official requests.

"I don't see why not," answered Harold, "filling out authorizations is no problem because we have the original documents. However, whether they get honored without a formal request is another thing. I don't know how their filing system works. Let me think about this for a while. This might be a lesser challenge than to get a vehicle."

Karl thought about his connections and all he could come up with was Fritz, but Fritz was SS and the Wehrmacht ran the depot. Any SS driver would have been subject to suspicion. They needed someone else. "Why don't I ask Dr. Felder if he needs some special food or something? If we can comply with what he needs he might be able to help us," Karl voiced his thoughts to Harold.

"That would depend upon what he needs and the availability in the warehouse. You might as well talk to him. It's worth a try to get a car. But, please, don't promise anything, it might ruin the goodwill you are enjoying in the hospital," Harold agreed.

When they got up in the morning, they were told that there had been no air raids during the night. The Russian artillery had continued their barrage all through the night and Harold thought that they sounded a lot closer than yesterday. He had gotten up before 5:00 AM to make an early round of the nearby hospitals. He was still hoping to find his parents and he also searched for other tenants of the destroyed apartment building. So far, he had found three people who had lived two floors above his parents. They told him that they had not seen his parents during the air attack. This gave him hope that they might have been in a different shelter. Maybe today he would get lucky in his effort.

Karl went to the Catholic St. Hedwig Hospital, which was further away, but he had been told that they maintained an up-to-date database on civilian casualties. His visit was fruitless. There was no trace of Harold's parents.

By 7:00 AM they were back in the bunker and in Officer Bernd's office.

Harold told the Sturmbannfuehrer about his missing parents and Officer Bernd asked why Harold had not mentioned it earlier.

"I was thinking that they might show up within a day or two. My father was an air raid Marshal and he could have been any place. My mother could have been with my aunt. But by now, I think that they would have left me a survivor message among the rubble of the building. I am starting to get very worried."

Officer Bernd looked at his two young aides and then at their reports from the last two days. He liked the boys. Their reports were in an orderly fashion and covered every detail he needed to know about. "Why don't you spend today trying to locate your parents," he told Harold. "Take Karl along to inspect the rubble of the building again. He is pretty good at it and in your panic you might have overlooked something. I wish you luck, and don't forget to report back to me tonight."

The boys clicked their heels and marched out of the office. "Let's go first to the building and then to my aunt's place," suggested Harold as they left the bunker.

Fritz was already standing at the exit and handed the boys a paper bag with a small loaf of rye bread and a can of lard. "Orders from the Sturmbannfuehrer," he told them. He gestured to Karl to join him. "I know about the availability of a small amount of food.

Maybe 20 pounds of margarine and about 10 pounds of canned meat. It is not far from this bunker. We would need some tobacco to trade for it."

"How much Tobacco?"

"Counting my commission...maybe 10 pounds."

"At this time, I do not know if I can get that much. I will let you know tonight". Karl rejoined Harold who had waited for him.

"What was that about?" Karl told him about yesterday's conversation with Fritz and the present offer.

"If Fritz was a regular soldier, I would think that we might want to work with him. But with him being with the SS, let's think about that. I mean, we have been warned about their habit of playing by their own rules."

"What can happen to us," asked Karl, "we don't trade this for ourselves. It is for Frau Becker and the children. We could not eat 20 pounds of margarine if we tried."

"True, but depending upon the circumstances and that we gave the food to the children, I am a bit worried that we might leave ourselves open for blackmail. Today they want 10 pounds of tobacco and tomorrow they want 50. I have been warned by my father to be careful of the possibility."

Karl pondered Harold's apprehension. He was probably right to be cautious. Besides, he needed Harold's ability to obtain tobacco in the first place. Maybe it was best to tell Fritz that he was unable to get his hands on that much tobacco or for that matter, on any tobacco at all. He regretted that he had given Fritz the impression that he wanted to kungle. "You are right," he told Harold, "let's try to get some food directly from the Brandenburger Strasse Depot."

The boys used the U-Bahn for part of their way and then walked the remainder to Harold's apartment house. Karl started to inspect the larger pieces of rubble in the former courtyard and Harold checked along the street. They found several messages in different places but not a single one relating to the Kellner family.

"Nothing," said Harold, but there was no despair in his voice. He had searched the area before and somehow he thought that the absence of a note regarding his parents was not that bad. He still had hope.

"We should check back here a few more times," suggested Karl. "There were many tenants in this building and some of them might not have had a chance to leave a message. Let's go and find your aunt."

Harold's aunt lived in an apartment house on the Emser Strasse in Wilmersdorf. Harold described to Karl the modern building and told him that it even featured a sub floor with a garage for four cars. Karl knew where it was. He had passed this building many times as a small boy when his parents had lived nearby the Emser Strasse.

"Are there really still cars in the basement?"

"No, they were all requisitioned by the Wehrmacht a few years ago. It is a shame because there was also a great black 6-seater Horch, which belonged to the owner of the luxury building," answered Harold. "Come to think of it, I don't know of any civilian who still owns a car. The last ones disappeared when the Fuehrer declared 'Total War' and my uncle had to surrender his Opel. My father told me that my uncle would be compensated after the war, but he did not believe it would happen."

When the boys reached the five-story building, they were surprised that it was hardly damaged. They went up to the third floor and found a note on the door leading to Harold's aunt's apartment informing a would-be visitor that she had left Berlin. The note specified an address in Bielefeld and was dated four days prior. Harold was familiar with the address, but his parents had never mentioned to him that his aunt had left. Maybe it was a snap decision by her and his parents did not know about it.

Karl tried to cheer up his friend by sliding down the heavy oak handrail, which wound down the circular carpeted staircase. He made it all the way to the first floor when an old lady with a cane was coming up the stairs and interrupted him in his glide. While she was busy berating Karl for his juvenile behavior, Harold walked down and politely wished her a good day. He passed the lady and also Karl as if he did not know him, but he did not fool her because she looked at their uniforms and started to tell them what she thought of the HJ in general and of Karl specifically.

While Karl was still embarrassed and apologizing, Harold helped him out by informing the lady that he was looking for his aunt who lived upstairs and that he wanted to bring her a small can of lard. But his aunt had left Berlin and he was wondering if she might be interested in receiving the lard. The old spinster did not listen to him. She shook her cane at Karl and did not miss a beat in her lecture until Karl pulled the small can out of his pocket and offered it to her. Then slowly everything changed.

First she sniffed on the sealed tin can and then her face lit up. "Oh, you are so kind. I surely could use the lard. May I offer you a cup of coffee?"

Karl politely declined and Harold asked to be excused, but told her that he would be back to look for his aunt and at that time he would like to take her up on the invitation. She nodded her head and called after Karl, "Come back anytime you wish to slide down on the banister. You made it nice and shiny," but he was already out the front door and did not hear her anymore.

"Menschenskinder, I have not had such a verbal beating since I was ten years old and was caught in a U-Bahn tunnel by an inspector," he told his friend as they were walking back on the Emser Strasse.

"I thought she would hit me with her walking stick. I could see that she was ready to swing. Do you think she is nuts or just old?"

"How do I know?" answered Harold. "But now you see how fast you can go from less than nothing to hero."

Karl shrugged his shoulders, "Just forget it."

Their next destination was Dr. Felder's office in the Zoo Bunker. Karl introduced his friend and did not waste any time to tell the doctor about the plight of the KLV children in Halensee.

"We might obtain legal access to the depot in the Brandenburger Strasse, but we need a car or small truck. If you could help us out we might be able to bring you back some things for your hospital. Is there anything you need as bad as we need transportation?"

"You don't need to bribe me, Karl, you know that I will help when I can. Nevertheless, let me think for a moment. We are out of wound powder. 'Bayer-Leverkusen' brand if you can get it." He picked up the phone and told his aide, "I need a car and a driver to pick up supplies." He listened for an answer. "No, Hans will not do, I need Corporal Kurt Halder for this job." He listened again and told Karl, "Go to the exit. I will have a Red Cross truck picking you up. The driver will be a corporal. He is...." Dr. Felder was looking for words, "well, he is kind of a big man." He winked at Karl who did not understand what this could mean.

"A Red Cross truck is perfect," beamed Harold as they stood waiting on the sidewalk. The driver of the 2-ton truck was a huge corporal in a hospital uniform and a big white armband with a red cross. There was also a red cross painted on the side and on the back of the truck. The corporal mustered the uniforms of Karl and Harold and asked, "Where to?"

"Halensee," said Karl, "to pick up the authorization papers. Then to the depot in the Brandenburger Strasse."

The corporal stuck out his enormous hand, "Call me Kurt, never mind my rank. You must be friends of Dr. Felder. I am supposed to assist you." He turned on the corner to drive down the Kurfuerstendamm. There was some light traffic consisting of troop carrier vehicles, a solitary tank and some ammunition trucks. They did not see any civilians on the way to Halensee. Instead, they saw plenty of SS commandos walking the streets. The Russian artillery was getting closer. It was now over two nights and two days that they had not stopped shelling. So far, they were still hammering the outskirts. Karl felt sorry for the soldiers who were ordered to hold their positions. He could not imagine how they could survive.

"Are you still receiving burn victims," he asked the Corporal.

Kurt shook his head, "No, hardly any civilians at the present time. Mostly soldiers from the Seelow Heights battle. But what we are now facing is not a battle. According to our bunker commander, it will be a mass slaughter of our men unless the American troops reach Berlin before the Russians invade the city. I have not heard of any Wehrmacht reinforcements coming to our aid."

What Kurt had said was exactly what Karl and Harold feared and they could not think of a suitable answer. When they reached the old Dienststelle in Halensee, they saw that Frau Becker was just about to leave. Kurt stayed in the truck and Karl went to speak with Frau Becker while Harold got busy typing and filling out authorization papers.

"We just received the news that we are allowed back into one of our old school buildings in the Pfalzburger Strasse," Frau Becker reported. Karl knew about this building. He had attended this school in 1936. In the beginning of the forties, it had been converted into military barracks. "Did the military give it back to the school district?," he asked.

"Yes, the current Volkssturm Regiment moved out and there are no reserve units to take it over," answered Frau Becker, "I suspect we got it back because we still have over 200 children under the age of twelve without a home to go to. We are very successful in finding temporary homes, but not enough."

"Do you have your list with your food requirements," asked Karl and added, "I still cannot promise you anything, but Harold and I will try, and we have a small truck available. If we are successful, where do you want the food delivered? Here, or in the Pfalzburger School?"

"Bring it back here, please. I will be back when you arrive. We will double up with our women to guard it. We don't know anything about the present condition of the old school building. All we are told is that it is available for us."

Karl looked around, "Where are the children now? I don't see any."

"They are in several shelters in the neighborhood where we have some facilities to do the cooking." Frau Becker handed Karl her list of food requirements.

It was very short. If she had simply written only three words: 'Anything to eat', it would have been essentially the same. Karl handed the papers to his friend who was still busy typing. He marveled at the speed with which Harold had filled out all the different documents.

"I need Kurt's signature. Go get him in here," he said to no one in particular.

When the corporal entered, Harold asked him if he smoked. "Yes, of course, if I had any tobacco I would smoke."

"Sign here, and here, and over here once more, please," said Harold and pushed some papers in front of Kurt. "Hey, I asked whether you smoked and asked you to sign, I did not say anything about reading," he scolded Kurt when he saw that the corporal wanted to read above his signature line.

"Does my signature get me tobacco?"

"It will if you sign this," answered Harold.

"I understand," the corporal nodded his head and signed in the indicated places.

"Now you too." Harold motioned to Frau Becker, who did not take a second look at Harold's writings. She trusted Karl and if Harold was his friend, that was good enough for her. Besides, she was hungry. If her signature would produce food .... she was all for it.

Twenty Four

Kurt did not stop the truck at the entrance of the Brandenburger Strasse Depot but as instructed by Harold, he ignored the Wehrmacht sergeant on duty and pulled right up to a small loading dock in the rear of the warehouse. The activity next to the building looked very different to Karl than he remembered from his last visit. This time there was a long line of military vehicles lined up along the street and some of the drivers leaned on their horn. They were annoyed that the Red Cross truck seemed to have priority because the guard had jumped to the side and the truck had disappeared through the passageway. Harold had instructed Kurt to act as if he was in a deadly hurry.

"Act with authority and don't tolerate or answer any questions." Kurt nodded in agreement and padded Karl on the shoulders. "You will like the way I follow instructions," he mumbled to himself. As soon as the truck came to a stop, Harold jumped out and handed the storage master, a civil servant in a dark blue suit, all of his bunched up documents.

"Please excuse our urgency, but we need to be back at the hospital as soon as possible. It is a matter of life and death and we are late already."

The storage master was not very moved by Harold and slowly positioned the documents on the top of the paperwork which was already piling up on his counter. He was still trying to straighten out the crumbled official certificates when he noticed the impressive figure of the corporal, who came storming through the door.

"It is all there," shouted the brawny giant, "everything is signed and counter-signed. Don't study it, step to it. I need help loading. Where is everybody?"

When the corporal saw that the storage master took his time to clean his glasses and adjust his tie, he got visibly upset. "I have never seen such a slow pigpen. I need to keep going and if you don't hop to it, I will report every one of you!"

The civil servant beckoned to his storeroom helpers and leaped for cover when the beefy corporal hit his fist on the counter and continued, "Damned government employees! I really don't care if you never worked in your life before, but when I am here, I expect you to jump when I tell you something. Get me my food and get me out of here. NOW! God forbid we would be that slow at our job, everyone would die!"

Kurt swiped his arm across the stacked-up paperwork from the counter and ripped Harold's requisition forms from the hands of the storage master. "You don't understand do you? Jump! Jump!" He shouted at the blue suit and threw the papers in the air. "I don't like to be kept waiting while you are reading!" Another piece of paper sailed to the floor.

The storage master looked helplessly to Karl for support while his depot helpers were hurriedly dragging boxes of assorted food to the rear of the truck. Karl whispered to the civilian, "There is also a request for 20 units of cigarettes among the authorizations. If you don't have any we will take tobacco. Hurry before the gentle corporal gets really angry."

The station master, who already looked pretty pale, did not want to take the chance and produced in record time three large cardboard boxes from the storage room behind him. 'Here, take the extra carton of tobacco too," he told Karl, "just get this brute away from me. Look, look, he is destroying my counter and my filing system!"

Karl looked over to Kurt who had dragged the counter a few feet to the side and in doing so, the center drawer had fallen to the floor. He had not bothered to pick it up. Instead, he was holding a Leitz Ordner, 'a hand filing system' in his hands, and was ripping it apart. The colored indexes were flying all over the office.

"I will shred your whole place to pieces if you don't hurry up," he yelled at the dockworkers who were falling over each other in their effort to fill up the truck. They had never witnessed anything like that before. Most, if not all of the military, had been polite and very thankful when they received their rations. But, this maniac here was obliviously deranged.

"Chicken-shit civilian leeches, stand straight, leap or stand to attention when I talk to you!" The corporal continued to yell. Harold began to fear that Kurt might overplay his hand. He was also beginning to think that the corporal might be really insane.

"We cannot wait any longer," he pointed at the wall clock, "whatever you have loaded will have to do," he announced to Kurt who looked around the office as if he was looking for things to dismantle. When he did not see anything that needed arranging, he closed in on the storage master, lifted him off his feet and slammed him with his behind on top of the counter. "Sit, don't move, here are your papers, start working," and with that he gathered some of the papers from the floor and dropped them in the lap of the terrified government official. Karl thought he had seen enough and rushed out the office to close the rear doors of the truck. Harold went up to the counter and asked the storage master respectfully where he wished him to sign for the food supplies.

"I have no idea where your papers are. Just look at this mess. Please get the corporal away from us; I will sign off for you."

Harold looked around and had to agree that corporal had done a pretty good number on the paperwork. There were forms and authorizations all over the place. "His medication is starting to wear off. He has been under heavy stress, you know." He confided to the civilian, who did not dare to move and continued to stare at the remains of his office. "Just take him away from here and to his physician. He should not be driving a truck. He belongs in an institution!"

Harold joined Karl in the truck and Kurt returned the salute of the guard who had remained at the driveway entrance and was not aware of what had been going on in the office.

"How do you like that? They don't even wave goodbye. Did I do good?" he asked of Harold.

"Excellent, you almost scared me. What possessed you to jump all over the supply guy?"

"Heck, it was fun, and it was your fault. You told me not to tolerate any questions. So, I figured the best way to do this is not to invite any in the first place."

"I have to agree," said Karl, "that you two play well together. If I didn't know any better, I would think that you did this before." He shook his head in disbelief.

The corporal parked his truck again in front of the Dienststelle and began with the unloading. Karl went to get the women from the office and they formed a line to transfer the food into the building.

"Thank you, this should last us for a while. What is in these tiny boxes?" asked Frau Becker as she pointed to a large carton full of small cardboard containers.

"Medicated powder, I guess," answered Karl. He placed the box back in the truck and handed a handful to Frau Becker. "Please, keep a few for me, I'll be back to pick them up."

Kurt was done placing boxes of supplies on the sidewalk. "What do you want me to do with these?" he asked Harold, and handed him the original requisition and authorization forms bearing his and Frau Becker's signatures. Harold's eyes almost bulged out of their sockets and Karl started to swallow. "How...w w what?" Harold stuttered.

The corporal looked at the boys and shook his head. "You did not really think that I was nuts and leave our calling card behind?" He took the papers back from Harold and stuffed them in his pocket. "Don't tell me, I know what you want me to do with them. Now, where are my cigarettes?"

"Later," said Karl.

During the drive back to the bunker they noticed that the noise of the Russian artillery had moved closer. "How much longer do you think we have until they stop and move their infantry forward?" asked Harold.

"Maybe two or three more days and we will hear them coming," answered the corporal. "This is also why I had my fun with the stinking government employees at the depot. There is not enough time for them to trace our visit. We should do this more often while we still can." He looked expectantly to Harold.

"You mean at the same place?" asked Harold.

The corporal shook his head and looked at Karl. "He is your friend, right? I know a little dense can be cute sometimes, but you might want to watch him a bit."

They arrived at the Zoo Bunker and Harold handed Karl one of the cigarette boxes and took the tobacco one for himself. "The third one is for you," he told the corporal.

"It has been a pleasure," said Kurt when he shook their hands. "Call me when you need me. Captain Felder knows how to reach me."

Karl and Harold clicked their heels and stretched their arms in a salute to the disappearing truck. "Where to?" asked Harold. "We should have told Kurt to stop for a moment at our hide out."

"No," said Karl, "When three people know about something it is not a secret anymore. Stay down here while I run upstairs and thank Dr. Felder. I'll be right back." He had to wait a few minutes before he was able to see the Captain. "Thank you, Dr. Felder. I got you a box of medicated powder. I don't know if it is from Bayer-Leverkusen."

"How did you like the Corporal?" The Captain smiled. This time Karl understood the twinkle in Dr. Felder's eyes.

"You were right, he is...kind of hefty...and he does not seem to like civil employees."

"Hmm, yes, interesting fellow, isn't he? Well, I thought that you might need help. Glad that I could assist."

When Karl reached the street, he had to search for a moment for Harold who was helping a group of women and children to carry their bundles of bedding into the high-rise bunker. "They told me that they will not come out again before the Russians are here," said Harold as he walked ahead to the U-Bahn station. "Let's hope that their food supply will last that long."

The boys made fast work of adding the tobacco and some of the cigarettes to their stash in the hide-away, refreshed their water supply, and went back to report to Sturmbannfuehrer Bernd.

As Harold went up to the Officer's office, Karl walked over to Fritz, who again was on guard duty at the entrance. He handed him two small packs of cigarettes. "I was able to get something for you. Now you owe me some extra rations."

"Where did you get these?" asked Fritz.

"I kungled for them," lied Karl, and he went after Harold. Sturmbannfuehrer Bernd was already waiting for them. He was all excited and like always, did not bother to return the salute of the boys. "We found your parents, Harold. They are alive and well. I even have a message for you."

Harold had to sit down. His lips trembled and he was unable to speak. The last few days of despair and hoping had come to a sudden and unexpected happy ending. He had a hard time asking question and instead, opened the letter. The message carried yesterday's date and was from his mother and very short. It only said that she and Harold's father were in a government shelter when their apartment house had been destroyed. They were unharmed and on a civil employee transport out of Berlin. She loved him, wished him well and hoped to see him again. Harold recognized her handwriting.

After he had read it for the second time, he had gained sufficient control of himself to thank the Sturmbannfuehrer and asked how he had found out about his parents and how he had gotten hold of the letter.

"I know that we are evacuating some of our higher placed civilian officials. It is a flash order from General Helmuth Weidling. We are trying to get them out of the city before the Russians close in," explained the officer. "When you told me who your father was, I put one and one together and hoped that I was right and dispatched a Sturmman to the assembly bunker. The transport left yesterday. There were many letters left behind, but this was the only letter he found addressed to you."

Karl tried to make sense of what he knew about Harold's father and what he had just heard. "May I ask a question?" he asked.

"You may," answered the Sturmbannfuehrer.

Karl stuttered for words and then he clamped up. "I answered myself already," he said, hoping that the officer would leave it at that. He had wanted to ask if Harold's parents had been really evacuated by the Wehrmacht, or if the SS for some unknown reason had arrested them. He had stopped himself when he realized that he was about to question an SS Officer. Sturmbannfuehrer Bernd had been more than accommodating to him and had surely extended an effort to find out about Harold's parents, but to question him could be a fatal mistake.

"Good," said the Sturmbannfuehrer, "enjoy the good news. Tomorrow we will do some exercises and trial runs in the tunnels."

Harold thanked the SS Officer, who Karl thought looked a little embarrassed, but then he told himself that he was seeing things because he had a suspicious mind, and like with a few things during the last days, he might be mistaken.

The officer's mess was busy when the boys entered. They received the same soup as the day before, but this time the rye bread was freshly baked and there was plenty of it. There was even a large dish of Schweineschmalz (pigs lard) on the table and Harold used the opportunity to make some sandwiches for the next day. Karl had only one bowl of soup, but ate three sandwiches. Schweineschmalz sandwich was his favorite food, especially when the rye bread was fresh. He remembered that his father had never allowed fresh bread on the table. It had to be at least two days old, because then it would be easier to slice and the bread would last longer because the slices would be thinner. He missed his father, but tonight he could feast.

Harold did not look as happy as Karl had expected him to be. He was distracted and hardly touched his soup. He wrapped up the sandwiches for the next day in newspaper and asked Karl if he was ready to retire to their bunks.

"What gives?" Karl asked when they were alone. "I thought that you would be happy and jumping up and down when you heard the good news about your parents. Instead you are murky and obviously depressed."

"I am kind of happy that my parents are alive, at least yesterday they were, but I don't believe that they are being evacuated. I think that they have been arrested."

"Come on Harold, I don't think that they have been arrested, and for what?" He had feared to voice his suspicion to Harold and now that he heard that his friend was thinking along his own lines, he wanted to help him to maintain hope.

"My father had told me that this might happen, because he had some enemies in the administration which had ties to the SS."

"This is all you go on? What about the letter from your mother?"

"It is the letter which made me think in that direction. It was much too stilted. She never used in our conversations at home the term 'civil employee'. My father was always a government servant, never an employee. But, the letter reads: 'Civil employee transport'. Another clue is that she did not mention a forwarding address. If she forgot about this, there should have been another letter to let me know how I could contact her. No Karl, I know that there is something wrong."

"These are some pretty self defeating thoughts," said Karl. "We should start examining what we know for certain, and that is that they were not killed by the air attack. This is one good thing. We also know that they were still alive yesterday."

"This does not contradict my theory."

"Well then, let us examine what we don't know. We don't know for sure that there was no other letter. The Sturmman might have missed it. If another letter should turn up, your feelings will change. Tomorrow we will ask where the civilian assembly shelter is located."

"You just want to give me hope, don't you?"

"Yes, I want to give you hope, because there are enough reasons not to think the worst. Tomorrow we will start asking questions; in the meantime Good Night."

Karl's answers were factual enough for Harold to stop his negative thought pattern. He even managed a thin smile. "Thank you, Karl. You are right. Tomorrow is another day." He bunched up the blanket under his face. He liked to fall asleep with his head a bit elevated.

Twenty Five

The next morning started no different from the previous one. The whole city was in a cloud of dust and ashes, which obscured the sun. The Russian artillery was still relentlessly pounding the suburban areas of Berlin and slowly advanced their positions. Inside the bunker, the mess room was quiet. The few SS Officers present were not talking to each other and it looked to Karl as if they had received some distressing orders. Some of them studied a map of the city taped to the wall. When Karl went to inspect it, he saw that it was a street map. He turned to the officer nearest to him and asked, "I am trying to locate the shelter where the government employees are supposed to be. Do you have any idea how far it is from here?"

The officer turned to Karl and recognized him from the meeting last week in the Sturmbannfuehrer's office. He pointed on the map to the Augsburger Strasse, where it crossed the Passauer Strasse. "I don't think that they are there anymore, but this is where they were two days ago."

Karl thanked the Officer and would have liked to ask if he had any idea as to their destination but decided against it. He knew about where the shelter was. It was only a few days ago that he and Harold had been close to it. When they had examined the subway tunnels, he had also checked the ventilation shafts next to the Augsburger Strasse U-Bahn Station and he remembered that the Passauer Strasse was close to it.

He went back to his seat at the table and told Harold about the good news. "I doubt that there was an arrest by the SS. The officer would not have told me about the shelter."

"Good, how soon do you think we can go over there and check things out?"

Karl saw with relief that his friend had recovered from his gloomy attitude of the previous night and was ready to tackle the new day. "We need to see first what the Sturmbannfuehrer has planned for us, and then we take the train to the shelter."

Harold looked all over the room to find another copy of the Voelkischer Beobachter, the official Nazi newspaper. He wanted to double up the wrappings around last night's sandwiches. The original wrappings were soaked from the lard, which during the night had penetrated the bread as well as the newspaper. He was holding a big greasy lump in his hand and he was thankful when one of the officers saw his plight and handed him a few sheets of the latest edition. Karl hoped that the packages would survive in their pockets until noon. He loved to eat the bread when it was soaked and greasy. However, the newspaper wrapping bothered him a little because the printer's ink stuck somehow to the bread. But this was a small price to pay when you had something that good.

Sturmbannfuehrer Bernd had three SS men with him when they entered his office. "This morning, I want you to show these three Rottenfuehrers where the bulkheads to the Landwehrkanal are located. I also would like you to inform them about the exact locations of the third rail at the crossings of Gleisdreieck."

Karl, who usually snapped to the Sturmbannfuehrer orders, walked to the wall map of the U-Bahn system, looked at the three Rottenfuehrers and pointed to the Gleisdreieck station. "As you know, this is the major crossing of the railroad with the S-Bahn (the above ground City trains) and the U-Bahn. It is very confusing and nothing is marked on location. There are stretches without power and the trains roll on until they reach the next hot rail. I will show it to you, however, I strongly advise you to never approach these tracks without either Harold or me to guide you."

When he saw the Sturmbannfuehrer had a questioning look on his face, he added, "It will take more than a short visit and explanation to enable you to safely navigate through this spider web." The expression on the Sturmbannfuehrer's face did not change. Karl's face was getting red when he continued, "This crossing is already dangerous enough above ground with all the different railroad tracks. Furthermore, it is presently congested with supply trains, hospital trains and troop trains. The switches are all electrically controlled. They move substantial lengths of track without warning. If you stand on the wrong side and the switch gets activated, your feet will be trapped. As I said, this is above ground and in daylight. By night or below ground, it is almost impossible to explain or to teach. I suggest we don't even waste the time trying."

"Alright Karl, we understand," said the Sturmbannfuehrer, "but if something happens to you or Harold, we need to function. Please advise."

"Not much to advise," answered Karl. "We are talking about house to house combat in the Gleisdreieck area. City center. At that time the trains will have ceased to move and we can assume that the power will be off. You will be able to enter and defend this area without having to worry about the hot rails. Therefore, no wasteful instructions from Harold or me are needed. I feel that we should concentrate on the other areas of the subway system where we can guide your troops underground behind enemy lines."

"Well stated, Karl, thank you," beamed the officer. "There you have it, gentlemen. I told you that Karl and Harold know what is expected of them. Trust them and imagine what your combat mission might be. Ask your questions accordingly. I expect you back by noon."

It turned out that most of the Rottenfuehrers' questions did not concern the possible attack routes, but centered about the emergency exits. When Karl pointed out that the emergency exits might be blocked by rubble or collapsed buildings and that they might have to crawl through ventilation shafts, their initial enthusiasm faded. "I thought that you would show us secured routes and exits," complained one of them.

"Of course I will show them to you. They are all there, and if you follow us, you will know them as well as Harold and I do. I am just concerned that they might not exist when the circus begins. You will have to know secondary attack routes but don't worry, we will be with you to guide you."

"Thanks," said the Rottenfuehrer, "I think."

They entered the subway system at the Schilling Strasse and spent almost two hours walking the rails. They got used to the passing trains fairly quickly and while Karl pointed out the location of hot rails and switches, Harold directed their attention to the bulkheads next to the Landwehrkanal.

"Will you be carrying Panzerfausts," asked one of the men.

"I might," answered Harold, "it will depend upon our orders."

"Stupid question," he said to Karl when they had a moment for themselves.

"Do they expect that we will do their job? Or what?"

"Let it be. Just formulate your answers to what they want to hear. Their bravado seems to disappear down here. From what I have seen so far, they are already chicken-shit scared and that is just of the darkness. It will be easy for us to lose them and to disappear."

"Do you want to try this right now," asked Harold, "it would be fun to test your idea with this group."

"No," said Karl, "we know already that we are able to do that anytime we want. Now is not the time to raise their suspicion. Let them think that we are fanatical patriots and that they can use us."

"You are right," Harold answered, "let us invite their questions."

There were not many more questions and Karl was signaling to turn around and retrace their steps. His work light shined along the tunnel when he saw a big white chalk mark on one of the walls pointing to a semi hidden ventilation shaft. "Why did you do that?" he asked the group.

"Isn't it obvious," replied the oldest one back. "Suppose the Russians are also in the tunnel and we have to retreat. We will find the exits."

"Yes," said Karl, "and so will the Russians. Matter of fact, you will need to crawl because the shaft is narrow. They will be on top of you before you reach the outside."

"Nonsense," answered the Rottenfuehrer, "the Russians don't carry flashlights; they will not see anything." He pushed Harold, who had started to wipe off the arrow, to the side and aimed his own flashlight at Karl's face. "Look at him," he said to the group, "this boy is afraid to the point of being paranoid and combat has not even started."

Karl, being blinded by the light, shrugged his shoulders and raised his hands to shield his eyes. "Leave the mark, Harold, it is their call. We are just to serve as guides."

"I am glad to hear that you know your place, kid," said the Rottenfuehrer and lowered his light. "I would also appreciate if in the future you would keep your remarks to yourself. You are not in command and don't you ever forget it."

Harold could not keep his mouth shut. "You ever heard of tar torches?"

"If the Russians are carrying torches, we will shoot them that much easier," the SS man informed him.

Harold could not see Karl's face or hands, but he was sure that Karl wanted him to be quiet. The SS men were conferring to either mark the walls or not and decided to wait. They wanted to enter the tunnels later on in the day without the boys and see if they could find their way around without them.

The group was back in the Sturmbannfuehrer's office before noon and the SS men told Officer Bernd that they had wanted to mark the exits and ventilation shafts with chalk and that Karl had interfered. Bernd listened to them and sided with Karl that the arrows might invite the Russians to follow them, but it was their decision to mark or not to mark.

Karl asked if he could leave to check with Harold on the Pfalzburger Strasse School. "Yes, but don't spend any unnecessary time there. I need you two back here," said the Sturmbannfuehrer. Karl was already out of the door when Bernd stopped Harold. "Hold on, Harold, here is another letter for you. One of my men found it when they sorted the other letters that were left behind."

The Sturmbannfuehrer picked up a pile of letters from his desk, searched to find the right one, and handed it to Harold. After a fast 'Thank you' and a flawless salute, Harold stormed by his friend and ran down the hallway to the mess room. The ripped envelope did not make it to the table. It tumbled to the floor where Karl picked it up.

Apparently it was good news. Harold did something like a dance around the room and Karl could see tears of joy running down his face. "They have really been evacuated. They left me a forwarding address. They are alive and well. Karl, Karl, Karl, I am so happy, I am so happy, my parents are alive!" He repeated himself over and over again and waved the letter back and forth. He did not stop running in circles until Karl interrupted him.

"This is indeed great news and I am happy for you. Tell me about your letter on our way to the school."

"To the school? I thought that you wanted to use the time to check out the assembly shelter."

"I did, but now that you received this letter, we don't have to go there. Instead, let's visit the school. I'd like to see if Frau Becker has moved in." He grabbed Harold by the arm and pushed him out of the door.

"How is this letter different from the first one?" He asked when they reached the street.

"This is very different. It is as if my mother is talking to me. It is..." he searched for the right word, "warm and personal, not like the first one at all. And my father has added the address of their destination. You want to read it?" he asked his friend.

"No, you said that it is warm and personal. I am happy to see that you are your old self again."

They used the subway for part of the way and Karl remembered the lard sandwiches. "Why don't we eat while we have the time?" He fumbled to get the package out of his pocket. The lard had leaked through the newspaper and left a stain on the outside of his uniform jacket. He looked over to Harold and saw the same kind of stain. There was nothing they could do about it and they started to peel the newspaper off the bread. The wonderful heavy taste of the lard made up for the few print spots on the bread. Harold liked it so much that he declared that it was the perfect lunch treat.

They were still licking their lips when they started to walk the length of the Pfalzburger Strasse. Karl had a hard time recognizing his old school building. The main building was still standing, but the side building was gone and so were the tall Poplar trees, which had once shaded the schoolyard. Karl had liked the Poplar trees. He had always enjoyed the first fresh green leaves in the springtime. Now the yard was just a hill of broken cement pieces and it looked like the trees had been chopped down for firewood, because there were some stacks of wood piled up in a corner.

The boys found Frau Becker with several volunteer women in one of the classrooms on the ground floor. They had a makeshift kitchen set up and were busy with dispensing blankets to a group of children.

"Any newcomers?" asked Karl.

"No," answered one the women, "these are the ones we were so far unable to place with any families."

Frau Becker chimed in, "We don't expect any new ones because we have been told that there are no more transports coming into Berlin."

Karl nodded in agreement. "Yes, I was told the same thing. No one and nothing is coming in or going out anymore." He went over to her and gave her three packs of cigarettes. "This will give you a start when you need to trade for something. Did you bring me a box of the medicated powder?"

Frau Becker thanked him and reached into one of the many boxes in the room and handed him two small packets. Karl shook her hand. "I don't think that I will be able to come back to see you. I wish you well and...thank you."

Frau Becker went for her pocketbook and handed Karl a small piece of paper. "This is my new address. We moved in with my husband's sister. Our apartment house is off limits due to falling debris. I hope that you will survive the next week and when you do and need a place to stay, look us up. We don't have much room, but you and your friend are always welcome."

Karl and Harold thanked her for the invitation. Harold looked at the address. "I know the location and since we will survive, we will see you there when this is over."

Karl was stuffing the powder packs in his shirt pocket underneath his jacket when he felt the little box from the submarine commander. He had forgotten about it and pushed it out of his mind again. Harold was already a block ahead and was looking at a display case on a movie theater when Karl entered the street. The movie theaters had stopped showing feature films in favor of propaganda and newsreels.

"Hey, Karl, you want to see this," he gestured excitedly to a newsreel advertisement. It showed Adolf Hitler in the courtyard of the Chancellery pinching a little boy's cheek. Harold remembered the boy from a few days ago because he had been standing close to him.

"Where are you," asked Karl looking at the picture.

"I was standing four boys away from this fellow, to the right of him, I think." He studied the other pictures in the showcase. "There I am; this is when Artur Axmann pinned the medal on the guy next to me. I did not know that they took a picture of that."

"They sure took a lot of pictures. Think about it. These newsreels made it out of Berlin and they will be shown in every movie theater in Germany. This means that your parents will see them too."

"Not so sure about that. My parents very seldom go to a movie, but maybe you are right. They might hear about this newsreel and it was my father who was responsible for my invitation."

They were still looking at the pictures when they were rudely interrupted by a two-man SS patrol. "What are you standing around for? Why aren't you with your unit? We need to see your I.D." The smaller one of the two reached for Karl's winter cap and studied the silver eagle. "You are not entitled to carry an eagle on your cap," he announced and began to remove the emblem. In the meantime, Karl had managed to show his credentials to the other SS man.

"Give him his cap back, Franz. This fellow is a special aide to Sturmbannfuehrer Bernd."

"What gives with this eagle? Special aide or not, he is not entitled to wear this emblem." Franz was not impressed by Karl's title. He kept the cap in his hand and continued to remove the eagle. Karl reached in his pocket and handed the older SS man his service book, which identified him as a KLV leader and entitled him to wear the silver eagle.

"Franz, let's go. You don't know with whom you are messing." The taller SS man grabbed the cap from Franz and gave it back to Karl. "Sorry, you have to understand that we have orders to look out for drifters. You should not stand in front of movie theaters." He lifted his hand as if he wanted to salute, but then changed his mind. His eyes traveled to the grease spot on Karl's uniform, which caused him to look at Harold's uniform. It featured the same spot in the same place. He shook his head and grabbed Franz by his arm. "Let's go."

Harold had still not shown his ID when the SS men turned and walked away. Karl refastened the eagle and put the cap back on his head. He looked in the direction of the disappearing SS men. "In a way, we invited their examination."

"Yeah, right" grinned Harold, "they did not even look at me and I am the one in the pictures. I think they did not like you."

Twenty Six

Sturmbannfuehrer Bernd was reading and sorting his last orders when the boys reported back to him. Karl felt he had to mention the incident at the movie house, and he also wanted the Sturmbannfuehrer to know about Harold's decoration. Officer Bernd smiled at Harold and offered his congratulations.

Then his expression changed. "I received several situation updates. The Russians completed their ring around the city and we are now completely on our own. There is no relief available anymore." He pointed to the chairs and motioned the boys to sit. "As of this evening we, the SS, will open some of the warehouses and allow the civilian population to help themselves to whatever there is left. This includes food as well as clothing. After that, there will be no more food rationing. The food supply for the civilians will be down to zero.

"It will get very serious, very fast, because it will be virtually everyone for himself. Special SS commandos will be on the streets to enforce order. There will be also 'Flying Court Marshals'. They are empowered to execute anyone in uniform who is caught retreating with spare ammunition. Uniform means all military units, including the Volkssturm and the HJ."

Officer Bernd stopped long enough to help himself to some coffee from his thermos. "There are some other things you need to be aware of. In order to protect yourself from any misunderstandings, I advise you not to carry any weapons or ammunition when you traverse the tunnels."

"Furthermore, the high command has given the bunker commanders official permission to close the entrances when they are under direct attack. This means that our communication with each other might be interrupted from time to time. You might have completed your mission, but you are unable to return into the bunker. Should this happen, you are still under my command and you are to remain in the tunnels until we open up again. Any questions?"

"Not at this time, Herr Sturmbannfuehrer," answered Harold.

Karl focused his eyes on a spot on the wall, as he always did when he was unsure of what to say. "Karl?" asked the officer.

"Herr Sturmbannfuehrer, permission to talk freely?"

"Permission granted."

Karl was still not sure how to formulate his thoughts. "Herr Sturmbannfuehrer, we need your advice without sounding scared. You said that the bunker is going to be closed when under direct attack. How long are we supposed to stand down and wait for your orders, which might never come when we are overrun?" Karl got up and stood in front of the Officer's desk. "No, this did not sound or come out right, did it?"

The Officer took his time answering, "Sit down, Karl, yes it did not come out right, but I think I know what you mean. I am unable to give you personal advice. But, I can make a statement. Let me put it this way; you are a subway rat, and no self-respecting rat would ever be caught in a labyrinth which features exits."

He got up and his eyes met the eyes of Karl and Harold. "Stand by in the mess for your further orders. Dismissed."

The mess was empty, as it was already past 8:00 PM, but there was still the ever-present pot of soup simmering on a hot plate. The boys helped themselves to a bowl and looked for the bread. There was some left from the day before, and it still tasted great.

Harold was the first to speak, "I take it that he thinks of us as self-respecting rats."

"Self-respecting rats...which will not get caught," corrected Karl. He was holding his cap in his hand and began to remove the silver eagle.

"What are you doing," asked Harold.

"Are you blind? I will also remove my shoulder rope identifying me as a sniper. You heard that we are under the direct command of the Sturmbannfuehrer and that we are to remain in the subway tunnels. I don't know about you, but I don't need any more emblems or insignias. I will turn into a regular rat, indistinguishable from other regular rats."

Karl had succeeded to do away with the eagle, and replaced it with the regular HJ emblem, which he had carried on the inside of his cap. He took off his jacket, removed the shoulder rope and inspected the shiny greasy spot outside the side pocket. It really started to bother him. His father had taught him the first rules of self-respect, and they included keeping his clothing clean and immaculate. Lately it had been difficult to follow these rules, but it was reasonably doable. The only real problem he had was with his shoelaces. The rules of the HJ dictated that the laces extending from the bow had to be of equal lengths; meaning that the right shoelaces had to be equal in length to the left ones. This was easy enough to do when you had new shoelaces available. But this was not the case anymore, and to top it off, his shoelaces had been worn thin and he had finally ripped one in half. His left shoe now sported an extremely short lace while the other one was still within regulation length. He had shrugged it off as another minor casualty of the 'Total War'.

But, the grease spot on his jacket was something else. For him, it was intolerable. He looked around to find some regular writing paper. A napkin would have been better, but paper would do. He finally spotted a piece of cardboard on top of a garbage can. Harold looked on in amazement as Karl took the cardboard and rolled it back and forth over the edge of the table until it became soft and smooth. He laid out the jacket on the table and placed the cardboard over the grease spot. Then he heated up the blade from his Fahrtenmesser (HJ knife) on the electric hot blade. While he carefully heated the cardboard with the blade from his knife, the grease from his uniform melted and transferred over to the cardboard. He repeated this several times and moved the cardboard around until he was satisfied with the result. It was not nearly as good as it would have been with some ink blotter paper, or some old piece of flannel clothing. He had even singed the wool of the jacket, but the grease spot was now barely visible.

"You are a damned neat freak, that's what you are." Harold exclaimed. "Next thing is that you will be looking for your mother or some woman to iron the crease in your pants."

"My mother could never do it good enough for me," informed Karl, "I always ironed the pants myself. And also my shirts," he added.

Somehow this did not track with Harold. "Tell me, how do you live with yourself?"

"You know what," asked Karl, "I wonder the same about you. Give me your jacket."

"Don't you dare!" Harold wanted no part of this and moved to the far end of the table. The door opened and Officer Bernd entered the room. He sniffed the air, which carried a strong odor of hot pig grease and burnt wool. "There is definitely something wrong with the ventilation system," he remarked and filled his thermos with hot coffee. "Get ready to guide a platoon of six SS men to the bulkheads by the Landwehrkanal. You will leave in ten minutes and meet them at the Anhalter Station. No need to wake me when you come back. I expect your report tomorrow morning."

"What now, Karl? You always look like you want to ask a question." The officer wrinkled his nose and was apparently not in a good mood.

"Yes, Herr Sturmbannfuehrer. If I may, is this platoon carrying equipment or something? If it is, do you want it stored in one of the supply sheds close to the bulkheads, or directly at the bulkheads?" Karl slipped into his jacket. His face was a big question mark.

"Good thinking. Whatever they are transporting, pile it up in the nearest storage room."

As Karl advanced to the door, Bernd took a step backward and sniffed in Karl's direction. "God so help me. You have been too long in this room. Get going. You need some fresh air." He almost ran back to his office.

"Neat freak," grunted Harold as he passed Karl. "You almost poisoned our commanding Officer."

When the boys reached the outside, they expected it to be dark. But the huge fires ignited in the outskirts by the four day battering from the Russian artillery shed a sinister glow over the inner city. The inside of the subway station was filled to capacity. Even the trains were packed and Karl suspected that many of the civilians had adopted the running trains as a refuge. He listened to the rumors, which agreed that the fight for the inner city had started. Everyone had a different version to tell. Some told of infantry units fighting three miles from the chancellery, and others of reinforcements from Stettin.

When the train reached the Anhalter Station, they found the SS platoon waiting for them. It consisted of five Sturmman with large, heavy backpacks at their feet and one Rottenfuehrer who introduced himself as Richard Stein.

"How far do we have to go," asked Stein.

"About one kilometer, maybe a little less," informed Karl.

The Rottenfuehrer pointed to a wooden box behind him, "I might need some help with this." Harold grabbed at one of the handles to estimate the weight. It was heavier than it looked and he understood Stein's question. While it was easy to carry for a short distance, it would get heavier along the way. "You lead," he motioned to Karl, "I will help the Rottenfuehrer."

Karl looked at the box and estimated that it was too large to pass through some of the narrow passages between the trains and the walls. However, it might work if the men would be able to sit it down every time a train was passing. But, this would make for some awkward transportation. He consulted his watch and compared the time with the large clock in the center of the station. "Sit down on your packs. In another hour the train schedule will slow down to 40-minute intervals. We will enter the tunnel as soon as the first train of the night schedule leaves. This way we will be at our destination before the next train passes. He could see that Stein relaxed. He must have been worried about transporting his cumbersome crate.

The Rottenfuehrer padded his pockets, searched through his pants pockets and came up with an empty pack of cigarettes. In a helpless gesture he was about to toss the package between the rails when Karl stopped him. "Let me have that." He offered Stein and the other soldiers a cigarette from his own package and then stuffed some more in the empty pack. "Enjoy," and he flipped the box back to Stein.

As the cigarette smoke drifted to the next civilians, Karl could almost feel the resentment towards the smoking SS men. He got up and handed an old invalid his last cigarettes. "Please share them."

Harold followed his example and divided a pack of tobacco between the men in the crowd. Since Karl did not smoke, he could not understand the need of smokers and marveled at the instant change in attitude towards them. Miracle sticks, he thought to himself. I'll be damned if I ever get hooked on them.

The last train of the daytime schedule arrived, but hardly anyone got on or off. The train left the station and Karl got up to lead his group into the tunnel. The noise and cheering of the civilians behind them faded away.

"I think we started another rumor," said Harold, but no one heard him. Karl crossed the tracks a few times, advising the group where to step. They reached the first steel partition within fifteen minutes, and Karl stopped to point it out. "I'll show you the nearest tool shed where you can store your stuff," he announced and kept on walking.

"Halt. We have orders to assemble explosives at this site and also at the following bulkheads. Nobody told us to store anything," said the Rottenfuehrer, and he took a large battery operated work light out of the crate and started to rummage around in the box until Karl interrupted him.

"I have orders to show you a place where you are able to hide these devices."

"This is nice of you, Karl, and you can show us the place if you wish, but we need to follow our own orders."

"You cannot set up the explosives at this time; it is far too early in the game." Karl's tone was not pleading anymore but more like demanding.

"Karl, you cannot stop us, but I'd like to know why you are turning against us?"

"I am not turning against you, but the battle for the city center might never develop. When the high command sees that all is lost they might surrender before they order the destruction of our city."

"You are dreaming and hoping. Let me tell you that we will never surrender. Hitler's orders are 'Scorched Earth', and scorched earth it will be."

Harold tried to help his friend. "There is a hospital train parked within two kilometers of here. If you blow these bulkheads, the patients will drown."

"We don't blow up anything," one of the Sturmman chimed in, "We are technicians. We only set up the charges and the timers. The actual implementation is not our job." He talked while he connected a timer to one of the backpacks.

"Where will you be when this happens," asked Karl.

"I don't know," it sounded as if the answer came from both SS men at the same time.

"That's right. You don't know. Let's hope that you are not one of the patients in the train. Let's go back, Harold, we did our job." He started to walk, but stopped when the Rottenfuehrer grabbed on to his arm.

"Wrong direction, you still need to guide us to two more bulkheads."

"Follow me," Karl said and walked in the original direction. One of the SS men stayed back, strapping the backpack to the levers in the frontal opening of the steel gate.

They did not have to walk very far. The next steel separations to the Landwehrkanal were close to each other and it turned out that the group carried more explosives than they needed.

"We go back and double-up on the charges," announced Stein. "You can leave us alone now. We will find our way back."

"No, you won't remember where we crossed the hot rails," said Karl. "We don't want to be responsible if you trip up on them. We wait."

He suddenly pressed the Rottenfuehrer's chest against the wall and hollered to the group, "I hear a train coming, get down or stand straight against the wall!"

"Thank you," stammered Stein after the train had passed.

"Think nothing of it," muttered Karl, "my orders are to guide you. Do you wish to see where the hospital train is parked?"

"You don't give up, do you," asked Stein.

"Don't tempt me. You don't know how close I am," garbled Karl, and then louder in the direction to the group, "Are you done?" There was no answer.

It was well over thirty minutes until the last of the technicians reported back to the Rottenfuehrer. "Ready," said Stein, and Harold took the lead on the way back. They parted company in the Anhalter Subway Station and wished each other well.

"So, we were right all along. The SS wants to flood the tunnels," said Harold on the way between the subway station Friedrichshain and the Friedrichshain Bunker.

"Yes, and I doubt that the Wehrmacht knows anything about it," added Karl and pointed to the red sky. "You would think that it is enough what the Russians do to us. I simply cannot understand why we want to add to this and destroy our own transportation system." He stopped walking and listened intently to the noise in the air.

"Did you hear that howling sound?"

"You mean the whistle and then the howling?" Asked Harold.

"There it is again." This time the sound seemed to come from a different direction.

"It must be the Stalinorgel (Katyusha). I have never actually heard them, but this is not artillery. They must be still far away." Karl listened again but the awful sound was gone.

The boys broke into a run, crossed the street, and did not stop until they were inside the bunker. "What's your hurry," asked the SS guard on duty.

"We think that we heard the Stalinorgel," said Harold.

"Nonsense, the Russian line is still over five kilometers away. You must be mistaken." The SS guard was surprised by the frightened expression in Harold's face.

"Believe me, this sound will scare you too," said Karl, and went after Harold to the staircase. The Sturmman laughed and went outside to listen. He did not hear anything other than the pounding of the artillery. When he came back in, the boys were gone.

"What is a Stalinorgel," asked Harold when they reached their sleeping quarters.

"I don't know exactly. I heard that the explosives are rocket propelled. They are fired in bunches of four or six, I think. The rocket engines cause the terrible sound. I even heard that the Russians made recordings of it and then played it back over loudspeakers before they attacked Warschau. The purpose was to demoralize us. We should ask Officer Bernd about it."

It was almost 5:00 AM by the time Karl found some sleep. Three hours later, they stood in front of Sturmbannfuehrer Bernd's desk and reported about their mission with the SS detail.

"I was afraid that they were placing explosives," said Officer Bernd. "The high command only told me to assure that the SS commandos had access and guidance to the subway system." He pushed himself away from the desk and walked to the wall with the U-Bahn map, which was dotted with pins and little flags. His face seemed to have aged during the last night and his uniform was wrinkled. He looked like he had slept at his desk. "I was ordered to a briefing at the Fuehrer's bunker last night and it was utter chaos." He walked back to his desk and turned around to face the boys. "I tell you this because I might get replaced or arrested at any moment, and I have become fond of you and I want you to survive." He took his time talking, and Karl could see that the officer was choosing carefully what he wanted to convey.

"Like many of us in the officer corps, and maybe you too, I had thought that the Americans would team up with us to fight the

Russians. This will not be the case. We know now that the Western Allies have reached the Elbe River and General Eisenhower has ordered them to stand down. Most, if not all, of our own western division surrendered to them without a fight.

"All of our eastern division have been destroyed or splintered up and at this time we have less than 60,000 men to defend the inner city. This includes the Volkssturm." He looked deeply into the eyes of the boys. "All of the available Panzerfaust weapons have been issued to the HJ. The few HJ units which are left are now under the command of the SS and ordered to defend against the tanks. Hitler's orders of the 'Scorched Earth' includes the destruction of every bridge, government building, bank building, even our prized museums; actually, anything of value to the enemy. But it does not stop there. He also wants everyone who is able to carry a weapon to fight 'til his last breath'. Surrender is out of question. All he wants the Russians to find is scorched earth." Bernd stopped and wiped his forehead. "The few officers who openly objected were immediately arrested." Again he wiped the sweat from his forehead. "I fear they have been already executed."

Karl was the first one to break the silence. "If we destroy everything of value, what is there left for the survivors to live for?"

"Nothing," answered the officer. "Hitler does not want any survivors."

Karl needed a while to digest the answer. "What did you do to think that you would get arrested too?"

"I did not do anything, at least not last night during the briefing. But everyone knows that I always objected to the willful destruction of our city. I think the only reason that I am still alive is the also well-known fact that I am a loyal officer, and we are short of officers."

"Is there not a difference between loyal and fanatical?" Karl wanted to know.

"Yes, Karl, there is, and this is why I fear that I will get arrested. Everyone knows who is a fanatic and I am not one of them." The Sturmbannfuehrer sat down again. His voice was almost toneless. "I will not leave the bunker anymore. If you don't find me when you return from your missions, it means that you have to follow my over-riding order and that is to stay alive. It is much better to live for yourself than to die for someone's idea."

"Thank you, Herr Sturmbannfuehrer, for confiding in us. Please be assured that we will obey your order." Harold got up and pulled

Karl with him. The boys wanted to salute, more out of habit than out of conviction, but like most of the time, the officer waved them to leave.

Twenty Seven

The room was busier than the last few days and the boys had to wait until they found a table to eat their breakfast. Not much of a choice, dark rye bread with honey ersatz and hot coffee.

"Have you seen those guys before?" Harold motioned with his head towards a corner table, occupied by three SS Police Officers.

"No," said Karl, "take your bread and let's get out of here." He pushed his chair back and left without waiting for Harold to follow.

"What got into you," asked Harold when he caught up.

"Nothing, it is just that these guys with their metal shields across their chests give me the creeps. I don't want to be around them. Did you see their boots?"

"Well, I could see that they were not barefoot. What about their boots?"

"Harold, it is time that you become more observant. Their boots were not only spit-shined, they were also brand new. And there are no brand new boots available." Karl had turned the corner towards the staircase. He wanted to go down to the entrance to see if Fritz had any better food for them. Harold was right behind him. "So, what about it? Where do you think they obtained the boots?"

"Only one possibility. They must have either cleared or ransacked a warehouse. You know about warehouses. Any idea where footwear might have been stored?"

"No, sorry. I only remember that my father told me about a general merchandise warehouse and this was, I think, near the Hallesches Tor. Let's ask Fritz, maybe he knows."

Fritz was at his usual place and was hiding a small can of Braunschweiger wurst under his heavy coat. "This is all I could get you for your cigarettes," he told them. "You have a better chance than I do. You are allowed to roam around."

"Any idea how the SS Police got their new boots," asked Karl.

"They got new boots? I could surely use some myself." Fritz lifted his right boot and the boys could see that the sole was paper-thin. It had even a small hole on the side.

"Maybe you can ask them when they leave the bunker," suggested Harold, as he followed Karl back to the staircase. "What do you intend to do with the can of wurst?" He wanted to know.

"I will see the Sturmbannfuehrer to ask about our orders. You go to the mess and get some bread. We'll make a sandwich and we eat it right away. I am hungry. The artificial honey doesn't cut it."

Sturmbannfuehrer Bernd had been sleeping in his chair when Karl entered the office. He had knocked on the door and when there was no answer, he had slowly opened it to glance around. "Come in Karl. Get a rest for two more hours and then I want you to inspect the situation in Gleisdreieck. Take Harold along. I need an estimate of how many civilians are below ground. I also need to know if the hospital trains between here and there have been moved and where they are now. Come back as soon as you have the answers."

Karl went back to the mess. He was passed by the SS Police detail, which stopped in front of Officer Bernd's office. To his relief, he heard them rapping on the door and figured if they had come to arrest his Sturmbannfuehrer, they would have not bothered to knock.

The boys had just finished their wurst bread and were ready to lie down on their cots when a runner summoned them to the Sturmbannfuehrer's office.

"These are my subway aides, Karl and Harold," he introduced them to the policemen who said nothing. Karl saw that one of them was an Oberscharfuehrer, an equivalent rank to his own, but the SS, and especially the SS Police, outranked the HJ. The other ones were regular SS Policemen.

"Please guide this unit through the tunnels to the Gleisdreieck Station. Their mission is to search and identi..."

"Never mind what our mission is," interrupted the Oberscharfuehrer, "as long as they understand theirs. Where are their weapons?"

"I ordered them not to carry any weapons on this mission. They need to be fast and unencumbered because after they guide you to your destination, I need them back here as soon as possible."

The Oberscharfuehrer was not satisfied with the answer. "Our Fuehrer, Adolf Hitler, declared 'Total War'. You have two able HJ members under your command and you ordered them not to carry any weapons?" He turned to one of his men. "Make a note of that, Dettleff."

"Just a moment," interrupted the Sturmbannfuehrer, "put that notebook away." His voice was hard as steel. "Now listen to me, Oberscharfuehrer, and stand at attention when I address you. As a courtesy to you, I offer you my aides. However, they are under my command and they stay under my command. On this mission to guide you underground to Gleisdreieck, they don't need to carry weapons. They are not engaging an enemy. They are temporarily your guides and I don't think that you need any protection. If you think you do, get your own reinforcements.

"You can leave without them or I order them to guide you. However, under no circumstances whatsoever, will they be under your command. You have exactly twenty seconds to decide." The policemen looked at each other and accepted the offer.

The group crossed the street with Harold leading and Karl staying between the Oberscharfuehrer and Dettleff. As soon as they entered the subway station, Karl recognized what the purpose of the police mission was. They were looking for deserters and started to I.D. the civilians.

This could take hours until we reach Gleisdreieck, he thought. "Why don't we proceed through the tunnel? No runaway is crazy enough to stay in the station across from the bunker. However, once you reach Gleisdreieck, you will see all kinds of fugitives."

The Oberscharfuehrer was annoyed by Karl's suggestion, but then he reconsidered and asked, "Do you mean in the tunnel under the station or in the rail road station above?"

"I think that you would find more in the station above ground." Karl wanted to spend as little time as possible with the detail and he wanted them out of the tunnel. As far as he was concerned, this was his and Harold's tunnel and he did not like the idea of showing the SS Police a safe way among the hot rails.

The Oberscharfuehrer reevaluated again. He was up for promotion and the more deserters he caught, the better his chances were. "We take the train to Gleisdreieck," he announced to the group.

"Karl will show us how to work our way between the upper and the lower stations."

"Good Idea," agreed Dettleff, "I don't like to be in the tunnels anyway. Which train do we need to take?" He looked from one side of the platform to the other, not sure which direction the trains were running. He spoke with a northern German farmer's dialect and Karl had the impression that this might be the first time that the policeman was in a subway station, because he looked exceedingly uncomfortable.

"We will take this one," said Harold, and pointed to an approaching train.

As soon as they reached Gleisdreieck, Karl took over and directed the attention of the group to the location of the heavy switches and the crossings of the S-Bahn (City trains) with the railroad tracks. Harold caught on to what Karl was doing and explained in great detail where the hot rails from the U-Bahn ended and started.

Strangely enough, the SS policemen were so concerned with their own safety that they did not notice what the boys were doing. "Enough already!" exclaimed the Rottenfuehrer after listening for the third time to Harold about the tricks of avoiding the hot rails. "We will never remember even a fraction of what you are telling us. This is more confusing than helpful. We now know enough and we are where we want to be. You are dismissed." He left the boys standing on the bottom of the stairway to the upper platform and disappeared with his men in the crowd.

"That went pretty smooth. Let's find the hospital train." Karl was just as eager as the SS men to get away from each other.

"You were so dedicated and concerned about their safety that you forgot to ask them about their boots." Harold grinned and stepped to the side to avoid a kick from Karl aimed at his lower leg.

The hospital train, which was parked a week ago on a spare rail on an elevated section of the U-Bahn, had been moved. It would take them hours to look for it and they still might miss it. There were too many possibilities of where it could be. If it would have been parked on any other station, they could have split up and searched in the opposite directions, but not here at the cross roads of the major train routes. "Let's find the stationmaster; he might be able to help us." Karl decided to keep their time above ground and away from the bunker to a bare minimum.

He had good reason to do so. The Russian infantry had moved through the suburban area and was heavily engaged with the retreating Wehrmacht units in street-to-street fighting. The Russian artillery had been moved forward and was now shelling the inner city. There were fires and exploding shells all around them.

"The hospital train was moved in the tunnel towards the Anhalter Bahnhof Station. It is parked on a side rail," the stationmaster told them when they finally located him.

"Can you estimate how many civilians are presently in your station?" Harold wanted to know.

'It could have been around 8,000, but this was yesterday. Today we are in the process of shutting down and suspending all train traffic."

The boys were suddenly aware that their relative safety had disappeared. They were within minutes of the combat zone and had to get back to the bunker. Harold did not need any encouragement. He knew they had to run. Karl was next to him when they reached a departing train in the direction of Friedrichshain. The train was filled to capacity and the boys had to press and push to avoid being trapped in the self-closing doors. The train stopped at the next station but nobody got on or off, and the doors closed again. They made it within one station before Friedrichshain.

The train came to a halt in the middle of the tunnel. First the lights went out, and then the train rolled along without power until it finally came to a stop.

The doors stayed closed but were not locked. The power failure must have triggered a failsafe switch. Harold was the first to leap off the train. Karl wanted to follow but was held back by screaming passengers. "Don't jump! You will get electrocuted!"

"How can that be?" he shouted back. "The power is out!" He freed himself and jumped down. Harold had waited for him and was now running beside him. They had only their small dynamo flashlights, but the beams were enough to keep them moving at a pretty good clip.

That was until they ran into a bunch of people who had spilled over from the Friedrichshain station. They reached the platform, which was swarming with civilians. It was barely illuminated from some emergency lights. Harold barreled ahead and in his effort, must have stepped on a few feet or some people because Karl could hear screaming and cursing coming from his direction. They made the exit and stopped when they reached the street level. There were no exploding shells nearby, however. they could hear them whistling nonstop overhead. The bunker doors were still wide open, but it took a lot of effort to get through the crowd and to the staircase.

Sturmbannfuehrer Bernd looked more rested than in the morning and he listened to the Karl's report without interrupting. "Our phone lines don't work and we will have to rely on communication runners for the time being. I want you to sleep in alternating shifts so we have at least one of you rested up when we need you. Dismissed."

The boys went back to the mess and found out that the kitchen suspended their service. There was a small sign on the door that read 'Out of service'. No explanation if there was no food available or a shortage of helpers.

"I suspect that there is sufficient food in the bunker and that the cook has been assigned to flak duty," speculated Harold. "Are you able to sleep right now? I doubt that I can sleep and I am willing to take the first shift."

"You need to sleep when you have a chance to do so," said Karl. "Go ahead and take the first shift. I can sleep whenever and wherever I want to." He went to their quarters and while he was sleeping, Harold was summoned for emergency aid duty. Most of the wounded coming into the bunker suffered from minor injuries. The severely wounded were transported to temporary emergency treatment centers, with the nearest being one block away from the bunker. The next one was in the district of Charlottenburg.

The regular hospitals were unable to keep up with the onslaught of patients. Their hallways were filled with hospital beds and folding cots stacked on top of each other. The medical staff worked like Karl and Harold in alternating shifts. The worst injuries were most of the time fatal burn injuries. They were generally caused by the flamethrowers.

Karl relieved Harold in the evening and took over the night shift. When the morning came, it was impossible to know if there was an actual frontline.

The Russian spearheads of tanks had done their job and bewildered the defense line of the Wehrmacht. Karl had observed during his nightshift that the medical station of the bunker was running low on pain medication. He had dared to make a visit to the treatment center next to the bunker only to learn that they were equally running low. After Harold took his shift, Karl went to the Sturmbannfuehrer to volunteer for a trip to the Zoo Bunker hospital to see if he could obtain some medical supplies.

"I am unable to call them and we don't know if they have anything to spare. I hope that you don't make the trip for nothing," said Officer Bernd when he gave him the permission.

Karl went to find Harold who was not too happy about his friend's idea. "You must be tired. You worked the whole night. Let me get permission and you stay here."

"Yeah, the medical supply is the foremost on my mind, but I would also like to try and get us some food. It is now over 24 hours that we had anything to eat and I am getting hungry." Before Harold could think of another objection Karl was gone. So far there had been no fighting in the vicinity of the Friedrichshain Bunker, but he figured that he was safer underground and walked as fast along the tracks of the U-Bahn as he could. He passed some trains, which stood empty on the tracks, and he speculated briefly where the passengers might be when the pain in his stomach reminded him that they must have been hungry too.

When he passed the platforms of the stations, he saw that they were still filled to capacity. He reached the Zoo Bunker in record time, but was unable to locate Dr. Felder. Nobody else was in authority to assist him with his plea for medical supplies. He was about to give up when an idea struck him and he started to ask for Corporal Kurt Halder. Within a few minutes, he was able to find him. Kurt was working in the ammunition elevator shaft. His hands were greasy and Karl had forgotten how big they were. Kurt greeted him like a long lost brother and listened to Karl's complaint that he could not find Dr. Felder.

"I don't believe that you came all the way to visit with the captain. What is it that you want from him?"

Karl told him about the shortage of pain medication.

"Pain medication, I understand. What else?"

"Well, yes I can use something to eat."

"Wait right here in the elevator. I'll be right back." Kurt took off and Karl sat down on a toolbox, closed his eyes and was sound asleep when the Corporal returned.

"I have about thirty pounds of medication, but only one small box of Knaeckebrot. Do you have transportation?"

"No," said Karl, "I was hoping that you could help me. Otherwise

I carry it in a backpack if you can get me one."

"No medication, no transportation, no backpack, oh I almost forgot, no food," he shook his huge head, "I understand, let's go." He grabbed Karl by his shoulders and pushed him out of the elevator shaft. "Follow me," he marched ahead to the underground garage, which was filled with fully loaded ammunition trucks and various other vehicles. "Wait," he opened the door to a Kubelwagen and motioned Karl to sit in it. Shortly thereafter Kurt reappeared with a cart and several boxes, which he loaded in the back of the car. Being his usual self, he was already in second gear when they went through the open garage door and passed the guard who jumped aside the moment he recognized who was driving the car.

"Do you know where Dr, Felder is, or might be?" asked Karl over the noise of the crackling artillery shells.

"Yes." was the short answer.

"Well, where?"

"He worked so many shifts without relief that he finally passed out. I carried him out and I am hiding him in the back of my truck until he finished sleeping it off."

Without really thinking about it, Karl turned momentarily around and glanced at the rear of the car. Kurt came to a stop in front of the Friedrichshain Bunker and shook his head again. "I thought that Harold was the slow one." He helped Karl to carry the few boxes beyond the doors and handed him the box with Knaeckebrot. "I will tell the captain that you asked for him," and he took off before Karl finished thanking him.

Twenty Eight

Karl did not trust Fritz to guard the pain medication. Instead, he asked him to send for Harold. In the meantime, he sat on the boxes and was almost asleep again when Harold arrived and helped him to carry the cartons up to the Sturmbannfuehrer's office.

"Well done, Karl, the wounded will be very thankful." Officer Bernd was glad to have Karl back in his fold. He looked at the Knaeckebrot in Karl's hand but did not ask any questions. "See to it that you get some rest."

It was not until 2:00 AM next morning that the boys were summoned back to the Sturmbannfuehrer's office. "We have confirmed that some of our remaining tanks stopped the Russian infantry from crossing the Moltke Bridge. We want to insert one of our roll commandos (assault team) to re-secure the bridgehead. What would be our chances of getting the commandos behind the Russians?" He looked expectantly at Karl.

"How many soldiers in your roll commando?" asked Harold while Karl studied the wall chart.

"Normally 35, but we would like to double that number," answered the officer.

"No problem to get behind them, or among them, if we exit through this ventilation shaft." Karl pointed to one of the little flags on the chart. "The exit gate at this location is next to the entrance of a large housing block, which extends all the way to the bridge." Karl looked once more at the other nearby flags on the chart.

"Any second thoughts, Karl?" asked the Wehrmacht Officer who was already in the room when the boys entered. "I will be leading the assault commando. Our lives depend upon your local knowledge."

"No second thoughts, Herr..." Karl was looking at the officer's uniform to ascertain his rank and when he saw that the shoulder bars had been removed from the uniform, he continued, "The housing block will give us the cover we need to exit. Before you commit your commando, I will get up and see if we are clear and get out of your way. The success will depend upon the speed of your troops to exit the shaft." He wanted to add that it would also depend on whether the Russians had flamethrowers nearby, but decided to wait until they were on location.

"Ready to go?" asked Harold

"Wait," Karl turned to the officer, "What weapons are you carrying? You will not be able to crawl through the ventilation shafts with heavy machine guns."

"Hand grenades and light machine guns," answered the officer.

"Good, we are ready when you are." Karl opened the door for the officer to exit and motioned to Harold to pass. He stood for moment in the doorframe, waiting for some possible additional instructions from the Sturmbannfuehrer and when none came, he saluted and left the office.

"Where are your troops?" He asked the officer who had identified himself as a Lieutenant to the boys.

"Across the street; in the subway station."

When the group left the bunker, Harold stopped and looked up. There was nothing to see except low clouds reflecting with an eerie glow from the fires around them. It was the screaming and whistling sounds of the Stalinorgels that made him look up. The frightening and reverberating noise made his hair stand up, not only on his head, but on his skin as well.

"How far away are these rockets," he asked the Lieutenant.

"Far enough not to worry," answered the officer.

"Not to worry; how do you know?"

"Simple, the rockets travel so fast that they hit you before you hear them therefore, as long as you hear them they are traveling elsewhere."

"Thanks for the assurance; not very convincing. Let's run for it."

The Lieutenant wanted to answer, but the boys already sprinted towards the subway entrance. The station's emergency lights barely illuminated the mass of shelter-seeking civilians. The soldiers of the assault team were standing in clusters around several sergeants who came to attention when the Lieutenant appeared. Karl told Harold to bring up the rear in case someone stayed behind and entered the tunnel. He encountered a problem right away, which he had somehow missed and not considered. Since he had a small dynamo flashlight, he could illuminate the rails and walk at a fast pace along the tracks without bouncing into the walls but with six or seven men behind him, it was pitch dark and this slowed his group considerably. He stopped and waited for Harold to come within shouting distance.

"You take the lead, Harold. Walk slow enough to keep the commandos together. I will run ahead to the nearest storage shed and get us the tar torches we saw last week." He turned to the two soldiers who had kept pace with him before. "Follow me." He took off at a fast clip and the two soldiers had no problem keeping up with him.

They passed a partially deserted train, which had stalled when the power went out. As he passed by, he flashed his light up to the windows of the train, but was unable to determine how many people were hiding. He knew they were there because he could see some through the open doors. When he came upon the storage room, he could see that someone had tried unsuccessfully to break down the door. It must have been people seeking additional shelter or wanting to find out if there were any useable supplies.

His strange key did the job. The torches were in the box just as he remembered them and he passed a bundle to the first soldier who had entered the room with him.

The next soldier received a likewise bundle and as Harold's column reached the shed, the torches were already lit and laying on the ground ready to be picked up as the group passed. The torches had been stored to provide emergency lightning in case of a power failure and illuminated a much larger area than Karl had anticipated. The Lieutenant gave Harold a pat on the back.

"This will help. You guys are great," and he hurried after Karl, who was again rushing ahead. Harold waited until the last soldier had passed and extinguished the remaining unneeded flares. He left them on the ground next to the door, which he locked again. He was just as surprised as Karl at the great illumination the torches provided and put his flashlight back in his pocket.

The assault commandos reached their destination in less than an hour and when Karl climbed into the ventilation shaft, they stubbed out the torches and sat on the ground to rest. While the noise of the fighting above permeated the tunnel, it was extremely louder as Karl neared the exit grate.

It was one of the exits he liked because of the wider opening. He huddled under the opening to listen. There was no shooting nearby, but he could hear extensive gunfire in the distance. Otherwise, he could only hear from time to time, the howling of the Katyusha rockets.

Karl rechecked in his mind what the Sturmbannfuehrer had told him about the Russian's position at the bridge. Accordingly, he had chosen this exit and he should be behind their lines. The grate was left unlocked from his previous visit and he tried to lift and shift the grate out of the grooves holding it in place, but it did not move.

"Let me do it," he heard the Lieutenant behind him.

"We do it together, but you stay down while I investigate." Karl moved over just enough so that the Lieutenant was able to help him. This time the steel frame moved and Karl stuck his head out to look around. Since it was still nighttime, it was difficult to see very far. He did see, however, that he had been right about the location of this particular shaft. The exit was right alongside the apartment building.

He double-checked the vicinity and then crawled out, keeping himself next to the structure's wall. He reached the main entrance to the building, which was only a few feet away. Its huge double-doors stood open, wide enough to allow a car to pass through to the courtyard. The rear building across the demolished yard was halfway gone and still burning. He could see that the staircase in the front building seemed to be still useable. Karl waited and listened for a few minutes to make sure that no one was around. When he was sure that he was alone, he slowly moved back to the shaft.

"Go down," he whispered to the waiting Lieutenant and edged himself through the half open grate. "It's all clear. You should have no trouble getting your men out."

"Thank you, Karl. Any suggestions?" Ever since Karl had handed out the torches he was impressed enough not to be above asking for counsel.

"If I were commanding an HJ detail, I would move two of my men with a machine gun to the building's entrance to provide cover for the group. But you know more about combat tactics than I do."

"Right, I do," agreed the Lieutenant. He went to the bottom of the shaft and conferred with his sergeants. Two of them would be the first to move out and to provide the cover. He would then be the first one to follow and then his men and the last ones would be the remaining sergeants.

"Thanks boys, wish us luck. You can return to the bunker any time after the last of my men is in the open."

Karl stepped next to Harold and watched in awe how fast the assault team left the tunnel. He wanted to follow them to close the entrance when Harold stepped in front of him. "My turn. It would take you forever to pull the cover back in position," and he climbed up.

Karl had no problem with that. He knew that Harold was a lot stronger than he was. After Harold came down, they waited a minute to hear if their group had engaged the Russians and when they did not hear anything, they started back. When they reported back to the Sturmbannfuehrer, he had another assignment waiting for them. Actually, it was the same mission as before, except this time they were guiding about 200 men under the command of an older corporal. By the time they had reached the infiltration point, it was daylight.

Harold had taken point at the exit. He was slowly lifting the grate and scanning the street when he saw a Russian tank in the entranceway of the building they wanted to get into. It was a T34 and did not move. It just sat there. It was a frightening moment because he did not know if he had been detected. The tank had a machine gun mounted on top with a protective shield and a gunner lying prone behind it. This meant that this tank was not part of a spearhead. It was a component of the actual combat force. Harold knew the difference because the corporal in charge of the infiltration platoon had told him that the regular T34's could not elevate their cannons sufficiently to wipe out units on rooftops of the apartment houses. Nor could it fire into nearby cellar windows. It could destroy the whole building of course, but this was not an option when the Russian infantry was advancing through the settlement complex. They had solved the problem with the gunner on top of the tank.

Harold took care to move the exit grate slowly back into position. "What do you want to do," he asked the corporal after he had reported to him the location of the tank.

"Step aside and let me take a look," said Karl, who wanted to see for himself before he would suggest abandoning this exit and moving the unit closer to the bridge.

"No," the corporal intervened, "we will take the tank out." He asked his sergeant behind him to hand him a Panzerfaust.

"We only have two of them," the sergeant informed him. "We can call for an HJ unit. They have the training and carry plenty of them."

"Training," answered the corporal, "you mean they have more guts and I will not have boys doing my job."

He must have moved the grate too fast or too high, because the Russian machine gun opened up and sprayed the exit. Little pieces of shrapnel found their way into the shaft. The corporal waited until the gunner had to change the ammunition belt and fired the Panzerfaust point blank at the tank. There was a deafening detonation. Even down in the tunnel beneath they could hear the crackling subdued explosions as the ammunitions inside the tank went off.

The corporal, who was halfway out of the exit when he fired the weapon, dropped back, and when he did not hear or see any supporting Russian infantry, he sprinted towards the burning tank and took cover next to the entrance.

"Do you want me to get out and scout the street corner to see if there are more tanks?" Karl looked at the sergeant who hesitated to follow the corporal.

"No, I would rather stay with you, but here goes." The sergeant signaled his troops to follow him and disappeared through the opening.

The first six soldiers carried machine guns, but the remainder just left their heavier weapons behind. "What do you want us to do with these?" Harold pointed at the small arsenal and looked at the soldier who had just dropped a bag of hand grenades at his feet.

"You hand them up to us after we are out, dim shit. Don't start a conversation." Karl intertwined and stepped aside as another soldier nearly dropped his ammunition box on his feet.

There was no way he could lift the heavy box over his head into the shaft and he considered opening it to lighten the load when one of the last soldiers pushed him out of the way and started to pass the gear up into the shaft. Harold helped him and went up behind him to take a final look around. The explosion from the tank had caused the entrance to the building to collapse. The ashes and dust mixed with the smoke was hard on his lungs and he was still coughing when he reached the bottom.

"I did not see where they went and I closed the grate. Hopefully we were not observed and invited any visitors." Harold was spitting while he was talking. Karl took the lead and they went back to the Friedrichshain Flak Tower Bunker, which now had become the target of the long-range artillery. The exploding shells around the subway exit and the bunker made it suicidal to cross the street. The boys where hunkered down. They waited...and waited. It was dark when the artillery barrage finally slowed down. Karl was more than hungry and chanced to dash to the entrance of the tower. The massive doors showed severe scars from the artillery shells but were mechanically undamaged and partially open.

He waited behind the entrance until Harold arrived, who was still suffering from his coughing fits.

"We need to get something to eat before we report to Bernd. He might send us immediately out again," Karl observed his friend who was bent over trying to catch his breath.

"Yes, I agree. Food would be really welcome." Harold managed to say before he started to cough again. The boys went up to the mess only to find it closed.

"This looks pretty bad. Let's go and see Officer Bernd. Maybe he can get us some bread or something." Karl lured his friend to follow him to the Sturmbannfuehrer's office.

The Sturmbannfuehrer's office was locked and the boys deliberated about using their cigarettes or tobacco to kungle for food. This would mean that they would have to leave the bunker. They were still discussing possible alternatives when the Sturmbannfuehrer opened the door. Apparently he had been sleeping in his office because he was still yawning when he stepped aside to let the boys enter.

"I will get you some food," said Officer Bernd after the boys finished their report. "We closed the officer's mess because of some misuse and thievery going on." While the boys wondered who would steal the Kunsthonig or the watered down jelly, they were glad to hear that they were getting some real food, or so they hoped.

It turned out to be cold pea soup with some bacon bits swimming in it. There was not much of it, hardly a bowl for each of them, and it did not relieve the hunger pain, but it was better than nothing.

"What's our next assignment?" asked Karl, and he went to study the wall charts.

"You will..." the telephone which was working again interrupted the Sturmbannfuehrer. "Good news," he told the boys after he hung up the receiver, "The troops you guided succeeded to keep the Moltke Bridge in our hands." He looked at Karl, "You most certainly found the right infiltration point; well done."

Harold was still fighting to keep his urge to cough under control. His lungs must have been severely irritated and he was fighting for air. "I will be all right if I could just get some water to drink," he told Karl, who was watching him.

Sturmbannfuehrer Bernd summoned a runner, who returned with a feldflasche, a flat tin bottle with a felt cover, filled with water. "Better?" He asked Harold, who started to sip on the bottle and wiped tears from his eyes.

"Yes, thanks. How can anyone breathe this stuff and still be able to fight?" He looked at Karl, "How come you are not coughing," he wanted to know.

"I was not topside after the tank exploded. You must have gotten a full dose of the stone dust covering the streets." He faced Officer Bernd, "Is there any chance that I can do the next mission by myself and Harold can rest for a few hours?"

"You both will be able to rest for a few hours. We will wake you about 2:00 AM. By that time Harold should have recovered. According to current reports, our hospital trains are retreating. They are being pushed and pulled towards the inner city by soldiers of the Wehrmacht. We need you to scout and ascertain if and where Russian troops are entering the subway system. Dismissed."

Harold wanted to say or ask something, but Karl snapped a salute at the Officer and grabbed Harold by the collar and pulled him through the door towards their sleeping quarters.

"It's time you learn to disappear when you are dismissed," he told his friend, who made a detour to the washroom to refill his water bottle. "The next mission is perfect for us. We can split up for awhile and one of us can check on our hideaway and get us some more cigarettes from our stash." Karl searched the sleeping quarters for his blanket or any other blanket. They were all gone. The Sturmbannfuehrer was right after all, there was some thievery going on. "It looks like someone needs the blankets more than we do," he commented to Harold who had finally stopped coughing.

Twenty Nine

"Time to get up; it is past three and the Sturmbannfuehrer wants to see you." The runner waited long enough to make sure that the boys were awake and left the room. Harold's coughing had stopped completely and a few minutes later, they were standing in Officer Bernd's office. Besides the Sturmbannfuehrer, there were two more SS Officers in the small room. They all stood in front of the city maps and moved the little pins and flags to different locations.

"How are you doing Harold," asked Bernd, and Karl thought that he could see genuine concern in the Officer's face.

"I am doing great," answered Harold, "may I keep the water bottle?" He patted the field bottle, which was hanging from his belt and smiled when the Officer nodded his approval.

"Your orders from last night are herewith cancelled. You have two separate assignments this morning. One of you will guide Officer Winter to the subway station Kottbusser Tor, and the other will guide Officer Traubach to the Rummelsburger Landstrasse. You will need to come back as soon as possible. Any questions?" He looked first at Harold and then at Karl. "Of course, Karl again, why am I not surprised?"

"Officer Winter's destination is no problem. But Officer Traubach's target is not close to any U-Bahn station. Do you want us to guide him to the nearest subway station, or directly to his destination?"

The officers consulted the map again. "This is not an exclusive subway operation. Officer Traubach does not know the city. You will need to guide him directly to his destination. Underground or above does not matter." Sturmbannfuehrer Bernd looked directly at Karl. "Either one of you know the destination better than the other one?"

Karl spoke up again, "I know exactly how to get there, but..." he had another question.

"Now what?" Officer Bernd was getting impatient.

"Is there a staff car we can use, at least for part of the way? If we need to walk, it will take us a minimum of two hours, even if we use subway shortcuts."

"If there was a car and driver available, I would not need you. I am afraid that you will have to walk. Hurry up otherwise the Ruskies will beat you to it."

Karl looked at Untersturmfuehrer Traubach. "Ready when you are."

Traubach saluted the Sturmbannfuehrer and motioned to Karl to follow him out of the office. Karl could not help himself. "I think that this will serve for breakfast," he said to Harold and closed the door.

The Sturmbannfuehrer was speechless for a moment. He looked from Harold to Officer Winter and back again to Harold.

"I don't recognize Karl anymore. He was always polite and never spoke up," he said to both of them.

"Karl is hungry," said Harold, and as he walked to the door, he parroted his friend. "Ready when you are," and held the door open for Officer Winter.

"Doesn't the HJ salute the SS?" Untersturmfuehrer Winter asked Officer Bernd.

"They usually do. We have been working them pretty hard. Maybe they are both hungry."

Winter shook his head in disbelief. "Hunger should have nothing to do with discipline and respect." His demeanor was stiff and demanding.

Officer Bernd seemed relaxed in his question, "Tell me, Untersturmfuehrer Winter, have you ever been hungry?"

"No, Herr Sturmbannfuehrer," answered Winter.

"Dann halt Deine Schnauze. (Then shut up.) We need these boys; besides you can trust them with your life." He returned Winter's salute and waved him out of the room. Harold did not hear the exchange between the officers. He was already waiting at the staircase.

The Russian long-range artillery had resumed the shelling of the bunker's vicinity. When Officer Winter and Harold reached the exit, there was no sign of Karl or Untersturmfuehrer Traubach. The night clouds above them glowed in sinister colors ranging from hellish red to dirty yellow, with a constant flickering of blinding white between them. The thunder of the exploding grenades and the howling of the Katyusha rockets left no doubt that the fight for the inner city had begun. Officer Winter took a deep breath, "Battle sky," he said to Harold, "a battle we cannot win." When he received no answer, he indicated to Harold to sprint across the street.

A few minutes later they disappeared in the U-Bahn tunnel. Karl and Officer Traubach were already a few hundred feet ahead, but in a different direction.

"We will take the subway tunnels for the initial leg of the walk. It is a bit farther and will take us about ten minutes longer, but we will be safe from the artillery shells." Karl was anxious to put some distance between them and the flak tower.

"Don't tell me that you feel better with the Stalinorgels exploding around you," said the Untersturmfuehrer, fifteen minutes later when they attempted to exit near the Schlesischen Tor Station.

"You are right," said Karl, "this is even worse." They were standing below the ventilation grate in an airshaft close to the Spree River, but did not dare to leave the tunnel. The Russian Katyusha rockets were exploding all around them making it impossible to leave the measly protection of the shaft.

"I wanted to exit this side of the river and cross it above ground at the Markgrafendamm. This would have been the shortest route." Karl motioned the officer to follow him back into the tunnel. "It would be easy to cross the river using the subway tunnel. We don't have to walk all the way to the next station. We could try the nearest airshaft on the other side. However, you should know that this would add about thirty minutes to our walk, because we will have to follow the bend in the river. Or we could wait here until the Russians point their rocket launchers to a different target."

"I would like to keep moving. Let us see what the other side looks like," answered the Untersturmfuehrer.

A short while later they were relieved to see that they made the right decision. There were no explosions near their new exit hole. This side of the Spree River was not even under fire. It seemed that the current Russian objective was to level the vicinity of the Schlesischen Tor Station.

"Is there a major route we could be following, or do we have to walk through these little side streets?" It was still too early for daylight and the officer studied the small street in the eerie light from the clouds' reflections before he climbed out of the vent.

"We are a few minutes away from the Koepenicker Chaussee, a major thoroughfare, which leads directly into the Rummelsburger Landstrasse. Both of the streets are almost endlessly long, at least a few kilometers." Karl passed the Untersturmfuehrer and started a slow trot without looking back.

Officer Traubach tried to keep up with him. The whole area looked devastated. There was nothing but burned out housing blocks around them. They passed a few Volksturm and HJ units also doing double-time, but in the direction of the Russian mortar line. Karl had the feeling that they could be in hand-to-hand combat any minute.

The SS Officer slowed down to catch his breath. "Give me a break. I am not in shape to keep up with you." Karl stopped and looked back at Traubach, who trailed him by a few steps.

He was about to answer when he saw an armored military vehicle coming up behind them. It had the big black German cross painted on the front and while it first appeared that the heavy Hanomag truck tried to skirt around them, the driver finally obeyed the Untersturmfuehrer's signal to stop.

"I want you to take me to my unit at the power plant on the Rummelsburger Landstrasse." The strict command, issued in a steel-hard voice together with the imposing uniform of the SS officer left the driver, a Wehrmacht sergeant, very little choice. His face showed that he regretted that he had stopped but when he heard the destination, his expression changed.

"Hop in, if you don't mind sitting in an ammunition truck. I have to tell you that I am loaded to capacity, but I am going to the same location." He motioned to the officer to sit beside him and then pointed at Karl and to the cargo section.

"Hold on a second. No need for the boy to risk his life. He needs to go back anyhow." Untersturmfuehrer Traubach was about to thank Karl for his service when the Sergeant interrupted. "Go back? Where to? He cannot retreat, this is a battle zone."

"Not to worry," answered the officer, "He is unarmed and has to report to the SS headquarters. I will write him an order to assure his safe passage."

Karl had followed the short dialog with some apprehension. He wanted to get back to the relative safety of the U-Bahn tunnel, but he liked the idea of receiving a written note or order from the officer. He hoped that it would carry weight in case he needed it.

"Tell Sturmbannfuehrer Bernd that you accomplished your mission and relay my thanks. Here are your orders; be safe." He handed Karl the note and slapped the steering wheel of the truck, which the sergeant took as an order to drive. Karl did not even wait for the truck to move. He stuffed the order in his pocket and started to jog back. He did not stop until he reached the airshaft.

Without wasting any time to relax, he descended to the bottom and walked back in direction of Friedrichshain. Unfortunately, it was a short walk. When he reached the area of the Schlesischen Tor Station, he was slowed down by insurmountable debris. He could not imagine that this was caused by a hit of the Russian artillery. Even a direct strike was hardly able to cause this much damage. He speculated that some German demolition unit had triggered the devastation to stop the Russian infantry from advancing through the tunnels. He went back to the ventilation shaft he had previously visited and dismissed with Officer Traubach.

When he got there, it was no different than before, except that it was now dawning and the first daylight showed more of the horrendous destruction caused by the still-pounding Katyusha rockets. He decided to walk back underneath the Spree River. This time he bypassed the airshaft they had used to exit and walked all the way to the next U-Bahn station. The platform was overflowing with the same mass of refugees as in all the other stations.

"Do you know how far we are from the Russian line," he asked the nearest woman who was sitting on a pile of boxes.

"No. I have no idea, but I heard that they might come down the entrance anytime."

Karl estimated that she must be in her late thirties. She had been crying and was shaking when she spoke. He felt helpless and sorry for her. "I am sure that we have some fighting commandos above who will stop their descent," he tried to encourage her.

She lifted her head and looked directly at Karl. "I see that you are wearing a uniform. Why aren't you up there with them?"

"I am just a messenger boy running errands for the Flak Tower commanders." Karl excused himself and scanned the platform to find someone who might be able to answer his question or to kungle with him a slice of bread for the few crumbs of pipe tobacco he had found in one of his pockets. He cursed himself for leaving his stash of cigarettes in his hideaway.

"Karl? Karl Veth?" He heard a male voice next to him. He turned and recognized one of his former Volkssturm trainees. He had liked the fellow and respected him because he was one of the fastest learners in his group. The old man was bald, except for a few white hairs on the back of his head. He must be over 80 years old, thought Karl, although he remembered that he was pretty agile for his age. "Yes, that's me. I remember you, but I am sorry, I forgot your name."

"Reichert," was the answer. "You taught me how to handle the phosphor bombs." The old guy pulled Karl next to the stationmaster's cubicle. "I thought you were a sniper? What happened to your shoulder rope?"

"I am still a sniper. Must have lost my rope when I changed my uniform."

Karl was glad to see that this fellow had survived the Volkssturm training but when he looked closer, he noticed that Reichert was wounded. His lower left arm was badly bandaged with a dirty shirt. When Karl looked in Reichert's eyes, he could see the old man was in pain. "When did this happen?"

"About three hours ago. It was still dark and I followed my unit, who got out through the main exit when two T34 tanks appeared from the cross street. Our HJ commandos took them out, but the tanks were followed by an infantry platoon and I think that as of right now, we are holding our position at this station. I was hit by a bullet or something in the crossfire." Reichert looked down on his arm and shook his head. "Freak injury. It happened before I could even get a single shot off."

Karl pulled a small first aid package from his jacket pocket and fished out the 'jod' antiseptic solution. "Sit on the floor and let me clean you up." He removed the bloody shirt from Reichert's arm and inspected the wound. He was glad when he saw that it was not a serious injury. A bullet or shrapnel had grazed Reichert's arm and caused the bleeding. After Karl had cleaned the gash, he applied a clean dressing and bandage from his kit. "Don't touch it for a few days. Let the ointment work." He gave Reichert two pain pills. "Take one right now and use the other one if you have trouble falling asleep."

The old soldier swallowed the pill without water and tried to stand up again. He did not do too well and was still shaking. "Thanks

Karl. I don't know where my unit went. After I got hit, I took cover between the steps and came down here again. I think that I was stunned for a while. All I remember is that some woman wrapped that old shirt around my arm."

Karl thought that men over 80 years of age should not have been drafted in the first place and he was certain that Reichert was unable to hold a gun in his left hand or to steady it sufficiently for a decent shot. "I think that your role as a soldier is over. You should be with your family." Karl looked around to find Reichert's gun. If possible, he wanted to take the old man to his home. But to do this without being accused as a deserter, they would be better off to leave his gun behind. "Where is your gun," he asked.

"I must have dropped it on top of the stairs," answered Reichert. He shrugged his shoulders and supported his left arm with his right hand.

Karl picked up the dirty shirt from the floor and fashioned a sling for Reichert's arm. He hesitated for a second to place the bloody rag around the old man's neck, but then he decided that it was helpful as it indicated a more serious injury.

"How far are we from your home? Where do you live?"

"On the other side of the Spree River. On the Wrangler Strasse, close to the Zille School..." Reichert wanted to add something but stopped when he saw Karl's serious expression.

Karl knew the Wrangler Strasse, but did not know where the Zille School was located. "I don't know the school. Give me a nearby cross street."

"Pueckler Strasse, in the general direction of the Kreuzberg." Reichert pointed to the westbound rail track. Karl contemplated the answer because the Wrangler Strasse was on the west side of the Spree River. He had two options. The obvious one was to walk back in the tunnel and exit at the Schlesischen Tor Station, but he knew that the last section of the tunnel was caved in. He just came from there and had been forced to turn around. The other option was to exit either right here or through a ventilation shaft close by. This would mean that they would have to surface in the middle of the housing fight, which seemed to rage on this side of the Spree River.

He listened to the gunfire above and questioned in his mind how many of the surrounding streets were already in Russian hands. "Follow me. If I walk too fast let me know." Karl helped Reichert to climb down from the platform and entered the tunnel leading back under the Spree River towards the Schlesischen Tor. He wanted to take his chances at surfacing in the nearest airshaft before the collapsed section. This shaft had been impossible to exit because of the incoming Katyusha rockets, but they might have shifted to a different target. He had heard that the rocket launchers were mounted on trucks, which constantly changed location to avoid being targeted by the German defense.

Reichert was right on his heels when Karl climbed up in the vent to take a look around. To his relief, he saw that he had made the right decision. There were no more incoming rockets. They had done their job and leveled the whole area around.

"Hurry, we have a chance to get out and through the ruins before the rockets start in again." Karl reached down to grab Reichert by his jacket and pulled him up. "Can you take the lead from here?" he asked, but Reichert was already a few steps ahead of him. Apparently he knew this area better than Karl because he went into a slightly different direction than Karl had anticipated. Reichert was eager to get close to his apartment, hoping the building would still be standing.

It still took over forty minutes of running; first through almost leveled streets, then around the piles of burning wreckage, until they reached a section of the city that showed considerably less damage. Reichert pointed to their destination. It was a typical Berliner apartment house from the 20's and only the top stories were gone. The lower floors still seemed to be in decent condition.

"Look Karl, there is my apartment, on the ground floor." Reichert, in spite of his age, broke into a sprint and avoiding a heap of rubble, dashed through the tall main entrance door. Karl, who was a few steps behind him, stopped at the door. As far as he was concerned, he had done his job and he was ready to find his way back to the flak tower. "Karl, please come in for a moment and meet my family." Reichert stuck his head out of the door and pulled Karl into the small, but nicely furnished apartment.

Reichert's wife seemed to be in her late 70's, and she was more than happy to see her husband again. "How bad is it?" she asked, and pointed to the arm in the sling.

"This is more for looks than necessity," Karl informed her, and removed the rag from Reichert's shoulders. "He was lucky and will be as good as new. Just give him a few days."

Reichert introduced Karl to the remainder of his family; his granddaughter and his great grandson, who was maybe 3 years old. The little boy was shy and tried to hide behind his mother's dress.

"We cannot offer you anything to eat, but would you share a cup of coffee ersatz with us?" asked the granddaughter.

"Of course he will," answered Reichert and pressed Karl, who wanted to leave, back on a chair.

"I really do not have much time, but I would be happy to accept."

"Listen to me," said Reichert, "within a few days this nightmare will be over. We can hide you in the back of the building until the fighting stops. You are too young to be another casualty of this insane war," he looked with searching eyes at Karl.

"Thank you," said Karl, "I know you mean well, but you were fighting too. If you were not hit in your arm, you would still be out there and I am sure that you would not be hiding."

"Look at my family," answered Reichert, "I was fighting for them and I still will. But you, what have you to fight for? You need to survive and then start living for yourself. Living for yourself should be on your mind."

"Well, yes, I agree with that part, but in the meantime, I might be able to help someone, like I helped you. If I need to hide, I will. But right now, it is too early for me to give up...and thank you once more for your concern." Karl could see the disappointment in the old man's face.

"Look here, Herr Reichert. You know as well as I do that the SS will execute me and your family if they find me and suspect that you were hiding me. I sincerely appreciate what you are trying to do for me, but we are better off to pass on this idea. Please don't worry about me. I intend to survive. Take good care of your arm." He got up to leave and was once more stopped, this time by Frau Reichert.

"Karl, thank you for bringing my husband home. Please remember where we live. We hope that you will survive and when you do, you will need civilian clothing. We have plenty of it and will be happy to help you."

They shook hands with each other. Karl patted the head of the little boy who had been leaning against his mother, and left the building.

Thirty

By the time Karl reached the Friedrichshain Bunker it was late in the evening. He had been constantly forced to seek shelter from the never-ending artillery barrage, which the Russians leveled at the vicinity of the flak towers. So far there had been no street fighting this side of the Spree River. HJ and Volkssturm units at various points along the river had stopped the Russian infantry.

The door to the Sturmbannfuehrer's office was closed and locked and because Karl wanted to report back to him, he knocked for a long time on the chance that the officer was just sleeping. He was still standing in front of the door when Harold showed up with a small cardboard carton in his hand. He had returned from his assignment earlier in the afternoon and like Karl, he had found the door to the office locked.

"What are you carrying," Karl asked looking at the carton.

"Come on, I'll show you in our quarters. We will try his door again later before we get some shut-eye." Harold pushed Karl ahead of him down the hallway. He seemed to be in an excellent mood, which was instantly infectious when Karl inspected the contents of the parcel.

Besides several packs of cigarettes, there were also two small tin cans of corned beef and several packs of Knaeckebrot. "Happy?" asked Harold. "I went to our hideaway to get some cigarettes to kungle and this is the result." He smiled as he started to open the cans.

"We should only open one can," suggested Karl, "we don't know when we will get something to eat again."

"Nonsense, we have these cigarettes to trade and if all fails, we make another run to our stash. We have sufficient food for at least two weeks. So let's celebrate and eat while we can."

The cans were 250 grams each, about half of a pound, and the boys wolfed them down in record time.

"Dessert," announced Harold, and he pulled a tin of Fliegerschokolade from his pocket. Karl had never eaten this delicacy. The round tin measured about three inches across and contained three wafers of good tasting chocolate.

"Why do they call this Fliegerschokolade," he asked.

"Because it is laced with some stuff that keeps our pilots awake when they are on a long duration flight. At least that is what I have been told. The pilots call it Chocacola." Harold broke the third wafer in half to share the treat equally with his friend. Karl decided to munch it together with a few slices of the dried Knaeckebrot and it was delicious. "We should try once more to see the Sturmbannfuehrer," he suggested after they finished eating. He got up from the cot and took a package of the Knaeckebrot along to offer it to him.

"Come in." Bernd was behind his desk and looked rested.

After the boys finished their report, he gratefully accepted the bread and started to eat right away.

"I thought that we had plenty of provisions in this bunker, how come we don't get anything to eat?" Harold was bold enough to ask.

"Yes, I thought the same. Matter of fact, we all had been told that food was not one of our problems. I also think that the food is actually here, but someone is playing games with it, but not for long. I assure you that I will find out what is going on." The Sturmbannfuehrer did not seem to mind that Harold had asked this unpleasant question. He pulled a small green notebook from the shelf behind the desk and opened it to a new blank page. "This is just for my personal information. We don't know what the next few days will bring and we still hope that we will be saved from the Russians by the western allied forces, which are still standing on the Elbe River. But, in any event, I've grown fond of you and would like to know where I can contact you in case we get overrun and the war is over." He looked at Harold, "I know where your parents went, but if you were missing, where would you be here in Berlin?"

Harold wavered and almost said, 'In the U-Bahn airshaft in the

Uhlandstrasse, corner of Kurfuerstendamm'. He looked at Karl for help and his friend jumped right in. "I will be in the Berliner Strasse Nr. 26 and I hope that Harold will be with me. We have been invited by Frau Becker to stay in her apartment until we find our parents."

The officer had seen the hesitation in Harold's face and was not too happy about Karl's rapid answer. "You wanted to say," he asked once more.

"I was not sure how to answer, because my Dienststelle is closed and I forgot about Frau Becker's invitation."

Officer Bernd wrote down the address and turned to Karl. "You answered already and I guess that you don't have an additional address?"

Karl gave his best impression of thinking. "Yes I do," he said, "in case Frau Becker's apartment gets destroyed we might be at a friend of my parents. Emser Strasse, corner of Duesseldorfer Strasse. I know the house, there is a Kneipe (beer restaurant) on the ground floor, but I don't know the number."

"Well, then this will have to do," said the Sturmbannfuehrer. "I also wrote down my home address in case you want to see me after the war." He ripped out a page from the rear of his notebook and handed it to Karl, who kept it in his hand and stared at it.

"Does this mean our job is done here? Are we dismissed?" He wanted to know.

"No, not by a long shot, just the opposite. This means that from now on it will get serious. Should the Russians elect to bypass or surround our flak towers, we will lock up tight and you might not be able to come back in from your missions. In this case, I hope that you will be smart enough to disappear. However, I would like to visit with you when this is over." He got up and placed the notebook back on the shelf behind him. "Tomorrow morning I have a slightly different task for you." He looked directly at Karl. "I want you to get close to the Kreuzberg Station. Supposedly there is an old brewery with stables for their horses. Do you know where this is?"

"No, Herr Sturmbannfuehrer. I heard about an old brewery close to Moabit, which had purportedly plenty of horses for their delivery carriages, but I don't know of any stables around the Kreuzberg." Karl did not really trust any horses and he had been especially afraid of the heavy brewery horses that pulled the platform wagons, which were loaded with beer kegs. Whenever he had seen one approaching, he had always crossed the street before they came close to him.

"I know where the stables are for the dairy horses," offered Harold.

"Yeah, but the dairy horses have all been drafted to assist moving the artillery around," said Bernd, "I want you to shoot a horse and bring back the meat. You have to be fast and disappear back in the nearest subway tunnel to avoid being robbed by the civilians." He went to the map on the wall and pointed to one of the colored pins. "As far as we know, there is a stronghold of an HJ unit reinforcing this street corner position. You will obtain your guns and ammunition from them. I already wrote an order to that effect." He gave Harold an envelope.

"I can shoot a horse, but I don't know how to butcher one," said Karl. He felt mighty uncomfortable at the aspect of carving up an animal.

"Get one of the HJ members to assist you. Promise them part of the meat; you will not be able to carry a whole horse by yourself. You will have to think on your feet. No more questions? Get going before daybreak." The Sturmbannfuehrer started to shove the hesitating boys out of the door when he remembered they needed backpacks. "Wait; take these along to transport the meat." The rucksacks were scuffed, discolored and well used, but would serve their purpose.

"We got this assignment because you are a sniper," Harold accused his friend as they went down the hallway.

"You don't need to be a sniper to shoot a horse," Karl informed him. "Have you ever seen a beer horse? I mean up close? They are not like your tiny taxi carriage horses. A beer wagon horse is so huge you can't miss it," he explained, "You just put a handgun to its head and pull the trigger."

"I would rather jump two subway trains or a bus before I get even close to a darn beer horse," decided Harold. "You had the training, you shoot it."

"If I have to shoot it, I will, but I will be at least 50 feet away from it. I will not get any closer. I think that they will eat you if they can reach you." Karl was adamant about it.

"A fine soldier you are, shooting a horse from 50 feet," mocked Harold, "the Fuehrer would be proud of you." They were still arguing who was the more refined city boy, when they fell asleep.

When they left the bunker before dawn, they were awed again by the menacing colors in the clouds. The most frightening reflection was the deep red outlines interwoven with black. Even though the boys had gotten kind of used to the howling of the rockets, the intimidating sky together with the terrible battle sounds was still unnerving and they hurried to get off the street and into the subway station. The trains had stopped running two days prior and the crowd had spilled far into the tunnels. The smell of feces and urine was overpowering. It took the boys well over an hour until they reached the HJ unit they were seeking.

The overall commander of the trenched-in defensive position was an SS Hauptscharfuehrer (Master Sergeant) with the name of Schlueter. Besides the HJ unit, there was a platoon of SS, two German Tiger tanks and a platoon of Volkssturm soldiers. Schlueter just glanced at the order from the Sturmbannfuehrer to supply the boys with guns and sent them over to the HJ commander who was about 16 years old and of equal rank with Karl. His name was Schroeder. They did not know each other because Schroeder's HJ unit was from a different district than Karl's.

Schroeder handed the boys two rifles. Both of them were the heavy old 7.92 X 57 Mauser Gewehr, named 98, with a bunch of ammunition, hand grenades, two Panzerfausts and two handguns. He lifted the backpacks from the boys and when he saw that they were empty, he filled them with more hand grenades.

"Do you know where the local brewery is or where their stables are located?" Asked Karl as he ripped the Rucksack from Schroeder's hands and removed the grenades. "We need the packs to be empty to carry meat back to the bunker."

"What brewery? What meat are you talking about?" Schroeder looked confused at Karl. "We are not from this district. Our unit is from Tegel. I thought that you were part of the reinforcements we are waiting for."

"We don't know of any reinforcements." Harold was a bit worried that this defense group might retain them. He considered them greatly inadequate for holding the wide street crossings in front of them. "We are under orders to shoot a horse and bring the meat back to the Friedrichshain Bunker." When he saw the skeptical expression in Schroeder's face, he hurried to add, "You are supposed to help us in exchange for some of the horse meat."

"Now you are talking!" The prospect of fresh meat worked like a charm. The Obergefolgsschaftfuehrer was eager to assist and went to SS Officer Schlueter to inquire if he knew of any horse stables in this area. It turned out that the SS leader was just as clueless as the boys.

"There is no brewery even close to here. Let me see your orders again." He squinted at the brief note and shook his head, "This makes no sense at all. You must be at the wrong location. It is also dated April 26th and today is the 27th. You are one day late, where have you been all this time?"

"We were ordered the leave at daybreak, which we did, and it is still early in the morning. We are to report back in the bunker by noon." Karl wanted the SS Officer to drop his questioning. He still hoped that there was a brewery around and he wanted to scout the area for the stables. "If one of your men is from the country and knows something about butchering, we could sure use him. In exchange we will share some of the meat with you."

Schlueter, who apparently was well fed, revolted at the thought of eating horsemeat. He was about ready to lecture the boys when he saw that one of his tanks started to move. "Who is giving the orders to move?" he shouted to the Volkssturm sergeant standing next to the tank. Then he heard the second tank also rev up.

"Orders from the Fuehrer Bunker. You are ordered to move out immediately to strengthen the bridgehead at the Moltke Bruecke." An HJ messenger on a motorcycle handed Schlueter a brown envelope and was gone before the SS Officer had a chance to open it.

"Moltke Bruecke, that's straight up the street. You cannot miss it, but we are happy to show you the fastest way," Karl volunteered.

"No, I will find it. You have your own orders. Get on with it." The SS Officer left the boys standing and signaled to his troops to follow the tanks, which already moved in the direction of the Spree River.

"The father of one of my boys was a butcher. He knows something about meat cutting. He can help you as long as you send him back with some of the meat." Schroeder was not about to lose the prospect of extra food. "But I need one of you to take his place." He looked expectantly at Harold. "No problem," answered Harold and turned to Karl, "Don't worry about me. Good luck with the horse. I will go with this unit to the bridge."

Karl was not happy with the turn of events, but he told himself that Harold would have been of no help in cutting up a horse. He was torn between having a butcher on his side or ordering his friend to go with him. The HJ leader made up his mind for him. "Georg," he summoned a member of his group, "give your Panzerfaust to this guy," and he pointed at Harold. "Take his empty backpack and assist this Oberscharfuehrer," he pointed at Karl, "to butcher a horse. Don't come back without any meat," he added.

Georg, who was maybe 14 years old and a big boy for his age, grinned at Karl for approval. "Where is the horse?"

"I need to find one first." Karl gave his Panzerfaust and his handgun back to Schroeder. "Feel like going through some subway tunnels?" he asked of Georg, and also handed a handful of ammunition back to Schroeder. He had decided to take only two cartridges for his rifle. He knew that he needed only one to kill a horse. The other one was more or less for backup.

Georg seemed to like his new assignment. He even offered to carry Karl's rifle as he went with him to the U-Bahn station. Due to the imminent street fighting, the station was crammed to the top with civilian refugees. There was no way to enter the tunnels through the main entrance. Karl was sure that he remembered a ventilation shaft nearby, but due to all the rubble, he had a hard time finding it. Georg had no idea what a grate to an airshaft would look like, but eagerly helped in the search.

"Which direction will we be going?" He asked after they finally found the buried grille.

"We will go under the river to Moabit," answered Karl, "We need to find the brewery stable to get our horse." He slowed down when he heard Georg's answer.

"You are seeking to shoot a brewery horse?" He asked in bewilderment. "My father was running a Rossschlaechterei (horse butchering shop). We helped to butcher the remaining brewery horses well over six months ago. I know where the stables are in Moabit because we picked up the horses that were declared unfit by the artillery to drag their cannons around. I can take you there, but the stables are empty. You will not even find horse shit anymore, much less a living horse waiting to get slaughtered." The initial enthusiasm in his voice changed to disappointment.

Karl stopped walking. He had his small dynamo flashlight out to illuminate the tracks and kept pressing the lever to keep it active. This was terrible news and he felt stupid that he had essentially traded his friend for a now unneeded butcher boy. "You were so raring to go with me. Where did you think we would find a Horse?"

Georg's answer startled him. "Well, from the Ruskies, off course. You know the little ponies they use to pull their supply wagons?" Georg's voice sounded bubbly again. Karl had not been in the frontline above ground and while he had heard about the Mongolian

Panje horses, he had never seen them. "It should be doable; if we get close enough and you are a good shot." Georg continued, "I will cover you while you take out the Panje driver and shoot the horse. We run to the cart, cut up some meat, and disappear back in the tunnel. Before the Ruskies know what happened, we will be gone."

Karl liked what he heard. The subway tunnel system was almost created for this operation. Maybe they could even plunder the wagon. "Have you ever seen such a Panje cart," He inquired of Georg.

"Yes, a few days ago when I was hiding with an SS commando on the rooftop of an apartment building in Tegel. A Soviet infantry detail had stopped advancing below us and did not know our whereabouts. They had run out of their fighting spirit when they got out of their drunken stupor and sobered up. They waited for their provisions to catch up with them. Mostly they waited for their vodka, I guess."

He stopped for a moment and Karl used the pause to inquire, "Did the provisions arrive with the cart?"

"Yes, and from what I could see it seemed that the driver was also totally drunk."

"What did you do?"

"Personally, I did not do much, but the SS used their hand grenades and wiped the Soviet group pretty much out. Some of them might have survived, I don't know. We retreated from the rooftop after we dropped the grenades."

Karl studied Georg, who told him about the encounter with about the same voice and indifference he would have used if he had been reporting about a vacation trip. He must have seen a lot of action during the last days to be so emotionally detached. "You just gave me an idea. Let's plan this a bit. I think I know how to get us behind the lines and back again."

Thirty One

The boys had reached the last station before the river and Karl decided to rest for a while before they continued to advance further below the river.

The platform on this station was, like the previous ones, without power and only a few emergency lights illuminated the area around the stationmaster's cubicle. The area around the exit was standing room only because many of the refugees were now also Volkssturm soldiers who were seeking temporary shelter without being accused of being deserters.

Karl spotted an empty space further back on the edge of the platform next to a young woman with a little boy close to her. "Do you mind if we sit for a while next to you," he asked the young mother who did not look up. She just lifted her little boy, who was maybe 3 years old, on her lap and continued talking to him. The little boy was softly crying and did not respond to her or to Karl who undid his rucksack and sat in the empty spot next to her.

As Karl had expected, the people on the other side of him also moved a little more together to make room for Georg. While Karl was thinking of questions to ask, Georg stretched out, rested his head on his backpack and let his lower legs dangle over the tracks.

"Tell me," Karl started, "You said that the Russians you encountered ran out of their fighting spirit when they sobered up. Are they always waiting for vodka to get drunk again, or are they being replaced by a secondary unit equally drunk?"

Georg opened his eyes again. He had almost fallen asleep. "Karl,

I don't know. I think I told you everything I observed. But why are you always referring to the fighting troops as Russians? Why don't you call them Soviets? I mean, in the few days of combat I witnessed, I only saw Mongolians. I don't recall seeing a true Russian soldier. Alive or dead."

"That is an odd question to ask," answered Karl, "what is the difference if I call them Soviets or Russians?"

Georg wondered if he had heard correctly. Could it be that the HJ leader really did not know? "There is a huge difference, Karl. The front line fighting Soviets are all Mongolians and they don't fight if they are sober. They are a different breed of people than you or I, or for that matter, the Russians. The Mongolians don't follow orders. I doubt that they even understand what an order is all about. They are just a bunch of normally harmless people, but when they are drunk, they almost turn into animals."

"They will charge our machine guns and no matter how many we kill, they just climb over their fallen comrades and keep on coming until either they run out of troops or we run out of ammunition. You mean you did not know that?" Georg started to worry that he had teamed up with a clueless and combat inexperienced partner.

"Yes, I heard that the Russians," he stopped to correct himself, "the Soviets have no respect from our MG 42, but I thought that they were charging because they thought that we eventually will run out of ammunition."

Georg shook his head. "No, the Russians are too smart to commit combat suicides." He changed his position to stretch further out on the tiled platform. "As long as we are resting, do you mind if I sleep a little?"

Karl had no objection and tried to get some sleep himself. He shifted around to find a more comfortable position as he overheard the young mother talking softly to her boy. "Please don't cry. I don't have anything to feed you. Look at me, mommy is hungry too." She lifted the little boy from her lap and was holding him tight. "Maybe tomorrow we will be able to eat again, and maybe, in a few weeks daddy will also be home again." The little boy tried to understand what the mother was telling him, but kept on sobbing. "Please don't cry. Maybe tomorrow... maybe we will have something to eat again... Maybe tomorrow we will eat again..."

The mother repeated herself over and over again and used a kind of a soothing singsong in her voice. All the time she was crying herself.

Karl could not listen any longer. "I'll be right back. Please watch my backpack," he told the woman and disappeared from her side.

He moved through the crowd and whenever he came next to a man he shined his flashlight on the other's hand. Finally, close to the exit he found what he was looking for. His light illuminated a hand with dark tobacco stained fingertips. "I have two cigarettes. Do you have some food to kungle," asked Karl as he sidled up to the man who was of medium height and wearing an expensive overcoat. Karl wondered how this fellow had avoided the Volksturm draft when he noticed that the stranger dragged his left leg. This might be the reason, he thought to himself.

"Yes, I have two slices of bread," came the fast answer.

"No, not enough. I have a little brother who is hungry too." Karl made a vague hand movement towards the far side of the platform.

"Well, if you had more cigarettes I might have more food," said the stranger as he hobbled between the people to the more lit up area by the stationmaster cubicle.

"Let's see first what you are offering." Karl suspected that he might have found a black market trader. The stranger opened his coat and Karl stood back in surprise. The lining of the coat featured several pockets. There were some loaves of bread protruding and Karl could see in the dim glow of the emergency lights something that looked like salami. Underneath the arms, below the seams of the sleeves, were also some wristwatches dangling from safety pins. No question about it, Karl had stumbled on a black marketer.

"Take your pick," said the trader, "I offer you a loaf of bread and the salami and your choice of a wristwatch for 20 cigarettes." He moved out of the circle of illumination, back into the darker area.

"Not so fast," countered Karl. The hasty replies and actions of the marketer told him that this habitual smoker was out of cigarettes. The kungle had turned in his favor. "I will give you 10 cigarettes for the bread and the salami. You can keep the wristwatch."

"Deal," was the immediate answer. The trader reached in his lining and gave Karl the bread and the wurst. His act was again way too eager for Karl.

He expected some conditions and when the marketer stayed quiet, he pulled the cigarettes from his pocket and began to count them out. This was a bit difficult because he did not want to drop the food. He had barely counted to five when he felt the hands of the trader pressing hard against the sides of his throat.

"Stop counting, you bastard," whispered the marketer, "give me all your cigarettes, or I break your sorry neck."

Karl's trained reflexes kicked in and without a wasteful second, he stepped down with his right foot on the left shoe of the attacker. His hands went up, behind the neck of the trader, and as he pulled the man's head down, his right knee went up to meet the face of the unlucky man. He was unlucky because Karl must have stepped on a sore nerve or some old injury. As the trader was spitting blood and a tooth, he was groaning and rolling on the floor, clutching his left foot. Karl slid his HJ knife back into the sheath. His reaction had been so automatic that he did not remember when he had drawn it.

"Count your blessings that you did not pull this stunt on my friend. He would have killed you." Karl felt an impulse to kick the trader's face, but then he just bent down, collected his bread and a second loaf, plus the salami and the cigarettes he had dropped. He got up and tapped the two nearest persons on the shoulders. "There is a black market trader with food lying on the floor." While the bystanders looked down and around, Karl slipped away. He simply disappeared in the dark cluster of the people around him.

The mother was still rocking her boy when Karl emerged next to her. "Tomorrow is now," he announced, and handed her the bread and the wurst.

The mother was speechless and stared at the food treasures in front of her.

"H- h, how can I thank you?" she stammered.

"Don't worry," said Karl, "just feed your little boy and make sure that nobody sees you eating. There are some bad people around here."

He sat down in his old place rubbing his neck where the trader had hurt him.

The woman was too hungry to protest. She began breaking one of the loaves in little pieces and fed the dry bread to her child. "Thank you, thank you," she whispered, when to her surprise, Karl handed her a packet with ten cigarettes. "They might come in handy, but only kungle with people you know." He smiled at the little boy, who had stopped crying and was now happily chomping on the bread.

Georg had slept peacefully and almost fell off the platform when Karl woke him up. "Give me ten more minutes, please," he mumbled, still half asleep.

"Alright, fifteen more minutes, but then we have to move." Karl agreed and started to daydream about his younger brother and his little sister, who were somewhere in western Germany. He hoped that they had something to eat.

He felt sorry that he was unable to help them, but at the same time he was glad that he was here in the station, providing some food for the little guy next to him, whom he did not know.

By the time Karl woke Georg for the second time, the young mother was asleep. "We need to move on." Karl was reaching for his rifle, but Georg snapped it away from him. "I carry, you lead." They grabbed their backpacks and were gone before the woman woke up.

When they reached the airshaft Karl had targeted, they were on the other side of the river and it was dark. Karl carefully moved the exit grate out of the grooves and waited for a moment until he lifted it up some more to look around. He could hear small arms fire in the vicinity of the river, but there was no fighting close to them. He was sure that they were behind the Soviet line. Again he scrutinized the immediate area, and when nothing moved, he crawled out of the shaft towards a burnt out vehicle about ten feet away.

The vehicle turned out to be an old delivery truck. It would give him the cover he needed, but he did not know which side of the truck he had to position himself on. Georg had followed him, bringing Karl's gun along. He was taking cover on the opposite site of the vehicle. The boys had emerged not far from a street crossing and were quietly debating whether to stay or to move closer towards the crossing and the side streets.

Karl scanned the area a little closer to their position when he thought that he saw the outline of a body not twenty feet away from him. He studied it for a while and when he detected no movement, he crawled towards the shape. It was a dead German soldier. He had bullet wounds in his head and part of the face was gone. Karl lifted himself up on his knees to see if he could spot any more bodies. The more he looked the more he detected. He counted six more silhouettes, none of them moving. He crawled slowly from one body to the next. All of them were German. The ones without bullet holes in their heads had their throats slashed. Karl got up and walked deeply bent back to the damaged truck.

"Are you tired of life," Georg hissed at him and pulled him down.

Karl shook his head. "They are all dead and there is no movement anywhere."

Georg was flabbergasted by the greenness of his partner. "Germans or Soviets," he asked.

"All Germans," answered Karl.

"Did they still have their wristwatches, rings or shoes on?"

"I did not check for their rings or watches, but yes, they still had their shoes on."

Georg pressed Karl deeper into the dirt and lowered his voice to a whisper,

"Then any minute we will see the Mongolian women. They always follow close behind the combat zone to rob the dead bodies of valuables and cut the throats of any survivor."

"Some of them had already their throats slashed," Karl whispered back.

"This only means that there are women among the fighters. The women are the most ruthless foe you could face. How long do you want to wait?"

Karl did not understand. "Wait, for what?"

"The Panje wagons follow the dead bodies to avoid enemy contact. Since the bodies have not been robbed, they will show up sooner or later. I only wonder how long you want to wait because the women might be here any moment."

Karl was unclear about the time issue. The simple order to shoot a horse in a stable had turned into a combat mission. He was sure that the Sturmbannfuehrer would not have ordered him behind the fighting lines to shoot a Panje horse. But here he was, and he had to make a decision.

"We will wait one hour, but not a moment longer." He checked the gun Georg had carried for him and took a position behind the fender of the front wheel. While he was concentrating on the cross street in front of them, Georg watched in the direction of the river. The small arms fire had not stopped and was only interrupted by some occasional machine gun blasts. He estimated that they were close to one Kilometer behind the combat line.

The squeaking sound of a wheel alerted both boys at the same time. It came from the cross street and seemed to be advancing in their direction. Karl saw the Panje wagon before Georg and was surprised how small it was. A little horse, not bigger than a pony, emerged from the darkness. It eagerly pulled the little wagon and Karl could make out the driver who was hunched over a board or something on top of the cart. The reins of the horse were in his right hand. The way the cart was advancing, it would pass within fifty feet of them. Karl once more studied the area behind the Panje carriage. There was nothing else moving, just the wagon coming closer. "I shoot, you run and start carving," Karl whispered to Georg, who laid his gun down and pulled his knife.

A few seconds later he heard Karl's gun. It sounded like it was a single shot but when he saw the driver spinning around and the horse falling down, he knew that it must have been two shots. However, the driver got up again and clutching his right arm, he ran screaming back in the direction he had come from.

"You missed," yelled Georg, and he took off towards the cart. Karl was right next to him when they reached the wagon. He was amazed at the speed with which Georg cut and butchered the horse. Karl was laying flat on the ground, stuffing the steaming bloody meat in his backpack and starting to load the second one when a few tracer bullets blasted above him into the wood of the carriage.

He carried his rucksack in front of him and dragged Georg's pack behind him as he double-timed back to the truck. Georg had dropped his knife, darted to the vehicle and started to return a few shots as Karl continued to the airshaft, dropping the packs down waiting for Georg. The very next thing he saw was the cart exploding and turning over on its side.

"The tracer bullets must be hitting the vodka or some ammunition," Georg shouted as he jumped down the shaft on top of their backpacks. Karl followed him, pulling the grate back in position as he descended.

'That was too close for me," said George, as he strapped his pack on his shoulders. "How come you missed the driver? He was so near to us." He wanted to look into Karl's eyes, but it was too dark in the tunnel to see his face.

"I did not miss," he heard the answer, "I don't kill. I just wanted to take the driver out."

"You did not even do that. The bastard came back and almost killed us," mumbled Georg, but it was loud enough that Karl, who walked in front of him, could hear him.

"Nonsense," Karl bellowed back. "Nobody shoots with his arm socket gone. And it was gone; the driver was right handed. The tracers must have been fired by some troops behind him."

It was unclear if Georg was satisfied with the answer. He had one more thing to say, "You might want to change your priorities if you wish to stay alive."

Karl did not answer. The way he figured it, he had done what needed to be done and they were now safely on their way back. He was thinking about which U-Bahn exit might serve best for both of them.

They walked the tracks for over thirty minutes, passing some parked hospital trains and a few dark station platforms. The smell of human excrement always increased in the immediate vicinity of the platforms. Nobody bothered or even noticed the boys, who walked quietly with their full rucksacks on their backs and their guns dangling from their necks in front of them.

Karl had decided to leave the subway close to the Mohrenstrasse. He knew the area fairly well and it was the easiest way for Georg to connect with his unit. He was also afraid that they might be robbed of their precious meat. He thought that it might be best to hide the rucksacks in one of the service sheds and see what the situation was on the streets before they parted their ways. The next service shed was only a few meters away and after the boys had placed their goods on an empty shelf, Georg suggested that they should stay and use the shelves as a makeshift bed to sleep for the remainder of the night. Karl agreed. This was by far a more pleasant place than the stinking stations. He locked the storage room from the inside and within a few minutes they were sound asleep.

"What time is it?" asked Georg a few hours later.

Karl tried to get up. His throat was still hurting and he hit his head on the shelf above him. "It is past 7:00 AM, time to get going."

The boys had nothing to eat but the horsemeat. They reasoned that they would find some fire in the streets, which would serve to grill the meat.

One more hour without food would not kill them, but they were sorely tempted to chew on an uncooked piece of the sweet smelling rump.

"Let's take a look around and then come back and get the packs." The boys took their guns and Karl locked up the shed as they left.

The next ventilation shaft was not too far from the Mohrenstrasse, exactly where Karl had wanted to be. He was the first one out and found himself on the sidewalk of the Friedrichstrasse. He watched for any activity nearby and after he had determined that the sounds of the fighting line were at least 500 yards away, he motioned to Georg to join him. They were in the government and financial district of Berlin. Most of the office buildings around them had been pretty much destroyed. Artillery barrages had leveled whatever buildings had partially survived the air attacks. They were still deliberating whether to get the meat first or to look for some suitable fire when they were interrupted by a sharp command behind them.

"Drop your guns and turn around very slowly!"

As the boys followed the order they found themselves staring at the shining breast shields of an SS flying court marshal detail.

Thirty Two

Karl had no idea where the two SS men had come from. "I am under direct ord.........." he started when he was rudely interrupted.

"Shut up, you swine! Hand over your ammunition!" the SS man shouting at him was a Rottenfuehrer and he spoke with a heavy Bavarian accent. He was close to six feet tall and towered above the boys.

"I don't have any ammunition. I spent my last cartridge taking out a Russ..." Karl stammered.

"I told you to shut up, you miscarriage of a dog!" There was no question that the SS man was from Bavaria. His choice of words and his accent left no doubts. The boys had dropped their guns and Karl tried to stay calm and struggled to open his shirt pocket to show his credentials when, his hand and arm were being bent back and upwards by the second SS man.

"Let me show you my........." Karl started to say when he was interrupted again.

"You must be a Polack that you don't understand. I want your ammunition, your bullets, and your cartridges. I want all of them and I want them now!" The Rottenfuehrer was now yelling at Georg while the second SS man had still not said a word. He was busy searching the pockets of Karl's uniform for ammunition. Georg attempted to say something and was also interrupted by the well-built SS man.

"What have we here," he smiled at his partner, "A dirty bloody uniform. These boys must have been retreating from the front line." He had snatched Georg by his collar and was inspecting the sticky substance on his hands. "This is indeed blood," he decided.

"It is horse blood!" screamed Karl.

"Of course it is, my boy," answered the Rottenfuehrer, and then it seemed to Karl as if the sky had fallen. Everything happened so fast that his mind had difficulty to keep up transmitting to his consciousness . . .

Georg had emptied his pockets, which contained three rifle cartridges. At the same time, the Rottenfuehrer raised his handgun and fired a bullet through the forehead of Georg.

"This is number two as of this morning," he roared, "This will teach you not to retreat with ammunition." He looked straight at Karl who thought that his last moment had come.

He looked thunderstruck at Georg's dead body lying crumbled up on the street. A small circle of blood started forming under his head. Karl's knees gave out and as he slid to the ground he lost control over his bowels. He soiled himself in an instant and as he was revolting at his condition, he waited for the bullet to end it all. The bullet never came and as he regained his senses he heard the SS men arguing with each other.

"Put the gun away, you idiot. You almost shot a special aide to a Sturmbannfuehrer!" The SS man without the accent had read Karl's ID card and tried to stop the Rottenfuehrer from committing another execution.

"I don't care if he is the son of a Sturmbannfuehrer. This guy here had cartridges in his pockets and he was abandoning his unit. It is our job to execute deserters."

Karl scrambled to get up and both of the SS men took a step backwards.

"Look at this boy. He shit all over himself. He knows that he is guilty. I wish that I could find a cartridge on him." The Rottenfuehrer was not giving up and the handgun was still in his hand. Karl had never felt so powerless. After the initial shock, he was now rearing to take some kind of revenge, but he knew that any action at this time would be his death sentence.

He gritted his teeth and counted backwards from the number eight. He knew that he had to occupy his mind in order to maintain control over his feelings. Slowly he lifted his head and studied every feature of the Rottenfuehrer. He was sure that he would never forget him and in an instant, he knew that he would take revenge for Georg. He did not know how, only that he would. His inner core belief system had changed a few degrees during the last five minutes. Actually, it had changed a lot.

"Stand straight like an HJ member and not like the shit-head that you are, and don't you dare move. I still don't know what I will do with you."

The Rottenfuehrer was still steaming with excitement. He reached down and with his partner, lifted the lifeless body of Georg from the ground. Both men carried the corpse across the street towards the nearest lamppost. Deserters were to be hung. When they reached the streetlight, they laid the body down and turned around. The street was empty. Karl was gone.

"Where is that guy," fumed the Rottenfuehrer, "Now you see that I was right. I should have shot him while I had the chance." He took his 9mm Mauser out again and raced to the spot where they had left the boy standing. Nothing. The crossing remained empty.

"What is this? He cannot simply disappear. I hold you responsible if we don't find the kid."

Both of the SS men took their time and studied every door and window along the side streets. They did not notice that the grate on the sidewalk had moved a few inches from its previous position. Karl was standing in the tunnel a few feet from the airshaft. He was in full control of his senses again and his breathing was back to normal. Just the stench coming from his pants was a reminder of the past fifteen minutes. He did not expect that he would be followed, but he waited anyhow just to be sure. When he did not hear anything, he went back to the tool shed to pick up his backpack. He could only carry one, so he left Georg's pack behind. Hopefully the meat would not spoil until he had a chance to come back.

The way back to the Friedrichshain Bunker was easy compared to the happenings of the past night. Within an hour he was passing through the entrance of the flak tower and climbed up the stairs with the horsemeat on his shoulders.

"Welcome back," said the Sturmbannfuehrer when Karl came through the door. "Harold came back last night and was worried when you had not shown up by this morning. He almost went searching for you." Officer Bernd sniffed in direction of Karl's uniform. "Now this is not quite as ghastly as the last time you stank up the office," he sniffed again, "but it is awful enough to warrant a change of uniform. Go get Harold for me. He should be in the mess. We are serving again, and then take a shower. When you get back,

Harold will have a clean uniform waiting for you."

"Well, I don't think that my jacket needs replacing, but I sure could use a clean pair of pants. I still have a fresh pair of underwear in reserve. What do you want me to do with the meat?" Karl had decided not to report about the execution of Georg. He liked the Sturmbannfuehrer. He even trusted him a bit, but not enough to report anything detrimental about the SS. Besides, Officer Bernd had not asked any questions about the origin of the horsemeat. He probably assumed that Karl had found a stable and Karl was not about to volunteer anything.

"Harold will take care of it. Get cleaned up and something to eat and then report back to me."

Karl took off for the mess and found his friend eating a bowl of potato soup. The moment he opened the door, Harold backed off and sniffed the air.

"Holy cow, did you take a swim in the sewer?"

"I will tell you later, right now you need to report to the Sturmbannfuehrer." Karl was not in the mood for long explanations.

The shower water was hot and he took a long time to clean himself. When he was done, he found Harold waiting in the mess with a clean pair of winter uniform pants and his usual big boyish grin on his face.

"You smell clean alright, but you still look terrible. What is the blue spot on the side of your throat?"

Karl had totally forgotten about his encounter with the marketer. "Uh, this here," he rubbed behind his ear, "this is nothing. Menschenskinder, Harold, these pants are way too long."

No matter how he tried to adjust them, the pants were designed for a person at least five inches taller than he was. He looked down at his legs and could not see his shoes and the pants were dragging several inches on the floor. Then he pulled the pants up and the only way he could clear his shoes was when he fastened the belt just underneath his armpits.

Harold was amused by the attempts of Karl to adjust the pants to his body size. "Boy oh boy, Karl, unless you cut them off they will never fit. Let's have 'em back." He took the pants and left Karl standing in his shorts. A short while later he was back. He still had the same pair of pants in his hand, but in the other hand he had also a pair of shoelaces.

"Put them back on again and sit down," he ordered Karl. He

bound the laces at the end of the pants around Karl's lower legs. "Stand up and fold the waistline down."

Karl cooperated as well as he could and wound his big leather belt around the doubled-up waistline. He could not see himself and was just glad to have clean clothing against his skin. Harold, on the other hand, was having a field day trying to dress his friend and could hardly contain himself.

"I have seen clowns in Circus Krone who looked less funny than you." He turned Karl around several times to inspect him from all sides. "No, you might get away with this outfit when you just walk around. But the moment you try to carry something or try to run, you will wind up flat on your face."

"Now what," Karl asked.

"We will have to 'borrow' a pair of pants," was Harold's short answer.

"Borrow, from whom?" Karl rubbed again the sore spot on his throat.

"From someone as short as you are, preferably when he is sleeping." Harold went to the soup pot and served Karl a hot bowl of potato soup. "Don't worry, I'll take care of it. Take your time eating and then report to Bernd. Your jacket will cover your waist."

"What about my legs?" Harold did not hear him anymore. He remembered that he had seen something like a laundry/cleaning facility in the basement.

As Karl was relaxing and eating, his mind went into overtime. Every time he closed his eyes, he saw images of Georg's face and of his lifeless body. He opened his eyes again only to see flashes of light around him.

I must be hallucinating, he thought. He had heard that this had happened to people after they had experienced severe shock. I cannot let this happen to me, he thought again, and tried the method he had been taught by Dr. Felder. He counted back from the number eight and as he counted, he tried to imagine the shape of the number. It worked. The more he concentrated to see the numbers in his mind the more he regained control. The images from Georg dissolved somewhat, and the light flashes stopped.

"Day dreaming? Look what I got for you." Harold stood in front of him and twirled a deep blue pair of pants in his hands. Karl was glad to be interrupted in his misery. "They are not regular HJ issue, but they will do."

"Thank you, Harold, where did you get these?" When Karl saw the disapproving expression in Harold's face, he corrected himself. "Never mind, I know, don't ask."

The newly 'borrowed' pants fit much better, and they had now a spare pair on hand, which in an emergency, could be used by either one of them. When the boys showed up in the Sturmbannfuehrer's office he did not even glance at the pants, he just sniffed the air.

"You did good Karl, our horsemeat is presently 'schmoring' and we will enjoy it later on." He went to the U-Bahn chart on the wall. Most of the little pins and flags, which were before cluttered all over the map were gone and the few remaining ones were now in a tight circle around the 'Innenstadt' (city center).

"To make it short, I have no good news. The Soviet forces gained control in the outlying areas and some of them are already advancing towards the city center." The Sturmbannfuehrer pointed on the chart to the location of the Zoo Flak Tower, indicated with a white pinhead. "Between the Zoo Bunker, the Humboldthain Bunker and our own Friedrichshain Bunker, we have less than 30,000 troops left with maybe another 15,000 Volkssturm members. We are supported by less than 1,000 tanks, and we are facing three major Russian forces exceeding over one million troops and in excess of 20,000 tanks and pieces of artillery."

Bernd stepped back from the chart and pulled out the chair from behind his desk to sit down. His gray hair was matted and without any sheen. His eyes were tired and deep in their sockets. "Sit down boys," the SS leader talked as if he were in a trance. "I received orders from the OKW this morning that the subway system is to be flooded. All the charges have been set and only need to be triggered. I refuse to carry out the orders and I expect to be arrested or shot before this day is up." His posture did not resemble the officer the boys used to know. He sat hunched over his desk and his hands supported his forehead.

"If you know that your decision of refusing orders is the right decision, and if you expect an imminent arrest, why are you waiting for it to happen," asked Harold. He threw a questioning look at Karl and when he saw no objection he continued. "Herr Sturmbannfuehrer, Karl and I are able to make you disappear. Nobody will find you until you decide to come out of hiding."

The tired officer glanced around the room and then connected with Harold's eyes. "Yes, but then what? If my fellow officers don't kill me, I will get shot by the Russians or banned to Siberia. Not much of a choice. But I will think about it." He waved the boys out of the office and when they closed the door Karl could hear him saying, "Stand by in the mess. I might need to talk with you again."

Harold kept on walking but Karl experienced another anxiety attack. He was leaning on the wall and his eyes darted sideways and back, but without focus and his breathing was fast and shallow.

"Dang," said Harold coming back to Karl. He was just about to make a snide remark when he realized the seriousness of Karl's condition. Without asking any questions, he pressed his shoulder under Karl's arm and dragged him to their sleeping quarters.

"Lay down," he said, and looked for an additional blanket to cover Karl. The very moment Harold had attended to him, Karl was feeling better; as a matter of fact, much better. In the hallway he had feared for a moment that he was losing his senses, but then Dr. Felder came back to his mind and the various conversations they had after their encounter with the Russian tank in Poland.

Dr. Felder had worried at that time that Karl might experience some severe stress symptoms. His previous advice proved invaluable now. "You need to relax your mind," the doctor said. "If you are with someone, you need to talk with him; if nobody is around, count backwards from a single digit number, visualize the number and if possible, assign a color to it." All of Dr. Felder's advice has always been simple, maybe even primitive, but it always worked.

Karl sat up on the cot and looked in the direction of Harold. "Sit down, please. I need to talk to someone."

As Harold listened, Karl told him about Georg and the execution squad. After he was done, he felt a lot better and silently thanked God to be alive.

Harold and Karl never talked about God. For Karl, his relationship with God was a very personal relationship, and he felt very good about it. It was definitely not up for discussion. Not with Harold or anyone else.

After Karl finished his narrative, he started to relax. His heartbeat slowed back down to its regular beat and he knew that he had just experienced a perfectly normal reaction. Most of all, he knew that he was not in danger of losing his mind. He looked up at Harold and fully expected some ridicule in regard to his soiled pants, but Harold's habit of making fun at Karl's expense did not kick in.

Instead he asked, "Will you be able to recognize the

Rottenfuehrer if you see him again? I mean if you would see him across the street, could you point him out for me?"

Karl got up from his cot and paced the room. "In a way, I hope that I will be able to forget him in time, but right now? Yes, I would recognize him." Karl was staring at a spot on the wall. He wanted to say some more, but decided against it.

A runner came storming into their room "The Sturmbannfuehrer wants you on the double."

Karl was the first one in the office with Harold right behind him. "We suffered massive Volkssturm casualties," Officer Bernd announced, "Right at the entrance of the bunker. Get down there and help where you can. When you are not needed any more come back up here."

The boys worked for over two hours with various HJ rescue teams to carry the wounded across the street to the subway entrance, where they were loaded in one of the parked trains. It was not a designated hospital train and there were only two doctors on hand to treat about 150 soldiers. As it turned out, they were the casualties of a Katyuska attack that had completely leveled the area around the bunker. The soldiers were part of a reinforcement group assembled to relieve the fighting units around the Fehrbelliner Platz.

When the boys reported back to officer Bernd, their uniforms were ripped and bloody and dirty beyond recognition. Even their faces were a sweaty mess.

But so was the face of the Sturmbannfuehrer.

"Get back in the subway tunnel and rescue anyone you can. Our very own SS bastards blew the bulkheads and the water is coming in and rising."

Karl wanted to answer that the water could only rise to a certain level, but the Sturmbannfuehrer pushed the boys into the hallway and closed the door.

Karl shrugged his shoulders at Harold. "If we tell them that the Landwehrkanal is busted, we will create a chaos in the station." As they were running towards the staircase, they heard the muffled but unmistakable sharp crack of a 9mm handgun behind them. Both boys turned and looked at each other.

There was no one in the hallway. Harold was the first to understand what happened. "It must be Bernd," he hollered at Karl, and ran back to the Sturmbannfuehrer's office. The lifeless body of the SS officer was slumped over in his chair and his handgun was on the floor. He must have shot himself in the temple.

"Get one of the guards," Harold was shouting at Karl as he closed the door from the outside.

Karl went flying down the staircase right into the arms of three SS policemen who came storming up. With firm movements, they pushed Karl to the side and continued up the stairs and stopped in front of the Sturmbannfuehrer's office. Two of them drew their weapons while the third one, a Hauptscharfuehrer, (Master Sergeant) who was not a policeman, stepped to the side of the door.

"You are too late," said Harold, who had retreated a few feet.

The two SS policemen took no note of him and busted into the small cubicle. "The swine of a traitor killed himself," Karl could hear their shouts of disappointment as he raced up the stairs again with Fritz, the entrance guard leader, right behind him.

The two Sturmmen were dragging the corpse of Officer Bernd out of the office and down the hallway while the Hauptscharfuehrer went around the desk and started to open the desk drawers.

"Get out. I am in charge of bunker security," announced Fritz to the non-commissioned SS Officer.

"And you will remain in charge," said the young blonde officer. "However, I am the new holder of this office. I am now in command of the U-Bahn defense units. Here are my credentials." He took a single sheet of paper from his top pocket and laid it on the desk.

Fritz picked it up and read the brief order. It identified the Hauptscharfuehrer, with the name of Albrecht, as commando leader in charge of the 'inner ring' U-Bahn system. It carried the current date and was signed by General Mohnke, the dreaded SS defense commander of Berlin.

Fritz, however, was not entirely satisfied. "This looks authentic to me, Herr Hauptscharfuehrer Albrecht. However, you need to go up to the fifth floor to have this document countersigned by the bunker commander. Until then, you cannot stay in this office or remove anything from it."

Fritz was so obstinate, almost threatening, that the Hauptscharfuehrer considered to pull rank on the security officer, but decided against it and went up to see the commander on the fifth floor. Fritz stayed for a few minutes inside the office and then closed and locked the door from the outside. Karl, who had watched the exchange of words between the SS men from the hallway, wondered why Fritz had stayed in the office.

"What do you make of that?" he speculated to Harold as they went down to hurry across the street to the subway entrance.

"Nothing," answered his friend," You have to stop thinking about things which are not directly related to our survival."

"That's exactly what I have been wondering about," said Karl, "I am just trying to connect the dots."

Thirty Three

The subway station was in turmoil. Karl noticed that the water had already stopped rising, but so far it did not look like it was receding. There was really not much the boys could do to help. The rumors were flying around again. Most of them were about drowned children and wounded soldiers. The latter ones supposedly drowned in the hospital trains. Every one of the civilians scrambling out of the tunnels reported about a different incident.

"Now would be good time to disappear to our hideaway. Our commander is dead and no one knows about us," suggested Harold.

"Let's not decide on that right now," answered Karl, "We still might be able to help a lot of people. But, I agree to check on our place. We need to know if it even still exists."

Since the water stood over three feet in the tunnels, the boys decided to walk part of their way through the connected basements of the apartment houses. But every so often they had to walk on the streets. They were stopped a few times by SS patrols, but Karl's credentials still carried weight. None of the patrols knew about the suicide of the Sturmbannfuehrer and since the boys carried no weapons, they were always released after a few threatening questions.

Most of the questions centered about the fact that they were walking on the street although they were designated to transverse in the subway tunnels.

Karl had a standard answer. "The U-Bahn has been flooded and we are on the way to the next station to determine the extent of the damage."

When they finally reached their hiding place, it was already dark. The entrances to the Uhlandstrasse Subway Station on the Kurfuerstendam were barricaded and a sign proclaimed 'Flooded - Closed'. In spite of the barricades, there were still some people emerging from the lower platform.

"How high is the water level?" Harold asked the next person coming up. It was an older woman, a little bit over 5 feet tall. She was severely limping and it took her a while to understand the question. "Not too high, she answered, "maybe a foot above the platform level. But you should not go down. There are bodies floating over the tracks and there is no place to sit or sleep down there." The dress below her waistline was dripping wet and Karl felt sorry for her.

"Do you have a place to go to," He asked her.

"Yes, I live not far from here and I think my apartment is still undamaged. But, two days ago the main gas line going through our basement got smashed. I think that there are still some poisoned bodies below the rubble. It just smells terrible. I am afraid that the subway will start smelling the same."

"Do you need any help," asked Harold.

"No, I am fine, thank you just the same." Her voice sounded almost fearful and as she eagerly shuffled away, she left a small trail of water on the sidewalk.

Karl ducked under the barricade and went a few steps down. He wanted to see the maximum height the water had reached by looking at the walls of the entrance. "Our stash should still be dry. I don't think that the water went that high." He came up and was about to crawl under the barricade to get out when Harold tapped his head. "SS coming; get down." Karl laid down flat with Harold right beside him. The SS patrol inspected the entrance on the opposite sidewalk and it looked to the boys as if they were trying to find shelter from the artillery shells, which again pounded the length of the Kurfuerstendam. The boys crawled away in the darkness without being noticed.

A short while later they were removing the rubble on top of the grate covering their hideout. Harold went down while Karl watched on top.

"Everything is dry and fine." Harold gave Karl two packs of cigarettes and a small tin of corned beef as he inched out again. "Why don't we stay here? We have food and blankets and could easily hide here for two weeks."

"Yes, we could do that," answered Karl, "if we would know for sure that the war would be over in two weeks. But what if there really is a super or wonder weapon? We cannot simply reappear. I think that we should report back to the new commander and see what his orders are. We might be able to help some of the soldiers in the hospital trains." Karl was indicating to Harold to get back down and followed him into the airshaft. The exploding artillery shells were just too close to stay above ground.

"You must be out of your mind," Harold was upset, "Why are you talking about a super weapon? You know that it doesn't exist. We will get overrun within a day or two and we both know that the Mongolians are not taking prisoners in Berlin. If we really want to survive, we should stay right here."

Karl knew that Harold was right. Their chances of survival were much greater if they stayed right where they were. Due to the blankets they had stashed away, their little shelter was almost cozy and the water level was more than eight feet below their resting place in the wall. "Look, Harold, you can stay here if you want to, but think about it, we survived this long. One more day of action will not get us killed. Let's keep a clean record for one or two more days."

Karl was almost pleading and Harold felt kind of sorry for his friend who was apparently not thinking right. "I did not think you were that loyal, Karl. However, I will not stay behind. I will go back to Friedrichshain with you."

Karl shook his head, "Loyal? No, Harold, I am only loyal to a certain degree. But I do think that we still could help some of the trapped civilians. Nobody knows the emergency exits better than we do." Karl wrapped a second blanket around himself and pushed some of the provisions out of the way. "For right now, we stay put. We should eat something and wait until it is safe to leave."

They opened a package of Knaeckebrot and had some of the water they had saved in glass milk bottles. A few hours later, the shelling slowed down and the boys were on their way back to the flak tower. To their surprise, there was hot coffee and bread and jelly in the mess room and they helped themselves before they reported to their new commander. Hauptscharfuehrer Albrecht was the opposite from Sturmbannfuehrer Bernd. He was maybe 22 years old and brazen. When the boys entered his office, Harold observed that the uniform of the Hauptscharfuehrer lacked any kind of medal or indication of actual combat experience.

"Where were you last evening?" His voice carried no accent, which caused Karl to think that their new leader came from the area of Hannover. He wondered if Albrecht had any understanding of the Berlin U-Bahn system or if he even ever rode in a subway car.

"We were ordered by Sturmbannfuehrer Bernd to assist civilians escaping from the flooded tunnels." Karl was back to his short replies, but apparently he should not have mentioned officer Bernd.

"The Sturmbannfuehrer was a traitor. His orders were invalid and you should have waited until you received your new orders from me."

"We had people drowning in the tunnels. They needed our help," Harold tried to help his friend.

"People? You mean civilians. It served them right. They should have stayed in their apartment shelters. Their very presence in the tunnels hinders our defense effort." Harold wanted to answer but the Hauptscharfuehrer cut him off. "You stand at attention when I address you and only speak when asked." Harold snapped to it and in a somehow perverse way he was happy about the officer's abrasive manner. He was sure that pretty soon they would be in their hideout because his friend would not take much of this abuse.

Karl was standing close to the wall. He had noticed that the small green notebook from officer Bernd was gone from the shelf behind the desk. However, all the other items still seemed to be in their usual places. He turned to face the subway charts and studied the small circle of flags. There were still a few pinned right in the center of the city. All the other ones had been removed.

"What are you looking at?" The Hauptscharfuehrer barked, "There is nothing left in the subway for you to do. You will not leave the bunker anymore. You are herewith released from your former duty and will report to the flak commander on the fifth floor for reassignment." He waved at the boys to leave when he noted their dirty uniforms. "Halt, you are a disgrace to the HJ. Get cleaned up first. On the double."

There was turmoil outside the office and then the door flew open and two tall SS men entered. Harold noticed that they had the metal shields of a court marshal detail hanging over their chests.

"Knock before you enter!" shouted the Hauptscharfuehrer.

"We were ordered here to retain one of your subway rats to guide us through the Friedrichstrasse U-Bahn station." Harold was already in the hallway waiting for Karl, who stood frozen in the doorframe.

"We need that boy right now," continued the tall SS man in a heavy Bavarian accent.

"There is a fast assignment for you," ordered the Hauptscharfuehrer as he looked at Harold who had entered again. Harold had within a split second connected the Bavarian accent with his friend's behavior and was now blocking with his body any view of Karl, who edged sideways out of the office. "Alright, both of you go," hollered Albrecht, "but report back to me before you see the bunker commander for reassignment. I might have more work for you than I thought."

Karl was racing down the staircase taking two steps at a time. "I'll see you in the station, second track," he yelled at his friend who was following him with the SS men. Karl wanted to get into the darkness of the tunnel before the SS detail leader had a chance to recognize him.

"Where do you need to go," asked Harold when they entered the station.

"We want to go to the tunnel where the deserters from the front line try to infiltrate with the civilians," answered the Rottenfuehrer. "We don't know exactly where this is, which is why we need you to guide us."

Harold nodded in agreement and waited for Karl, who was now standing next to them, to take the initiative. "Det is so dufte einfach, imma an da wand lang, imma an da wand lang," (This is easy, follow me along the wall). Karl spoke now in a unique Berlin accent, which he never used, but was capable of. It completely disguised his voice.

There was no love lost between the people of Bavaria and the people of Berlin. The Berliner thought of the Bavarian as stupid mountain ranchers, mixed blood from earlier Roman soldiers...after all, you could clearly see it on their brown skin...The Bavarians on the other hand, thought of the Berliners as people with a big mouth, a real big mouth...but what really infuriated them was the well known fact that the people from Berlin could back it up.

Karl already had a plan. He was thinking of guiding the SS detail right behind the combat zone. Let them exit at an airshaft and then drop down and lock the exit grate in place. With any luck, this would place the detail right between the fighting troops and the Mongolian women. He could not think of a nicer place for the court marshal unit to be.

The Rottenfuehrer sickened when he heard the Berlin accent. It grated on him since he had arrived in Berlin and to make it worse, he could barely understand a word of it. "Get away from me, you rotten shorty, and stay behind." He looked at Harold. "You speak like a normal human being, you lead." He did not waste another look at Karl, who used his best accent to tell Harold which direction to take.

The water in the tunnel was still standing one to two feet high, which made their walk uncomfortable and annoyed the SS men. "There has to be a better way than to get wet and dirty," complained the second SS man, a regular Sturmman, who usually kept quiet.

"Shut up," answered the Rottenfuehrer, "The flooded tunnel will entice many deserters. I expect that we will be very successful."

The group had walked for about twenty minutes and was still a mile away from the point Karl had in mind, when he heard some guttural voices way ahead in the tunnel. "Listen," he ordered. The SS policemen pulled their handguns and pressed their ears to the wall. When they did not hear anything, they started to walk again. Harold took the lead again, but was walking a lot slower. He trusted the ears of his friend; besides, he thought that they had already passed the street-to-street combat zone above.

The Sturmman cursed when his foot hung up on something below the water line and he landed head first in the water. "Quiet," Karl reminded him when the SS man splashed around. Up to now he had not used his flashlight and was not about to do so in spite of the Sturmman's plea to look at what was hindering his walk. The Rottenfuehrer however, put his gun back in the holster and pulled out a powerful flashlight. He played the light over his buddy who finally untangled himself.

"Light out," hissed Harold. But, it was already too late. Shots from straight ahead reverberated in the tunnel and a few bullets whistled by the group. Karl and Harold were taking cover in the water while the Rottenfuehrer pressed himself against the wall. He still had the flashlight lit which invited a few more additional bullets, but all of them missed.

Apparently, a Soviet combat unit had either penetrated the tunnel or at least taken a position in it. Since the first shot rang out, not even a minute had passed and now both of the boys were as wet as the Sturmman.

"Back, back," roared the Rottenfuehrer and in his hurry to retreat, he ran into his partner pushing him back into the water. Karl could not see this but the cursing of the two SS men left little doubt as to what was happening. "Halt your cussing. I can't hear the Russians. They might be just a few men and I can lead you around on the second track. Then we blind them with our lights and take them out." Harold was disgusted at the SS men's behavior, but his words fell on deaf ears.

"Insane," screeched the Rottenfuehrer, "You are insane. I don't want to die in this tunnel. We have to run."

Karl did not wait for a different order. He started to walk back where they had just come from. The water hindered all of them from breaking into a run. However, the Rottenfuehrer managed to take the lead by roughly pushing his partner and the boys to the side. Karl used this opportunity to whisper to his friend, "Let's split up. We meet at our place." Before Harold could answer, another few shots screamed by them and this time the Sturmman got hit.

"My leg, I got hit in my leg," he yelled and tried to hold on to the Rottenfuehrer. Karl pressed the lever of his light and could see that the Rottenfuehrer freed himself by punching the Sturmman in the face.

"We need to carry this man," yelled Karl at the Rottenfuehrer, who kept on walking.

"Let him be," he bellowed, "He is a weakling anyhow. He does not deserve to live."

"Next airshaft. Try to get him out through the next airshaft," Karl was keeping his voice down, trusting that Harold understood. He did not have time to lose if he wanted his backup plan to work. He labored to overtake the Rottenfuehrer, who was walking fast and gasping hard and struggling to stay ahead of Karl. Behind them they could hear some splashing and Karl was hoping that it was Harold with the Sturmman.

"Can you hear them coming? You need to run faster," he hissed at the Rottenfuehrer when he passed him. He now constantly pressed his dynamo light, partially illuminating the wall on his left. He estimated that he was close to his destination and slowed down to examine the wall, but still blocking the Rottenfuehrer from getting ahead of him. He was looking for the bulkhead to the sewer line and when he saw the indention half way up the wall, he pointed it out to the SS man.

"Let's get up here. There is an emergency exit behind the steel door." Karl wanted to climb up first to open the bulkhead, but was brutally thrown back in the water by the Rottenfuehrer who had almost given up but got a second wind when he saw the rungs in the wall. He climbed up and in doing so he was also trying to step on Karl's hands and head, who had recovered from the toss in the water and was now coming up behind him.

The Rottenfuehrer lamented and cursed as he tried to move the steel lever to open the partition. "Let me help you," said Karl, but the SS man pushed him back again and finally managed to open the steel gate. In his hurry to escape, he did not become aware of the foul smell from the sewage canal. He lifted himself through the opening and started to descend on the other side when he noticed that the water was higher than in the tunnel he was escaping. He was holding on to the rungs on the inside and standing on the ledge the boys had detected before. "Hell," he screamed, "how deep is this?"

It seemed to Karl that the Rottenfuehrer wanted to climb back up again, but this was not to be. Karl already had the heavy bulkhead halfway shut when the SS man had moved down the other side. With a firm effort, he closed it all the way and the heavy steel lever fell back in place. He had wanted to say something fitting to the head of the flying court marshal squad but in the excitement of the final struggle, he found no words. He was in a cold sweat, shaking and feeling miserable, but his mind directed his thoughts to Georg and he felt better. Not much better, but enough to get a hold of his emotions.

He listened for some sounds from the direction of the Russians, but it was quiet. The last thing he had heard was some splashing, which he attributed to his friend. Before he kept on going, he took a moment to collect his thoughts. If he wanted to serve with the flak units in the bunker, he needed to exit now, close to the station where they had started out. In the last moment he decided against it because he also tried to envision what was happening above. Due to their brief encounter with the Russian combat unit in the tunnel, he knew about where the fighting line had to be. It seemed to him that the Soviets had bypassed the bunker and if that was the case, they could already be close to Harold's and his hide out. It was decision time. And he decided to live. He kept on walking.

Thirty Four

Karl was able to continue through the U-Bahn tunnels until he reached the station close to the Zoo Bunker. But when he tried to exit, he saw a T34 Soviet tank advancing on the Kurfuerstendam. It was a frightful sight as the tank moved slowly and almost systematically back and forth spraying the cellar windows with its flame-thrower, setting everything it touched on fire.

Karl knew that the flak on top of the Zoo Bunker could take the tank out, but it seemed that the tank commander knew that too. He kept his tank close to the corner of the former café Kranzler and did not move any further towards the burnt out Kaiser Wilhelm Gedaechtniskirche. However, his machine gun raked the intersection whenever something collapsed or moved. If there ever was a killing machine, this was it.

Karl was waiting for the Soviet infantry to show up, but there was none to be seen. Instead, he saw a second and third tank taking up a position directly across from the subway station. They behaved like the tank spearhead he had encountered in Poland. They did not shoot. There were no machine guns mounted on top and no flame-throwers spitting fire. They just stood there like a monument.

Karl was shaking uncontrollably from the top of his head down to his toes. He did not know if this was due to his wet clothes or if it was sheer fright. He tried to sort out his thoughts and figured that this shaking might be a natural reaction to his weakness. He had not eaten since the Knaeckebrot in their shelter and that was close to 24 hours ago.

"Do you have a Panzerfaust nearby?" He heard a voice next to him. He looked to see an HJ member of his age, and like him, he was shaking and terrified. The boy had no weapon on him and his eyes were wide open in horror. "No," said Karl trying to make contact with his eyes.

"Then we are dead," said the boy.

"No, we are not," answered Karl, "we are still breathing."

"Yes, we are dead," insisted the boy, "Look over there, at the lamp post on the corner. That was my friend. He did not fire his Panzerfaust and he ran for cover from the flamethrower. The SS caught him a few hours ago. They executed him and hung his body up for all to see as an example. Then they herded us up and made us look at him. They are still in the station below us. We are not allowed to retreat."

"Cannot be," said Karl, "you have no weapon and no ammunition. You cannot fight these tanks with your bare hands."

The boy shook his head, "It does not matter. They want to use us as bait for the Soviets to use up their ammunition. We might not be dead now, but we will be before evening."

Karl looked around. He was lying near the top of the station exit. When he had crawled up from the platform, he had only seen civilians. He did not remember passing HJ units or an SS commando. He glanced at the boy next to him and noticed that his uniform was wet below his belt. He must have somehow crossed from the other side of the station. Therefore, the HJ and SS units could be still on the other side. However, if this boy had made it, the others could have too. He looked again at the tanks, which had not moved. The first tank had stopped using his flame-thrower and now stood close to the other ones. Only his machine gun was still active, shooting from time to time at seemingly nothing. There was still no infantry in sight. "What is your name and the name of your outfit?" Karl asked the boy.

"My name is Heinz. My outfit is from Tempelhof. We were 156 boys when we moved out yesterday morning."

Karl was astonished. "My name is Karl, but did you say 156? Down here in the station? How could I have missed you guys?"

"We are now down to about 30. We defended the airport."

The voice of Heinz was toneless and defeated. Karl considered his options. He could stay up where he was until the tanks moved. However, if the tanks decided to roll to the entrance and spray the steps with their flame-throwers or with their machine guns, his chance of survival was less than marginal. He could slither back in the tunnel but if there was really an SS squad waiting, this was not much of an option either.

"Did your unit or the SS unit follow you from the other side of the station," he asked Heinz.

"I don't know. What's the difference?"

"Follow me," Karl said, "stay low and no more talking."

Slowly he crawled backwards down a few steps and then stopped and turned on his stomach to see if he could spot any uniforms directly below him. He could not see far enough into the dark station to be absolutely sure, but he took a chance by sliding all the way down to the platform. Nobody stopped him and when Heinz appeared next to him, he decided to press their good luck. He stepped down from the platform, which was barely covered with water into the deeper section of the tracks. Heinz did not hesitate either and within a short moment, both boys were in the safety of the dark tunnel.

Karl wanted to get at least to the next airshaft, but he hesitated when his dynamo light illuminated a floating body in front of him.

So far he had not encountered any drowned victims and even now he was not sure if the body in front of him had drowned or was maybe trampled to death in the initial panic when the tunnels were flooded. Not that the cause of the death mattered, but Karl was getting afraid being in the foul water. It was bad enough with all the filth and excrement floating around, but now the addition of dead bodies really concerned and frightened him.

Heinz apparently had none of these misgivings. He simply pushed the body out of the way and waited for Karl to take the lead again.

The next ventilation shaft proved to be unsuitable to serve as an escape. It was totally buried under debris and the boys were unable to push the grate open.

"Is there another shaft like this somewhere?" Heinz wanted to know.

"Yes, there is," said Karl, who was relieved to see that during their short walk together, his new companion had somehow perked up.

A short time later they succeeded in opening the grate of the next shaft. They were now close to the Uhlandstrasse and it was almost dark. They looked up and down the Kurfuerstendam, but besides the continued shelling by the artillery, they could not see any activity.

"How do you feel about us going back to the station? We might be able to get some of your friends away from the SS," Karl asked, as he searched his mind if this was a good idea and if he would be able to pull this off. But, he reasoned, if he could just get one more boy to safety it would be worth it. Then again, he had also to consider where he could hide the boys. He looked into the eyes of Heinz and saw that the terror was gone, but his answer was still slow.

"We could try it, if you think it would be possible, but where would we go from here?"

"One thing at a time," answered Karl, "I cannot possibly know where we will go from here because I don't know what it will look like when we get back here." He padded Heinz on the shoulder. "Stay here for awhile. It might take me some time, but I'll be back."

"Wait," said Heinz, "will it take you more than an hour?"

"It might. I want to see if I can find a secure place for your group."

"If I am not here when you return, I will be in the tunnel trying to connect with my unit." Heinz sounded eager to help his friends.

Karl heaved himself out of the shaft, moved the grate back in its place and walked slowly along the nearby front of a former clothing store. He was within fifteen minutes of his hideout and he wanted to see if his friend had made it. Maybe Harold had an idea of how to proceed.

What he thought was a fifteen-minute walk turned out to be twice as long. He was constantly ducking in and out of the shadows and sometimes when he thought that he saw something moving, he waited before he went on. By the sound of the small arms fire, he reasoned that the Soviet infantry must still be at least ten blocks away. The Soviet tanks he had seen near the Zoo Bunker must have been a spearhead without any back up. It was really confusing because there was no real battle line. All he knew for sure was that the Soviet infantry had bypassed the armored bunkers and was now shredding the remaining German defense units street-by-street and house-by-house.

Harold was indeed in the hideaway when Karl arrived. He was lifting the grate and waving at Karl when he saw him entering the courtyard.

"Did you get the Sturmman out," Karl asked.

"It was not easy to make him climb up the ventilation duct. Once he was on the street, he just sat down. He was not seriously wounded, but stinking mad at the Rottenfuehrer to leave him behind. He asked me to get him some medical help. I ran into a unit of the Volkssturm and sent them in his direction. Then I came directly here."

"Good," said Karl and told Harold about Heinz and his unit.

Harold nodded his head, "Yes, I also saw some bodies strung up not far from here at the Guentzel Strasse lamp posts and also further down on the Ludwigkirchplatz. They all had signs attached to them."

"Signs?"

"Yes, some ripped up cardboard, they read something like: 'I am hanging here because I refused to defend my Fatherland'. There were some other signs, but it was already dark and I did not stop to decipher them."

"Any suggestion where we could hide the boys from Tempelhof? If we are able to get them out, that is." Karl wanted to get back to Heinz.

"Yes, but first we have to make sure that no one can get up to us from below. I started to throw some debris down the shaft, but then I did not know from which side you might be coming in."

There was plenty of rubble close by and in no time at all, they were done with their job. The shaft below their shelf was now blocked.

"I have to get back to Heinz. What's your idea of a safe place for the boys?"

"Let's eat something first, and then I'll show you."

Karl was so hungry that he wolfed down whatever Harold handed him. He did not even know what was in the tins.

"Remember the older lady who came out of the Uhlandstrasse station?" Harold talked while he was chewing on his bread. "She mentioned a broken gas line and some dead bodies in the basement. We should inspect the basements of the buildings she referred too. They would be easy to find because I watched her when she left."

"And then what," asked Karl.

"Let's go and find the buildings. If there are still some corpses in the basement, then none of the tenants will enter the cellar. We can place the boys in the basement and move the dead bodies near the entrance. That might be enough of a deterrent for the Russians to enter and search."

It did not take more than thirty minutes and the boys found that the basement in question lent itself almost perfect for their purpose.

All of the upper floors of the building were gone and the entrance to the basement was also nearly impossible to detect. Actually, they found the entrance only because of the awful smell coming from below.

"What do you think," smiled Harold.

"This might work. The boys would only have to stay in here for a few days." Karl admired his friend for his resourcefulness. It was almost midnight and the fighting had still not come any closer, but this could change at any moment, and they had to get off the streets sooner rather than later.

When Karl approached the air duct where he had left Heinz behind, he was in for a pleasant surprise. The boy had been back to the station where he had made contact with several members of his unit and they had been able to enter the tunnel unseen by the SS squad.

"We hoped that you would come back. Right now we have 14 boys lined up down here, and more might be coming." Heinz appeared changed. The possibility of staying alive had been enough to charge him up and he was impatient for Karl to carry on.

"Look," said Karl, "you might have to hide for a few days in an awful smelling place. But, there is a much better chance of survival than in the subway station. Harold and I," and he pointed to Harold, "will get you some food. But then you are on your own."

Harold led the way back to the basement and the boys, from time to time, left a member behind to guide any latecomers to their shelter. By the time the morning broke, they had guided 22 HJ members to the relative safety of the basement. Karl and Harold were almost tempted to stay with the group. They felt at ease to be surrounded by comrades and except for the horrible smell, the basement was almost pleasant. There were some air raid shelter cots to sleep on and to their surprise, there was also a whole shelf of glass bottles filled with water.

Karl instructed them how to form a 'body movement detail' to bring the corpses up to the entrance and also, how to leave a portion open to allow fresh air to enter. In the meantime, Harold made several trips to their little shelter to bring the boys some food.

"Make yourselves some observation holes and have one of you

on the lookout constantly. Wait at least a full day for the combat zone to pass before you come out. And under no circumstances are you to keep any weapons down here. If you feel that you need your weapons, then stash them somewhere else. The Mongolians will slit your throat if they find the bunch of you armed." Karl reminded Heinz of the obvious and shook his hand.

"Do you think that one day of waiting is sufficient?"

"No, I think that I would stay hidden until the food runs out. But, in any event, one day is the bare minimum."

Karl shook hands with all of the boys and wished them well.

Harold was already waiting for him and they went together to their own shelter. The courtyard where their airshaft was located had suffered some additional damage during the night. The remaining walls surrounding the area had all been leveled by artillery guns, but the shelter entrance was still accessible.

"What date is today," asked Harold.

"April 30, but I may have lost a day. It might be May 1st already." Karl was not so sure himself. The events of the last days had been a blur.

"Should we stay here by ourselves or would we be better off in joining the group in the basement?" Harold wondered for the third time if they had made the right decision.

"We stay here, because we know that we are safe in our place. If we team up with the group, we are no longer in control. Any mistake by any one of them can cost us our lives." Karl was adamant. "Did you leave us any..." he did not finish his question because he heard the grinding of chains coming from the street. "Down, down," hissed Karl as he pushed his friend down the opening. It was not a second too soon. As the Russian tank rolled into the courtyard, it also opened fire and strafed the remaining ruins from top to bottom with its machine gun. Karl had barely enough time to pull the grate on top of him and when he heard the roar of the flame-thrower, he rolled himself sideways into their shelf.

The tank driver took his time turning the big monster right and left and blasted the whole area with his machine gun and flame-thrower, which was nothing more than ruins and rubble.

The acid smell of the flame-thrower caused the boys to cough uncontrollably and they pressed themselves deep into the ledge.

For a moment they had visions of being cooked as the inferno passed over the top of the vent shaft. The heat was so oppressive that for a few seconds, it was impossible for them to breathe.

Fortunately, the flame-thrower did not linger over the airshaft entrance and continued to sweep the area.

Satisfied that nothing was alive or moving, the tank driver continued on his way by simply rolling his brute over the walls of the ruins onto the next street. The whole action of the tank did not last more than ten minutes, but for the boys, it seemed like an eternity. Harold was the first one to recover, but he was still fighting for air as he pushed himself away from the wall. He could hear the diminishing sound of the chains and tried to touch the grate, testing to see if it was too hot to move.

Karl was holding him back. "Don't," he managed to say.

"It's not hot," Harold assured him.

"Psst, quiet, there might be soldiers following the panzer." Karl wanted to wait a lot longer than Harold, who was impatient to look around.

It was nearly impossible to distinguish anything between the noises above. They could hear other chained vehicles further away and now and then machine gun blasts. None of this was close to them and they assumed that there was no defense unit in their immediate vicinity. They knew that the Waffen SS would put up a fight around the Zoo Flak Bunker, but that was about a kilometer away. They had also observed several Wehrmacht columns during the night and they overheard that there was a defense line being established along the Schillerstrasse, which was only a few blocks away.

Karl had been right with his precaution. Within a few minutes they could hear shuffling footsteps. They seemed to be right on top of them and as Karl tried to determine if this was many or just a single soldier, he noticed that his heart was beating so hard he thought it was loud enough to alert the soldiers. He made an effort to slow his heartbeat down and looked over to Harold who was motionless kneeling next to him. There was no sound coming from his direction and Karl concluded that it must be the blood pressure in his ears giving him the impression that his heart was beating too loud. He shifted around in the meager space he had and discerned that he could no longer hear his heartbeat. It must have been his blood pressure.

"Have we waited long enough," asked Harold after another twenty minutes.

"I don't understand your hurry to make a mistake." Karl had

made up his mind to stay off the street anyhow and wondered what Harold thought he could possibly gain from looking around and maybe getting discovered.

"Alright, then we just eat and sleep." Harold moved the blankets around and made himself comfortable. "You have not told me how you got away from the Rottenfuehrer. Was it the same guy who executed Georg," asked Harold as he searched through their stash to find some Knaeckebrot.

"Yes he was, and I did not get away from him. He got away from me," Karl answered.

"He took off?"

"Well, not exactly. He was so afraid of the Russians that he climbed into the sewage system to escape."

"Really? There is no exit from the sewage system. What did you do?"

"I closed the bulkhead behind him." Karl's answer did not betray his emotions.

Thirty Five

All through the remainder of the day they could hear small arms fire and machine guns. From time to time they could hear running and footsteps. Every time the footsteps came close, they could also hear the rasping sounds of Russian soldiers communicating. When the evening came, the combat noises increased.

"I think the Waffen SS from the Zoo Flak Tower is staging a counter attack," Karl speculated.

"How so?" Harold had not enjoyed being in their shelter all day. Patience was not his strong suit and if it had been up to him, they would have left their hideout right after the sounds of the first Soviet soldiers diminished.

"I can clearly hear the different sounds of our Tiger Panzer. Don't you notice that the Russians are running and screeching in panic?"

Karl had a hold of Harold, who wanted to sneak a look again.

"Yeah," agreed Harold, "I can even hear the Germans yelling and exchanging orders."

The combat noises came from the next street over, and only now and then they could hear someone running through their courtyard.

By midnight however, it sounded like the SS was retreating again and shortly thereafter, they could hear that a German unit seemed to re-group right above them within the rubble of their area. By now they could differentiate between the hard sounding steps of the SS boots and the mushy sound of the Russian shoes or whatever they were wearing.

Karl could hear the sharp German commands to take cover around the former gateway of the courtyard and wait for the Russians to enter their territory. However, the Russians engaged them differently than the SS had expected. The Russian infantry had retreated, and then all of a sudden there were the loud screaming noises of Katyusha rockets howling above them towards the Schillerstrasse. At the same time and under the cover of the deafening noise of the Katyushas, several Russian tanks moved in from the street and their flame-throwers opened up on the surprised and now trapped SS troops.

The indescribable awful terrible stench from burning flesh and the screaming of the burning bodies sent shivers of terror down the spines of the boys. Fortuitously for the boys, none of the SS men had been close to their grate and the tanks were concentrating their assault on the corner where the Germans had dug in. It was an entirely uneven match of men with rifles and handguns against the killing machines of the tanks.

It was over in less than ten minutes and the tanks spitting bullets and flames kept on moving towards the Kaiser Wilhelm Gedaechtniskirche and the Zoo Bunker. The screaming of the dying stopped as fast as it had started. Even if the boys had wanted to help the wounded, there was nothing they could have done.

Karl, as well as Harold, was mortally scared and unable to move. When Karl had finally gained control of his senses and said something to Harold, he received nothing but silence in return. But after a long while, Karl could hear Harold mumbling, "The screaming, the terrible, terrible, screaming; I cannot get them out of my ears."

The morning came, but the sun was unable to break through the oppressive battle dust. The heavy guns from the flak bunkers fired point blank at the advancing Russian tanks, which were burning and disabled all around the Reichs Chancellery. However, the Soviet infantry could not be stopped. The boys could not possibly know if there was a distinctive front line. All they could hear was the still ongoing small arms fire in the neighboring streets, and the screaming of the Soviet women when they came running through the courtyard robbing the corpses of their final belongings.

Even though both of the boys were hungry, they were unable to eat. The massacre of the previous night had somehow affected their stomachs and when Karl looked at Harold, he could hardly recognize his friend. The ever-present big boyish smile was gone.

Harold was lying on his back and staring at the low carved out ceiling above him. There was a deep wrinkle under his vacant eyes, and Karl wondered if his friend would ever be the same again.

"Harold, snap out of it. For heaven's sake, we are alive and I think that the worst is behind us." Karl tried his best to get Harold to react, and he was relieved when he noticed some eye movement.

"Is it over?" Harold finally asked.

"I don't know," answered Karl, "but we survived so far and I believe the end must be near." He crawled out from under his blanket and up to the grate, which was covered with dust and minor debris.

"Are you finally ready to take a look?" Harold became interested in the efforts of Karl.

"Yes, it is daylight and we might be able see something, but first I want to listen." Karl pressed himself against the steel cover above him and strained his ears. "One thing seems to be sure, there is no more fighting in our immediate area." As he tried to lift and shift the grate to the side, he triggered a minor avalanche of dirt and muck. The dust again caused coughing fits.

"If we could rise above the ground level, it might be easier to breathe," speculated Harold. "We are practically suffocating because we are in the midst of this filth."

Karl watchfully moved the grate far enough to the side to enable him to take a peek. "There are plenty of footprints in the dirt around us." Karl cautiously lifted himself higher out of the shaft.

"You think we can move around without leaving tracks?" Harold was also sticking his head through the opening.

"Yes, I don't think that our tracks will be noticed in this mess."

Both of the boys were now standing upright but ready to drop in an instant. "You are right," said Karl, "It is much easier to breathe up here." Both of them filled their lungs with the cleaner air. It was not really that much cleaner, but it was far better than in their shelter.

"Now what? Where to?" asked Harold.

"Nowhere, let's just relax for a moment and then we have to get something into our stomachs before we leave this place; if we leave it at all today."

Karl rearranged a few cement fragments around the grate to afford a better view of the courtyard without having to stand up. Then he went back down to their shelf and opened an unmarked can. He looked surprised at the contents, which was cooked beans. He did not know that beans came in tins. The beans floated in some kind of thin soup, which was a lot tastier than just plain water.

"Harold, you have to try this," he said quietly to his friend who did not hear him. He had disappeared from the entrance. Karl liked the taste of the bean soup so much, that he finished it before he decided to look for Harold.

He spotted him about 30 feet away leaning over the unmoving shape of a soldier. He wanted to call him back, but then he figured that Harold would come back on his own. However, he was concerned that some follow up Russian units might surprise him, so he threw a small stone in his direction. Harold looked up and returned to the shelter. His face was ashen and his movements were slow when he sat down on the shelf next to Karl.

"None of the bodies have any rings or watches on their charred remains."

"What about their boots?"

"Boots? I think they are molten to the bodies; there is hardly enough of a body left to be buried on any of them."

Harold had his head between his knees and brushed Karl's hand away when his friend was offering him a wafer of the Fliegerschokolade. "I can't eat," he said.

Karl understood, but he also knew that his own appetite had returned when he had tried the watery soup. He searched the remainder of their food stash to find another unmarked can for Harold.

He interrupted his hunt when he noticed something unusual.

"Listen, Harold! Do you hear anything?"

"What? You don't have to shout to get me to listen." Harold was not moving and kept his position.

"I don't hear anything; I don't hear anything." Karl repeated and got up to stick his head out of their hole. The stillness around him was almost supernatural. For weeks they had been immersed in sounds of artillery, bombings, rockets and the rattling of tanks. Karl looked at his watch. It was 3:00 PM and the battle noises were gone. However, some far away jubilant shouting and singing very faintly disturbed what first seemed like utter silence.

Harold pushed Karl out of the way to listen for himself.

"I don't hear anything either," he said as he fully stood up outside the shaft. "You think our troops surrendered," he wondered out loud.

"Hard to say," answered Karl, "but most certainly the fighting has stopped."

"What do you think we should do?"

"For right now, let's enjoy the silence and the fact that we survived. I don't think that we should go anyplace. Somehow I don't trust this situation. I think now would be an excellent time for you to eat something." Karl went back down to their stash and came back with an unmarked can. He opened the tin with his knife and offered it to Harold. "Here, regardless of whether you have an appetite or not, this might just do the trick."

"You are right, this is good," agreed his friend, "now leave me alone, I can take care of myself." As stubborn as he was, he did take the chocolate Karl offered him again.

For a while they sat in silence. Each one had his own train of thought and Karl became aware that he could finally think a thread of thoughts all the way through to its completion without any interruption.

"What's that noise?" Harold was the first to hear it and then Karl could hear it too. It sounded like a loudspeaker, and the sound came nearer and nearer. "It must be a loudspeaker mounted on a vehicle," said Harold.

Finally they could discern the message, which was repeated over and over again: "Berlin has surrendered. All of the remaining German fighters, wounded or not, drop your weapons and come out of hiding and assemble..."

Although the message was always the same, the place of assembly changed as the truck with the loudspeaker advanced from one district to another.

"Let's go," said Harold.

"Go where?"

"You must be deaf. Didn't you just hear where we should assemble?" Harold got ready to leave their place.

"Are you nuts, Harold? Yesterday we disobeyed the SS to fight until our last breath, and now you want to answer the bugle call of the Soviets?" Karl was stunned at his friend's behavior.

Harold stopped in his tracks. "Then what do you want to do," he asked in bewilderment.

"Nothing, absolutely nothing." Karl almost shouted at his friend. "We have food. We have water. We stay here and if possible, we observe what happens to our troops at the assembly points." Karl was pretty firm to stay put.

"Then let's observe right now. Maybe we could use the subway tunnels to get to the assembly points. At least one of them should get us close enough to see what is going on." Harold was just as resolute, but bent on moving on.

"Alright," said Karl, "if this is what you want, we should compromise. I agree that we should observe, but in civilian clothing. Let's find Frau Becker. She promised to help us and at one time confided to me that she had civilian clothing for us."

"Let's get on with it," approved Harold, and went down with Karl to stuff their pockets with cans and cigarettes. When they got out, Karl helped Harold to cover the grate with some of the rubble. Just in case they had to come back.

They used the basements and courtyards of the apartment ruins as cover as they went slowly along the Uhlandstrasse towards Frau Becker's last address and arrived there shortly before sundown.

Along the way, they had waited out various Mongolian units, which combed the streets looking for the German women. The many screams coming mostly from cellar windows confirmed that they were successful in their search. Very often the screams ended abruptly with a single gunshot. Neither of the boys said a word as they tried to stay out of sight.

When they lastly arrived at Berlinerstrasse 26, nobody answered their knock on the apartment door. Karl was about to give up when a door further down the hall opened. An old invalid stood in the doorframe and beckoned the boys to enter. He turned out to be Herr Becker.

"Come in, we were hoping that you survived, but we did not expect you this fast. My wife is hiding in the cellar next door. We barricaded the entrance with some furniture. You can see her tomorrow." He was a WWI veteran and the boys could see that he had lost a leg. His hobble was slow and strained, but his face was one big smile. "You must be tired. You can sleep here on the floor in the kitchen. I will get you some blankets."

"We don't want to impose on you and sleep here," said Karl, "We just hoped that you could help us out with some civilian clothing."

"Of course, but where do you want to go?" asked Herr Becker.

"We wanted to go to the assembly points," answered Harold.

Herr Becker looked at the boys and his face showed his concern.

"Don't go there. They will just herd you into freight trains and transport you to Siberia. Believe me, I was a prisoner of war in WWI and I was in Russia in the forced labor camps. If I hadn't lost my leg, they would have never shipped me home."

"Thank you, Herr Becker, answered Karl. "We know that you mean well and for tonight we will accept your offer and sleep here. By tomorrow we will decide."

"Good," said Herr Becker, "Tomorrow is early enough to decide."

"Are you hungry? We will gladly share what we have. However, it is not much."

"Thank you, we brought some provisions with us and you are welcome to them." The boys emptied their pockets and the old invalid gaped at the food in front of him. They also gave him most of their cigarettes. After all, they still had some left in their hideout.

Herr Becker boiled some water to brew coffee ersatz and then joined the boys in their meal. In a way, it was a festive meal. Even though they only had some liverwurst and Knaeckebrot, it was the relief from the pressure and from the uncertainty of the last weeks that made all the difference.

"Good night," wished Herr Becker, "Tomorrow you will talk with my wife. I am sure that she will come up with some good ideas for you."

The boys stretched out on the floor and covered themselves with the blankets. "We continue to exist," said Karl, who was too excited to sleep. That the war was over and to have survived and to be finally safe was almost too much to comprehend. He thought of his mother and how much he wanted to see her again, and of his little brother and sister. He was full of joy to see them real soon, and in his mind he pictured their reunion.

Then he thought of his father and hoped that he had also survived. Then he thought again of his mother. His thoughts were like a wheel, with no beginning or end, just repeating themselves.

Harold also twisted from side to side. Like Karl, he was wrangling with his thoughts and trying to find a soft spot on the hard floor. By 6:00 AM however, the boys were sound asleep.

Shortly thereafter was the crashing sound of the front door being broken down. Hard boots kicked Harold and Karl in the sides and harsh Russian orders interrupted their sleep. Harold opened his eyes and caught a fleeting glimpse at the boots of the intruders. One of the boots had a small hole on the side. Karl turned to see what was happening when a sharp voice with a Russian accent woke him up completely.

"Karl Veth?"

"Yes," Karl managed to answer and looked up to see a Russian officer with a green notebook in his hand.

"You are under arrest!" Hard hands pulled him up and pushed him out of the door.

Germany had surrendered and the war was over. However, the terror for the Berliner civilian population had just begun.

AUTHOR'S NOTE

First and foremost, thank you for reading **Loyal To A Degree**. I must admit that the story was difficult to tell at times because it is based on my own experiences in Berlin toward the end of World War II. Writing it meant not only remembering, but reliving experiences that have spent many years buried in the back of my mind.

I had a discussion with a friend of mine while I was in the process of writing the book and when I told him what it was about, he asked me what had inspired me to write this story now, after so many years had passed. I told him there were several reasons, but the most compelling is the fact that not many books about the war, if any, were written from the perspective of a 14 year old German boy who was drafted to fight for a cause he did not understand. There are plenty of books about the heroic actions of officers, pilots, and so forth, but nothing about the common foot soldiers - young boys who had barely reached their teens.

By telling this story, I hope to give a voice to the many, many young boys who did not survive the war. They were not heroes, nor were they villains. They were simply boys doing what they were told and what was expected of them in a time when doing anything less was punishable by death.

Karl's story does not end with **Loyal To A Degree**. He faces many more challenges in the days after Berlin falls and surrenders to the Russian army. **Trust To A Degree** is the second book in the series and the release date will be announced on my website. If you would like advance notice of when the book is coming out, be sure to add your name and email to the form on the website at **www.horstchristian.com**.

Best regards,

Horst Christian

ABOUT THE AUTHOR

Horst Christian was born in Berlin, Germany in 1930. His father, a mathematician and a banker, taught him to read and write before the age of 5. He discovered his love for writing by the time he was 10 years old and wrote vacation reports and several articles for the German school periodical "Hilf Mit."

When Horst was 10, he entered the "Jungvolk," a subdivision of the Hitler Youth, which was mandatory in the Berlin school system. He then entered the Hitler Youth at the age of 14, also mandatory, and continued writing for the Hitler Youth periodicals "Der Pimpf" and "Die Deutsche Jugend Burg."

His favorite pastime was playing in the U-Bahn (subway) tunnels. While other children played soccer, Horst, with a few other likeminded children, explored Berlin by riding the subway trains.

Drafted to help defend Berlin against the Soviets at the age of 14 because of his unique knowledge of the subway system, he served as a guide for various SS demolition commandos.

In the early 1950s, Horst immigrated to the United States and became a US citizen after the mandatory 5-year waiting period. He loves to travel and has visited all 50 states in the US, most of Europe, Canada, Mexico, the Caribbean and some Central American countries. He now resides with his wife Jennifer in Idaho.

HorstChristian.com